NIGHTRISE

NIGHTRISE

By William Scott Martin

Edited by Alcy Frelick

Cover Design by Sarah Francia

2018
Polar Night Press

Copyright © 2018 by William Scott Martin

Cover design by Sarah Francia
Edited by Alcy Frelick
Book design by William Scott Martin

www.polarnightpress.com

First Printing: February 2018
Polar Night Press

Ordering Information:
Quantity sales. Special discounts are available on quantity purchases by corporations, associations, and others. For details, email the publisher at polarnightpress@gmail.com.

ISBN-978-0-9992170-0-9

Dedication

This is dedicated to my nephew, Charlie.

Acknowledgements

Special thanks to Alcy Frelick, who edited this book. Thanks to Sarah Francia for providing the cover art. Thanks to Jason Travis for the lettering and finalizing the cover.

The printed version book uses Palatino Linotype font for the body and subtitles, and Centaur for the chapter headings and titles. Headers are Garamond. All are licensed for use in PDF documents.

Text embellishments are from Nymphont by Nymphette, and free for commercial use. For more information, visit <http://www.dafont.com/nymphette.font>.

Prologue
Farewells

THROUGH WIND-TOSSED snow and the steam of a steeping brass kettle, the warrior could merely twist his head to look out from one world into another. The north face sloped into gradual plains and gentle streams, and past the horizon milky with stars were farmlands and cities for endless miles. That was home, and now the past.

The future was south. A land ragged with cliffs and forests, like primordial giants had rended the land open to fallow with the wildest imaginable things. A carpet of woods that would not give an acre for free, thick and unruly as it was unplowed by man's feet, interrupted with cascading rivers. His new world, the place they called the Nightlands.

He was taken out of his introspection by the whine of the kettle. He'd found the flattest rock on this plateau, beat the snow and ice from it, and smoothed out a sitting rug so heavily embroidered he could almost feel the fish leaping out from it. Something told him he should not risk such a fine work of art, with the wind throwing ice in every direction, but it was an old concern. It kept the stone from seeping the warmth from him, and besides, he would be keeping nothing. Not the carpet. Not the kettle. Not his sword or chain armor on his back. Not even the porcelain cup on his palm, which begged to be filled with something hot.

As he poured, the steam struck him in the face, instantly softening his skin. In truth, he was less drinking tea and more the hot water, since he'd used up most everything in the ascent and had nothing left for the Nightlands. And as he sipped through cracked lips, he supposed it was appropriate things worked out like that. Such a civilized activity hardly fitted such a savage place.

It wasn't the smell of tea, but emanating warmth, which tempted the riding stag back to life. Branch, as the warrior had taken to calling him, had been sitting so still by the fire he might have been mistaken for a snowdrift. And now Branch the stag made curious eyes at his master. It wasn't long before the stag shuffled forward through the snow without standing, not willing to suffer the cold.

"You want some, Branch?" the warrior asked.

He held the cup to the stag, giving his muzzle an affectionate stroke, ruffling up tawny silver fur. One delicate dip of the tongue, and that was all the animal needed. It lowered its head to the warrior's knees, with its antlers to the side, and closed its eyes. They would need each other's warmth to get through this night.

The warrior was called one name but gave himself another. His new name would be Ossen. The rug, the kettle, the cup—all belonged to the man who bore his old name. When it came time to make his descent into the Nightlands, he sighed, eased off his armor, set aside his ax, lance and javelins, and grasped his scabbard just below the hilt, so that the blade was balanced in a loose grip. He was now stripped to his bare chest and leggings, and at that moment he felt as weathered as the icy rocks beneath his boots.

Other than his sword, there was just one legacy of his past life left. Branch, whose cloven feet hobbled unsteadily after him, antlers stiff to the wind and snow that whirled about. It was strange how that stag's face could express so much with so few human features; it was all in those begging eyes. They harkened back to the journeys and battles they had both shared together. Branch could never understand why they had gone through so much, but he had been unquestioningly loyal like only an animal could. But now senses and instinct communicated something that language never would. Something would change forever between master and animal.

"Go home, Branch," said Ossen.

The animal took a step forward into deep snow, but tentative and hesitant. For all the razor cliffs and precipices that surrounded them, it was Ossen he watched.

"It's over, Branch. Go home. Your kind was meant for the plains."

Ossen would've bled himself dry if it helped Branch understand. But there was no reason in the animal, the stags for all their pride and pomp were beings of emotion. They would never understand the subtle and alien rules of civilization, he would take this abandonment as betrayal no matter what Ossen's reason.

He took a step forward, wrapped his arm around the beast's warm neck. Through the muscle and fur and skin was the dull throb of the animal's heavy heart.

"The reason why I liked you so much is because I never needed to talk to you," Ossen chuckled at his own little bitter joke. "But it's over, Branch. Everything I was is gone. I'm not your master anymore, that man doesn't even exist. In the Nightlands, stags aren't for riding, they're for food. Go home."

While he still embraced his old friend, Ossen reached out for the bridle's buckle. But the stag sensed it, bristled, and shook his master off. The stag circled around some distance up the slope, onyx eyes shining.

"You're going to make this difficult. Curse you for making me do this." Ossen let a breath pass for resolution to move him. When it did, Ossen knelt, plunged his hand into the packed snow, and closed his hands around the first rock he could get his hands on.

The animal turned its eye to the stone Ossen clutched, his fingers not quite long enough to fully wrap around it. Branch bristled and flinched backward as Ossen flexed his hand.

"Run, Branch! The next one's for real!"

He didn't lie. The rock bulleted quickly out of his hand, viciously enough that the stag jumped and hurtled back up the slope. It echoed and clacked against the cliff but was far wide of where Branch stood. Ossen wasted little time in getting another stone. He knew Branch enough to know he wouldn't give up easy.

And indeed, the damn animal stuck its head over the edge, one final glance to see if his one friend and master was leaving for good. And Ossen's response was a rock, this time bigger, quicker, and only a little off the mark.

Hails of arrows. Lances. The teeth and claws of so many beasts. All these things Branch had courageously faced. It seemed a testament to their bond that he should flee from something so simple as a thrown rock. But it was a good thing it should, the weight was not in the stone but in the message it sent.

There was a sensation that ice lurked just beneath the skin, and though Ossen shivered and shook, nothing broke it. But the air changed just beneath the snowline. In relief, Ossen went to his knees, put his hands to his shoulders, and rubbed. He didn't expect to thaw himself out, but he needed the strength to make the descent before dayfall.

He even considered waiting for *it*, for the sun, to scourge the cold right out of him.

It was a foolish thought, even Ossen knew that. He was nightfolk, and the sun would drive men like him mad. He just hoped some force could whisk him to a safe place, to pour him hot water and gently touch his brow out of pure concern.

But it wasn't the Daylands anymore. It was here the charts ended, the sages shrugged, where young men dared each other to tread but none had quite the courage. This was the place where monsters long thought vanquished still roamed. Here lived the force civilization hoped to hold back. Down the narrow paths, flanked by sheer cliffs, and between the clawing, hungry trees were the true Nightlands. Places that promised no shelter except what you made for yourself.

It is on the threshold of that world when Ossen looked down, and realized his abdomen was sticky with blood.

He held the black substance to his eyes. A woman once called it "red", but like all males of his species he was entirely colorblind. No matter, it had the same meaning red or black. Ossen knew his stitches had opened somewhere on his descent, and that he'd been bleeding for some time. He dreaded to look behind, to see between his footprints the drops of blackness he had laid all the way down.

At least now he'd know enough to apply pressure. But he wasn't sure what good that would do, when the monsters would catch his scent.

Even with that, even if his back was scourged of skin and his stomach eating its emptiness, he would still be better out here than in the Daylands. If the open sea had offered any chance at all, even that would have been better.

The vultures were already starting to notice Ossen. They made long, drifting ovals, hovering in the air with broad, unbeating wings. When Ossen stumbled, or he gripped his stomach, they seemed to inch a little closer, ready to supplement their rotten diet with fresh flesh. If it came to it, it would be too little to drive them off with rocks, and his sword served more as a crutch than a weapon.

Yet, the only relief within the dark embrace of the woods was from the sky. Already on the threshold of death, he sensed the eyes of many creatures, looking on him whether in fear or hunger. Whatever beings lurked within the forest posed a less immediate threat, and so Ossen felt no choice but to push on.

It was not the animals that clawed at him. It was the vegetation. Snaring, scratching, biting. Things pulled at his feet and resisted his entry. No matter how he lifted his feet, he would catch on something, break some vine, snap some branch. This place had its own way of swallowing sound, and now that Ossen was between walls of wood rather than rock, it seemed the echoes died to single, final bursts, into, he was sure, pairs of twitching ears.

He tightened his grip around the sword. He was glad he brought it, but he knew even that would need to go. Like everything he'd discarded on that mountaintop, it was last reminder of who he once was, and what he could have been. An artifact of the man that had to die if he was to have any life at all. He just couldn't shake the feeling that he still needed it—if not now, later.

What he needed was a compromise. He would hide it in a place only he would care to look—as a last, tenuous thread to his old life. He found an old hollow that would do the trick. Inside the rotted trunk, among the maggots and spiders and all matters of wet crawling things, he placed the sword, as delicately as he might place a child to bed.

His eyes lingered on it for a good long time, strands of moonlight dancing on the gilding. How proudly and gracefully he once wielded it, and how many countless days he held it to his breast as he slept. The sword was so close to him it might have deserved a name, but he never thought to give it. And now, he wanted to remember every rock and tree to seal its hiding place in his mind.

Ossen tore his eyes away. At that moment, his chest clenched painfully, and his stomach seized, like it was squeezed by his own body's pressure. It stopped him—*am I dying?*

No. As the feeling subsided, it wasn't anything like that. It was simply sadness that had struck him. Simple, but strong. And as Ossen staggered on, eating the feeling.

He was wounded, exhausted, and now, unarmed. There was no point for predators not to be bold. A cat, with saber-like claws perfectly formed to rip through undergrowth, emerged from the shadows without any need for stealth. A feline tongue slipped out and moistened its whiskers.

He had no reason to think it, but he had half-expected to walk through the forest unopposed. Perhaps it was a blind presumption that there was some mercy in the universe, but that assumption now crumbled. This cat, much too small to pose a threat in any normal circumstance, saw him as the weak, helpless prey he was.

Without his sword to grasp, he leaned over, wincing painfully, and picked up a branch. The best he could do was snap it to make a sort of cudgel, but Ossen could already feel it was so rotted that it would come apart the moment he struck anything with it. It would do as much damage as a wet scarf.

The cat was cunning enough to see that. Even as Ossen crushed the stick with both hands, and waved it in threat before him, it wouldn't retreat, it wouldn't even flinch. The cat's cleft lips only wet further.

There was no point in running. Ossen inched forward, waving his stick, hooting out and hollering, speaking in the cat's primal tongue. And suddenly, the cat turned and zipped right back into the shadows. But when Ossen heard the creak of a drawn bowstring behind his ear, he knew it instantly it was nothing he did.

It was not a steady bow. It was held by shaking hands, the girl's shoulders were not properly squared, and the arrow was not pulled back as it should.

"Drover?" she asked.

Ossen shook his head. "Warrior."

"I am not an herbalist," the woman said, as way of apology.

"Weaver is just fine for this," said Ossen.

The woman gave Ossen a curt nod, and then plunged the needle into his stomach. It was every bit as painful as the wound it treated, and Ossen's only reprieve was that the wound had been burning so badly they had the effect of dulling one another. And yet, once the needlework started, the woman performed her task confidently and competently, just like she was mending two pieces of cloth.

Her tongue went between her teeth as she worked, a sign of focus and concentration, and Ossen watched the woman a while before he passed out briefly from the pain. She had a contemplative, gentle expression, even under intense focus, and Ossen liked how her black hair cascaded behind a pair of long, pointed ears.

"They were right," said Ossen, smiling gently, despite the pain.

"Who was?" asked the woman.

"You're like me," Ossen flicked the point in his own, slightly shorter ears. "You have pointed ears. So do I."

The woman had no idea what to make of the remark, so after a glance she returned to her work.

"What's your name?" asked Ossen.

The girl's eyes flick upward. "Minda. Daughter of Mana."

The Monster

Part I

Chapter One
The World as It Is and Was

S O THE ELDERS SAY: "Ours is an old world, and the past is incomprehensibly distant. Once was an age where there was only one sky. Set with a great burning orb, it was called 'day'. They were times of barbarity and misfortune, as only monsters, ghosts and demons dwelled beneath the sun." Life hid in dusty burrows away from the searing fire.

Such was the time before speaking creatures. Yet, whatever gods controlled the universe, they chose to set in motion a second sky, a velvet shroud to give the surface shade. Under the dark, demons and ghosts retreated, life crawled out of the burrows, living creatures multiplied, and the first man spoke the first word.

The speaking man set himself apart from all the others who crawled and slithered the earth. He walked upright, and used his tongue and throat to form words instead of grunts and bleats. From speech arose thought, and thought gave birth to civilization. They were the great folk, "mankind" in their own lost language, and though they spread their works across the face of the world, there came a fall. The gods, forever inscrutable, brought a hammer to them, their empires collapsed and decayed, and nature reclaimed the ruins. The people who were once one were now smashed into a hundred pieces. One of those shards became the nightfolk, and another became the dayghosts. One had sovereignty over the night, the other contended with the demons and beasts of the day.

The two peoples were bound, for each had strengths to balance the other's weakness. Wherever there were nightfolk, soon would come dayghosts. And though they traded, defended each other, and sometimes lived together, ancient but unforgotten law decreed *never would they meet*.

Laws eroded, the empire that wrote them turned to dust, once practical concerns morphed into mystical taboos. Both sides kept faithful to an unwritten treaty, and only few knew why.

It was a task reserved for able-bodied men, but as a young boy Chev made the journey through the wild lands to the flat black obelisk at the edge of the forest. They called it the "trading stone", and it was so big Chev had to go on the tips of his toes to see the surface. It was covered in dizzyingly arcane runes and indents so big each could swallow his head. He had a hypnotic attraction to it, he would've stared until his head hurt if Ossen hadn't swooped from behind, stooping over the rock with a hand full of black and white pebbles. In earnest he worked, taking and dropping pebbles for purposes Chev couldn't guess.

In the distance, past muddy fields and a well-trod trail, lay the village of the dayghosts. It was hard to imagine the strange creatures that lived inside; bizarre beasts who would come out in the burning day, labor and labor to pull plants out of the ground, and crawl back before dusk. They belonged in the stable of household spirits that misplaced tools and spoiled meat. Chev knew well, from the warnings he was told, that they weren't to be pestered.

To lay eyes on one was to be cursed forever.

Ossen didn't open his mouth much. Not just this journey, but his whole life as well. So it always came as a surprise when he did.

"Do you understand the runes, Chev?"

Chev shook his head.

Everything Ossen did seemed practiced, even for something as simple as pointing a long, powerful finger at a vessel of white pebbles. "The dayghosts have left a message for us. See how the symbol above it is straight like a bone? They need meat. Look here," Ossen pointed at another symbol, and a hole full of black pebbles. "They'll give us linen in exchange. It's a good trade. We'll hunt for them six stags, bring them the meat and furs, and they'll bring us cloth."

Chev nodded, mouth parted. He thought he understood now: each of the symbols meant something. But the shapes looked like nothing; like scratches an animal might make by accident.

Ossen scooped up a handful of pebbles, and placed them deliberately in each of the indents. "Now we make our request. I need metal tools. I'll offer them some gourds of honey in exchange. You see where I put the stones? You need to learn each of them. One day, when I'm gone, it will be your task to talk to the dayghosts. You need to negotiate with them. Drive a hard bargain. Offer them refuse and take from them treasures."

"I will, father."

Once he realized what he'd just said, Chev clapped a hand over his mouth and blanched. Ossen looked down at him, fixing him a dangerous look. Chev already knew what Ossen was to say.

"It's for your sake nobody knows, boy, not mine."

"I know," said Chev, "I know. I'll be careful, I promise."

Ossen's stare lingered for a while, but it was a look of concern rather than anger, before he hastily rejoined the trading party.

Was it a happy childhood, or an unhappy one? As an adult, on reflection, not even Chev knew.

But he would always remember that moment he came to the *realization*. He was only just old enough to be aware that he thought, when at a random passing moment inner lightning burst and Chev suddenly understood how different he was from everyone else. For a good minute he could do nothing but stand wild-eyed, just weighing everything in his mind.

All the other children had dozens of siblings. Chev was only ever alone.

All the other children were raised by the community. Chev was only ever taught by his mother and her mate.

All the other children's mothers had different men stay in their burrows. Minda only ever had Ossen.

This was the manner Chev realized how alone he was. It was like he lived alongside the tribe rather than as a part of it. And the more he thought about it, the more obvious it became. The other menfolk, their eyes would pass right through him, they would not greet him or touch him. If they interacted with him at all, they were always restrained, like every word had to be picked carefully.

Only Ossen seemed to give him any passing affection. And he was not an effusive man.

Ossen was typical of most nightfolk in that he was tall, there was a silver sheen to the skin and black hair that stood high on his tall forehead. A pair of pointed ears jutted out from the sides of his head, moving the same direction as wind-brushed breeze. But every other feature he had spoke to his nature. Like how his lips sealed so well, to show how unpracticed he was at opening his mouth, and his keen wolven eyes; deep gray and wary most the time, but hungry and fierce when they needed to be.

He was a hunter like most every man in the tribe, but that's where the similarity ended. Ossen was never with them when the community sent their hunting parties, and never partook in their loud boasts and chest-beating. Never wore trophies, never dressed himself with teeth, skulls and skin from fresh kills, never came with sacks laden with gifts for his mate. Ossen was a man who only ever hunted alone, and whether successful or not it never showed on his face. He made straight path for his burrow, and to Minda, each and every single dawn.

He could not have been any more distant and still be part of the tribe. And yet, the few times he was gone for extended hunts, Chev noticed. The air was colder, the horrors of the deep forest seemed that much closer, and the stares from the other tribesfolk drilled that much further. He was an often distant sentinel.

The night Chev was old enough to walk gracefully, Ossen took him hunting. Such was Ossen's manner that he hardly ever offered instructions, he simply let Chev watch him work. This was Ossen's territory—fashioning tools, catching and roasting suckerfish, tracking and ambushing prey. When they sat to rest, Ossen would draw in the ashes of the campfire.

"This rune means 'health'. This rune means 'fire'. You put them together—it is the act of burning wounds. You understand?"

It seemed like the hundredth rune that night, and Chev had watched so intently his eyes ached; rubbing them only dried them out quicker. But still, he nodded and struggled to keep his vision from blurring.

Ossen continued on each trek. Chev learned continuously—runes that represented certain kinds of wisdom, runes that meant certain animals, runes that meant a certain type of rock. It was a bewildering array, and Chev couldn't imagine what he'd need so many for. But Ossen still taught him, and Chev took it on faith this was important; Ossen didn't teach unimportant things.

Sometimes there were such lessons. Other times, the clouds would part and the stars shine down on distant mountains. Ossen would look to the horizon as though remembering.

Only once he said: "Past those mountains are the Daylit Lands. There's no forest there, just big cities of the dayghosts, and fields for miles and miles with nothing to protect you from the sun. That was my home."

So that was that. Ossen *was* a stranger to the tribe. Chev thought it odd that he had come from so far away, but it hadn't occurred to him to ask why. By the time he'd ever think to do so, it would be too late.

One particular night Ossen and Chev were following stag tracks. They chased it far too long and too far, but Ossen was single-minded. He paid no heed to the unfamiliar forest, where the vines grew thick, and underbrush snared and bit. Chev kept glancing at the shadows, sensing pinprick eyes out in the foliage. His heart thumped, his legs were unsteady and twitching to run back. But Ossen was focused, and that kept Chev grounded—he couldn't be unmanned around him.

Ossen peeled back an especially thick shroud of brush. There was a clearing, and in the center was the stag, laying on a rock. Chev, bewildered, assumed it must've been asleep, but then he saw its belly. Split open like a cavern, dug out like a mine, some monster had taken its insides. The nightmarish image seared like the sun into Chev's eyes.

But Ossen stooped over it, brushing off the flies.

"*Bone-skins*," he said, a finger drifting over a claw mark. "Monsters. We need to leave."

Chev gladly followed Ossen back to the village. At some point of safety, Ossen knelt to Chev and spoke very clearly.

"Chev, if you ever see a bone-skin, you run, you fight, or you let it kill you. Chev, never, I mean *never*, talk to the bone-skins. You understand me?"

Chev nodded.

"Good."

This was not a village in any recognizable shape. During the day, something could wander right through and not see any sign of habitation. It was by design, as these nightfolk erected no structures; they made burrows beneath ancient trees, a single entrance drilled between roots, protected by thorny brush. The tree itself formed the support beams, and inside, the nightfolk sheltered through the hostile day. The village, as it was, was simply a collection of such burrows.

Only a vast, rotted out tree stump served as a central landmark, set upon a slight rise. It must've been a mountain of a tree once, something that really speared the horizon, making the mighty oaks around it shrubs by comparison, to the point where the whole town could comfortably assemble within. It made for quite the sight as one entered the village, the lord of the forest in its day, still on its throne, big roots clamped into the earth like gripping fingers.

Across the way, serving as a border between the village and the forest, ran a rocky stream of clear water, alight by nearby fireflies and the stars. Campfires dotted between the foliage. Muffled through vegetation and canopy were the sounds of village life. Ringing tools, laughter close and far, and whispered gossip were the birdsong.

As Ossen emerged from the woods, he regarded it all with a grunt.

Warm nights like this one brought the whole village out. Women in their dozens grouped beneath the shelter of boughs, at looms or nursing children or knapping tools. They suddenly came silent as Ossen and Chev splashed across the creek. Chev felt rather self-conscious that they'd failed to catch anything, so his cheeks went hot and he kept his eyes downward. Ossen, as he always did, marched on without regard.

The eyes of the village women were bad enough, but it got worse for Chev. The main hunting party returned at the same time, and they emerged laughing and teasing, at least half their number with animals draped around their shoulders. Chev would go out of his way not to be seen by them, but Ossen hadn't those instincts. Ossen and this hunting party came to face each other. Their laughter died suddenly, as though infected by Ossen's severeness; there was this intolerable, unending moment when they stared at each other. The confrontation was full of discomfort, and it was clear the other hunters sought an excuse to turn away. They eventually gave up, and didn't bother giving Ossen a reason for their wide berth.

A throng of boys followed closely behind, laughing and slapping one another and doing little games. Chev froze for the spectacle of one boy throwing a dirt clod at another; in seconds there was a screeching fight. They fought for fun, with stick spears and leaf knives and twine slings of dirt ammo. Chev knew their names, he'd seen their faces, but he couldn't call even one a friend.

His mouth went slack as he watched on, there was a split in the crowd and he was eye-to-eye with a girl his age. Sana, daughter of Serra.

They were staring, staring silently at *each other*, and Chev didn't know why. But for some reason, it was fine. She had nice eyes. Like rocks glinting after rain.

"Are you coming?"

Ossen's voice pulled him out of the trance. He blinked and turned his head to find the old hunter staring down at him from across the way.

"I want to stay outside," said Chev.

Ossen shrugged. "Don't stay out too long." And with that he descended into Minda's burrow.

When Chev turned, Sana was gone.

Her absence felt like a blow. There were things Chev didn't quite understand. Like what had made his heart pound and his feet go numb. The strange girl Sana, who Chev had never properly talked to, had taken something of his with her when she walked away.

Chev didn't know what it was, but he did know turning away was the thing that had stopped him from finding out. It was Ossen who had made him turn. Chev whispered: "It's Ossen's fault."

It was the first negative thought he ever had about the man, a simple statement that bloomed into a profound truth the more Chev ruminated on it. Before long, it broke a wall Chev had built inside. Out came a stream of bitter thoughts, parading themselves, each bearing Ossen's face. Chev had a dark image in his mind where Ossen was a looming shadow, his long arms and legs stretching and forming a cage. On the other side was the tribe; the friends he deserved to have. The men he deserved to learn from. On the other side was Sana.

He longed to be on the other side.

But somehow, an invisible hook fixed him to that man, *that stranger,* made from fate and circumstance. By an accident of birth, this was a man who was merely his father. Merely his father and nothing more.

Chev was kept from sleep by a mind darkly churning, it kept him rolling in his bedding with an uncomfortable pain in the stomach and a feverish sweat on his forehead. By dusk, he felt thoroughly beaten by his own sleep, a layer of salt and grime had come caked to his skin as he stirred awake.

And now the sun had set and the ordeal was not over. He broke fast with the cause of his distress sitting across from him, even glancing in Ossen's direction made fresh that same poisonous feeling. He kept his eyes fixed to the floor, but even so the way Ossen sipped his stew caused Chev tremors, unable to ignore each sharp slurp, that greasy, sticky sound, as Ossen sucked and lapped. The points of Chev's ears shivered to its discordant rhythm.

Chev's stew was beginning to congeal. Minda, one to be stern without raising her voice, set aside her weaving and prodded the bowl, a clear sign Chev was to finish his meal no matter the condition. Chev dutifully drank it, the lukewarm venison made lumps in his mouth. But it could've been rancid and Chev wouldn't have noticed. There was a flavor of an idea that got him suddenly excited.

He resolved not to follow Ossen hunting tonight. Instead, he would go out hunting with the tribe; *his people*. The community he deserved and *needed* to be part of. He drew up the speech he'd give Ossen in his mind, anticipating the moment when the old hunter would be left dumbfounded by its truth.

Now, as Minda wished them farewell, it came time. They emerged from the burrow, the sun only having just fallen. Chev had rehearsed over and over what he'd say to him, yet somehow, as he turned to Ossen's impenetrable eyes and set lips, it was like that stew was still stuck in his throat.

"Ossen," his voice cracked and shuddered, feet making trails in the dirt, "I'm not hunting with you tonight."

He had expected Ossen to react strongly—to be angry, to demand obedience, or to shrink down on his knees and beg forgiveness. Or at least to look lost for words. But Ossen did the worst thing possible: he tightened his already thin lips and shrugged. "I'll see you come dawn, then." And he went into the woods.

In the center of the village Chev stood alone, fixed in place staring at the part of the forest Ossen had disappeared into. He got that same feeling that kept him up all night—horrid churning. It ate through his stomach.

Outwardly, he was silent. Inwardly, he was incoherent with curses. When he broke out of paralysis, the first thing he did was stomp a small plant until it was nothing but a broken twig and crushed leaves. He felt no better for it.

Mother's burrow was just behind him, but retreat felt too much like defeat. No; he knew now was the time to go do what he promised himself. Somewhere, the men and boys of the village gathered for their expedition. He could join them, hunt with them. Show everyone he was just like everyone else. Bask in the warmth of their newfound companionship.

But as he saw the throng near the forest, his legs suddenly got very heavy, like they were clad with tree trunks. It was the cacophony of sound, of laughter, their little private banter exchanged so fast it was like a dizzying new language. One of slapping, punching and teasing yet never in anger. He couldn't imagine being so completely embraced by *anyone*.

Perhaps he was like Ossen—an outsider encroaching into a community he didn't belong. Still, he went forward step by fearsome step. His hope was someone would see him and welcome him, integrate him seamlessly and painlessly into the group. But things were as he feared. As he came closer, the more eyes fell on him, the more silent the group became. Laughter turned to discomfort. Eventually, no one made a sound.

Everyone was staring. The village men, boys younger and older, a sea of slitted eyes and pursed mouths waiting for him to act. Chev had to say something—and quick. But as much as he wanted to, nothing came to mind. Blood rushed up to his cheeks, his mind a vacuum.

"Boy, why don't you go to Ossen?" said one, finally breaking the silence.

"Yeah, go to Ossen."

"No space for you."

Wordlessly, and wanting to run, Chev stepped backward. The most shameful outcome seemed now the only option. He was most certainly scurrying off into his mother's arms. It was all he could think of.

"I'll take him."

Grizzled words split the world. Chev twisted toward it—a wizened old nightfolk, with skin like gnarled wood, and limbs just as long and tested. There were mad sprouts of silver hair from his chin, and he sounded words as much as he spat them. His lips didn't seem to fully cover his crooked, horse-like teeth

"I'll take him," the old man repeated.

The hunting party was a chorus: "Yes, boy, go with Varnas. Go with Varnas."

"C'mon boy," Varnas said, sweeping around, "things to do. Let's not dawdle."

A soft blow with a stick broke Chev out of his confusion, and he stumbled to catch up. This man was shockingly energetic for his age, both in his stride and his conversation. He rattled constantly from subject to subject, losing track of his old points before making new ones.

"—No one follows me anyway. They tried to put a shawl on me, call me an elder, as if I'm some darned fogy who can do nothing but sit around. 'Wise' is what they call useless people, you know that? Well, look how old I am, I never left these woods, never will. I'll die doing something important, I promise you. What was it? Yes, not as agile as I was, but I got somethin' whole lot better: smarts. That's how I can get away with walking around alone, yapping as though these woods weren't full of pawcats and ursars. That reminds me—"

Chev tried to listen, but he ended up only following the man, into some mysterious corner of the woods. Toward the deep forest. Near where Ossen had tracked that stag, slain by some monster called the bone-skin. The vision of its carved-out belly shook him.

Chev had to say, "This is too far."

"Don't be a pansy. We hunt smart, not stupid." With that, Varnas approached a patch of ground. Under any normal conditions, Chev wouldn't have even acknowledged it, but he noticed something—a diamond carved in a nearby tree, the undergrowth bulged slightly and unnaturally.

Varnas went to his hands and knees. A long, twisted arm grasped something in the undergrowth.

"Ah—looks like we got sumthin'. Oh, it's a biter! Nasty lil' thing. Here we go!"

Varnas pulled out a big sturdy cage, within bounced a carcoon, hissing with hair raised in rage. A long striped tail flapped menacingly.

"Oooh! Looky, heh, good one! Come on, boy, more traps today. Do something useful and carry it, will ya?"

Before Chev was ready Varnas had already tossed the cage over. He clapped his hands over it in panic, the creature inside twisted and rolled, and gave Chev a heart-stopping hiss.

"Grab the handle, you fool boy! It's gonna bite!"

Sharp little teeth smashing against the cage had Chev momentarily paralyzed. He had to juggle the thing until he could get the handle.

"Got real lucky this time. Carcoons bit shy of Nightfolk, don't like to live where we do. Very nice fur. Very soft. Let's see if we got some more."

That night they found three in total, and by the end Chev was stumbling with a tower of cages filled with pissing hissing creatures.

"Not a bad haul. Three of 'em. Normally get one or so. Good job, boy. Let's take a break."

They took a seat on a fallen trunk. Chev gratefully set down the animals, growing deaf to their bouncing and hissing.

Varnas folded one leg over the other, grunting pleasantly. "I used to hunt with the best of 'em. I could still probably do it, too. Bit clumsy now, don't have the energy for it. A whole lot easier to trap. Maybe not as glorious, but what's glory gonna do me now, huh?"

"Why did you take me?" The question had weighed on Chev the whole time, and now it sprung out of him.

"What I did what now?"

Chev enunciated clearly, annoyed he had to repeat himself: "Why did you take me?"

"Huh? You mean out trapping? Well, thought you could use the company. They didn't look too keen on taking you. Don't know you too well but I never saw you lazing around. So what? Was it something wrong? Do you need a reason?"

Chev shook his head. "You were the only one that would. Everyone hates me."

"Everyone hates you? Oh no, boy. Nobody *knows* you. You spend so much time with that oddball Ossen you're practically a stranger. These are traditional sorts, they don't know how to deal with things they don't understand, y'see? That's all. Don't hold it against them. Me? I'm too old to understand *nonsense*, if you get me. Don't have the patience for it. Jerky?"

Varnas offered a Chev a strip of venison meat. Chev gently pushed it away.

"I'm not hungry," said Chev, folding his arms.

"More for me, then." Eagerly, Varnas bit down on the whole hunk of jerky. He continued to talk, open-mouthed, hardly stopping to chew. "Now this, this is *good*. You can taste the sun innit, hell to look at but nothing beats it for jerky—"

"It's because of him. Ossen. He's the reason they all treat me like a stranger."

Chev broached it suddenly, his young brow tight and wrinkled. He looked like a little sour man, hunched up the way he was.

"Now, now, don't say that—" Varnas waved his head indecisively. "Sure. Maybe people treat you a little odd because of him. He runs his mouth sometimes, he's moody, acts strange. All sorta things. But I know, the elders know, everyone knows, what he does, it's not on your head. You're not him. I just don't understand how Minda puts up with it, that's all. So when people treat you the way they do," Varnas searched for the words, "they don't know *how* to treat you. That's all."

Chev nodded. Slowly, not in understanding, just in acknowledgment. "I want to know what's wrong with Ossen."

Varnas laughed uncomfortably and scratched the back of his head. "Well, it don't feel right telling you. You might be a bit young for it."

It was a brisk journey back to the village. Chev was worried Varnas would ask him to carry the cages somewhere else—he was more than through with hissing carcoons. It was to his relief Varnas dismissed the boy with a pat between the shoulders.

"You did a good job, boy. Hardly a complaint outta you. Except the ones about—you know what I mean. Go on kid. Go home. Have fun. Or something."

Chev was wordless. He stared the direction of his home. For some reason, it felt like such an arduous journey, and he was hesitant to start it.

"So uh... you just gonna stand there or something?"

Chev shrugged.

Discomfort was written on Varnas' face; he looked toward the boy and his own burrow, the pile of carcoon cages that had begun to rock violently. "Well, those carcoons aren't gonna skin themselves. Come out with me anytime." He waved a hand goodbye before he pulled up all the cages.

Chev felt nothing but empty-hearted. There were things he could not share with the Varnas. Like how, at that moment, he would've done anything to go home with him instead, and not that cold and dismal place Minda's burrow had turned into. Not while the stranger called Ossen dwelled with his mother, bedding in furs that didn't belong to him, eating food and wearing clothes lovingly crafted by his mother's hands.

It didn't matter whether Ossen was close or not. When people saw Chev, they saw Ossen right next to him, like a phantom clinging tight to his shoulder, and there was nothing that would fix it.

So he decided he *wouldn't* go home. He'd rather sit on the banks of the creek, fold his arms, and wait for dawn. The sun would hurt, but whatever pain would come was purifying compared to the sickness he'd wrestle with at home. He'd even take it as a favor if a monster came to bite his head off. Among the frogs and crickets, with the waters gurgling nearby, he would wait until peace came to him.

The whole village was supposed to be in their burrows by now. And yet, a figure watched from the shadows, a furtive hand against a tree trunk. Chev pretended not to notice—he didn't care if it was a monster out to attack him. But it approached very cautiously. And it came out into the moonlight, face shining.

She was curious. That was all Chev could read from Sana's expression.

It was the worst person who could've found him like this. Chev's heart thumped even as he shrunk back, pulling his knees to his chest. He hadn't wanted to share this misery with anyone. He twisted his head away, but Sana, in deliberate motions, took the ground next to him.

She wasn't quite waifish. Her most startling features were her eyes and hair, both as black as oil, yet she seemed only brighter for it. With the air so still, only Sana's gentle breath seemed to stir. She had read Chev's mood; she stayed silent, only tossing a pebble into the waters for idle amusement. They shared the sight of shimmering moon-lit waters running over river stones, for a good, long time.

"You don't have to hang around me," said Chev, finally.

"I want to." Sana's voice didn't brook doubt.

"No. I don't *need* you to hang around me. I'm good alone or not."

"Okay." Sana lifted herself onto her feet, so she stooped by the waters, "So then I won't bother you if I sit close."

"I don't care. Sit as long as you want. Sit until the sun melts your skin off."

"Is that what you want to happen to you?" asked Sana, unable to stop a giggle, "You're gonna sit here for the sun? What's that gonna do for you?"

Chev fidgeted, unable to answer.

"Besides," Sana picked up an especially shiny, especially smooth river rock, and held it to her eyes as she spoke, "it doesn't melt your skin off. You just get sick and blind. One of my mother's mates had sun sickness once. He was in his furs for weeks, and when he was well again, she was so glad to be rid of him." Sana flipped the stone into the air and caught it, an eye aglitter. "Your mother really likes Ossen, doesn't she?"

"Yes," admitted Chev.

"He must be real special then. Though it's gotta be cold in your burrow, with it just being you and all."

"It's all the same to me," muttered Chev, not really wanting to answer.

Sana's smile turned sad, the shine in her eyes died down. With caution, and watching for his reaction, Sana took his hands, making a silvery orb of weaved fingers. Chev twisted in surprise, but he didn't pull himself back. Her fingers were too warm and too soft for him to wrest away.

"I really want you to be part of the tribe, Chev," is what she said.

Chev was boiling hot inside, burning like the sun shone on him, and he found himself swallowing for all of the things that lodged in his throat. When she let go, the little smooth stone was glittering in his palm, still wet from the creek bed.

"The sun burns, Chev." A caress over one shoulder, and she had said all she wanted to. Chev had no clue how haunting this moment would become.

Sana's encounter had him sitting just a little longer. Chev wasn't curious anymore how the sun would boil off his skin, he just waited for his heart to slow. The night was warm and the blooms were out. Moths with spiral wings danced along the moonbeams. A grasshopper mounted a nearby cattail, and seemed to watch Chev for a time. There was a sleepiness to the air, Chev quickly lost track of time.

By the time Ossen discovered him lounging by the creek, the sky had turned muddy with light. Ossen prodded him with the blunt end of his spear, and looked down on him with his narrow gray eyes.

"Come on, Chev, Minda sent me to get you," said Ossen.

Chev rose up from the patch of cool moss. This man's stony unmoving face was the last thing he wanted to see. "I know."

"Monsters stalk the night as well as the day. You know this. You shouldn't be so far from others."

Chev was on his feet, puffed up defensively. "I can handle myself. I can run fast. I can climb. I can kill monsters, if I wanted."

"Right," Ossen said. "I'm sure you can. It's your mother I'm thinking of. You'll make her sick with worry if you're not home before dawn."

Ossen had carefully fed Chev's pride. Feeling the bite of the elements, Chev gladly took the bait. "Of course."

They went back together, in silence. It was a good thing that Chev walked behind Ossen, because Chev kept a hateful expression fixed on his face, and it grew more severe with each step. The boy hadn't stopped thinking, he watched Ossen's lean body sway with every practiced footfall. The clues Chev had gathered, from Varnas and from Sana, worked themselves into a complete picture. Chev felt he was grasping at a truth everyone feared to tell him. The obvious, finally, was being made clear.

Just as a ray of sunlight first struck across the sky, Chev suddenly ran up to block the entrance to Minda's burrow. The boy lit up with defiance, while Ossen scratched his rugged cheek without any particular emotion.

"Isn't it time you moved on?" asked Chev.

Ossen's sigh was ragged with exhaustion. "I knew this was coming."

"It's that I know my father, isn't it? That's the reason everyone hates me."

"I don't want this conversation now, boy. I'm tired. I want to go to my furs."

Chev stepped to block Ossen, folding his arms like a proper guard. "I'm not stupid. I can see how we're different from everyone else. I can see how everyone treats us. I didn't get it until now. The problem is you not leaving like you're supposed to. And I'll stay here 'till the sun comes up, if it means that you'll leave us alone."

Chev didn't know what he expected out of Ossen, but it was anything but a smirk. There was nothing amusing about it; it was the contemptuous expression of a man who knew better. "Minda has always had the choice to be left alone. I have always had the choice to leave. Neither of us want to. Neither of us ever expect wanting to. You're not going to change that." When he moved to pass, Chev took another step to block him. "Step aside, kid."

"Tell me why then. Tell me why you did this to me. Because I'm supposed to be normal, I'm supposed to be like them!"

Ossen shrugged. "You can be like whoever you want to be, son. All I did to you was give you life. I can't tell you what to do with it."

"That doesn't answer my question."

"The answer is that they're afraid of me, boy. Because they're small-minded and superstitious, they're afraid."

"Afraid of what?"

"Afraid I'll kill their children."

Chev was so horrified he couldn't speak. Seeing Chev's reaction, Ossen settled into that same smirk.

"Son, I'm not from around here. I had no one but my mother and father to teach me everything I knew. And damn boy, I know a lot. A lot more than these small tribal types. You see, I've traveled far and wide, seen a lot of things. I've read books. You ever even seen a book, boy? Didn't think so. Outside this little forest, there's stuff you can't even imagine. I used to hunger for the sight of them, I used to chase after the destiny they all said was mine, but now I'm just tired all the time. I'm looking for contentment, and Minda's the only person who has ever given me peace. So I don't give a lick what these small minds think. I could crush this little place in a day if I had the mind to. So let them whittle their lives with their little problems. Now let's go inside. Minda's waiting for us."

Chev was not over what his father had said, but his aura seemed to shift as he crouched into Minda's burrow. He forgot all about his hatred as he followed behind. Suddenly, *this man*, the man who happened to be his father, turned from a loathsome figure into an enigma that had to be solved, under the space of a minute.

Neither of them knew they were being watched. And yet, a fellow nightfolk man unfurled from the branch he perched upon, and grinned toothlessly about what he heard.

Chapter Two
And Peace Came to Its Own End

MINDA AND OSSEN were silent people, but in different ways. Ossen spoke like his lips were heavy and tight, Minda had full, light ones that tended to flutter open while she thought. This was especially true as she worked the needle. One thread in, another came out. Slowly, vines crept up shawls, graced with nightblooms and curving leaves. Fish danced and nightbirds sang. Anything she made was beautiful and mesmerizing, to see that Chev didn't need the woman's sixth sense.

The women called this sense "color", the mysterious, secret markings etched on all things. Men were blind to it, so Chev could only trust that it existed. Women could perceive it, but only lightly. Legends said that only a dayghost could see it fully. To the dayghosts, the world was awash with supernatural light.

When Chev was especially young, he would tell Minda that he was trying very hard to see *color*. She thought this very funny, and she picked him up by the elbows and kissed him. She had a sweet smile then, and even now, though lines creased the corners when she curled her lips, and her brow started to fold over her eyes. Her skin had dulled from moon-lit silver to ground pebbles and her once sky-like hair fringed with white like river froth.

Yet, however Minda and Ossen looked, however they aged, and whatever they said or didn't to one another, when Ossen came from a long hunt in the woods he had no thoughts except climbing into Minda's furs. Every night, his form melded into her contours, folded an arm over her stomach, put his head atop her breast, and slept. Every night, Minda welcomed him with a quiet glow and snuggled into the security of his arms.

Tonight, Chev expected to go hunting. But Ossen had different plans, he inclined his head toward the enormous rotted stump in the center of the village.

"I have to talk with the elders tonight. You can go into the woods, if you wish. You're old enough now to go alone."

"They'll ask me to speak to them too, one day. Won't they?" asked Chev.

Ossen nodded.

"Then I want to see them too."

Ossen gave another nod, this time with the slant of a smile, and they struck out toward the elder's hall.

It was a short climb up the stony outcropping where the great dead tree once stood, titanic crumbling roots made arches over the path. Passing into the central chamber, Chev and Ossen found themselves in open air, with the river of stars above providing all the light they needed. The elders perched atop their wooden pedestals, swaddled in blankets, each looking like a bird with a shriveled, prune face.

They addressed Ossen directly. "Greetings Ossen, of the Daylit Lands."

They all crowed in turn, and it turned out to be a dry discussion of village affairs—stag populations, aggressive pawcats, dayghosts and the trading stone. Business was brisk and pleasantries were minimal, still it all went over Chev's head and he started to drift off into some fantasy.

But as things drew to a close, one of the elders spoke: "Ossen of the Daylit Lands, you're an asset to our tribe, and through your demonstrations of loyalty and competence you have proven your trustworthiness. It is in this light I ask:" The elder bent to pin Chev with his eyes. "Why do you risk all this by bringing *that boy* here?"

Chev jumped, alarmed at suddenly being the focus of attention. And Ossen visibly pulsed; the temptation to say something angry was not easily squelched. "Is the boy not your kind?"

"All of us know *whose* kind he is," said one of the other elders, in a voice dripping with suggestion, "With the sort of eyes cast on you, you'd be advised to deflect suspicion rather than attract it."

The hunter was thrust into a mood that could barely be held back. His hand clenched and unclenched, his teeth ground, a vein popped out from his temple, yet still, his voice was steady and his words chosen carefully. "I'm not trying to hide anything. Any conclusion you make is your own. Are we done?"

"Of course. Unless there was something else?"

"No," Ossen twisted around and headed out the door, Chev in tow. When the elders were out of sight, Ossen broke. He tightened his fist, and pounded the elder's tree so hard bark flew in strips.

"Ignorant! Ignorant fools! Damn closed-minded fools they are! I'll—"

Ossen stopped himself as soon as he met eyes with Chev. He dropped his hand—pieces of the rotted tree bark crumbling out—and answered the question lodged in Chev's mind.

"It's like I said boy. They don't hate you. They fear me."

"I need to know why," said Chev.

Ossen's face shriveled up with a snort, like he needed to think about it. "I suppose you do. It's because I know you, and you know me."

"I've known that. I don't understand *why*."

"Listen, Minda and I—we don't run our lives like they do. They do things the way they do things, and we do things our own way. I wish they understood that. And, sometimes, I think they will. Until then, I do the best I can for the elders. Not for myself, but for you and Minda."

As Ossen and Chev turned to head home, Chev overheard Ossen mutter, "And sometimes, I wonder if I'll have to *make* them understand."

It had been four summers since Chev confronted his father outside Minda's burrow. The old hunter had brought it up only once. On that night, they were both working on something outside the burrow. Chev was lost in his concentration on the arduous task at hand, and they had not spoken a word until Ossen, out like shooting star, asked, "You still hate me, boy?"

Chev had to think about it. Not because he didn't know the answer. Simply because he couldn't imagine why Ossen would ask. "No."

"Good, good," muttered Ossen. And that was that.

In truth, as the years wore on, Chev had changed. Ossen had spoken ill of the elders; a blasphemy in this community, but he had done it so brazenly and casually that Chev couldn't help but respect it. It took a lot of time and even more reflection, but eventually Chev took some pride in being so different from the others. No longer did he dread going home alone while all the other children thronged together. He proudly did so, and all the stares and words that once proved so piercing seemed to just glance off him.

It was the power that Ossen showed; there was a romance to thinking his father had been some great adventurer. Suddenly, every wrinkle and scar on Ossen's beaten skin seemed to tell a tale, and Chev was attentive to whatever the man had to teach him.

Then there was Sana.

Chev hadn't stopped thinking about her, not once. He wondered if he could share a burrow with her one day, though Chev wasn't sure if it was a plan or just a fancy of his. Sana was not far from having her own place, and Chev was close to breeding age himself. In any case, it would take time, and so Chev contented himself with just her friendship.

These were peaceful days. They had their time, and they came to their own end.

The name "Feska" never sat well with Chev's ears, even before it made Chev want to gag and spit saying it.

It belonged to a fellow tribesman. Ossen didn't like him, but no more than he disliked most people. Chev only knew of him because of his infamous smile: most of his teeth had been beaten out him, and what remained looked to be calcified over his gums. Like Ossen, he hunted alone, but unlike Ossen he did it like a pawcat, stalking from the canopy and throwing himself on the backs of prey, hunting dagger in hand.

One particular night, Minda joined the tribe in celebration while Ossen busied himself in the burrow.

"You go ahead," he had told Chev, "Your mother likes them. I can't stand the festivals, to be honest. Dealing with those people, it's work is what it is. Go ahead, and take care of your mother."

So Chev went. There was a big fire in the center of a clearing, surrounded by dancing and drumming and a tornado of moths swarming like a thick blanket. The laughing and bouncing shadows were disorienting, but his instinct was to seek out Sana. At these sorts of gatherings there was plenty of horseplay between men and women; teasing, slapping, chasing. He was already calculating how many boys he'd need to fight to get Sana's attention.

Sana was certainly out there, but that was not who Chev saw first. The bonfire licked at a scene beyond the flames; a craned figure and Minda's flickering face. The figure grabbed her, she twisted out of its grasp and fell hard on the ground. Similar scenes were playing out everywhere, but with joy and laughter. Minda's eyes were wild with terror.

Alarmed, Chev bounded across. He fought past the heat of the fire and trod over embers and loose food. Someone cursed him for something. He didn't care. All he saw were Minda's burning eyes. As he drew close, both figures faced him, the pause giving Minda time to tear herself away with indignation.

The man's voice was smooth but oily, and contrasted starkly from his twisted features. "Relax, boy. I was just talking to your mother."

He was so distorted by flickering light and shadows that Chev didn't recognize this man at first. Then the man smiled, and there was no mistaking the teeth that were so distinctly his; a calcified ruin of gums and twisted bone. It could only be Feska.

Chev wanted to say something, his throat was tensed like stretched sinew, but Minda pulled Chev away quickly by the shoulder. Feska's malignant stare followed them all the way to the edge of the feast, until they were safely out of earshot.

Minda spoke with her fingers, in the same manner she might tell Chev off. "Don't talk to Feska. More than that, more than anything else, *do not tell Ossen*."

"I can't let him talk to you like that!" said Chev.

"Swear on the ancestors you won't tell Ossen."

"Father and I can —"

Minda interrupted him with a glare and the sternest voice that Chev had ever heard from her. *"Swear on the ancestors!"*

Chev swallowed back any protest, instead whispering urgently, "Please tell me you're not letting him do this to you!"

Minda's face broke into tenderness. Two fingers brushed aside Chev's hair. "I'll handle him. Trust me. A woman knows how to do this. Now, please, *swear*."

Chev didn't like leaving his mother at this man's mercy, but her eyes begged for trust. "I swear. On the ancestors." Chev hastily amended.

"Good, good. Now go find that girl you like, Chev." She patted him on the shoulder, and turned away.

"Will you be fine?"

"I'll be fine," she turned, flashing a studied smile, "I'm just going home."

Chev didn't trust that smile.

He didn't look for Sana. He was so preoccupied he went straight to his spot next to the creek, just to sit and watch the stars. It didn't help with the uneasy feeling he had, though he promised his mother he wouldn't bother about Feska, the image of the man stuck in his head.

When daylight approached, Chev lifted his aching head from the bed of moss at river's edge, and he saw *him*. Or he thought he did, because the figure that stooped in the canopy with the horrific grin evaporated. After a moment of breathless searching, Chev chalked it up to a vivid imagination, and put it out of mind.

But as the week wore on, it was clear Feska had the sort of face that could conjure itself from any shadow, between the boughs of trees and plumes of foliage. Chev doubted his imagination was this vivid. He grew certain he was being watched. He had no place to feel safe.

And if he couldn't tell his father, he had no one to tell at all.

One night it left him blind to Sana's approach. She stooped down next to him. "Found some new stars?"

He jumped, kicking his feet up. "Oh, Sana," he said, relieved. "Sorry. I was just thinking."

"I was thinking too. That's why I'm here. I saw you at the festival, you know."

"Oh, yeah," Chev recalled it like he'd been there years ago and not just a week.

"Yeah," she swallowed, and her voice wavered, as though volunteering her inner pain, "I thought you were looking for me."

"Sana, I was." Chev propped himself on his elbow to face her. Though she smiled, her chin was just slightly lifted. The only hint she felt indignant. "I even thought about you after. I just got distracted."

"By what?"

Chev searched for the word. "Personal things."

Sana's voice wavered as she sighed. "Chev, of course you're allowed to be with any girl you wanted, but I would've appreciated—"

"It's not that, Sana." Chev sat up. "I haven't had a lot of time to think about things. I'm a bit of a loner. You know that. But," Chev hedged, biting his lip, deep in consideration, "there's nothing that'll threaten our friendship. That's not even a question. Heck, if it weren't you, who else?"

Sana gave a relieved giggle, but it was clear she held something back. Especially as she looked at him with such watered eyes.

"It's good to see you with the rest of us, at least. You should try it more often. People have started making jokes, you know. It's mean, and I stop them, but there's only so much I can do. I've heard some call you a *drover*."

A *drover*. A wild man and exile, refused by all women, not much better than a beast, driven to haunt the forest in packs. As much as Chev didn't like it, he saw where the rumors came from.

"I'll try," nodded Chev.

They sat together for a little while after that, but Chev was too distracted to make good conversation.

And as he went home, he saw Feska again. This time, Feska didn't slink away so quickly.

Chev had enough. He'd had enough days ago, but he'd kept it in dutifully. There was no keeping it in now. He stormed into his mother's burrow, and after briefly checking to see Ossen was gone, he asked directly, "How long has it been going on?"

Minda was lined with apprehension. "What?"

Chev had to word things circuitously. "That *thing* you don't want your mate to know. How long?"

Minda sighed. Out of embarrassment, she danced around the answer. "It's hard to say. Not too long. You know, I don't really notice anymore. But if I had to say, I might say a few years."

"A few years!"

"It's not as bad as it sounds."

"You have to tell Ossen."

"No!" she shouted, like out of a panic. She took a breath, closed her eyes, collected herself, and said, "No. Ossen cannot know."

Chev's gaze bid her continue.

"Ossen doesn't understand how our community works, he'll make a terrible mistake. If they banished him—I don't know what I'd do."

"Tell me a plan, mother. If you don't, I'll kill Feska myself."

"Give me a few days. If that doesn't work, I'll talk to the elders. They can control him."

"And if the elders do nothing?"

"Then..." Minda swallowed, "then we'll see."

Chev wanted to have faith that Minda would fix things, but he slept on it uneasily. He was to pretend he didn't see Feska, but tonight Feska made that impossible. To Chev's crawling skin, he had chosen to sit in the branches across from Minda's burrow, a nasty sight first thing after sleep. There was a gleam from a blade he was sharpening, it hung in the canopy like a baleful star.

Chev was ready to hurry on, but Feska addressed him. "Greetings."

"Hello," answered Chev, vigilant for any movement from the stooped shadow.

"You've been watching me recently."

Chev retorted with an appalled, angry response. "It's the other way around, Feska."

"I am where I've always been. You've just been paying more attention. That's the thing about a cut, it's painless until you notice it."

Chev nodded toward the weapon. "That's a very nice knife."

"Of course," Feska grinned, "it's a daymetal knife. You know daymetal? Only dayghosts can work it. Perhaps I can give it to you one day, when my time comes. It depends on how our relationship evolves."

Chev snorted derisively. "You can keep it." He started off to the woods, but he was arrested by a question.

"You're Ossen's, aren't you?"

Feska was being very direct, far more direct than anyone else had been, treading around the subject carefully like the taboo it was. It was bold, but Chev didn't want to dignify it with an equally straight answer. "Perhaps. Mother doesn't tell me."

"I think you are. I should say, I *know* you are."

"You can't know."

"I do, I've been asking around. It's a funny thing, none of the other men say they've shared furs with your mother. And yet, here you are. Only person I haven't asked is Ossen."

"You don't ask him because you know he'll kill you."

Feska let out a laugh, his wide, thin lips peeling apart. "It's not like everyone doesn't already know, kid. Everyone just is too damn polite. I know different. We are a people of hunters. I wait, I stalk, I kill. This is how we do things here, but you and Ossen don't understand that. You'll learn though." He tilted his head to the horizon. "Go on then. Get running. Bounce out of here, little doe."

Chev had a little knife of knapped obsidian, and only old thin leather kept him from cutting his hand as he gripped it tighter. But Feska's knife was bigger and sharper, of daymetal no less, and the man was much more dangerous than any creature of the woods. Chev couldn't take the risk, he left slowly, with one eye on Feska.

Chapter Three
They Forced the Sword

IT HAD BEEN a while since Ossen and Chev had hunted together. But Ossen extended the invitation, and Chev took it.

He came to regret it: he was melting with Minda's secret, and Ossen was quick to sense something was wrong as Chev dragged his feet and waffled over simple directions. Even so, they managed to track a small herd to a copse; a dozen or so piglets, lead by a mother as black as soot, snuffling the ground and foraging. Ossen gave the hand signal, Chev pulled back his bowstring, but was so tensed by rushing thoughts that he pulled too hard and the string snapped. The whipping sound startled the herd, and they went shredding through the underbrush.

Ossen shook his head as he checked Chev's bow. "It's an old sinew," he said, a pool of string in his palm, "but you still shouldn't have pulled that hard."

"Sorry."

"Poor luck tonight, but there'll always be a second chance. You hurt your hand?"

Chev inspected his palm. The string had whipped his palm, leaving a mark. "No. A little maybe. It was my fault anyway."

"As long as it doesn't kill you, you can always make up for it later. Let's go home, give that hand a rest."

Ossen pulled his son up, and they both trudged back to the village.

"Something interesting?" asked Ossen after some distance.

Ossen had noticed Chev scanning the forest canopy. The boy quickly recovered from his surprise, and stuttered a response. "No, nothing," he said, before gluing his eyes to the forest floor.

"It's that pest, Feska, isn't it?" Ossen sighed.

Chev's heart pounded, his ears went hot. "How did you know?"

"The man is everywhere. Difficult not to."

Chev was so relieved, he chuckled. "Minda was wrong. She said you'd kill him."

"For being a strange man that hangs out in trees? Of course not." Something then struck Ossen, and he stopped to fix Chev a suspicious glare. "Why would Minda think I'd kill him?"

"Just..." Chev flushed, and he couldn't think of anything quick enough, "I..."

"What are you keeping from me, boy?"

"Not anything!"

"He do something?"

Chev knew what he was supposed to say, but he couldn't bring himself to lie about it. It was like his jaw came unhinged and lost power to form words. He only looked dumbly on as his father formed his own conclusions.

"I knew something was up," said Ossen. He broke into a run back to the village. Chev raced after him, brambles making their mark as he raced through the forest. Chev was just fast enough to see Ossen throwing himself into the burrow.

Inside, Ossen made a line for his belongings and pulled out a spear. Minda's senses flared, she rushed to grab his arm, and they caught each other in their glares. A whole, wordless exchange took place, and whatever they communicated with one another, it passed in tense silence. Ossen relented; in frustration he threw the weapon against one of the support beams, clattering uselessly to the floor.

Ossen paced to the other side of the burrow, his voice a growl. "What do you expect me to do?"

"There's nothing you can do. I'm going to see the elders."

"They'll do nothing. They've never done anything."

"That isn't true."

"They've never done anything for *you*."

To that, Minda had no answer but a slight frown. But she still gathered herself up, and wrapped a shawl around her shoulders. "The moment *you* try something, they *will* act," she said. "I'll see them right now."

She left, yet there was no patience in Ossen; he was ready for murder. He stooped on the floor, obsidian knife in hand, anxiously watching the entrance, glowering with those wolf eyes of his. Though Chev knew his father would never hurt him, there was such an aura of repressed violence that Chev feared approaching, the very shadows he lurked in seemed darker and hotter for his presence.

It was difficult to even place a comforting hand over the shoulder. Chev was worried he might spring like one of Varnas' traps, but he hadn't. He was a closed pot, still simmering, still pressuring to explode.

"Why didn't you tell me?" asked Ossen.

"Mother asked me not to."

Ossen considered that for a while. "It's not your fault," he concluded, "It was so easy to see. Stupid, blind fool I was, I didn't want to deal with it. I should've stopped this before it became a problem. No more, Chev. I swear to you, from now on, I'll take on anything in our way."

He snorted and stooped like animal, his head nodding to his own inner dialogue. Ossen was making himself dark, silent promises.

When Minda came home a little later, her face told the story of a long conversation without resolution. Her shawl dropped from her shoulders onto the ground.

"You were right," she admitted.

Ossen didn't seemed pleased about it. "The next time he tries something, I'll kill him."

"Just wait. He'll lose interest."

"I've known men like Feska my whole life. They only understand strength, Minda."

"You are an outsider and he is not. They'll always side with him. You have no choice."

"Give me a night, Minda." Ossen stood from the ground, and threw back his shoulders. "I can do what I always said I could do. Then no one would bother us again. No one would dare."

"I told you: I told you a thousand times, that's the *last* thing I want. Let it rest, Ossen. Please, tolerate them. They don't know any better."

Ossen looked to Chev, then back again to Minda. He was still drawn up, ready for action, but his mind worked hard.

"Fine. For you and only you, I'll let things as they are. But know the minute they do something against us, that's the time when I teach the lesson they sorely need."

If Feska had known Ossen's murderous inclinations, perhaps he would have chosen to do things differently. Or maybe it would have spurred him into bolder action. In any case, the very next night, Feska elected to reveal himself to Ossen.

Dusk had only just faded. Feska haunted the canopy above Minda's burrow, and Ossen either didn't notice, or chose not to notice. But this night Feska would force the issue.

"Ossen!" Feska shouted from his perch, "How is Minda? Sleeping well?"

It was clear just by looking Ossen had a million things he wanted to say, but he chose: "Minda doesn't want you," before pulling Chev away.

"I think she tires of you, that woman. She's got too much heart to tell you to go."

Ossen didn't even turn around. "That's because she wants me."

"I think you stick with her because no one else would take you, *drover*."

Ossen stopped.

He turned around slowly, his face looking like someone had peppered it—he had a crinkled brow, his eyes turned to knife-like slits. He said, very carefully and with great restraint, "You are fortunate that Minda is so reasonable. I could make you very, very sorry."

"The same to you, friend."

"No. I would make a waste of you. There wouldn't be enough of you for crows to peck. I could destroy you so completely it would turn to myth. Your name will come to mean falling to a terrible fate."

Feska smiled. "You're full of it."

"Try me sometime. I'll show you *all*."

"I'll take you up on it, friend," Feska leaned forward on his branch, "but not today. Some other time. When things are quiet, and you wouldn't expect it."

"I look forward to it."

It was only the night after when, just before their hunt, Ossen put his hand over Chev's shoulder.

"Take a break tonight, Chev. I need some time alone to think about things. I'll be back before dawn."

Chev was left alone, watching Ossen's enigmatic shadow meld into darkness.

Instead, Chev took advantage of Varnas' open invitation. He followed the old trapper into the forest, and despite offers, Varnas chose to do all the work himself. The tough trapper lectured between heaving piles of dirt.

"The most important thing... is to get... the pit deep enough... so that nothing... jumps out again... that's why I always set a marker... so no one... falls in." Varnas thrust the shovel into loose soil. "You are listening to me, boy? Aren't you?"

"Of course," lied Chev.

Varnas accepted it with a shallow nod. "That's good. I know... ugh!... that trapping's not as glorious... as hunting with your... own hands, but... trust me when I say... it has its own satisfaction..."

Varnas was the sort of man who could carry on a conversation by himself, which freed Chev to drift into thoughts which themselves drifted toward Sana. As soon as Varnas gave leave, he bounded off to that bend in the creek that he and Sana knew so well. He needed her right now like he needed water.

There were never any arrangements. One would show up if they wanted the other's company, and the other would come a little later. Sana came this night too, and, much to Chev's relief, talk revolved around mostly silly things: fresh gossip, old but timeworn jokes, and ancient dreams. Still, even then, the silences that punctuated her speech made it clear she was talking around something. She was about to broach a serious topic.

And it did come, after quite some hedging. "Chev, I've heard a lot of things about your mother's mate," she said.

It was the weight of her voice, and the cast of her eyes—this was a question she'd had pent up for a while.

"Mhmm," Chev was roused from a dreamy reverie.

"Is it true what they say? That he and Feska are enemies now?"

"Maybe." Chev tried to speak of it as though it had little to do with him.

"Then you have to be careful, Chev. Really careful."

"I'll be fine."

"You don't get it, do you?" her breath shuddered, "Chev, everyone thinks that Ossen is your father."

"I know what people think." Chev was brisk, making clear he didn't feel like talking about it.

"Chev, don't you know what that means?"

"Tell me, then."

Something disturbed Sana's voice. Its sweetness turned into a choke. "No one has ever told you?"

Chev rolled away, his hand falling in the grass. "Who would? Everyone pretends not to notice. And those that don't, well... Varnas says I'm too young, Minda doesn't like talking about it, and Ossen just doesn't pay attention to it. And Feska, what a jackass he is! I don't even care about it anymore, so I'm happy no one tells. I guess you're about to, though."

"You know the difference between us and the nightfolk of the deep forest, right?"

Chev picked a loose pebble, and tossed it into the water. "I dunno. They kill each other, worship dark gods, make deals with the bone-skins. Probably eat babies too. Never met one, and I don't care to."

Sana paused as though hesitant. "They *marry*, Chev."

"What's that?"

"It means they only ever mate with one person. The woman belongs to the man, as do the children."

"That doesn't sound so bad. It's like Minda and Ossen."

"That's right, Chev. It *does* sound like Minda and Ossen. Don't you see?"

"What? And that scares people?" Chev drawled sarcastically, "Makes perfect sense."

"No," Sana slapped Chev over the shoulder, "When two people do the marry, they set themselves apart from the community. A marry is unbreakable, except by death. And if someone wants to mate with a new person, they have to get rid of the person they have a marry with. Chev, *they have to kill them*."

Chev didn't connect the ideas at first. His brow crumpled: *marry, death, Minda. Marry, death, Minda.* So Ossen had to *die* if Feska wanted Minda. Was that it?

The theory turned out to be quite compelling to Chev. He would linger on it, but Sana wasn't done. She leaned into Chev's ear, and whispered.

"They kill the children, too."

Chev twisted to her. "That's absurd."

"I'm not saying what makes sense, Chev. All I'm saying is what I've heard."

Crickets chirped, birds droned haunting nightsongs, the silence left Chev to his thoughts. Sana didn't need to spell it out what she meant. If her strange story was right, Feska was after Chev, too.

"You don't need to worry about me, Sana. If it comes to it, I can kill Feska."

"Don't try. That's the only thing I can ask you. Don't even try, don't get yourself in trouble because of someone else's silly fight. Let the elders sort this one out."

Chev had already seen what the elders would do. But he didn't want to tell Sana that, and he didn't want her to know how close and sharp he'd been keeping his knife. There were so many things he could have unloaded on Sana, but he didn't. They stayed quiet, and so they spent some time listening to the rumble of the creek. The silence was what Chev preferred anyway.

But Sana's words still haunted him even after he left.

He'd spotted Feska later that day, though this was a rare time Feska was on the ground. Over his shoulders was an ursar skin, its fang positioned just over the brow, as if biting. It had to be Feska's newest trophy, as he boasted about it with some gathered hunters. Chev had never killed an ursar, he'd never even *seen* one, but he'd heard of it. A beast that needed a team of men to kill, and even then at great risk. And Feska wore its skin quite comfortably. Chev stared a little too long. Feska spotted him, and he turned his jagged grin to him.

It was startling how different he looked out of the shadows of the trees. Though he cut a short, bent figure, he was shaped like an ape, his torso and arms twisted with strength, scars accentuated the threads of his muscles, and his skin was pearlescent with health.

Ossen—had he a chance? Could a warrior defeat a hunter on his own terms? Chev wanted to believe Ossen could dispose of this man easily, but looking at Feska now, haughty with accomplishment and commanding the attention of gathered menfolk, it was hard to see a good outcome.

Chev went home early that night. Ossen was already there, deathly quiet as he threw himself into butchering a doe. It should have been such a routine task he could have done it blind, but there was none of his usual grace as his cleaver slammed into bone and sinew. Still, the meat made a pleasant stew, and what little conversation passed between the family was domestic and fixed on happier subjects.

Ossen was never one to distract himself on happier things. It meant the man was up to something.

Chev was right. It was late in the day, when the sun was fully out, and any decent nightfolk were fast asleep, when Ossen crept out from his furs, taking the utmost care not to disturb the woman he slept next to. Chev opened his eyes a hair's breadth. Ossen padded across the burrow, he considered his spear for a moment, then twisted suddenly to Chev. Chev shut his eyes just in time. The movement continued, he only heard a slight disturbance as Ossen—incredibly—pushed past the foliage that protected the entryway, and went out into the sun-drenched world. Chev jumped out of bed, seeing only that Ossen disappeared into the daylight, even his shadow evaporating in the sheer white.

Sleep shed from Chev, his heart erupting, newborn sweat appeared on his brow. He knew his father was bold, but going out in the daylight was pure madness. All his life, he'd only ever been told of the dangers of the day lit world—the fire it brought, the beasts that roamed it, the sicknesses it caused. Yet Ossen hadn't hesitated. He ventured into the burning land of dreams and death.

Chev crawled to the entrance on his belly, for fear a stray beam of sunlight would strike and burn him. The light was so thick it swallowed up even the leaves that covered it. Chev couldn't imagine what it would be like to see the sun with naked eyes.

But, Ossen had done it, so it must be possible.

His hand went to push aside the bramble, even being hot to the touch. He tried to get accustomed to it, like how one might dip their toe in water before diving.

It was only a matter of pushing aside the bramble.

Carefully, he did so.

He couldn't even see the Great Burning Orb yet, but the world was already afire. Every surface blazed with scintillating light, every piece of bark, blade of glass and dull rock became like a refracting crystal. Every drop of dew multiplied like stars, spider webs turned into galaxies. There was no sense in anything. Even squinting did nothing.

Chev couldn't imagine how Ossen could've stepped out into it. But somehow, he had. And Chev had to follow.

He did his best, but even shielding his eyes was unexpectedly horrible. His skin pricked with a burning sensation, and as Chev opened his mouth to cry in surprise, his throat dried. His lips split. Skin cracked and stiffened like leather; he hadn't even realized he could be this sensitive to the sun. But his father somehow withstood it, so he steadied his breath, and crawled out into the eye of the Great Burning Orb.

The worst mistake was to look up. It was the face of death, and more terrible than anything Chev could imagine. He could only withstand the sight for a fraction of a second before its fire stabbed right through his eyes and coursed through his skull. Chev fell back, blind, crawling back to the safety of the shadows. As vision came back it imprinted as a horrid black spot in his eyes—a dark sun.

It took a long time to be able to open his eyes again. The searing white end of the tunnel became a window into a different world, into the unimaginable dangers of the day. In the shifting illusions dwelled monsters and spirits. Somewhere out there was Ossen, his father.

What madness had possessed him to go out into that strange realm, Chev couldn't guess. All he could do was crawl back to bed and try to sleep. The next time he woke, it was Ossen returning home, just at the edge of dusk.

The elders sang tales of the dangers of day, and Ossen became a portrait of it. At dusk Minda rose. By habit, she turned to look at the man next to her—she screamed. Chev, already well awake, pushed his furs off and went to his mother.

Ossen was a terrible sight. One hand gently massaged his chest, and the other hung limp to the side. His face had turned dark somehow, tanned like leather might be, and lined with inexplicable wounds that followed the lines in his brow and around his eyes. As Minda reached to touch his arm, he drew quickly away.

"Stop," he moaned, "it hurts."

"What on... Ossen! What happened? What did you do?"

"Stop talking," he clutched his brow and curled away from Minda, "my head..."

Minda pulled him closer to take a better look. The outrage on her face was sudden.

"Ossen! You have daysickness!"

"Just a little. I'll be fine. I just need some rest."

"Ossen, why would you...? Why would you go out into the day? What were you thinking?"

"Please... stop..."

Minda gave Ossen a shove out of the furs. "You don't get to rest, Ossen. Not until you explain!"

Warily, and choosing to drop any protest, Ossen got to his feet. He sighed as he lifted up a new and strange object, one Chev had never seen before—it looked, for everything, like a narrow paddle made of leather, with a cross-like handle. It looked completely useless.

"What is *that*, Ossen?"

Ossen briefly debated what to tell her. "It's a weapon."

"A weapon?"

"A... dayghost weapon," Ossen notably hesitated.

"Ossen!" Minda clapped a hand over her mouth. "By the ancestors! What have you done?"

"It's just something I set aside a long time ago," said Ossen, putting aside the strange leather paddle.

"You have to get rid of it!"

"Why?"

"It could be cursed! It could bring us harm!"

Ossen sighed. "There's nothing cursed or magic about it, Minda. I'm not going to let Feska hurt this family, and if he tries something, *that*—" he gestured at the thing, "—*that* will protect us. Against that, Feska will be dead before he even hits the ground."

"If the elders find out—"

"—They'll do nothing. I'll make sure of that. The useless old bats."

"You'll make sure of it? What does that mean, Ossen?"

He didn't answer. He simply climbed back beneath the furs, grumbled something, and fell fast asleep.

Ossen's new weapon fascinated Chev—such a terribly strange object, and so terribly harmless. With sides of blunt leather and little weight, he couldn't see it doing much more than bouncing off someone, even a small animal would walk away with just a bruise. It made it all the more odd that it was so exceedingly crafted. The leather was smooth and black as the sky, being well-stitched with weaving strands of rawhide. Whoever made it went through the trouble of fitting a metal handle, with space for both hands to grip, crossed by a strip of steel that had no discernible purpose.

He wanted to touch it, feel the cool iron in his hand, but as he reached out, Minda bounded from across the room to slap his hand away.

"It's dangerous," she warned.

"Doesn't look dangerous," said Chev, though he nursed his hand it hurt more to be denied.

"Anything the dayghosts make are dangerous." She sighed, and turned back to her own work. "What was he thinking?"

Chev so dreaded mentioning he had followed Ossen into the day that it nearly jumped right out of his mouth. So many strange visions he saw, all felt like dreams, none he could give voice to, though he desperately wanted to.

Minda took a seat among her furs. "Chev, listen, don't tell anyone Ossen has been consorting with dayghosts, if you ever care to see him again."

"I won't."

"Don't let anyone know your father has daysickness, either, or sick at all. He's just resting today."

"I won't."

"Especially not Feska."

"I know."

"You know what Feska wants, don't you?"

"I know."

"If Feska tries to hurt you, come to me first. Let me fight Feska. You promise, don't you?"

This time, Chev didn't answer.

"Promise me, boy."

"I'll try."

"You're scaring me, child," Minda sighed. "Go on. Get out of here. Have fun."

"Have fun." Simple enough to say, but any hope that Chev could distract himself died when he stepped out into Feska's shadow. Tonight, as the night before, he chose to sharpen his knife outside Minda's burrow. Chev hurried past, pretending not to have noticed Feska's demented expression. Perhaps it was the clear sky and full moon, showing every lonesome tooth and twist of his lips, that made his smile especially disturbing this night. It was like something excited Feska.

Chev didn't want to think about it, so he threw himself into his own work, scouting for branches that might make good arrows. Still, a certain feeling grew by the hour, and by midnight it was impossible to ignore.

There were eyes on him. They glinted from the underbrush, bright and focused, but they flickered away as he turned to them, like shy candlelight. If it was a pawcat, it would shudder through the woods in retreat, and if it were an ursar, it would just attack. But these were not animal eyes. They belonged to methodical stalkers. Only nightfolk had such eyes.

Not Feska, who prowled from the canopy. Whoever stalked Chev did so from ground level, just past the curtain of vegetation.

So, Chev stilled his beating heart, kept his eyes to the front, and marched as casually as he could. If his stalker would not reveal himself, Chev would have to draw him out. He only hoped his caution would not give him away as he wandered past one of Varnas' traps.

Of course, when Chev heard the crush of foliage breaking and a smack of something hitting the bottom of a dirt pit, Chev grinned. Looking sly, Chev pulled his knife, and went to check what prey he'd caught.

The pit was just about twice this man's height, and there were grunts as someone hurled themselves up against side, never quite getting a handhold and sliding down each time. He looked up, the moon fell on his silvery face. A snapped bow lay at his feet.

He recognized this man; he was one of Feska's flunkies. "That you Darin? You were following me?"

"Throw down a vine, boy," said Darin.

Chev had never talked directly to the man, being fifteen or twenty years his senior, bearing the first lines of long life. Chev had also never even seen him alone—he was the sort of man who stuck to his group like a snail on a rock. But he was a lean, fierce man all the same; a good archer, if the stories were to be believed.

"Talk to me first," said Chev

"Got nothing to say. Forest doesn't belong to you."

"You were following me. Did Feska put you up to this?"

Darin swept the sweat and dirt off his face with his forearm. He'd gone quite flushed, and as he spoke he did so with a quiver.

"You can't leave me down here, you know!"

"So? Tell me why you were following."

"I said, I'll say again, I wasn't following you!"

"Darin, you're nowhere near the best hunter in the village. You're leagues behind Ossen or Feska. Don't pretend to me. So you better start talking or I'll— I'll..." in a fit of inspiration Chev pulled out his obsidian knife. "I'll show you what I'll do."

"If you cut a hair on my head, the elder's will get you. They're already damn close, too!"

"And if you hurt me, Ossen'll kill you!"

Darin snorted; an involuntary laugh. "That's just it boy, you fool kid. It's your father. Yes, we all know, boy. Have you seen how he acts? He's a bully, I know you can't see it. He shows no respect to the elders and the ways of this village. He keeps talking like he runs this place, and if we don't stop him, he will."

"Shut up!"

"He's sick, isn't he? Oh, don't answer, it's already written on your face. Feska was right after all. What instincts that man has."

Any retort Chev had died in his throat; somehow, Feska learned his father was sick. Which meant they knew he was vulnerable. Which for Feska was an invitation to attack. Chev rocketed back home, nearly skinning the soles of his feet, ignoring Darin's distant pleas. When he arrived the village was already alight with commotion, a crowd had gathered, focused on something near his mother's burrow. Chev's heart raced out of his chest, he pushed and shoved his way through a tribe fixed to their feet, cursing and damning anyone in his way. He made his way to the clearing in the middle, where a tense silence had settled.

The first thing he noticed was his mother's tear-ruined face. "Run away!" she cried.

Chev, so alarmed, lost any presence of mind, for Feska's face gleamed, his talon-like nails buried deep into mother's shoulder. His smirk twisted a fresh gouge on the cheek, black blood that went from his nose to the chin, like a second bloody mouth.

Feska looked on Chev with a queer expression, a portrait of expectant disappointment. "Looks like Darin failed," he muttered. His eyes bounced conspicuously between two men behind Chev.

It took Chev a moment to grasp he was communicating something, but by then, it was too late. Heavy arms clapped him like irons, then pushed him to his knees on the ground, bringing up a plume of dust. Unable to move, Chev's heart just pounded harder against his chest, screaming for blood and vengeance. Chev would see every finger Feska laid on his mother broken.

But Chev had immediately left Feska's attention. He directed it down Minda's burrow, shouting into its maw: "A correction, Ossen. Your son isn't dead. Yet. If you plan on making your heroic last stand, do so now."

All waited, but the burrow was pitch black. Nothing stirred within.

"This is what happens, Ossen." Feska drawled, his fingers dancing over his daysteel knife, "You have just this one, fragile woman and boy. You lose them, you lose *everything*. Isn't that right? Come out, Ossen. Now is the time to rescue your child. Do as beasts do, Ossen. Do as fathers do."

The inky blackness remained still. Feska peered deeper inside it, face contorting with ever greater frustration. Now he pushed Minda to the dirt, pressed a boot against her back—she cried out, as did Chev. Dirt spattered her, settling on her skin, crusting on her hair. Beneath her lips, spittle pooled on the soil.

Chev had devolved into unthinking, animal anger. The more he struggled, the tighter the grip became, but his wolven howls and growls drew Feska's attention.

"Calm down, boy," Feska flipped his knife, "You tried to protect her, I saw that at the feast, I respect that. But I wasn't after her. I was *warning* her, Chev, warning her about Ossen. Remember that night long ago, when you stood against your father? You tried to get him to leave your mother alone. Remember?"

Between the raging hatred that seared through him, Chev could only seethe. But though he tried not to, he remembered that moment clear as crystal. The night when Chev demanded Ossen leave him and his mother alone.

"Do you remember what he told you? It was the only truthful thing he ever said. He said, if this community ever stood in his way, he would destroy it."

Minda's voice was sudden and hoarse, "Then punish Ossen, not him!"

Feska pressed his foot down harder, to Minda's whines of pain. "The father does anything for his children. He butchers, he kills, he sacrifices all he can to save his own blood. That is why the boy must die. In the boy's death, Ossen proves his loyalty. Ossen finds redemption."

"Please!" Mother cried, "Please!"

Feska glowered. "Blame Ossen for what will happen next." He said to the men holding Chev, "Cut his throat."

"No!"

Minda must have screamed, but it hadn't sounded like anything a person could make, such a long, drawn out wail it was. He felt cold obsidian by the flesh of his neck, and the sharpness before it could even split his skin. Denial pulsed through him—for some reason, he thought if he could close his eyes, he would be transported away. But he wasn't dreaming, and neither was he dead.

He opened his eyes.

Ossen had lurched out, and leaned against the entrance of the burrow, his chest visibly heaving in the shadows. In his right hand clutched the strange dayghost weapon. The rest of him was terrible sight. Ossen had deep circles around the eyes, stubble coasted down his cheeks, and his skin was discolored by burns. As he stared murder at Feska, his pupils were veined black with blood.

Feska looked him up and down with disgust. "You're daysick, aren't you?"

Ossen pushed off the wall of the burrow, propelling himself toward Feska. His second hand went to the handle of the weapon.

Feska glanced at Ossen's absurd paddle. "Are you mad, too? What do you expect to do with *that*?"

Feska laughed prematurely. With a heave the leather scabbard flew off, and Chev saw the longest, brightest hunk of daysteel he'd ever laid eyes on. It was like a beam of pure moonlight as he hefted it toward Feska's neck. Feska died with mockery on his lips, his thin neck severed and his head launched into the crowd.

Chev was pushed to the ground as his two captors fearfully raised their daggers, but against the knives they were useless. The sword simply arced right through them, a gout of blood followed closely behind. The sword was so sharp it seemed effortless, but Ossen was heaving by the end, his shoulders and chest flaring. His eyes scanned the crowd with murder, and everyone smashed together to keep their distance.

A circle of onlookers formed around Ossen. Wide eyes from every angle, it seemed no one could turn away. As Ossen limped toward Chev, so did the crowd.

Ossen lifted Chev, whispering, "Go to your mother." Chev was quick to obey.

The hunter threw back his shoulders, steadied his breath, and stood tall despite the ravages of daysickness. He began to march; the crowd again following him, toward the rotted giant stump that house the elders.

Minda patted Chev's back, kissed him at the nearest place—his neck—and then went to Ossen's side.

"What are you doing?" she asked.

"You know what I'm doing."

"I'm trying to stop you."

"Why would you? They're useless, feeble, pathetic wastes of breath. Feska was right to fear me."

Ossen powered forward, through his own pain and between the roots of the great tree. The elders were mounted on their perches, warily eyeing Ossen's weapon.

"He's finally gone mad," one of the elders remarked, softly so it wasn't clear who had said it.

Ossen lifted his blade at the elders. It shuddered in his hands, made play with the moon and stars. "You gave Feska permission, didn't you? No... you *ordered* it."

Another elder crooned, "No, Ossen, we would do no such thing. Violence is not how we carry on our affairs."

"I've never met such a gathering of liars," Ossen stepped forward. "But here's where it ends. Where I come from, the man who commands the most swords rules. I once thought that so barbaric, I traveled far to flee from it, but now I see its wisdom. Rule by the sword can't be worse than rule by shriveled cowards. Now, I'll take this chamber, I'll take your seats and I'll make a throne of it. From this day forward, I'm *emperor*."

An elder crowed, "You wouldn't dare—"

"I *would*. If this is what I have to do to live in peace, then I'll *do* it. And none of this ancient tradition garbage will stop me—once I pile your bodies like rags, everyone will see how weak you always were."

One of the elders quivered to their feet.

"Ossen! If only you knew—everything you're doing right now is precisely what we feared from you. You have allies here. You could have worked with us. You could *still."*

Ossen lifted his blade to his shoulder. "It's too late to beg. You had your time to show compassion. At least die without lying."

He made a move to march forward, the sword lifted up ready to swing down. But a tremendous cry rang out, and Ossen froze. Minda stood by the entryway, Chev in her grasp, her arms clutched so tightly that she seemed to crush his shoulders.

Tears glittered down her face. "Will you kill them in front of Chev?"

In the drama Chev had forgotten himself. Only his mother's touch gave him any presence of mind. Yet, Ossen considered his lover's face carefully. His mouth was like a just-fired bowstring, vibrating between tenderness and brutal rage. But his grip never softened on his sword. He answered, "I will."

He took another step forward. Minda rushed for his sword arm. Ossen tried to shake her off, but she wouldn't let go.

Minda cried, "Kill me first, then! This is my village Ossen. Would you destroy *us?"*

"Destroy you?" Ossen was disarmed by the question. "Woman, this *council* would destroy you."

"This is my family!"

"I'm your family!" Ossen shook suddenly, in his anger he flared out.

He wasn't trying to hurt her, all he wanted was to push her off. It wasn't precisely clear how it had happened, but in a split second, Minda was cut by the sword, the tip slashing her arms. She fell back, the blood poured freely. Her shawl so quickly soaked into blackness. Her face turned dull like clay.

Ossen's voice shook, his black eyes watered. "You did that to yourself." But the shock was so evident. The man who was always so stoic stumbled backward, letting the sword rattle on the dirt floor. "Damn!"

Another elder lifted himself onto his twig-like legs. She intoned: "Ossen, you've shed blood on sacred ground. You've traded with the dayghosts outside of the clan. To top it off, you've grown power mad, and attempted to become a tyrant. For these crimes, Ossen, you are banished, to roam the forest with the animals, monsters, and the drovers."

Ossen sneered—he tried picking up his sword. But Minda had crawled atop it, balling up like a boulder.

He whispered, "Minda, please! I don't want to hurt you!"

Minda raised her head, tears streaming down her face. "You will have to!"

The moment hung. Ossen still tried gripping the sword, his face just as cold, but something inside fought him. He had no strength to pull it, not while he locked eyes with Minda.

He let go.

With a heavy sigh, his shoulders hunched, he marched to the center of the chamber. Resolving to end this with pride intact, he stated, "I will accept your banishment. There's nothing for me here anyway. And who would want to rule over worthless creatures such as yourselves?" He glanced at Chev. "Come boy. We're leaving."

The boy had watched the scene with wordless horror. His mind swirled with mixed loyalties; everything he loved had just raised hands against each other. It was paralyzing; in that moment he would mindlessly act on anything anyone asked of him. It was only his mother's intervention that stopped him from following his father out into the unknown. She clapped a bloody hand over his shoulder, and that stopped him.

"He's staying here," she told him.

"They'll never accept him," said Ossen, "he'll always be the son of the traitor."

One of the elders piped, "Your sins are not his. If you leave in peace, we will keep him like our own."

"They're lying," he said, but seeing solid opposition in every direction, he turned to Chev, and told him, "If you ever grow tired of these fools, I will be wandering the Daylit Lands. You will find me there."

Ossen was about to leave when he was arrested by a command, "Take your cursed weapon with you."

Ossen had no appetite to follow a command by the elders, even if he would have done it anyway. Even so, he glanced at once at Minda, chose it was better not to fight it, and struck a final comment.

"They're not ghosts, you know," said Ossen, "They're called *dayfolk*. They're flesh and blood, like us, and nothing about them is magic."

The sword carved a crescent in the dirt as he picked it up. Without looking back, he ventured out into the forest, and disappeared into its shadowed embrace.

Minda put on a brave face until they were back in the burrow, and then she collapsed in exhaustion. Chev cleaned and bound the wound on her arm and covered her with sleeping furs. But her sleep was elusive, interrupted by sudden sobbing and twisting and turning. Chev, with his heavy heart, couldn't even close his eyes. It was bright and burning outside when unconsciousness finally took him.

His dreams were strange and vague. A creature climbed onto his chest and pressed down on him a subtle weight. He tried batting it off, but it would become fog whenever he touched it. There was a piercing light that arrived and faded with equal suddenness.

When he woke, Ossen's sword was laid on his chest.

Chapter Four
A Monster that Speaks

YEARS PASSED. Chev's memories of Ossen never went away, but they dulled like old copper. So too the village began to forget, and just how they once kept silent about the scandal swirling around Ossen and Minda, they did the same for Feska's death. Uncomfortable topics were set aside, peace settled, normalcy returned.

For Minda, the memories remained fresh.

Only Chev could see it. Where others saw a smile, Chev saw Minda's disguise. Her laughter was even rarer. In unguarded moments, Chev often found her pondering the long scar along her arm, the wound Ossen gave her, the only thing she had to remember him by. He could try and fix things, persuade her to take another mate, but Chev already knew he had nothing but sweet words for her.

Unable to fix things at home, Chev threw himself into the world outside. He became something of a long-range scout, on the look out for new hunting grounds, and this self-imposed role gave him immense energy. No longer did he have the patience to listen to old folk crow on about the past—he favored action. Sometimes he barely stepped back home before wishing his mother farewell, bouncing out on yet another ill-defined expedition, wandering for as long as the night lasted and returning only as the sun rose. He came back—sometimes with only stories, other times with exotic pelts, plants, and artifacts. His mother's burrow became a dump for trophies.

Something else happened. He metamorphosed—his limbs long, his frame strong and lean, muscles threaded across his body. Now his jaw set well in his face, his eyes went the way of polished river stones, and he took on the gentle moon-like sheen of a healthy nightfolk man. He no longer shuffled about, heavy with a troubled youth, but with the lightness of assurance in his own strength and skill, and in the rare times he chose to speak, he did so with nothing to prove.

There's a distinct time when home is no longer large enough, physically and mentally. He saw how things were going, so he packed his few personal possessions and relocated to the bachelor's burrow, a barracks of sorts for the men of the village who weren't currently mated. It was nothing more complicated than a hall of hammocks.

Chev was not in a social mood when he first stepped inside, and mercifully, the place was empty. He set everything he had by his new home— a fur-lined backpack, jangling with tools, spears, cookware and clothes. It was everything he cared to own, but even those items only served as a cocoon around his prized possession: the Daysword. The weapon Ossen had set by him before he left. He reached inside just to grasp the metal of the hilt. There was an elemental coolness to it, like touching raw power.

There was a commotion, and Chev hastily extracted his hand. Two men had thrown back a curtain and walked in. To call these "men" though, felt like the wrong word—each were younger than Chev. They laughed at some unheard joke and had each other's arms around their shoulders.

"...And so, that's when Varnas says, 'Hey, I'm standing right here!'"

Whatever the joke was, they found it so funny they were practically slapping each other. One nearly flopped onto the floor as he clutched his belly.

Chev stood stupidly until both boys spotted him. They seemed equally dumbfounded.

"Look at that!" said one of them, "It's a Chev! Laven, what portent doth hold such a rare beast?"

"I dunno, Jaev. Better see the elders about it."

Unused to being the center of attention, Chev took it as teasing. He threw his concentration into unpacking, spreading out his things, growing familiar with the earthy scent of his new accommodation. Jaev and Laven continued to joke among themselves, even roughhousing a little, but Chev treated it like the everyday drama of nature and willed himself to ignore it.

He made his space, closed his eyes, and drifted into an early sleep.

Sometime later, a shuffling had Chev's eyelids fluttering open. He thought it was an animal rooting around the entrance, but then a shadow disturbed the light that filtered through the entrance. He let his eyes open slightly; a nightfolk shuffled his way in, his feet dragging behind him.

"Who'd come in at the break of dawn?" It was Jaev.

"Did Nalia *just* kick him out? Wow, it ain't his night, is it?"

"Shut up," cursed the newcomer, before throwing himself onto a hammock like he was dead, tired weight.

Chev sat up to see *Darin*. The very same who tried to kill him so many seasons ago. An energy passed between them as they caught eyes, like for a second they didn't know what to do about the other. Whatever Darin felt then, it ended with a grunt, and he flopped back onto his hammock.

Chev found waking into a new place oddly disorienting, his nose wrinkling to the strange must, the foreign, intimate resonance of friends talking. Someone was cooking something, someone else was laughing. Chev sat up and realized he had a headache.

"You coming hunting with us?"

That was Laven. Chev assumed he was talking with his friend, but Laven looked right his way with nothing but earnestness.

He rubbed his head; something in his skull decided to pound, like his heart had relocated where his brain used to be. "I'll think about it," he said.

Jaev swept his hand dismissively. "Forget it Lav, he's gonna run off into the woods alone, like he always does."

"Probably dreaming about Sana, heh."

"Probably? You ever see him when she's around? Goes clam quiet, then looks at her like she's the most distant star."

Chev kicked himself out of bed and set out to organize his gear. "You're just jealous."

"Jealous?" Jaev snorted. "Of course I'm jealous. Everyone is. Have you ever *seen* Sana?"

"She's hot," agreed Laven.

"Super hot. And she spends all her time hanging around you. If she invites anyone else to mate with her, I'll boil my foot."

"Better kiss your foot goodbye then, I think I've got a few moves," smiled Laven.

Jaev slapped him on the side of the head. "Moves? Ha! Bet you anything she doesn't know your name."

Laven rubbed where Jaev had slapped him. "Yeah, well, that's no obstacle. I was thinking maybe Chev could drop a good word for me when she dumps him." Then he turned and shouted: "Hey Chev, what would it take for you to drop a good word to Sana?"

"Your silence," said Chev, rubbing his temple.

Laven thought hard about that. "Was that a yes or a no?"

Jaev was professorial about it. "It's simple enough. If you stay silent, then he'll do as you ask."

"Yes but *how* silent? Am I supposed to just whisper? Or maybe not talk at all? Crap, Jaev, I don't think I could keep that up for more than a night. Hey Chev... hey!"

They had just noticed Chev quietly leaving. Reluctantly, Chev turned.

"What is it?"

"You didn't answer. You *were* gonna hunt with us, right?"

"I wasn't planning on it."

"Ah, damn, he really is a loner. Why you such a loner, Chev?" asked Jaev.

Another's voice boomed, and with its wooden tenor drew everyone's attention. "Forget it."

Everyone's head twisted about looking for the source of the comment. Then Darin made his presence known; he sat up from his hammock, and seemed to stare right past Chev to Laven and Jaev, like Chev didn't really exist.

"The boy is Ossen's brood, and just as arrogant as he was. No matter what you offer, nothing changes bad blood."

As way of conclusion, Darin laid back down, and wrapped his arms beneath his head.

Nothing changes bad blood.

In Chev's head, Darin's words metamorphosed.

Nothing changes *my* blood.

Ossen may be gone, but it seemed his legacy would forever stick to him.

Dark words gave Chev dark energy, which in turn drove Chev deeper into the woods than he should have gone. He couldn't tell himself that Darin had not spoken true. He *was* like Ossen. And to purge himself of Darin's poisoned words, he followed the creek as it made its course into thicker and darker woods.

Things grew here like they conspired to devour any path—curtains of vines growing between clumps of trees, and the waterway circling around massive mossy boulders and pillars of dirt held together by old knotted roots. Chev wasn't sure where he was going, it was simply a matter of heading where his nose took him.

It was by a muddy, silty bank when he spotted a singular nightbloom. The fragrance was gentle and had slight spice to it—but more captivating were the intricate layers of petals it beheld. Long stamens hung like cattails from the center, almost playful and inviting. Chev was hypnotized by it, and he immediately thought of Sana, and how it would look in her hair. Gently, he snipped it with a knife and pushed it carefully into his sash.

He wandered up the bank, the flower's spice having already gone to his head. The clearing was grassy and the ground soft like velvet, it would've made for a nice place to sit in the moonlight if he knew he could get home before daybreak. So Chev settled on a quick break to savor his find, twirling it between thumb and finger, watching it do its whirling dance. He did this until he felt the weight of the coming journey, compelling him to pull himself up from the grass and start off in the direction of the village. He drifted into a fantasy of Sana with her eyes aglow as she took the flower.

Chev stopped abruptly. There was a strange stick poking out from the ground, the end cut with a knife into two halves. He recognized it as one of Varnas' trap markers. Relieved, he took the long way around.

He hadn't expected at all for the ground to give away.

There was an enormous crack; Chev assumed it was the wind before he realized he was falling. He went into darkness, slamming into packed dirt. Winded and groaning, but conscious, Chev had the sick feeling he'd broken something. So he stretched his arms out, and, though unsteady, he tested his legs. They took his weight, Chev was both surprised and relieved.

He was, at worst, bruised. The relief didn't last long.

The flower...

It was a flat and sad thing now. He'd landed atop it, breaking the stem and smashing the petals. The thing swayed sadly by its own dead weight.

"*Sana*," he sighed. He could never show it to her, but a vestigial hope made him put it back in the sash.

The pit was deep. Even jumping and clawing at the sides, he could only reach an arm's length from the rim. So he tossed his spear over the edge and started his methodical climb, cursing Varnas with every clod of dirt he buried his hand into.

He couldn't imagine how the man would be so careless to misplace his own trap marker.

It was arduous work, he had to dig his own hand holds, and the soil was so loose he couldn't trust it to take his weight. Chev was almost spent when he finally touched surface—he pulled himself up by a tuft of strong grass, and he was about to throw a leg over, but then he came eye-to-eye with *something*. Something horrible. Chev forgot he was climbing; he lost his grip, and plunged into the darkness again, regaining himself only just enough to land on his rump.

The pain was nothing—it was his fiercely beating heart that was intolerable. He only processed the creature he had seen in pieces: bright, deep eyes, bent posture, bony limbs, ridged, malformed back. A pair of drooling mandibles, made from grinding molars. A description he once heard came to life.

A bone-skin.

Chev sweated like he had a fever. He suddenly recalled that stag he and Ossen once found, disemboweled by some ravenous force, the hunter's word a ringing bell. Things would only end in violence, that Chev already knew, so he reached for his spear—and then winced remembering he had thrown it over before his climb. He would be unarmed but for a measly stone knife.

The bone-skin leaned a little over the edge, eyes aglow and hungry. It spoke with a chittering, pitched voice. "You're not the old man."

"I'm not. So you can let me go."

The bone-skin made an irregular hiss—its version of laughter. "No, no, no. You are even better. I was-s-s not looking forward to eating him. Your people get very tough and bony in your age. But you - sweet fleshed, black mois-s-st marrow, mouth-melting livers-s-s - yesss, yes, yes. You will do nic-c-cely."

"Find some bush mice. I'm not easy prey."

"No, normally no... but at the bottom of the pit, without your sharp tools-s-s... oh excuse me, I'm just salivating at the thought. Daylight is coming, and as I recall your kind dislikes-s-s the sun."

Chev's heart was beating. The bone-skin was right—dawn was close. Chev was now reduced to making wild bluffs. He puffed his chest, hoping bluster would carry him through. "Far from it, monster. Try me in daylight, I dare you. I'll cut you to ribbons"

"Really? A nightfolk fighting in daylight? This I have to see. You s-s-stay right there, prey. We'll both wait for the s-s-sun, then we'll see."

There was some shuffling, and the bone-skin reappeared but in the branch over the pit, folding its skeletal arms and resting its head so that it was propped toward Chev. Chev had hoped for some respite, but as he stooped in the pit, he knew there was no resting within the creature's unblinking gaze. It seemed he didn't even have the space to think.

But Chev had to try, he put the creature out of mind and he wracked his head for a solution. Anything he could come up with came down to luck—that Varnas might come, that the bone-skin would fall asleep, that lightning would fry the damned monster. All the sorts of gambles that a good woodsman hated to take.

But there was no running, either. Daylight would be coming soon, Chev already knew he couldn't reach home before dawn. Any later, and this bone-skin would find Chev as day blind as any of the nightfolk.

Chev had to do precisely the thing Ossen had warned him not to.

He stood up, patted the dirt off his legs, and to the creature he *spoke*. "Bone-skin! What do I call you?"

The spiny, strange creature raised its head, suddenly interested. It pounced off the branch on all fours, and roved to the edge of the pit. "Our kind don't have names-s-s like yours do," said the monster, "but I suppose you could call me *Patienc-c-ce*."

It hissed, drawing out the last word in way that made Chev shudder.

"Patience, may we talk?"

"We already are."

"What could I give you so you'd let me go?"

The creature drew up. "There is but one bargain our kind deigns-s-s to consider. For pas-s-sage into our territory without molestation—one healthy child a year."

Chev never realized that cruelty delivered with such straightforwardness could cause the throat to dry up. The young man had to swallow, to suck in a breath, before he could speak once again. "That's a steep price."

"Only because you creatures-s-s are so attached to your brood. You are a fecund species, the brats get everywhere. What's-s-s one life?"

"We value all our people. We're a tight community—"

"So? Do you not have neighbors? Why not use their offspring?"

Chev held his disgust in. "We are not barbarians..."

"I care not what you call yourselves-s-s. I care of what fills-s-s my stomach, and that of my mate and brood. Will you do this or not?"

"I have to think about it—"

"It's all the same to me. I'll wait until s-s-sunrise."

Chev trumpeted out before the thing could leave. "No, no!" What he would say was already turning Chev's insides, but he opened his mouth and spoke, and tried to think as little of what he was saying as possible. "I accept."

The creature cocked its head to the side, the mandibles grinding to make an unnatural clicking sound. "Do you? I find this very s-s-surprising."

"Yes. I'll—" his mind and tongue rebelled at what he was trying to say, "—I'll bring you a child."

Again, that *hiss*. Mocking and grating, Chev wanted to cover his ears. After it went its course, the creature said, "I don't believe you, creature. But I'll let you go, and I'll look forward to taking the debt you'll owe me. We shall feast."

"You'll never get the chance."

Patience hissed once again—Chev expected it to say something, but it only loped back into the darkness. The air was, for a moment, heavy with silence, but with the monster gone life soon came back. The birds resumed their nightsongs, and the crickets chirped. Chev hadn't even noticed they'd left.

Even so, it was so easy to imagine the creature leaping out from the dark to clamp its mandibles over his throat—Chev was not sure whether he should climb. So he did it with great care, and as soon as he brought his head over the edge, he made a quick scan for the glowering, alien eyes of the bone-skin.

The spear was where he left it. He pulled it from the ground and, with one furtive glance back, threw himself toward the village.

Chev ran so carelessly he nearly stabbed a wide-eyed Varnas on the way. Somehow, his wrinkled face took on the bony ridges of that monster, and he stepped out from behind a tree so suddenly that Chev thought it could only be an ambush. Only Varnas' quick hands deflected the spearpoint into a tree.

"Watch it boy!"

Chev felt he had no time to apologize. "Run, Varnas!"

"Ah— hell! What did you—"

Varnas couldn't finish his thought before Chev broke for it. The old man was left following, each stride landing in Chev's footprints. He took Varnas bounding off knotted roots and the tops of boulders.

"Slow down, boy!"

"Keep running!"

They ran for a full hour. Day was coming, peering over the horizon, its fingers lighting the clouds with white fire. And in sight of the village, he collapsed. He spreadeagled on the soft mossy ground.

Varnas was only out of sight for a moment, but soon his springy tough body pounced into view, though notably slower than when he started. The run ended with a plodding walk, his back bent over, he nearly rolled between the roots of a big tree.

"My stomach cramped ten minute ago. Ah! Haven't run like that in a while." Varnas stretched an arm until it audibly cracked. "So what was it? An ursar?"

Chev shook his head, his voice was an exhausted wheeze. "It was waiting for you, Varnas. It was lucky it got me."

"Waiting for me?"

Chev winced with the intake of breath. "It moved your trap marker, hoping you'd fall in."

"Did it? The greater fool it is, then. The markers are for you folk, I never forget a trap. Was it a pack of drovers?"

"It was a bone-skin."

"A bone-skin?" Varnas whistled, impressed. "I should've listened to the elders, they said I was going out too far. How did you kill it?"

"I didn't kill it."

Varnas stared at Chev. "You didn't? How did you escape then?"

"I—" Chev swallowed, "I talked with it."

"Oh, Chev..." Varnas was at a loss for words, and suddenly his voice was brimming with worry, "Oh Chev, you've brought a hell of a disaster on our heads. Those things—you fight them or you run. You never *talk* to them. Anything but that. Didn't your mother tell you that?"

Chev shrugged, and he got to his feet. "I made it a promise, but I don't have to keep it. I'll simply never go back there. If it never sees me, it can't hurt me."

Chev was about to stand to go back to the village, but Varnas would not have it. He forced Chev's attention, seizing the young man by the shoulders, looking into his eyes until Chev would meet his. "Chev," Varnas said, "Once you promise tribute to the bone-skins, you *will* pay it. And, boy, you will pay until you have nothing left, then you'll take from others to give to them. You understand? If you don't give what they want, they'll take *everything* from *everyone*."

"If it tries," Chev pushed aside Varnas' arm, "then I'll kill it, personally."

Varnas gave a flat smile, like the statement was absurd on the face of it. "You say it like it's simple. I'll tell you what's more likely: when the elders find out you made a deal with a bone-skin, they'll give you over to them and then *spirits save you*." To punctuate his point, Varnas jabbed Chev's chest.

But Chev would not allow himself to lose face. He pushed away Varnas' finger, and then the man himself, stepping past and toward the village. "Sorry I even made you worry. Just let me handle it."

So Varnas followed with this: "What would you think if Sana found out, huh?"

That stopped Chev in his tracks. He turned a serious eye over his shoulder.

"The flower in your sash—bound for her, was it? Funny how sometimes things don't work out too well. There's no magic force bringing you good things in life. It's all here," Varnas tapped his temple knowingly. "Smarts and strength, boy. You got the strength—the smarts aren't quite there yet. You're as impulsive as your father."

Chev frowned, suddenly sure that Varnas was not so much different from anyone else. "The elders said, whatever sins Ossen had are not mine."

"You want the elders' protection? You got to listen to their rules. Otherwise you can go off and be a drover like the rest of 'em. Always free to do that." Varnas gave a smile, more genuine this time. "Lucky for you, I'm an old man with one last adventure in 'im. Together, we can fix this."

Chev looked searchingly into Varnas' face, to which Varnas gave smug wink.

"We'll need an ally, though. I have the man in mind. Think you have it in you to forgive an old enemy?"

Before dusk had even fully fallen, Chev pushed away his furs. He spent his first waking minutes ruminating on Ossen's sword, digging it out from the furs he'd buried it under. He could still remember how his father swung it through men like they were no more substantial than fog. In his nightmares, Feska's smiling head still rolled across the ground, dead before he even knew to be scared.

Such power, in such an unassuming shape.

Chev covered it back up. One day he might have to use it, he hoped it would not be today.

The others were still asleep. He broke fast on dried fish and fruit by himself. He clawed out of the burrow just as the sun had disappeared from view.

He and Varnas had arranged to meet.

The old man was leaning by a tree, his sleepy eyes came right as Chev approached. He picked himself up; prepared to hear what Chev had to say.

"I can't forgive him."

Chev expected Varnas to interject, but the old man betrayed no emotion. He waited for Chev to give his reasons.

"He tried to kill me," Chev finished.

Varnas shook his head, clucked with disappointment. "That's too bad, son. I was expecting a different answer out of you. What with the elders having given you a fresh start, you would be a big enough man to do the same for others too. Guess I was wrong."

"Do we need Darin? Aren't there better trackers? What about Jarv, or Bruus, or—"

Varnas cut him off with a shrug. "Probably. Probably those folks can do just as good a job as Darin. But would convincing them mean anything to you? This is more about what's on your inside than you think. You want to be like Ossen, always prideful and puffing out his chest to save some little face? Then you'll always be a danger to us, and I can't have that."

Varnas shrugged, and hobbled off back to his burrow.

"That's it?" Chev could barely believe he was being abandoned like this.

"That's it."

"You won't help me?"

"I won't help you."

"You'd leave me to the bone-skins?" Chev swept his hand toward the forest, ostensibly to the bone-skins that lurked within.

Varnas eventually stopped, but made a show of an exasperated sigh.

"I'll tell the elders, and they'll gather a party and deal with them. Nothing for you to do anymore."

"But if they find out I brought them..."

"They won't like it too much," said Varnas.

Chev swallowed an uncomfortable thought. *And if Sana finds out...*

Varnas made his way to the elders' tree, and Chev followed closely behind, begging all the while.

"Wait, wait, wait, Varnas! Maybe if we could just *talk* with Darin."

Varnas had a cheeky smile, "Hmm... if it ain't to forgive him—what about?"

Chev ran his mouth. "Listen, I'm not making any promises! We can still just have a conversation! Maybe he can see reason. Maybe we don't bring up Ossen or any of that business at all. Maybe he'll be willing to help out just 'cause."

Much to Chev's relief, Varnas stopped. But not without a perturbed look.

"You'll talk to him?"

It was tremendously difficult to say it, but Chev could just eke it out. "Yes."

Varnas nodded. "Then we go."

"Just be straight to the point. Don't go off on some nonsense, don't let him bait you into anger. Be, uh, *magnanimous*, ask for his help, *without getting mouthy* the way you do."

"I *do not* get mouthy."

"Sure you don't. But boy, this is *your* problem. Don't expect me to jump up and help ya."

With that, Chev was booted into Darin's direction.

They had joined a trading expedition to the dayghost village. As strong men picked up dayghost goods and hauled them back, Chev sidled next to a Darin considering the trade stone with a slightly strangled look.

It was a warm night. Lightbugs flitted through the air like mad stars. Fat toads croaked and hopped their way through the grass. One slapped onto the trade stone and then hopped right back off. But Darin was so focused on the runes all other things might as well have been invisible.

Chev cleared his throat. Darin twisted slightly to the sound.

"If you're going to break your silence to me, boy, this is a bad night to do it," said Darin.

"It's the only time I have," said Chev. He met his eyes, and shivered—he saw in him the men who had held him hostage that night years ago. For a moment, Chev saw Darin's head detached, his neck a cloven stump.

Darin's face grew grim. "Your sire murdered my friends, and only your mother stopped him before he moved onto the elders. She's the hero in all this. But I see more of *that brute* in you than her."

Any words about not taking any bait were forgotten as Chev's pulsing, hot blood went to his head. "It was only because you and Feska drove him to do it," he hissed.

"The only person who made him do anything was himself. If he'd acted like a man from this community he would have never been banished."

"You banished him because he scared you."

"Your damn right about that. I was scared of him, everyone was, power-hungry monster he was. And he did nothing but prove it, too."

Chev muttered bitterly, "I can't believe I'm supposed to forgive you."

"That's fine with me. I don't hunger for your good feelings, so you can take whatever is on your chest somewhere else. The only use I've got you for is reading these runes."

"Reading the runes?"

"Yes. You know how to read runes, don't you? Half of these symbols never get used. But look over there—" Darin pointed, "They poured all their pebbles into that little divot. No food. No furs. Just those things, into that one rune. I don't know it."

Chev eyed it closely. It took him a moment to recall what his father said about it. "I could tell you. But before I do, maybe I do have something I have to say."

"Then say it."

"I need help tracking a bone-skin. And killing it."

Darin seemed to clench at that. "I won't ask how you got involved in their kind, I don't want to know. But if it'll help the village, you have my bow. Now, tell me what those symbols mean. What do they want?"

Chev looked at the symbol. It was a set of two crosses, themselves crossed. Its divot was filled with so many black pebbles that the dayghosts placed a clay bowl to hold them all. "Sure," said Chev, "the rune means, 'weapons'."

When Chev went back, Varnas was making inquisitive brows at him.

"No hugging or tears. So what's that about?"

"We're fine." Chev answered like he was dismissing the question.

"You forgave him?"

"We made a trade, so we're good. He'll help us."

Varnas hissed, "Boy, that's not what I asked you to do!"

Chev shrugged. "The outcome is the same. What does it matter to you?"

He started off in the direction of the village, Varnas followed, ranting from behind.

"Before you start getting all silent and moody, I want you to think about what you've just done. To save your own hide you made a deal with a bone-skin. You know as well as me you run from or kill a bone-skin, and if neither of those things work, you damn well let it eat you. You want to bring bone-skins on us all?"

"Of course not," said Chev.

"Then you better prove you turned over a new leaf, because if you're gonna continue making deals with bone-skins there's no point saving you."

"Hey!" Chev suddenly flared, and he nearly tripped over himself to face Varnas, "You keep calling it a deal, but I didn't! I *tricked* it."

Varnas snorted. "Ain't no difference, once they know you can be played, you will be played. That's who they are, that's how they operate. They find idiots that think they're smarter than them, like you!"

Chev sighed. "Once we kill it, it's not gonna be any threat to us."

"That's hoping we get to it in time. That's hoping it doesn't call the *Feast* on us."

Chev blinked. "The Feast?"

"You don't even know the Feast." Varnas shook his head. "Well, that certainly explains a few things."

Chev was distracted by a sudden, unexpected sight. They had come across Sana, long black hair veiled her as she bent over to a copse of mushrooms. Chev was arrested by the sight of her, whatever he was about to say evaporating from his mind.

Varnas patted his back, and whispered. "We leave tonight, so go tell her what you need to." A slight push had Chev's heavy legs wheeling powerlessly towards her.

She didn't look to expect him. Wide eyes scanned him, soon lingering on the broken flower hooked through his belt.

Chev saw where she looked, so unthinkingly pulled it out, letting its limp stem flop forward. "It's for you. Actually, it *was* for you, but as you can see..."

Sana took it from his hands and broke off the stem. It was just a mass of bruised petals which pooled in her hand.

"I've never seen such a deep blue," she said softly.

"Blue?"

"Never mind. Thank you so much, it's very beautiful. I know you must have searched very hard to find it."

"You have no idea." Chev scratched the back of his head while surreptitiously scanning the forest for Varnas. "Picking mushrooms?"

"I was. It's part of being an herbalist and I—" she sighed, her prepared speech collapsing into a laugh. "Really, I just needed a reason to get out of the village. So there."

"I know how that feels," Chev nodded.

Her answer was enigmatic as she paced through the trees. "It's a different story for you." She sighed. "They're digging out my burrow right now. I should be there. But people keep asking me... things. There's only so many times you can dodge one question."

At Sana's stage of a woman's life, there was but one question people asked. But even Chev didn't want to say it, for fear of the answer. But, about to face a monster, he was also short of chances. And so he set fear aside, and asked. "Sana... I need to ask... about *our* future... perhaps you were thinking about me... as your next mate..."

"Oh, Chev, it's you." Discomfort fell across her face. "Probably."

Even that bit of doubt, Chev didn't like. He stepped up closer. "Whatever you need, Sana."

Sana took a seat on a mossy boulder. Moonlight struck her lovely face, strands of black hair fell around her ear, but the whole portrait was ruined by a twisted mouth. Doubts, it had to be.

"You're not around, Chev," said Sana, "I see you plenty, forest does too. But the people, they don't. They don't know who you are. You're practically a drover."

"What they have to say doesn't bother me—"

"It bothers *me*," said Sana, suddenly passionate eyes fixed on Chev, "I belong here, Chev, I'm a part of this place. Are you? I don't know. And if I have to choose... Chev, I don't know what choice I'd make. I don't want to make a choice at all."

"Tell me what I can do."

"Be with the tribe, Chev. Make an effort to know us. Let people see in you what I see in you. There are good people here, if you'd just give them a chance."

She had the sweetest smile in the world. When he answered, he was not sure whether it was to her, or to the soaring feeling that rose from his belly to his neck. But he said it anyway, and so went a promise: "I'll try."

But it was a half-hearted promise. Even Sana might have sensed that. But whether he could keep it was not in the forefront of his mind. He pictured the bone-skin, perched above and greedily eyeing them both. With that threat hanging over them, any other concern was meaningless.

If she ever found out, the disappointment would destroy her, and that would destroy him. He wouldn't let a tear fall down her cheek, and any degenerate monster that would hurt her would die by his hands.

Chapter Five
For Us, and Them

IT WAS A FEW hours before dawn when Darin emerged from the underbrush with bow slung over his shoulder. He gave Chev a grumpy acknowledgment before noticing Varnas.

"You too, huh?" Darin looked at Varnas without addressing him.

"He's helping us," explained Chev.

"I can see that."

Varnas grunted. "Don't make things complicated, Darin. The bone-skin threatens the village. We're going to kill it."

"Any reason this can't go to the elders?" Darin looked meaningfully at Chev.

"Ah, hell, Darin. Damn you for asking the right questions." Varnas spat into the underbrush. "If you can't trust Chev, try to trust me."

Darin nodded. "If you say so, old man. It's for the village. I just can't help but notice it's Ossen's spawn getting us wrapped up with bone-skins."

Chev stepped forward. "The elders said —"

"Don't use their words when you don't obey them," interrupted Darin, his bow jerking slightly.

There was a hostility that manifested as a heaviness between them. Chev and Darin had their chests out, glares smoldering like fire. Varnas quickly stepped between them.

"Hey, let's not kill each other before we kill the bone-skins. Can we do that? Good. Chev's going to explain himself afterward, aren't you?"

Chev hesitated. "Fine."

"See? Let's go."

Just before Chev had gone out, he had meditated on the hilt of the Daysword. At odds whether he should take it, he was torn over the dilemma. To not use it might cost a life. To use it might cost Sana.

His position in the village had always been tenuous, but now more than ever. He felt like a spider hanging onto a silken thread in a storm, the stain of Ossen's dishonor forever branded him, and only now he was protected only by the flimsy promises of wizened old crones and forgetful old men. No matter what the elders had to say, circumstances proved that the same hatred and distrust that nearly killed him years ago still beat through the veins of the tribe.

And now, as he stalked through the deep forest on the hunt of his life, he felt he was walking next to the personification of that hatred in Darin. Chev was only glad that the hunter was in front of him instead of behind.

Chev had taken the spear. Obsidian and wood it may have been but he still trusted it. He prayed that Darin's strength and Varnas' "smarts" would make up for any weakness.

Chev hadn't realized he'd drifted so far into ruminations until Varnas broke the silence.

"So... Nalia kicked you out."

Darin gave Varnas a hostile glance.

"I'm just making conversation," Varnas muttered.

"Don't you know to be silent during a hunt, old man?"

"You think I was born yesterday, boy? I'm just passin' the time until we actually *start* the hunt."

"Then please, get it out of your system before it gets us killed."

"What a pile of fun you are, Darin." Varnas smiled in spite of himself. "I remember when my first mate kicked me out. Oh what a terrible night it was. Day, more accurately. I'll have you know I was streaking buck naked to the bachelor's burrow. By the way, that was the same time I was the best looking man in the village, but also the laziest, so as you can imagine—"

"Please stop," said Darin, "for once Chev, say something!"

Chev shrugged, smiling. "I got nothing to say."

Varnas piped, "Of course not, he's the quiet sort. Actually, you both are. Except Chev's a little less angry and moody. A *little*."

"Hush," whispered Chev.

"What's that?"

"Hush!"

Darin raised his arm. Chev snuck ahead, leaping between roots so as not to break any branches—and then he was in the same bend in the creek he'd encountered earlier, open before him was the same black pit he'd fallen into.

"I saw the bone-skin here," said Chev.

Varnas picked up his trap marker and replaced it by the pit. "Damn thing did move it. It's gonna take a good minute or two to cover it back up."

"It climbed this tree," Darin noted scratch marks racing up one of the trunks.

Varnas put a milky eye to it. "Sure it's not a pawcat or..."

"No. Pawcats don't rip up the bark. But bone-skins, they puncture it. Look how deep the gouges are... it's a bone-skin all right." Darin shuddered. "I don't like this. They belong in the deep woods, not out here." He slung his bow over his arm, and made a steely scan of the woods. "It's decided, then. We *have* to kill it. We have to show that we won't cow to it and pay tribute like barbarians. We'll send a message that any bone-skin that comes into our territory will die, and we will do it so utterly they don't even think to try a second time. Come, it must be laired around here, somewhere."

Darin caught sight of some sign only meaningful to him, and he walked purposefully in that direction. Varnas and Chev followed from behind. It was a twisting path, full of unfamiliar brambles and snaring branches. Strange animals tittered, howled, hooted, and hissed from the shadows. They must've walked for a good half hour, chasing after Darin who moved at an alarming pace, Chev growing ever certain they were swiftly moving toward doom.

Here, not even moonlight penetrated the thick canopy. The fragrances were strange. The sounds were strange. They could sense uncountable animal eyes watching. There was no doubt about it. If there were deeper, darker parts of the woods, they could only exist in nightmares.

They were far from their village, and any nightfolk from here and out were drovers or savages. Chev and Varnas gripped their spears. Darin had an arrow nocked in his bow. He suddenly stopped.

"There's an outcropping with a cave," he whispered.

Chev tried to speak. "Is that—?"

"Don't speak. It makes its lair there. I think it does. Aim for the spots between the carapace." Darin gave them both a doubtful look. "At least, that's what I've been told."

Varnas stretched his arm. "No use in wasting time."

"Wait."

They both looked to Chev.

"We really going to march into its lair?"

Darin and Varnas exchanged uncertain glances.

Chev explained: "We have to be cleverer than that." He set forth his plan in whispers.

"This dry enough?"

Varnas dropped a bundle onto the heap of underbrush and twigs. Chev was bent over; he picked through it, flicking the pieces away that didn't fit his arcane specifications.

"That one, that one. Not that one. That should be enough. Right," Chev steeled himself, "Let's begin."

They were all on the tips of their toes as they approached the mouth of the cave, maneuvering around anything that might make noise. They all froze when Varnas stepped on something that snapped, but after listening to the stagnant air for a good while, nothing stirred. The rest of the way came without a sound.

The mouth of the cave was slightly shorter than Chev. He looked down into the cavern. Before him was a vacuous tube that wound deeply like a throat. The air that filtered out carried an empty sound, what Chev might imagine a stone sponge might make. The mere thought of venturing into its tunnels was paralyzing.

Varnas boxed his ear as a means to get him back to his senses, and Chev was grateful for it. He might've stared into that abyss forever.

He dropped all of the loose tinder just beneath the lip of the tunnel. One strip of bark, a handful of grass, and a wood stick. That was all Chev had to start a fire. He cursed himself for not bringing flint and steel. But he'd seen his father do this, so as Chev prepared he quietly recalled how his father had folded the bark to make a groove, then rubbed the stick ferociously to light the tinder.

He started his work, and it took a few good thrusts to find the rhythm.

Varnas bit down on his lip, suppressing whatever thought was on the tip of his tongue. Darin pointed his bow and gave a leery gaze into the inky blackness of the cave.

Chev's arm began to ache, his concentration divided; he couldn't help but flick his pointy ears to every echo the cave seemed to produce. The temptation to look proved near irresistible. But he kept reminding himself he needed the fire. If the bone-skin noticed him too soon, all would be for nothing.

He had a random thought. *Patience.* That was what it called itself.

There was a light, like from the belly of a firefly. Encouraged, Chev worked harder. Another spark born, then sparks. One landed atop the tinder. Chev blew it. It seemed to implode, a little flicker of fire gently arose.

"I did it," whispered Chev.

Varnas knew what to do now. He'd gathered some sturdy dry branches and he tossed a few of them on. In seconds, it would make a reasonable campfire.

"Light the torches, throw them in."

It was amazing how quickly the fire grew, blazing angrily as Varnas tipped a few cloth-wrapped branches. Chev with his strong arm tossed them as far down the cave as he could. Smoke, pitiless, poured out of the cave roof.

"It's working!" Chev cried out.

"I hear something!" said Darin.

What came from the caves was a sound fearful and terrible; a chittering and wailing, like panicked insects. Things scratching on stone walls and hurling themselves down passageways for safety. It became louder and louder, and the echoes multiplied.

"It's coming."

Unconsciously, Chev had made a terrible calculation. His squeezed his spear so hard he might've snapped it. "It's *they. They're* coming!"

Past the flickering torches and through the smoke, the bone-skins hurtled up the narrow tunnels, using their knife-like claws to hurtle themselves forward. Darin only had time to unleash one arrow before the next clambered over its dead companion.

There were no obstacles for creatures as these. They bounced easily from one side of the tunnel to the other. A bone white monster hurled itself through the flames, catching Darin stringing another arrow. There was a cry and a crescent of blood.

Chev was prepared. He thrust the spear between the joints of its bony armor. He had to put his foot against it to free his weapon. The thing whined, crawled into a ditch, and died.

Darin was breathing heavily, his cheek open from temple to chin. Any thought of escape ceased as a bone-skin launched itself atop Varnas. He lifted his spear just quick enough to skewer it in the abdomen. As Varnas struggled to free his weapon, another jumped out from the flames. This time it lunged for Chev.

Chev set the mandibles as a target. As it chittered and hissed, Chev thrust a spear into its mouth. He felt only soft tissue as he pulled it out. With it gurgling death it took some small measure of vengeance—the end of Chev's spear was ragged. The point had come loose. Chev was left holding a blood-covered stick.

"Damn!" Chev cried. *If I'd taken the sword...*

The dagger.

He pulled out his obsidian knife. Chev couldn't imagine the thing doing any damage. Certainly not to the monster treading out from the mouth of the cave.

Just behind the bonfire was a creature at least twice the size of the other bone-skins. Dancing flames revealed enormous bone-plated shoulders and a drooling insectoid maw. Fire glittered in its bead-like eyes. Even on all fours it came to Chev's chest.

The drone it made congealed into words, though Chev could hardly believe such a thing could even speak. From its grating maw was intoned: "You killed my children."

Darin hadn't wasted time; an arrow sprung from the bone-skin's eye. Its howl was like wind through a canyon, but still it leaped over the fires as though it were all over nothing. Varnas rushed to intercept it, but the monster lowered its head to lever Varnas with its strong back, flinging him like a limp rag through the trees. Darin loaded a second arrow, but the beast flailed out an arm and in the space of a blink Darin disappeared beneath the underbrush, unleashing tremendous snap as his bow broke like bone.

Chev was now alone except for the dagger in his hand, and even that could not stop trembling.

"You're not Patience," muttered Chev.

The bone-skin charged like a bull, arms swinging out like scythes. Chev broke away from it, rushing headlong into the unknown forest. He had to leap and twist through brambles and vines even as the bone-skin demolished them like twigs.

Chev was past fear. It was already onto regret. Regret he was so stupid to leave the Daysword behind. Regret he never told his mother goodbye, and that he'd never meet Ossen again. Regret that he hadn't really, truly told Sana how he felt.

Stupid pride and overconfidence made him leave the sword behind. Pride and overconfidence would be the death of him.

Burning set in Chev's lungs, he could only run so far and so fast. Things were so bad he saw the cliff rapidly approaching as his only means of escape. It turned out to be a rocky outcropping dropping into a river, foaming white eddies crashing below. Chev jumped without checking, any death being preferable to being torn apart by mandibles.

He refused to look down. He didn't want to see the magnitude of his mistake. The sound of fast-moving water grew to a tumult.

His body went into the water like a spear into flesh. It was cold, the temperature had him stunned and disoriented. He wasn't sure if he was sinking or surfacing, but by pure accident his head came above water.

It was still a struggle to stay afloat, but at the very least he was alive, carried by a brisk current into the deepest, most savage areas of the forest. The currents threatened to rip him to shreds but for a moment, relief. The possibility he might live reignited both hope and fear.

But it wasn't. Like a scouting wolf, the bone-skin popped over the edge of the outcropping. Chev moved to dive quickly, but the currents pushed against him too fiercely, and the creature turned its unnatural head toward him. On seeing him, the thing galloped back into the depths of the forests.

His mouth did Chev's thinking. "Get out of the water, get out of the water!"

Painfully, he paddled his way to the opposite bank and clawed his way up the mud. His plan was to disappear into the woods on the other side, but he wasn't fast enough. The creature made a ghostly image from between the trees, and then it loped out, sniffing and chomping at the shoreline, finding quickly a place to ford.

There was no outrunning it now. Chev pulled up some water grass and looked for a sturdy branch. He found something to grasp just as he heard splashing. Chev twisted to the sound. The creature waded briskly into the water. Not even the arrow lodged in its eye slowed it down.

Time meant he would have one chance at tying the dagger to the branch. The result was unacceptable, still, he bit off the remaining grass and pointed the newly-made spear at the bone-skin, jabbing the air in warning. Warnings were pretty much the only thing it was good for.

The creature tittered, it hissed, Chev nearly thought it would run. But the sound it made — a scraping, twisting, bony sound — was every bit a laugh as Chev believed it could manage. It threw itself toward him.

His meek little thrust did nothing. The point bounced off the bony hide and the spear was in splinters in moments. Chev now got the joke — it was delusion that he could hold the beast off with such a pathetic weapon. By the time Chev had the presence of mind to try and run away, the bone-skin was on top of him. Two fearsome claws slashed into Chev's abdomen, holding him fast while the pincers shuddered toward his neck.

Through the ferocious pain, Chev only managed to divert its bite from neck to collar. The mandibles dug into the soft flesh of his shoulder — he could feel his bone coming loose beneath the immense pressure. His chest, his shoulder, his everything, crushed and drained in a manner that felt unreal.

It would have been painless, if only Chev had accepted his fate. The bone-skin's mandibles would've beheaded him and then merciful blackness. But Chev still wanted to live, even though the possibility seemed more and more remote — he had done this all for a reason. Minda wouldn't forgive herself. He would never learn the truth swirling around Ossen. And Sana, always that point at the very end of the tunnel, a goal that kissed his fingertips. So, though the pain was excruciating, and the part of himself that only feared wanted to die, he still reached out for life, blindly grasping at anything that might anchor him in this river of death. His hand met the arrow sticking out from the bone-skin's eye.

Defeating the bone-skin was the last thing on his mind. He grasped it like a handle, twisting it incidentally. Now the bone-skin felt true pain. The pincers weakened, but not enough. There was still no escaping it. He would be eviscerated.

He needed only a little leverage. Only a little.

The bone-skin must have assumed Chev had blacked out when he let go of the arrow. But it was only to grab a rock. Slimy from the blood and water, he had to grip it tightly so it didn't slip. His plan came from adrenaline and not a thought of his own.

He hammered the arrow shaft into the bone-skin's brain. It sank by only a few inches, but it was enough. The monster went rigid for a half-second, and then it went limp like a sack.

But Chev didn't stop. He pushed it off, then pounded the arrow like a stake. Over and over, until the thing spurted out on the other side. Then and only then, Chev slowed, and wriggled out from under to let the monster slough off him into the river shallows.

The bone-skin made a big white boulder, sitting there as the water rushed over and around until slowly, the river turned murky with its blood.

It was more difficult walking through the thick forest than it had been running. Through blurry vision and unsteady gait, and carrying his trophy, the creature's head, Chev retraced his steps all the way back to the cave.

He heard his name called. Chev smiled in relief, forgetting all about following the trail of broken vegetation and fresh memories.

Varnas and Darin scanned the forest, hollering out for him. They sounded so scared, Chev couldn't help but be giddy. He couldn't wait to see the looks on their faces when he stepped out into the clearing.

Exhausted and bloody, they looked at him. There was relief without happiness.

Chev slammed against a tree trunk for balance, then held up the bone-skin's head. "I got it."

And then he collapsed.

There was light. A tunnel of light. Sounds of laughter. Chev might've thought he was dead. But would the other world have splitting headaches?

Knife thin slits opened to a thick layer of fronds. Light filtered down like looking up from the bottom of a lake. Somehow, night had turned over, day was bursting through, setting alight whatever paltry shelter they were in. He tried to swallow, but found his throat dry—like he couldn't breathe.

"He's up."

"Ah, the fool kid. Doesn't know how lucky he is."

"Deserves a long rest, that boy."

"Don't say it too loud. If that boy gets any more of an ego his head will explode."

"Welcome back to the world of the living."

Chev finally coaxed some moisture onto his lips. It was too bright, even as two shadows loomed by him. "Is it... daytime?"

"We're in one of Varnas' pit traps. Best we could do on short notice."

"Never say these things weren't useful." Varnas wheezed a chuckle.

Memories of the night trickled back. "We killed the bone-skins. Didn't we?"

"It was all you, kid. If we'd marched in there we would've been chow. You deserved the big kill. Even if it was *my* arrow that finished it."

Chev did a dry laugh. "I really hammered it in there, didn't I?"

"Yeah, you did. You're not as dumb as I thought." Varnas added, "Eh, sometimes."

"Shut up, Varnas." Chev laughed.

Darin's smile was rare. "Don't leave us out when you tell the story."

"Of course." Chev propped himself up on his elbows, squinted around in the tight confines of the pit. "Hey, maybe this'll help you with Nalia."

Darin ran a finger across his new scar, going the full length of his cheek. "Ah, you know maybe," he said sadly. "But probably not. There's things you just accept. It's the way we do things."

"Damn, Darin, don't sound like your life is over." Chev tried to sit up, and hissed at the resulting pain.

Both the other men forced him back down, chastising him as much as they laughed. Chev looked, a gross feeling hit him right in his belly. His chest was all stitch work. Sinew made a jagged line over his wounds.

"It mauled me. It really mauled me." Even Chev didn't know why he said it with a smile. Relief it wasn't worse, perhaps.

Varnas nodded. "And damn you looked an easy meal. It was damn lucky a pawcat didn't catch you on the way. Or a squirrel."

Everyone shared a drunken laugh.

Chev rubbed his eyes. "Thanks. Thanks a lot. I'm feeling... very tired."

"Rest, kid. You've earned it."

Was that Darin or Varnas? Chev was fading, his vision growing double, then quadruple, then black.

He only managed to hiss out one last word. "Thanks..."

"When I get home, I'm sleeping for a year," said Darin.

They had been trudging through the woods for only a few hours. They each felt heavy and exhausted from pain. Each was stumbling, falling over themselves as they wound their way towards home. Varnas looked ready to find the first tree to take a nap under.

Darin and Varnas were still smiling, elated by success. That feeling had long gone with Chev. When he slept last day, he had dreams. It wasn't the bone-skin he'd just killed that was chasing him. It was Patience. His rancid breath was always on the back of his neck, even after he woke.

Chev tried to quiet his own fears. He told himself, somehow, one of the bone-skins they killed had to be Patience. Even though none seemed quite his size.

It was a possibility he didn't want to consider, so it remained a shadow in his imagination. And he couldn't bear breaking good spirits by sharing his fears.

"Something wrong, Chev?"

Chev jumped, as if caught thinking. "No, nothing."

Thankfully, Varnas didn't push it. He shrugged, and continued chattering on about other things. Chev decided it was more constructive to imagine how he'd present the head to Sana. Once she knew what a service he'd done for the tribe, she was certain to take him.

That was, if she never found out he'd brought the bone-skins onto their heads in the first place.

Chev borrowed one of Darin's tools. He'd cut off the pincers from the bone-skin's head, and now busied himself drilling a little hole through the narrow section of the bone. Meanwhile, Varnas and Darin busied themselves cutting the flesh out of the bone-skin skulls. Two were already finished drying by moonlight.

"Look," chortled Varnas, modeling off a bone-skin skull sitting on his head, "It's a damn perfect fit. They're gonna piss themselves jealous when they see us wearing these."

Darin smiled knowingly. Chev gave Varnas a cursory grin. He'd just drilled out a hole, and he was stringing a thread through.

"A necklace?" Darin noted.

Chev nodded, a boyish grin plied his lips.

A few minutes later the trophies were prepared. The three of them were ready to parade themselves around the village. That was when Darin addressed Chev directly, though his eyes wandered and never quite met the one he addressed.

"What you were gonna say by the trade stone that night. I don't know what it was, but I just want you to know... Feska was wrong about you. If I was successful that night," Darin was ready to choke, "I would've done a terrible crime. You didn't deserve it. I thank every day you tricked me into one of Varnas' traps. That's the honest truth."

Chev searched for the earnestness in Darin. "If you'd joined up with Feska, Ossen would've killed you too. Falling into that pit saved your life."

"I know that," Darin shook his head, "but that's not the reason I can't stop thinking about what happened."

After some thought, Chev said, "I won't forget what happened, but I won't hold it against you."

"That's all I ask."

"Are you blatherers done droning on?" complained Varnas, "I want to show off these trophies! And then go to bed!"

What did a bone-skin skull look like? From a glance, no different from any other. Chev, Varnas and Darin walked into the village festooned with the things, and yet not even a murmur. Men and women walked past on ordinary business.

Then someone recognized Darin. He came simply to wish him well, but on seeing what he wore, he fell back; instinctive panic. That created interest. It drew more people. They were surrounded, murmurs sprouted like spring leaves.

"Look," someone cried out, "Bone-skin skulls!"

A clamor. The whole village emptied out of their homes, a pulse of excitement ran through each and every person. Talk couldn't be stopped. The three of them were the center of curiosity and interest. Soon, people were shooting questions quicker than any of them could answer.

A plump set of fingers grabbed at Chev's trousers. Another touched the skull on his head. Children broke like waves against Chev, all squabbling for attention. There was no controlling them. With smiles and laughter, Chev had to hold them all back.

Varnas had already been torn away by a crowd. He was in his element, finally given the captive audience he longed for; Chev could already hear the embellishments and endless digressions. Darin, on the other hand, had somehow forced his way out of the crowd. Chev spotted him in the distance beneath the shade of the tree, where he held the hands of the woman Nalia. He had his head inclined to her, they were so close their bodies nearly touched.

It reminded Chev that he had his own business, too.

There were still plenty of stragglers competing for Chev's attention, so he directed them to Varnas, and slipped away before anyone could stop him. Sana waited in the shadows of her freshly-dug burrow, head bent curiously to the commotion and the fuss. Something like joy and gentle surprise passed her face on seeing him.

"I should've known it was you," she teased. Her smile dropped on seeing the bone-skin skull sitting on his head. It had sunk to eye-level, so Chev had to tilt it up to get a good view of Sana.

"Hey," he said, suddenly stupid. Moonlight illuminated her in way that made her a vision, and something about the whole scene robbed him of words. He could only express himself in the simplest of ways. "I brought you a gift."

He held out the necklace. The bone-skin's pincers clicked with a myriad of black river stones.

"It's not as pretty as that bloom," he said, "but I thought about what you said. I wanted to tell you I'm not going away. I hope this proves it."

She took it, focused on it, let it drape like a garland in her hands. "I always knew it, Chev. I knew it, but I let myself be doubtful. I can't let other people's words distract me from what I know inside." She slowly inclined her head, and let him slip the necklace on. The mandibles fell across her chest, and the stones framed her moon-lit chin. She looked at him with deep moist eyes. "The burrow is nearly finished. I'd be honored—if tomorrow night— you'd be willing to share furs with me. If you don't want to—"

Chev's mouth moved faster than his brain. "Stop. I'd love to. Please have me."

His eagerness made Sana laugh. "I can't wait," she said. Suddenly, something behind Chev drew her attention. "I think Darin and Varnas need you."

Chev turned around. The two men were standing off a little bit, giving the space that they thought the couple needed. But it was clear Chev was needed. Chev gave Sana an apologetic glance, and he rushed over with a million aggravated thoughts.

"Can't you see I'm—"

Darin interrupted him. "The elders want to speak to us. And no, it can't wait."

"I already know what I'll tell 'em," declared Varnas, "I'll say, 'No, I won't join you in your stupid tree stump and rot. I'm content where I am, trappin' game, and I'll do it 'till the day I breathe no more.' And boys, just to let you know, I don't need no honors or commendations. I'll tell them all the credit goes to you two. Old Varnas is happy to be old and Varnas and that's that."

Every ounce of excitement that Chev had about Sana suddenly distilled into bitterness. He was still feeling the wounds of being torn from her, more pronounced than even the physical ones, and in his state any reason couldn't possibly be good enough.

As for Darin, he was unreadable, marching with them with a bent back and a pained expression.

The elders sat on their perches, eye glowing like cinders from beneath their shawls. There was no joy here. Only the gravity of terrible seriousness.

Varnas stepped forward, "Can't say I'm surprised that I'm being dragged here again. So I'll say now, and I'll say again, I don't want to be one of you. Life's too short to be wrapped in blankets waiting to croak. So—"

"Silence, Varnas," said one of the elders.

Varnas drew up, offended. "I wasn't done!"

"This isn't about you," the elder said.

Varnas suddenly got very quiet, retreating back with a hurt mutter: "I see how it is, then."

"You brought back five bone-skin heads. You claim to have killed them all. Did you?"

Varnas spat out, fist raised, "Well, we didn't pick 'em off the ground!"

"That isn't the question," boomed another elder, "Did you kill them all?"

"Is there any one of them left alive?" another piped a clarification.

"We sure did," Varnas nodded, "we smoked them out of their pit..."

Varnas continued talking as he always did, but it faded out for Chev. Patience's chittering head came to mind, an image that gnawed through any sense of accomplishment he might have had. The creature Chev had talked to, the creature Chev had made a deal with, the creature Chev intended to kill.

They all look the same, Chev comforted himself, *they all look the same.* Any one of them could have been Patience. He never got a good look at the monster anyway.

But still, the thought was there. Like Feska's ghost looking over his shoulder. A fear he only felt in his gut.

"You are silent, Chev."

Chev was alerted, he stood straight.

"Did you kill all of the bone-skins, Chev?"

Chev's tongue felt fat and numb. But he managed to say "Yes. We smoked them out of their tunnels. None were left alive."

"What I find disturbing," one of the elders piped, "is that this hunt was clearly organized. And yet, not one of you told us of this bone-skin incursion. Are you aware of the history of this tribe, any of you?"

"Of course," said Darin, "We fled the deep forests hundreds of years ago, to escape from the savages."

"To escape from the bone-skins," sternly corrected another elder, "and every custom, every way of life of this tribe was deliberate to stop these monsters. Chev, your mother's mate Ossen would have done anything to protect you. This is what we feared."

Chev shouted, "He would never consort with bone-skins!"

"But he would sacrifice the community to preserve his own blood. So short-sighted. And he proved as much when he murdered his own tribesmen to save you. We have much higher hopes for you. That you stand by your former enemy is encouraging."

Darin looked especially uncomfortable. Chev stepped forward, and declared, "I have risked my life to remove a threat from this tribe. Isn't that enough? Why must you interrogate me for doing you a favor?"

One of the elders coughed, and answered, "We are grateful. But we see the selfishness in your action. You did this to impress your lover Sana."

"So? Am I not allowed to do something to my own benefit? Can I not be a little selfish?"

"Not selfish in a way that threatens the community," intoned one of the women.

"In the short term, you removed a threat. In the long term, you may have destroyed us," said another.

"Bone-skins are strong and fast, but their greatest weapon are their tongues. They speak, and they remember. They remember those who are weak, they remember those who are strong. They especially remember those who wronged them. And they take vengeance on those who kill their kind."

"That is why all bone-skins must die," said another, with a tone of finality, "When we fight, we kill them all, or we don't fight at all. We will let none escape to rally the Feast."

That word again. It sent a shiver up Chev's spine.

"So we ask again, and we need you to be honest, no matter what is at stake. Chev, did you let one escape?"

Chev's throat went stiff.

"Chev? Is there something you want to say?"

"I only wanted to say I killed them all," he said.

There was a tension as the elders whispered among themselves, their ancient bodies turning to and fro. They came to a conclusion rapidly.

"You may go," said an elder.

"That's it?" Chev couldn't believe it.

"That is it."

Chapter Six
The Cuckoo's Egg

MINDA INSISTED CHEV spend the night. She'd made him something special—some sort of black bean cake, nearly every ingredient traded from dayghosts. The food was sweet, Minda's words less so.

"Don't take this to mean I'm not proud of you," she fired off breathlessly, "but you could have brought more than just two people with you. If you had, maybe they wouldn't have had to sew you up like... like... a torn shawl!"

"Mother, if we hadn't done it then, we would've put the village in danger!"

"Hush, you stupid boy. I'm talking to myself and not to you."

Such was the sort of talk that went on in Minda's burrow while she carefully fletched a bundle of arrows. Chev had the same guilty feeling as when he'd done something wrong by his mother. But the next dusk, she beamed him a contented smile a little after he had first stirred from sleep and crawled out from his furs.

"Chev, you're stupid and I love you. I beg you, never do anything like that again. Even if it's to save the whole village."

"I'll try," was the best Chev could do.

"You'll try," Minda sighed, "I suppose that's the best I'm getting out of you. I'll let you go then."

"By the way," Chev flushed as he was about to leave, and he spoke with an odd mixture of nerves and pride, "I'll be at Sana's for a while."

Minda blinked oddly, but it gave way to a smile. "Good for you, boy."

Chev felt the same way, and he left the burrow with a spring in his step. He had no idea he'd never make it to Sana's.

Somehow, Chev convinced himself he had just passed the struggle that would define the rest of his life. He couldn't think of anything more perilous than a bone-skin, not even Feska and his gang. From then on, no threat could be that insurmountable; it should have been smooth going into a future with Sana, however long that would last.

He was so distracted by the present that he never foresaw the inconceivable. His life would be derailed by something completely unexpected.

Jaev and Laven were about to approach him with an offer. If Chev had just stayed home, if Chev had refused, if anything could have stopped him from seeing them, another would have inherited his fate. As it was, their offer was so innocuous that Chev couldn't imagine anything going wrong.

The two young men approached Chev, and Laven asked, "We're going to the trading stone. Wanna come?"

Chev looked apologetic. "I can't move too much. But, if it's just walking..."

"Yeah," Jaev said, "we'll carry everything. It's just some exercise. Come on, hero."

And so the course of Chev's life changed completely.

For whatever reason, the dayghosts had asked for weapons, and in great quantities. The baskets were filled to the brim; some with bundles of arrows, others with axes of flint and obsidian, knapped knives, spears as sturdy as nightfolk hands could craft. It was a dizzying output, the expedition went out with enough weapons to outfit an army.

Chev watched the procession with idle curiosity. He thought of the Daysword, with its steel so rarely touched by nightfolk fingers, more straight and beautiful—and deadly—than anything their most skilled craftsmen could make. Chev didn't even have the imagination to picture how such a thing came to be. It was like they pulled it out of moonlight. And the people who could do such magic wanted *their* weapons. What an oddity!

He didn't think too deeply on it. But he wasn't the only person to have noticed.

Darin had a young scar across his cheek, and it suited him well. What suited him less well was the way he could only half close the near eye. When he blinked, it would sort of lag behind, making the exercise into a sort of wink. It was an odd effect as Darin came up to walk beside him. A basket of stone hammers on his back made his gait uneven and noisy.

"Never did I think we'd be shipping weapons to the dayghosts. I always thought it would be the other way around."

"Perhaps they're gonna try their hand at hunting," said Chev as he limped along, his wounds constantly reminding him with every step.

"Dayghosts don't like the forests. I think it's too far from the light for them. But who knows, they're a sun-addled people." Darin shook his head. "Nice of you to join us, by the by."

"I couldn't sit on my haunches all day."

"You certainly would deserve to," said Darin.

Hearing such a thing made Chev smile, especially as it came so grudgingly.

"Where's Varnas?"

"Sitting on his haunches all day."

"Ha! So much for dying on his feet."

"Even tough old trappers need a time out, I suppose."

They shared a smile together, and some silence.

"I saw you talking to Nalia," said Chev.

He nodded. "I did."

Chev elbowed him eagerly. "So? How did it go?"

Darin still had a lingering smile from the little conversation they had. He still kept it, but it seemed sadder now, like a reflection on good memories. "I told her goodbye. I told her I understood. I told her if she needed me, I'd always be around."

"Ah, damn Darin, I'm sorry."

"It's not like that," Darin interjected. "After so many years you still don't understand how things work around here. But you will understand. When Sana is done with you, you will understand. It's not our place to question. Just to accept, and to find something else to make life meaningful."

Chev shook his head. "I hate that. You sound so defeated."

Darin's basket shook as he shifted to face him. "And who am I fighting? Who won? That sounds like something Ossen would say."

Things were about to get pretty serious, a thoughtless comment went to the tip of Chev's tongue. But something rushed to Chev and slapped him painfully in the back. Laven wrapped an arm around Chev's shoulder. Unused to such close contact, Chev's barely-suppressed instinct was to twist out of Laven's embrace.

"This guy! One night in the bachelor's burrow, next night out! You broke a record, Chev!"

"It's wasn't Sana," Chev corrected, struggling for space, "I spent the night at my mother's."

"Don't ruin it, Chev. Everyone knows that it's Sana whose taking you in."

Chev sighed. "That is true."

"And you," Laven let Chev go, went to Darin's shoulder, "you old dog! Didn't see you either last night!"

Darin struggled from the weight Laven threw over his shoulders. "Please, Laven, I've got a full pack."

"Don't be such a pansy." Despite the taunt, Laven let him go. "But you still gotta tell me what you were up to."

Darin looked uncomfortable, but he admitted, "Nalia took me back for one more night."

Laven whistled. "Good for you! I knew something was up."

"We aren't back together. It was just one night." Darin said it like he was being accused of something.

"Of course," said Laven, "of course. Just don't let Jaev find out. He's a bit quick when it's about his mother."

"I don't blame him," said Darin.

"I hope to follow in your footsteps pretty soon. I think I found a girl who'll take me. Crossing my fingers. You guys can ask the spirits for me, right?"

Both Chev and Darin nodded strongly.

"Good, good. Well, I'm gonna hang back a bit. Gonna give Jaev a hard time. Wish me luck!"

As soon as Laven fell out of earshot, Darin whispered to Chev, "A bit annoying, isn't he?"

"You said it," agreed Chev.

The elders warn that it is when you least expect it when danger springs. They may have had in mind physical threats—monsters that rise out of loose dirt to snag the unwary, grasping vines that choke passers-by to water their roots with blood, river creatures that look like logs from afar but snap with teeth when close. Such things were common in the forests, there was nowhere truly free from them. New places meant unfamiliar horrors.

Chev would fall into just a trap, just not one laid by a hungry predator.

The horizon opened up as the forest gave way. The trade stone was not far, and baskets of goods littered around. The dayghosts had been productive. Further beyond the stones, they kept their endless fields of tall grasses and crops, a dirt path trailed between two muddy ditches, ending in a multitude of mounds that looked no different from tiny graves in the distance. Dayghost hovels.

"Can you imagine," Darin squinted at the tiny shapes, "there are people living in those things down there? And when the night ends, they'll crawl out, and toil as they bake beneath the Great Burning Orb."

"It's a different world," agreed Chev.

"I'm glad I'm not a dayghost," said Darin, "seems like a very hard life. You never get to see the moon or stars. Just the unending fire of the sun. No wonder they're so blind."

Chev had nothing to say, but he watched Darin for a while, as he perplexed on nature. Despite the new scar, Darin looked no more menacing for it. His face only expressed tranquility; it was difficult to imagine that man once tried to kill him.

Chev had never told him those words that Varnas thought so important: "I forgive you." Perhaps now he never needed to. Somehow, Darin must've known anyway.

The expedition was in good spirits. Raucous, almost. Nightfolk tended to be quiet, but Jaev was next to Laven and they were laughing loudly about something. No one bothered to quiet them, no one felt the need to. Even at this distance they wouldn't wake the dayghosts. Workers started unloading the weapons while Chev and Darin approached the trade stone.

Darin pointed. "Again. A symbol I don't know. What is wrong with these creatures?"

Chev knelt to inspect it. Even he didn't recognize it at first, three brisk lines beaming out from a semi-circle, but he closed his eyes and imagined Ossen drawing it in the ash.

"I'm confused," said Chev, finally.

"What with?"

"They want medicine."

Darin blinked. *"Medicine?"*

"That's the symbol."

"What sort of medicine?"

"They don't say." Chev scratched his head. "It just says 'medicine'."

"The elders will know what to make of it."

"Weapons and medicine," Chev said thoughtfully, stooping over the stone. "No meat or furs. There's something going on that I don't understand."

"It's not our place to puzzle it out. They're a strange people, those dayghosts. Incomprehensible."

Just then, there was a disturbance and they both twisted to see it. Jaev and Laven, minutes ago best friends, were at each other's throats, a pile of thrashing limbs twisting in the dirt. There was a rise of hoots and hollers as other tribesmen egged them on.

Darin sighed, sweeping a tired hand across his face. "I'll go see what the fuss is about. Go ahead and check the dayghost goods."

Chev lifted an eyebrow. "Sure. But Darin, let them have their fun."

"Don't worry, I will." Darin ran after them, shouting, "Hey, no eye gouging!"

Darin left Chev to set on his work. The dayghosts had done their part, baskets of varying sizes piled together as a haphazard mass. One was filled with bolts of cloth, another of ground grain, and another brimmed with dried fruits. Chev caught a subtle movement and sound from one of them, out of the corner of his eye, but as soon as he could try to track it down, a tide of chortles and whistles pulled his attention. Jaev apparently had Laven in an impressive headlock.

"Idiots," Chev shook his head. He was high on a sense of superiority.

The goods were passable as far as Chev was concerned, checking them started to feel like a ritual. Nothing was unexpected.

But then, the same basket moved again, and there was the sound of a faint squeal. "A piglet!" Chev exclaimed. With high hopes, Chev skipped right to the offending basket and peeled the top off.

The trap was sprung.

Chev reached to grab the piglet. It was a surprising struggle; not from the creature, but the oddly shaped basket which was very tall and narrow complicated by his still smarting wounds from the recent battle. After half-climbing inside, he finally got his grip around something.

It was warm, but it didn't move like an animal. Chev unwrapped the cloth that swaddled it. On seeing it, Chev's mind froze, his lips clamped together, and he stood dumbfounded with shock. It screamed and cried, and wheeled its tiny arms and legs.

It wasn't a piglet. It was a baby. And not a nightfolk's, either.

A dayghost child!

The mewling monster wailed at the moon, a tiny fur-covered thing, skin like a kitten's. Wet-nosed, big-eyed, broad-faced; it was so close to a nightfolk baby that the small differences were startling and alien.

Chev broke into a sweat, and into purely selfish thoughts. *Can I put it back before anyone sees?* The child's crying had already drawn some attention away from the fight. A band of curious nightfolk already were moving toward him.

There was no repossessing any of Chev's faculties. In a full-blown panic, wanting to run but unable to put the creature down, he froze. His heart thumped as a group formed around him. Chev held the monster tight to his chest.

"What?" Chev was defensive.

Asked one of the tribesmen: "What are you holding, Chev?"

"What's crying?" asked another.

Now even Laven and Jaev stopped wrestling, but the crowd had soon grown so thick that they had to approach on their tiptoes, craning their necks over a multitude of shoulders.

"Nothing." When Chev's lie was obvious, he shuddered, "Oh, this? Just an animal. I was about to put it back."

Chev's voice quivered too much to be convincing. Men approached to take a closer look. Curious eyes drew to the noisy, squirming bundle in his arms. Feeling the inevitable coming, Chev unwrapped it, and presented the beast to them. None of them, even Darin, knew what to make of it at first.

Then one of them sounded, in a voice of sheer panic, "It's a *dayghost!*"

"Quick, avert your eyes!"

Everyone twisted their heads away, eyes squeezed shut as though shielding themselves. Even Darin did the same.

"I don't want it!" Chev thrust it out at them.

"Don't look at it! It's cursed!" said one.

"Keep it away from me!"

"I'll put it back!" Chev practically dropped it back in the basket. "See, look! No more dayghost!"

No one could gather the courage to look at him to check. But Darin did walk forward, his eyes cast down.

"Chev," he said, "The elders will know what to do. We'll ask them. For right now—Chev, it's best if you walk apart from us."

"Walk apart?"

Darin sounded apologetic. "I'm sorry Chev, I don't know how curses work. It's just for a little while, until we can talk to the elders."

Chev walked forward to plead with Darin, and Darin quickly pulled himself away, as though Chev were some kind of searing fire. Chev looked on him, confused and betrayed.

"I'm sorry, Chev. It's not you. I don't want to be cursed. The elders say, night is our realm, and the day is theirs. And never are we to meet."

Chev spoke quickly, restraining himself so he could string his sentence together. "Cursed? I'm not cursed. I was only near it a little bit, and I didn't even know what it was! Surely the ancestors would understand! I thought it was an animal!"

Darin lifted his hands defensively. "I don't know Chev, I just don't know. This has never happened before."

"What do I do? Please, someone take it!" Chev pushed the basket toward the hunting party, and everyone shrank back as though presented with diseased meat.

"Keep yourself together, Chev!"

"Won't anyone do anything? Do I get no gratitude? Didn't I save you all from the bone-skins!"

Darin approached cautiously, a tentative hand out, unable to summon whatever he needed to lay it on his shoulder. "Don't be like that, Chev. We only wait because the elders are wiser than us—"

"And you, Darin," Chev turned to him with narrowed eyes, "You tried to kill me. And I let it go. Now this."

They all huddled together, scared, and now wordless. Carefully, Chev picked the child up again from the basket.

It was wailing, streams of tears wetting its velvety cheeks. Little arms and legs pounded the air. Such a strange and fragile creature to have so much power over proud courageous men, each either or both hunters and warriors.

And as Chev watched it whining and crying, he wanted to join its tears. Dreams started to disintegrate with each glance at its wet cheeks. It was no use telling the men anything. He spoke to the baby instead, let his useless words die in uncomprehending ears. "I was supposed to move in with Sana tonight."

As far as Chev was concerned, life had just ended.

The trip back to the village had been dead silent except for the wail of the child cradled in Chev's arms. Chev sometimes looked down it, watched its mouth curl open and scream. Its little eyes seemed permanently wrinkled in the throes of its tears.

"Sorry," Chev told it, "I'm not your mommy or daddy."

It didn't listen. There was something horrible in its cry, pitched to crack something inside Chev. He didn't have blood cold enough to ignore it, but neither was there anything he could do.

"I should've left you," he whispered, "I should've left you, but I couldn't, I couldn't."

There was no one in sight except for the path well worn back to the village. In his deliriousness, Chev plotted how he'd smuggle the child into town without anyone finding out. He even considered losing the child on the way, leaving it and hoping somehow it would fend for itself once day came. But any plan he conjured was insane and full of flaws. It was simply a mental exercise in denial, and it would only serve to set him up for disappointment.

Chev didn't come up with anything, and so the worst possible outcome transpired. Before the village even came into view, crowds had already gathered. He knew they were all waiting for him, because he was only thing they were watching.

Sana was in the crowd. She had to be in the crowd. Chev was certain of it. And if he just kept his eyes to the ground, perhaps he wouldn't have to compound his shame by seeing that deathly expression on her face.

It was strange how temptation worked. Chev couldn't bear to lift his gaze, so somehow he couldn't stop himself from doing so. He did it just in time to see Sana, just one face between the shoulders of hundreds of curious villagers. He looked just in time to see her lips drop in horror.

They made space for him to pass. What formed was a straight line, right back to Minda's burrow. It would be a long night.

Chapter Seven
A Vision Through the Sun

IT MAY HAVE BEEN just an excuse to get away from the village. It may have been a means to silence the mewling child in his hands. It was a combination of both. Chev was up before anyone had a chance to see him sneak towards the creek. Now, it was just a puzzle in how he'd get the child to drink.

The best he could do was gather one of the broadest leaves he could, fold it up like a vessel for the creek water, and carefully, drop by drop, fed her, giving the child enough time to cough and swallow.

"There, there," he said, "Please… please stop crying."

Even Chev didn't know how much it sounded like pleading. And it didn't work. The child cried. Cried itself to exhaustion, only to wake a little later, and cry once more.

"I'm well past my nursing age, Chev."

Minda was trying to explain why she could not feed the mewling child held to her breast, even as a fuzzy paw tugged hungrily at the shawl.

Chev, meanwhile, was on the tips of his toes, circling around like a lion in a cage. Whenever the child wailed, his hand went to his temple and he squeezed his eyes shut. Minda couldn't guess what the exercise did to help him; but he paced around so aggressively that she swore if she blinked too long Chev would be gone before she opened her eyes.

"How am I supposed to feed it, then?"

Minda didn't know what to tell him. "Perhaps we aren't supposed to. It's an animal, it's supposed to be beneath the sun. If we leave it out, maybe it can fend for itself."

"You're fooling yourself if you think that creature is going to be anything other than pawcat food out there."

"Chev, you won't want to hear it, but what are we nightfolk supposed to do with a dayghost? I know you've become attached, but..."

"*Attached?* I'm not attached!" Chev shook his head, went to it, and prodded its little belly, "I don't want it, but see! It's helpless. Even if we can't do anything for it, we have to *try*, don't we? At least until we can give it back to the dayghosts."

Minda looked very grave, but after a sympathetic smile she passed the child to Chev. "Chev... young lives are fragile. Even for nightfolk. Most don't make it to your age, and this isn't even our own kind. Please understand Chev. It's almost certainly not going to make it."

Chev didn't look at his mother, just at the child in his arms. Wailing so desperately—and for what? The sun? Chev couldn't bring it. Food? Chev couldn't feed it. He couldn't even whisper empty comforts into its ear. He was helpless to save it as it was to save itself. The only option left was to watch it die.

He suddenly found the wisdom in Minda's suggestion. It would only serve to break his heart to sacrifice so much to save it, only to have it die in his arms. It would be so much simpler to put it outside, to bathe in the sunlight their people were born in, and let it spend whatever time it had left. It felt even merciful, somehow.

"Ossen," Chev choked out as he stared at the dayghost's black eyes and tear-stained cheeks, "he said that they aren't ghosts. That they're people like us."

"That doesn't mean they're the *same* as us," Minda said, wrapping her fingers over Chev's shoulders.

"No," Chev was thoughtful, "they may be different from us. But, mother, I have to try. Even if it comes to nothing, I have to try."

Just then, there came a shuffling from the entrance. Someone was making their way into the burrow. Chev twisted to face Darin. The man blinked unevenly, the result of the wound across his cheek. Chev still wasn't used to it.

"The elders have summoned you," said Darin. "Bring the child."

The elders wanted to be with the child alone. It should have been a comfort, to have the child out of his presence, but with his back to the elder's hall, he could hear its cry pierce through the rotted wood, muffled as though miles away. He imagined how it must be to look through its dayghost eyes, to see a bunch of wizened, strange aliens picking through its swaddling, prodding it, handling it with roughened hands in their cold, clinical inspection.

At the very least, the child would be beneath the great river of stars. It wasn't the sun, but it was the closest thing the night had.

Chev was called back in. They'd left the child in a pool of cloth, in the center of the room as though it were some offering on an altar. Chev came forward to scoop the naked creature back into his hands.

"I'm afraid our worst fears have come to pass," said one of the elders. "The child is female."

"Why's that so bad?" asked Chev.

"Because you are doubly cursed," crowed another elder, into Chev's other ear. "Cursed with exposure to the dayghosts, and cursed by the bond."

"Bond?" Chev struggled with the concept.

"It is the dayghost custom. You touched it, you are bonded to it, and must remain with it. It is their most ancient and terrible law."

Chev held the child tighter. "But we are not dayghosts. Why would we follow their laws?"

"Trust our judgment," boomed another, "We cannot know their ways."

Chev's voice started to break, like a tide desperately clinging to a shore. "But I don't want it! Please, take the child! Break the curse!"

Chev held out the baby as far as he could. The elders acted as though the child exuded some repellent force, but somehow managing to retain their balance as they leaned away on their perches. They squawked out protests as a singular cacophony.

One voice managed to break out. "It's not our burden."

"How do I break the curse?" asked Chev.

"It is said only by death. We will leave the rest to you, Chev, Son of Minda. Go now."

When Chev left the elder's hall, it was to a village silent and empty. There were no children playing, no men preparing for hunts, no women at their crafts. Chev was ready to think he'd stepped into graveyard when Varnas pulled himself from the stump he rested on.

He spat something substantial from his mouth, then put a cloudy eye to the child. "Let your arms rest a bit, I'll take it from you."

"Varnas? Are you sure? You're not worried about the curse?"

"'Course I'm sure. Give me the baby, before I change my mind."

Chev handed it over, and the child didn't pause to stop crying.

"What are you going to do with it?" asked Chev.

"Give it back. Oh don't look at me like that. You didn't think I was going to adopt it, did you?"

Chev was silent. He rather hoped he would.

"No," continued Varnas, giving the child a light toss, "just wanted to see the dayghosts for myself. Hairy little feller, ain't he?"

"She," corrected Chev.

"Oh," Varnas made a quick glance, "oh yes, I see that now. You'd think it'd get awful itchy with all that fur, beneath the sun?"

Varnas gave it another little toss, giving it little smiles in an effort to cheer it up. It wasn't working, and Chev looked increasingly aggravated, especially as Varnas threw the baby higher.

"I'll take her back now," said Chev.

"Sorry, Chev," Varnas gave Chev a grin as the child was passed back, "didn't mean to get you worried and all."

"I wasn't worried," snarled Chev, cradling the child, "I just don't want to deal with a dead kid."

"Well, darn, I ain't that bad with kids..."

"You know what the elders told me?" Chev cut in, gritting his teeth down at the moaning, whining baby, "They said I was cursed. That I was bonded to the child forever. They said I can't leave her for the rest of my life."

It dawned on Varnas was Chev was saying. "Oh, Sana."

"If it weren't for this... this *thing*... I would be her burrow right now. Chev, why did the dayghosts give this to me?"

"Don't be a fool. Nobody gave it to you, you just pulled it from a basket."

Chev shook his head. Varnas swore the corners of Chev's eyes grew wetter, certainly his voice began to croak, as though strained through a tightening throat. His nosed crinkled as he spoke, "They did give it to me. They left it the basket meaning for one of us to take it. *Why?*"

Varnas searched desperately for comforting words. "I don't know dayghost hearts, Chev."

"Nor do I. But I have to find out. If not... Varnas, what if I did the unimaginable?"

Varnas shrugged, "You got me there, I couldn't imagine it."

"Don't be clever," Chev sighed, glancing up at Varnas, "You know what I'm asking."

"I know," said Varnas, contemplatively, "You do what you need to do, Chev. I'm only asking you leave it to the last."

"You're wise, Varnas."

"Not *wise*," Varnas corrected sternly, "Just *smart*."

"Right."

Chev's arms tightened around the infant.

"Please, hold it for a *minute*."

Minda shook her head. "I don't know how to take care of dayghosts, Chev."

"I'm not asking for you to adopt her, I just need you to watch her. I'll be right back."

Minda face fell. "It's a 'her' now? Oh Chev, it's not one of us, let it go!"

"I keep explaining:" Chev spoke as though he'd gone over it a million times, "I'm just holding *it* until I can figure out what to do. Please, mother, just *watch* it."

Minda screwed her eyes in thought. "Come back before dayfall."

Having finally convinced her, Chev emerged from the burrow. He wound the perimeter of the village, keeping his head low, avoiding the sound of any sort of village activity. He was not in mood to be even be seen.

The east was growing a ruddy lightness, wispy clouds soaking some of the remaining inkiness of night. Dawn was coming soon, Chev didn't have much time. And yet, outside Sana's burrow, things slowed. Each valued minute drained in indecision. Deep in that tunnel was Sana. Chev hesitated to imagine what she was doing right now.

Courage came to him finally, but only because time forced his hand. He stood by the mouth of the tunnel, and cried Sana's name.

It was Laven who came out.

Chev recoiled at the sight of the young man. It was the inevitable implication more than anything, as he squinted in the growing light in his half-naked form.

"Who's that?" Laven couldn't see through the rising dawn.

"It's me, Chev."

"Can't you see we're busy?" Laven said it too loudly, directing his head into burrow. Chev got the sense he was more advertising his loyalty for Sana to hear than talking to Chev.

"I just want to talk to Sana. Just for a minute."

"Well, as you can see," Laven was, again, conspicuously loud, "Sana doesn't want you, so you can scurry off."

"Laven! What's with you? You called me a hero last night!" Chev shook it off, clearing his mind. "I don't care what you're doing. I just want to talk to Sana."

"Sana has no time for you," he bellowed.

"Don't be an obnoxious ass, Laven, you've marked your territory. I beg you, let me speak to her."

Just then, there came a woman's voice from the burrow. "It's fine, Laven, I'm coming up."

She came, the moonlight falling over her, revealing her slowly. She turned Chev's heart into molten rock. A girl, now a woman, the earliest bloom of her adulthood. Her black hair stoked fire, eyes obsidian and silver, set in her ethereal starlit face. Chev yearned to reach out and touch her, but he could only see her over Laven's shoulder.

"It's alright, Laven, you don't have to protect me," it was a soft command.

Laven looked indecisive, between further bloviating and obedience. Sana repeated herself, this time more sternly.

"You don't need to protect me, Laven. Please leave us alone."

With a brisk grimace he retreated into the darkness. Sana only spoke when she was sure he was gone.

Sana asked, "What do you need, Chev?"

"So you chose Laven?"

"Don't tell me this is why you're here." Sana sighed, her gentle neck twisting, "Chev, it's painful to see you. I feel sick knowing you're so close. But what am I to do? You were cursed. And that's not something either of us have control over. Chev, I have to choose someone."

"But... you *promised* me..."

"Why do you torture yourself? Chev, you knew what I would tell you. Everyone knows now you have the curse. I'm an herbalist, not a shaman, I can't break curses. So what would you have me do?"

"I didn't come here for that. I came to say I was going on a journey. I'm going to see the dayghosts."

Sana flinched with disbelief. "Like Ossen did? Didn't you learn anything?"

"I don't care if it's dangerous, I don't care if everyone will hate me for it. I'm already at the bottom now and I have nothing to lose. Sana, if I break this curse, will you take me?"

Sana bit her lip, and receded in thought. "It would be unfair to Laven."

"And it's not unfair to me? Sana, tell me. Would you take me back?"

"Of course, Chev. Don't doubt me."

"Good. That's what I needed to hear." Chev turned around.

"Wait."

A shiver of thrill went through Chev to hear her so worried. He watched as the young woman silently debated herself.

"Are you really going to see the dayghosts? Right now?" she asked.

"I was planning on it," he replied.

"There's a plant out in the woods. It's light green with yellow—I mean to say it's spade-shaped and has prominent veins, each branch has a fan of seven. We call it a Sunleaf, and it's magic. Crush the leaves, rub it over your skin. It will protect you from daylight."

Chev drew a mental image of the leaf. He thought he remembered something like it. "How do you know this?" he asked.

"It's a woman's secret."

"A woman's secret?"

"Yes. We have many of them. Don't tell anyone I taught you how to Sunwalk."

"Sunwalk?"

Sana rolled her eyes and smirked. "Yes. Again, please, please don't tell anyone. I have to go now. Stay safe, Chev."

She retreated back into the darkness, stepping around Laven. He glanced surreptitiously to see that Sana had gone, and he quickly whispered to Chev, "Sorry, Chev! I didn't mean anything I said. I was just putting up an act for her."

"I could tell," said Chev.

"Listen, you're still a hero. I promise I'll put in a good word for you. Maybe the next time she chooses a mate?"

Chev lazily threw up a hand as farewell, "Thanks."

"You're a hero, brother! Make us proud!" And with that they parted.

Chev found the leaf Sana described, but he wasn't sure how much to use. He ended up stripping a whole branch. Crushing the leaves left a milky, sticky sap which Chev smeared over his arms, shoulders, and face. He felt gooey all over, like he'd been at home all day sick, and the cool night air left his skin chilled. He wasn't eager to put this new Sunwalking magic to the test.

He wandered back to Minda's, as he promised, right before day blazed across the forest. Minda gratefully gave the child up to Chev, but was immediately suspicious as Chev put together a pack.

"What are you doing, Chev?" she asked.

"I'm going to meet the Dayghosts. I'm returning the girl."

"Chev!" Alarmed, she was off her furs, and grasping Chev's arms. "Do you *want* to be cursed? And in the day? Are you mad?"

"I can't be cursed any more than I already am. Besides, I'm going to Sunwalk."

Minda was lost for words at that, stuttering and hedging. "*Sunwalk? How is that—* What did you— There's no such— *Who taught you that?*"

"The women's secrets are getting out," said Chev as he tied a shawl over his head.

"So that was why I smelled sunleaves," Minda said. "It'll protect your skin but it won't protect your eyes. Don't look at the sun.

"I'll try."

"Maybe you're better off not going, Chev. It's dangerous in daylight. What if they won't take her back?"

"We'll see. Hand me a walking staff."

She retrieved a stout branch. There was resistance as Chev took it, like she was reluctant to give it up.

"I asked you to come before dawn. Now, please, just come back."

"I will. Wish me well. Daylight awaits."

It was easy enough to say, but it was more difficult to do at the edge of the burrow, when the sun saturated the ground in front of him. The amount of light that blazed was alarming, it looked hot to the touch. He was as reluctant to walk through it as he would be through burning coals.

He'd done all he could. He was swaddled in shawls, stinking of sunleaves. The child was on his back, still weeping and crying out for food and love. A walking stick would serve him when he was weak. Fear was the remaining wall.

The child wasn't getting healthier. Even since he'd picked her up out of that basket, her cries became more labored, like wheezing. It coughed, and coughed again. The child was at its limit.

If he didn't move fast, she was sure to die.

He stepped out into the sun.

It was like that time so many years ago when he'd tried to follow Ossen out into the day. It was a strange netherworld of refracting crystals. Blazing white overwhelmed all his senses, but it didn't burn him like it once did. As light poured across his skin, the mysterious energies made him tingle. It left just a pleasant warm sensation.

Chev nearly didn't realize the child had stopped crying. In bewilderment he thought it'd died, so he quickly stripped her off his back. He only saw gummy smiles in that face, cooing and contentedness.

They really are children of the day, Chev was awed.

He held the child to the east, and whispered to it, "Look, girl! The sun! The sun!"

The child's eyes flared with new fire. Day lit her with profound warmth.

Minda was right. The sunleaf protected the skin but it did nothing for the eyes, so Chev kept his gaze lowered to the path through the forest, where things weren't so awfully bright. Occasionally, as the path turned a little toward the sun, Chev would be forced to draw the shawl down past his eyes, and hope that his innate sense of direction would keep him from straying into the wilder parts of the forest.

These paths should have been so familiar, but cast as they were with the fires of day they were more foreign than even the deep woods. Looking straight ahead, the landscape was a jumble of flaring lights, so bright one melted into another. The sun would filter through the canopy, making even the earth look as liquid fire, ever shifting by the whims of the wind. Every turn with every horizon passed, the light changed angle, drawing out new shadows of alternating inky darkness and eye-burning whiteness.

There was no getting used to such a surreal landscape of extremes.

At the very least the child had quieted. For some reason, it took some comfort here, and it had drifted into sleep on Chev's back. The only reminder of its presence was a tiny hairy paw that rested on Chev's shoulder. He didn't know how the child could have slept; he felt so exposed. Primitive fears grasped him. Giant birds might swoop down to snatch him. Ursars could chase him and devour him. And stranger beasts still—swarming stinging insects, hunter packs, big-mouthed lizards. He stuck out like a black pillar against white, and there was no darkness to retreat to.

The forest began to clear. The vast, empty white sky revealed itself, only punctuated by some mad-looking clouds, each shining nearly as bright as the sun itself. Chev squinted around with his hand over his eyes. He recognized the trade stone, so unreal looking as it was casting odd shadows. The dayghost village would be close.

Until then, he hadn't considered how the dayghosts would react to him. He hoped they were not as superstitious as his own people, but it was just that: a hope. And so he marched. The path was muddy, and sucked at his feet. The dayghost fields grew rampantly around him, a breeze grazing the crops and bringing the scents of agriculture—manure, wood and smoke. The smoke was especially pungent.

In fact, Chev started to doubt the fires were an illusion caused by shifting lights. He looked up, the black streaks coursing through the sky confirmed the truth. The dayghost village was burning.

Chev hurtled toward it. He could remember the village once as being distant daubs of shadowy huts set in the midst of great fields, but some force had come through and reduced them to black skeletons, black even by the roiling light of the sun. Fires were just burning out like dying stars. There was not any sign of life. Not even from the birds.

Again, the girl started to cry.

He wandered the ruins. Rather than thinking, he was feeling. He was a mirror for the emptiness around him. Silence had fallen, leaving only crackling as flames devoured the rest of the village. His mouth was slack and wordless. He was the observer sent to witness the end of an alien people.

The child moaned and wailed, beating Chev's shoulder. Though alien herself, her emotions were too easily recognized.

Something lay on the road. Chev had seen such things many times — the dead lay very flat and still in a way the living could not. Many times had he passed animals like that — he always wished them well wherever they were — but this one had two arms, two legs, and so was too similar to his own kind than he liked. Approaching it made Chev feel he was disturbing a deep rest.

The dayghost was dead. Someone had pierced the female with an arrow, and now dull staring eyes couldn't even reflect the sun. Chev could picture it still alive: she was a flat-nosed beast, short but broad and well-suited to long days working fields. Fine fur covered every inch of her, and where nightfolk had hair she had a luxuriant, coarse mane, now flattened out and sullied by dirt and filth.

The arrow gave resistance as Chev pulled it out, but seeing the arrowhead confirmed Chev's suspicions: daysteel. This one was killed by her own kind.

The child was wailing and crying even more intensely now. Chev thought it was the smoke, but as he pulled it from his back the child reached out desperately, incessantly to the dead body. She was even close to wriggling out of Chev's arms.

Oh no.

But it was as his mother said. For this creature so different from himself, there was nothing he *could* do. So, knowing it would accomplish nothing, he spoke to it.

"You knew this was coming, didn't you?" he asked it. "That was why you put her in the basket. But I'm sorry. You were wrong. We can't take care of her, we don't know how. The best I can do, is reunite you. You can both share the sun you love so much."

He laid the child atop the woman's breast — the child clamped down immediately — and then one by one he placed each dead arm over the child. It was like they were embracing. It was a bitter reunion, yet the child was silent. Mercy willing, perhaps it didn't know the difference. Things might even be peaceful for it. Maybe it wouldn't notice as it moved from the day-lit sky of one world to the next.

"Rest in peace," he told it.

He walked away heavy-hearted, but sure in the feeling this was the best outcome. The child could die alone in fear, or it could pass peacefully in the arms of its mother. The choice, he reasoned, was never really his anyway.

Chev was at the edge of the village, the voice in his head finally growing quiet. But then, a piercing cry. Worse than any the child had made before. Something had happened. Something strange. Something terrible. Something wondrous. And in Chev's mind, a latent precognition said if he didn't want his life to change forever, he should not turn around.

Fear kept his eyes straight ahead. His heart made his legs heavy. Before he knew it, drawn by the cry of the creature he'd somehow become responsible for, his feet made a slow circle back to the village.

He didn't want to see. For all things he wished he was blind. But the corpse's arm was outstretched beyond any illusion or trick. Held aloft like a gem on a pedestal was the child. Whining and wailing. Begging for something to come take it far, far away.

The elders say, some birds come to give their young to others, so that they might grow attached, and take them and raise them as their own. This was the nature of the trap Chev had fallen into. Its teeth had finally sunk home.

Chev left with the burden he had meant to discard, wail more piercing than ever. But its desperation had nothing on Chev. He didn't so much walk as slide his feet forward. He was falling straight ahead, back into the safety and shadows of the forest he'd never left before.

Idly, he scratched beneath his shawl. Something had come off—a flake of skin, dry as an insect husk. He thought so sluggishly that it took him a moment to realize it was his.

"The sun," he moaned. The leaf's ichor was drying off.

He weaved his thin fingers across his forehead, and found he was as hot as baked stone, the sweat only served to make him sticky. His armpits and legs chafed raw.

It was sunsickness. He needed to get underground.

The world he moved through was a blurry haze of light. There was nothing that didn't have a searing glare to it. And yet, as he trudged on, some clear shape resolved from the mirage of light and shadow. It was a man, impossibly tall, who stepped out of memory. He was of serious countenance, especially as he dipped his head to look down on Chev.

"You're a figment of my mind," said Chev, blinking upward.

"But that doesn't make what I have to say any less real," said Ossen, his voice echoing off the distant walls of the world beyond.

"Please, tell me what you have to and leave."

Ossen looked off toward the horizon. "It will never be as simple as that. The conscience you deny will ever hound you. You cannot escape it. Only in the depths of daylight will it ever be given voice."

"I have a clear conscience. I've only ever done what I thought was best," said Chev.

"You made the deal with the bone-skins. You brought their eyes on your community. The same community you hold dear. Or claim to."

"I don't claim anything," said Chev, "Minda, Sana, Varnas belong to the tribe. There are no people closer to me in the world. And I killed the bone-skins to protect them."

"No. It is as the elders said. You killed the bone-skins for Sana, and for yourself."

"And so? What does it matter? I still did a good thing."

"You seem to care little that *Patience* still stalks the forest."

Angrily, Chev kicked up some dust. "And how do you know I didn't kill Patience in that den? They're all the same. I don't need to talk to you."

Chev marched forward, through the pillar of shadow and light that made the illusion of his father. But the voice that boomed in his head was never clearer.

"You know well that none of them were Patience. Why hadn't you told the elders?"

"I didn't want to worry them."

"LIES!"

The word was so loud Chev clapped his hands over his throbbing temples. He stumbled off-path, finally smacking into the rough bark of a tree.

My head... Chev's temples felt like bursting dams.

"You wanted save your own skin!" the voice slithered into his ear.

"I didn't want to die!" Chev cried out, "I thought I could fix it!"

"You were wrong!" the voice boomed.

"I can still fix things!"

"You sacrificed the community for your own selfish desires!"

"It's not true!"

"It *is* true!"

The last illusory words rang out over mountains and forests, an eruption over the whole world that only Chev could hear. Chev could think only about how much it hurt—the physical pain of his head being smashed like a drum. He ground his head into the bark of the tree, moaning with tears falling fast down his face.

They were not tears. This was too hot to be tears. It could only be blood.

Now the voice was gentle. Chev felt a hand on his shoulder. Like the wind, it hushed. "Shhh."

Was it Minda's voice? Chev swore it was.

"Now you know our fears," it said.

"I can't give up the things I love," said Chev.

"We do not ask you to. All we ask is that you love us. And do not betray us. We are the tribe, Chev. In us is everything you could want. In life we will supply you. In death we will honor you. Taste our blood, find it sweet, make it yours."

Chev's licked slowly across his upper lip. His tongue was too dry to moisten it, but he tasted hot, coppery wetness anyway.

"Rest a while. Ease your burdens. Here, look, we have already lightened your load."

"Lightened... load..." Chev moaned.

The voice was right. His back *had* felt lighter. Like something had eased off his shoulders on the journey. Without thinking about it, he slid down the tree trunk, closed his ravaged eyes to the day-lit world.

Patience. Patience. Patience.

Through the blindness of unconsciousness, a child's cry pierced through. He swam slowly towards it. Life stirred back into his arms and legs.

He felt like he hadn't moved in whole cycles. But that couldn't have been the case—it was still the same sun he was baking under. Somewhere, beyond the searing white light, the same child weakly cried out. Chev wondered how that could've been.

"I dropped it," Chev realized.

That made him scramble. The sudden movement caused his skin to split, but he barreled toward the noise, his eyes ripped open for the shadow of the child. What Chev pounced on could have been a stump or a rock, but it felt soft—and it reacted to Chev's touch. Its cry quieted as Chev brought it to his chest.

It was meaningless looking at it to see if he was right; Chev's eyes felt like ground sand, and they struggled to focus. Gentle touch was all he needed. The girl's fur was soft and fine, even more so than the cloth it was wrapped in. A child's gentle hand reached to touch his.

"There you go, there you go," he cooed to it.

Just then, something emerged to block some of the light from the glare. At first, Chev thought it may have been Ossen's figment again, but this thing loped out on all fours. A pair of mandibles chattered as it approached.

Chev laughed at it. *An illusion of Patience.* His own mind taunted him with images of the foe he feared still alive. But, the creature was of stunning detail. The clean curves of the white bone, the spiny back ridge, the sunken malicious eyes. It even cocked his head, as though curious. Chev wondered what torments it'd hiss at him in his delirium.

"You're s-s-sick," it said.

"That's right," Chev slurred drunkenly.

"I told you I wanted a *healthy* child," said Patience as he peered at the tiny alien in Chev's arms, "I'll come back tonight. Make sure the child has no illnes-s-ses."

"Come back tonight," Chev cried out at the monster as it loped away. "You come back tonight! Ha! I'll show you!"

Chapter Eight
Patience

A RARE SIGHT—the elder's chamber was so full that there was barely an inch of floor left open. Hundreds of faces, but not one smile. Elders perched vigilantly from their pillars, men knelt uneasily by the fire, women clutched their youngest children. The only sound was the mewling of babes and the shushing of the mothers.

The waiting was difficult, but after a long time five members of the scouting expedition filed in, each taking places by the fire. Only Darin kept standing. He had sunken shoulders to match his tired eyes, even his scar seemed deeper and blacker.

"Chev's account was accurate," he said.

Chev wasn't moved by his vindication, only nodding to himself. For everyone else: rumors instantly ripped through the gathering in waves of murmuring. Only an elder silenced it.

"One person shall speak at a time," said the elder.

Another elder spoke: "Give us a full report, Darin."

"There is little else to say that Chev hasn't already said," said Darin, "We came across the remnants of a battle. We didn't want to get close, but we didn't need to. Plain as the moon that dayghost bodies had been left to fester. Every building was burned. Everything of value was stripped."

"And did you see what force attacked them?"

Chev was wrapped in furs, shaking from sunsickness, but he still managed to hoarsely cry, "It was other dayghosts, I know it!"

"Silence Chev," one of the other elders spoke through crackles. "You've already broke the laws of this community by dealing directly with the dayghosts. You have nothing left to say. Continue, Darin."

Darin made a split-second glance at Chev, as though he had no confidence in what he was saying. "It could have been a monster. It could have been dayghosts. I don't know."

"Where do we get our grain?" a woman cried.

"I have no tools!" said a man.

It was a collective realization; and with it came a cacophony of panic that even the elders had difficulty silencing. Like a wave everyone was on their feet, murmuring and rustling about in their places. The cries of children grew louder. The crows of the elders could barely be made out.

Still one elder had enough vitality to boom his voice, "Enough!" The gathering fell silent and still.

"We'll have no panic. We have plenty of dayghost goods to tide us over until we find a new trading partner. New expeditions will have to do until then. We might have to travel further, but we *will* find one."

Something inside Darin had been breaking, but in the brief silence that fell, he went to his knees. "I should have known," he moaned, "Weapons, medicine? I should have known immediately! *War!*"

"Do not blame yourself, Darin," said an elder, "even had we known, there was nothing we could have done."

His legs unsteady, blinking through his faded vision, Chev pushed off a walking stick and got to his feet, and spoke in a dry, scratched voice. "There *was* something we could have done. We could have sheltered them. We could have protected them."

The same elder boomed: "You have been told not to speak!"

"No!" Chev was defiant, pounding the stick into the dirt, "I *will* speak! And you *will* look!"

Leaning with the stick beneath his armpit, his shaking, spotted hands unwrapped the bundle he carried. As soon as it was clear what was inside, the room collectively turned their heads.

"It's the dayghost!" someone cried.

"Don't look at it!"

Chev held the sleeping child out. "See? It's just a being like us! They aren't monsters or spirits!"

"Put it away," said an elder.

"And you," Chev turned, addressing the elders, "For all your poking and prodding, you can't even look at it!"

An elder said, her head still turned away, "We didn't make those laws, Chev. They are as old as our race."

"So you say," said Chev, wrapping the child back up. "This is all that's left of the dayghosts. And if you aren't going to do something, I will."

"Where are you going?" asked an elder.

"Just as I said, I'm gonna do something," said Chev.

Walking stick in one hand, and the child bundled in his other arm, Chev hobbled out from the elder's chamber, stepping over village folk and brushing aside anyone else in his way. The din of fruitless debate boomed from the chamber, and Chev felt glad to be out. The night air was fresh, and though the skies were knotted by clouds things still felt lighter outside. Rich fragrance cleared his head like water.

He looked at the child. He'd had it for a few days now, and its cries were weaker and it slept uneasily. The rise and fall of its chest seemed so desperately fragile. The child needed food. And without any help, Chev had to improvise. He something, *anything*, that might fill her tortured stomach.

He walked the short way to the creek, setting the girl down, slipped off his furs, and strode into the waters until it came ankle deep. He made a trial sip—it was cool and fresh. He pulled a leaf, a broad one like a spade, and collected a fair amount of water.

It was a careful operation now. Chev slid the tip of the leaf into the child's mouth, and gently let the water flow in, stopping to let the child cough and swallow. He did it until all the water had drained. Meanwhile, Chev's eyes darted across the forest, hoping his eyes would latch onto something edible.

A branch weighed by berries was so inviting. But Chev knew well enough that only a woman's magic color vision could discern poisonous berries from the edible. Chev's solution lay in a rotting log. Wading over, then stripping off some bark, wood maggots writhed fatly just beneath. Their little white bodies, pale even by the moon's light, made a kind of milk when ground up with a rock and mixed with a bit of water. As a boy, he used to pop them whole and alive in his mouth and let their fibrous bodies explode between his teeth to his boyish thrill. For Starlight, she'd need to suck the paste off his finger. He only wished there was a way to make it sweeter for her.

The leaf was left to float away down the creek. The child Chev inspected for signs of health and strength. Her gurgling was a little louder now, and she wiggled more vigorously. Chev had to take whatever comfort he could out of that. It struck Chev, at this moment, if he took away the fur, drew out the ears into points, narrowed its face a little, the child wouldn't look so different from nightfolk.

"What's its name?"

A voice from the wilderness. Chev twisted around to the source.

"Sana? What are you doing here?"

Sana had been sitting on a nearby rock, how long Chev didn't know. There was a twist to her lips that could have been a smile or a frown.

She shrugged. "Just watching."

"I tried, really, I tried," Chev explained, setting the child gently by the creek, "but there was no one to give her to. But I know somewhere out there, there's a place for her."

"It's alright, Chev. Telling you about sunwalking... it was wishful thinking. On my part."

Chev was confused. "Sana..."

"No," Sana shook her head, and suddenly that twist in her lips revealed itself as something sad, "no. Ancestors, no. You know as well as I do that just giving it away won't break the curse over you. When I saw you still holding it... you don't want to know how I felt, Chev."

"Maybe it was like when I saw you with Laven," said Chev.

"Maybe." Sana grinned, but it was an uncomfortable, passing one. "I wanted to give you back this." She reached to take off her necklace.

Chev jumped out the water, and seized her arm, "I gave it to you, it's yours."

"I can't wear it," said Sana.

"Please don't give it back," begged Chev.

"I *have* to!"

Sana slammed her palms against Chev's chest, her eyes reddened. It was so sudden and intense that Chev stepped back, feeling like she might plunge her hand into his chest to rip out his beating heart.

"I can't have you hanging on my neck, Chev. It's too much for me. Please," the necklace rattled in her loose grip, "take it back. Forget about me. Find someone... *something* else."

Chev looked at the necklace he'd made for her resting in her hands. The bone-skin's mandibles were perfectly smooth and white, remembering well how it was to cut them out from the creature's head. Would he ever feel as invincible? It seemed a bitter triumph to savor now.

He took the necklace and clutched it tight in his hands.

Sana was about to leave, when she turned back. "Sunleaf. It also works if you already have sunsickness. Just chew it."

"Thanks," said Chev.

Chev followed Sana's advice, folding a few leaves beneath his molars and grinding them. It soothed him somehow. His headache subsided, and rubbing the leaf sap over his skin relieved the itching.

He watched the child wriggle around between the roots of a tree as he treated himself.

"Used to the night now, are you?" he said.

The baby cooed. Perhaps it hadn't the energy to cry anymore. Perhaps it just got used to the way things were.

"Don't worry," he told her, "I'll find something real for you to eat soon. And then we'll go out searching. I'll find dayghosts to take care of you."

Chev picked up the fragile creature. It was drifting somewhere between sleep and wakefulness, its furred cheeks resting in the crook of Chev's arm, finding some measure of comfort. From that angle, and with the moonlight hitting it in just the right place, Chev saw how it was not so different from him.

Wood maggots would not make milk forever. Perhaps there was some sort of plant with milky sap. A wise woman could know. Ideas fluttered around, ideas that stopped as soon as he heard the whimper.

It came from within the foliage, behind a curtain of vegetation. It sounded to Chev like a small animal in suffering. Chev curiously stepped over the obstructions, and the sight behind the bushes made him burn far more intensely than any sunsickness.

Scent of blood. Pounding heart. Uncomprehending eyes.

Patience. And he was with Sana. A claw sealed her mouth. A bloodied maw rose from her arm. Her dismembered arm. None of the ways she bent made sense. And her eyes—so white, so wide. Nothing could have expressed pleading so soundlessly.

Mandibles clacking together. Blood like spittle falling from hungry teeth.

"Lucky for you, she'll be alive a little longer. I've dec-c-cided to make it painful."

Its voice. Not rattling with excitement as it once had. Dull and cold and ruthless and emotionless.

"*You.*"

"Deal is off, after you s-s-slaughtered my brood," said Patience, "Run home. I want you to s-s-see what you've wrought, and then, I want to kill you while you des-s-spair."

Chev jumped away and rushed for Minda's burrow at full speed. There were no fears of ostracism now. He needed the Daysword, and to damnation whatever people thought of it.

The sight was surreal, and even having it transpire in front of his eyes, he couldn't quite believe it. Bone-skins, their segmented bodies, crawling down from trees, skittering from branch to branch, loping on the ground. Screaming men and women. People being devoured. Insectoid monsters emerging from burrows like ants from mounds.

He was deaf to the child in his arms.

The melee was a blur, but the path to Minda's burrow was, for this moment, clear. He sped for it. It took just a moment for his eyes to adjust—but he could clearly hear the sound of heaving, and crunching, the panicked cries of a woman.

One of the monsters was atop his mother, struggling. His anger rose so quickly he wanted to charge in with his bare hands, to do anything to wrest the dirty creature off her. But he swallowed his overwhelming instincts; he pulled the Daysword out from under his belongings. He would get the satisfaction of plunging the blade between the segments of the monster's carapace.

It hissed and scrambled to pull the sword out, but all it did was give the angle Chev needed to lever the monster's head right off. Its mandibles continued snapping even detached, and its body did a jittering dance off into the side of the room.

His mother's chest rose and fell, covered with scratches and gouges. It filled Chev with nausea to see her so wounded.

And I brought it on her, he reminded himself.

"Chev," she whispered.

"You're not hurt?"

"I don't know," she said. "You have Ossen's sword. So you kept it all these years."

"He left it with me," said Chev, "We need to get you out of here."

"Don't bother, Chev. They called the Feast on us. So use that sword, Chev, and don't be shy about it. Cut a swathe through them. Find Sana."

Chev gently handed the child to Minda. "Can you take care of her?"

Minda shook her head. "I can't protect her. I can't even protect myself." Minda laboriously rose from the floor. "It... *she* is safe in your hands. And nobody else's. Take care of her, Chev."

Chev nodded. The world outside was screaming and crying, and Chev quickly packed the child into a brace. Secure, he gave his mother a final glance; she nodded, and he plunged into the tumult.

It was vertigo of bloodshed and chaos. A cacophony of incomprehensible destruction. Slipping past the mortal struggles of the only people he'd ever known, his hearty sword held in two trembling hands, Chev prayed it wouldn't slip at a crucial moment.

So much to do, but he couldn't even set himself in a direction.

"Kill them all," he told himself, willing his grip stronger, "*kill them all.* Like they would kill us."

Her reminded himself, in a methodical, deliberate way, that Sana was being tortured by the monster called Patience. He ran toward the last place he had seen them, the burden on his back bouncing with each stride.

A man on the ground was barely holding off a bone-skin with a spear. He would be eviscerated if Chev hadn't sliced off the monster's legs and driven a sword through his back. The bony carapace only gave so much resistance.

"Varnas," Chev said in recognition.

Varnas grinned beneath sheets of glistening bone-skin blood. "Boy, you been holding out on us? That weapon..."

"Forget it, Varnas. You in good enough shape to kill bone-skins?"

"Still got some blood left in me. Might need a shoulder to get me on my feet."

Chev offered it, and Varnas helped himself up. His wispy beard was weighed by clumps of sticky blood.

"I've got to get Sana. Can you protect everyone?"

"Everyone? Tall order. Only safe place is the big tree."

"Get everyone there. I'll be right back."

Chev only had time to give Varnas a reassuring pat before racing away. He heard Varnas shout, "Yeah, because we really couldn't use you right now! Damn fool!"

Chev plunged into the woods. They were familiar, but in the adrenaline and urgency Chev couldn't put his thoughts together. He was spinning around, filtering the sounds of screaming and bloodshed from the village, isolating that from the Sana's cries.

"That way," he told himself.

It was only an educated guess from only a few moments of study, but it was good one. The foliage was all too familiar, and he emerged from the shrubs heaving. And the drag marks, blood scraped the ground like a single drawn claw, disturbing the low plants and branches. Patience was drawing Sana into the forest.

Chev chased down the path to the very end. It very nearly wasn't quick enough, and the scene dredged recent horror. One arm was cut from the elbow, Patience worked on the other arm now, starting from the wrist, mandibles grinding a horrific sound. One eye fluttered open and Sana, barely alive for the pain, struggled through dried, cracked lips to mouth for help.

Two hands on his sword, Chev lifted it like a moonbeam into the air. He hoped his sweat-slick hands wouldn't fail him now.

Patience looked up from his victim and hissed—"You s-s-still bring the child. There will be no deals-s-s."

"I'm taking your head," said Chev.

"And with a dayfolk s-s-sword too... haven't you been bus-s-sy?"

"Shut up and fight," said Chev.

Patience did shut up. It abandoned its prey and paced around, seeking a weak point to attack, bony carapace writhing and twitching— perhaps meaning to feign. But Chev was disciplined by necessity, knowing full well panic would kill him and Sana. So he sealed the hilt in his tight grasp, ready to hack Patience's head when it came within reach.

It came like as suddenly as a falling star, doubts about the slimy handle of blade. It was like he saw the future, of him swinging and missing, of the blade glancing off the hide, of him being too slow to save himself.

And Patience could sense that doubt, because what Chev thought would be a feint turned out to be a leap. Four claws raced at him—four claws and snapping, blood-covered mandibles punctuated the air.

The swing came too late. Like in his vision, the blade glanced off impossibly. The whole sword went hurtling into the undergrowth. In panic, Chev grasped the empty air for it.

Mandibles snapped at the straps of the pack, slicing through. The child went tumbling out onto the ground.

Chev figured the next target would be his neck. Or it should have been. Risking a vision of Patience disemboweling him, Chev forced his eyes open. But the monster was struck by greed, its claws digging wildly at the ground while sunken eyes gazed longingly at the child.

"Prey, you didn't told me you captured a *Dayfolk* child..."

Had Chev thought clearly about his next move, he would have never dared do it. But Chev was fueled by seething anger and fear, and before reason took him, Chev pulled the baby to his chest, and placed his obsidian knife to its throat.

"Call off the Feast, or I'll kill it."

"You aren't serious. You're bluffing," said Patience.

"Try me."

"I can't call it off," Patience whined.

"You lie."

Patience made a strange sound, like a growling click, it pulled itself back—it was the sound of desperate uncertainty. And then it hissed, louder now, growing to a piercing screeching that resonated several times after it was over. Chev held his ears tight, but it did little to muffle the sound.

"It's-s-s done," said Patience, "now, hand it over, before I call on it again."

Chev couldn't will himself to let go of the child, or the knife. But he didn't resist as Patience came to gently nudge aside his arms, and take the dayfolk.

"All is forgiven if you bring one of thes-s-se a month," said Patience, and then he loped into the darkness.

"You sacrificed it," moaned Sana, whispering through weakness, "you sacrificed it for me."

Chev scooped Sana into his arms. Not all of her... her right arm discarded on the ground, and her left wrist hung uselessly from her arm, reminding Chev how a broken branch looks still hanging from its tree.

"I didn't sacrifice her," said Chev. "I lied."

With his free hand, Chev picked up his sword.

The trip to the village felt like a journey, Chev was fraught by pain. Sana was so deeply in shock that she didn't even notice how he was stumbling and teetering on his two legs, but they made it back together. There was a quiet of sorts over the village. Sounds of mourning replaced the agonizing screams. The dead were surrounded by loved ones. People moved past empty burrows and bodies in a kind of stupor. Chev felt as if they were stepping into a nightmare tale told by the elders.

The chamber of the elders was burgeoning with all the people who could still walk. Warriors had weapons at ready, unable to quite believe that peace that had come so suddenly. Chev took Sana down to where the wounded were being laid out, and he set her gently down. Laven nearly jumped out over the wall when he saw them.

His voice was aquiver, and he tore at his clothing and long black hair. He looked at Chev, then at his mate and cried, "Sana—no!"

"Don't worry about me," croaked Sana.

Sana and Laven continued talking quietly—Chev couldn't bear to listen, Sana's leaving still felt terribly fresh. He turned and sought out Darin, who stared dumbfounded at the forest, looking terribly old with all the lines in his face.

"They called off the Feast," said Darin to Chev, "that's... unprecedented."

"They're coming back," said Chev.

"Why do you say that? What do you mean?" then Darin saw the shimmering metal by Chev's side, "Isn't that Ossen's sword?"

Chev didn't answer right away. Instead, he took several steps back, built up a gravel in his belly, before clambering onto what was the highest point in this assembly: a couple of bare rocks. When he addressed the tribe, he did so to milling, desperate people: "I'm going after the bone-skins. Anyone able to carry a weapon is welcome to come."

"Are you mad?"

Who said it, Chev couldn't know. But it was little different from the multitudes of questions suddenly thrown at Chev. The array of protests were bewildering, Chev found himself dizzy for chasing after each line of thought.

"It's my fault," Chev finally shouted.

That silenced the people.

"They're here because of me. I spoke to a bone-skin. I did it to save my own life, and since then I've been trying to fix the mistake I've made. Hate me if you want, punish me however you see fit, but as I see it we've got one opportunity, one chance, to turn this around. I've come to understand that these bone-skins are scared of us. They can entrap us, ambush us, extort us, but they can't fight us on even ground. Now, *they've* made a mistake. We know where they are. We can track them. We can fight them and destroy them. Never again will this chance come. So I beg you now: do what you want with me afterward. But please, now, follow me and help me fight. I'll go no matter what anyone does, but I can only win if you help me."

Indecision rippled through the gathered nightfolk. They all turned to the elder that emerged hobbling out from the great tree. The shawled figure, like a limping crow, looked closely into Chev's determined countenance.

The elder asked, "So you lied? You intended to cover your misdeeds by attacking the bone-skins. Was that it?"

Chev gritted his teeth. "Yes."

"And, when you come back, will you accept any punishment we choose for you?"

Chev let out a breath.

"Will you?"

Chev nodded, "Yes."

"Then," the elder steadied himself, "prove yourself. Follow them into the woods, as you said, and kill them all. All who can follow, should."

"I'll do my best," Chev told him. He lifted his sword to the gathered Nightfolk. "Everyone willing, gather your weapons. Follow me."

Chev didn't turn to see who was following him, he marched straight in the direction the bone-skins had gone. Varnas appeared on his side to his right. And Darin to his left, his two fingers already on his next arrow. There were feet drumming the earth behind him. The tribe was following.

Darin scanned the forest and sniffed the air before he pointed in a direction.

"They went that way," he said, "The boy is right. They're gathered in one place."

Arrayed behind them were a hundred tribesmen and a couple of dozen women, all bearing axes and spears and bows in bewildering makes and varieties. Among their number, Laven, looked paler than usual and uneasy behind a flint ax-head, and his friend Jaev, not much better. But it was the sort of reluctance that was normal and sane before heading into battle. Chev had no doubt, when the time came, they would find their courage.

"We should wait for them to separate," suggested one man.

"Nonsense," chastised Varnas, "If we let 'em scatter, we'll never get them all."

Chev nodded, and he spoke quietly as he scanned the woods in front of him. "They think we're licking our wounds, mourning our dead. They won't expect us."

"What do we do?" said another man.

"If they're all gathered we can surround them. Fan out, keep silent. And on my signal, charge."

"What signal?" came a voice from the back of the warband.

Chev thought about it briefly. "When I charge. That's the signal."

Varnas whispered, "What kinda signal is that?"

Chev shrugged. "It's the best I could think of."

They marched. On the way, Darin came up beside Chev. The man had thus far avoided looking directly at Chev, but now drew Chev's attention in a low, tuneless grunt. Chev looked sidelong his direction.

Darin still refused to look directly at Chev. He stuck his chin proudly toward the forest, and delivered his message in a halting, repressed way, like he could barely tolerate civil conversation. "Just so you know, if either one of us doesn't make it, I want you to know that Feska was right. About everything."

That was that. Darin turned away, making things abundantly clear and leaving no room for retort. All the progress he thought they'd made was for nothing.

The hissing and growling of bone-skins grew louder. Sensing danger was close, Chev bounded ahead, diving into brush to scan the clearing ahead. Just a handful of bone-skins would have been too many, but before him was a sea of twitching, jittering carapaces, like animated bones, clacking restlessly around a rock. The dayghost child's hapless cry rose above the macabre gathering.

In a gathering of alien beings, it was strange that Chev could recognize Patience. Perhaps it was the way he paced with such violence and menace, in the middle on all fours, snarling and snapping at his fellows.

"—How can You Ones-s-s not s-s-see why this is-s-s special?" said Patience, "Why would You Ones-s-s throw away s-s-such opportunity?"

"Our Ones-s-s do not call off the Feast," said an ancient bone-skin, loping out from the crowd. His bones had gone from white to off-color, and seemed brittle with advanced age. "Fear is-s-s our weapon. If the nightfolk do not fear us-s-s, they will not give the tributes-s-s."

"Fear of the Feast is what controls Those Who Feed Us. Without it, Our Ones must hunt as pawcats do," said another.

Patience growled defensively, "This is what This One has fores-s-seen. This One has seen our fresh territory grow scarcer and scarcer. This One has s-s-seen there are not enough tribes for all of our broods. This One has s-s-seen that Our Ones will fight Our Ones once again. Outside these woods, pas-s-st the mountains, are the Daylit lands. Ours-s-s could be the Holders-s-s of those lands."

"The Dayfolk ones-s-s are too difficult. They have armies and weapons made from s-s-steel. They drove Our Ones-s-s from the Daylit Lands-s-s in Our Ones-s-s times."

Patience made a clacking hiss, rather like he derided the weakness of those around them. "This-s-s has not always been so. In Our One's times Those Who Feed Us turned on one another, dayfolk and nightfolk both, to bring tribute. S-s-such a time can be brought on again. Nightfolk bring Our Ones-s-s dayfolk meat."

"And what of their taboo?" said the ancient Speaker, "They cannot lay eyes-s-s on one another. How can they attack one another?"

Patience paused thoughtfully. "The nightfolk ones and dayfolk ones know the other's weaknes-s-ses. Should war aris-s-se between them, they would slaughter one another until none are left. This is-s-s why there is-s-s the old law. But laws-s-s become forgotten with time. They forget why they came to be. It becomes-s-s-superstition. Thes-s-se nightfolk ones have forgotten. Now they can be trained. They are the s-s-seed. We will us-s-se them. Our Ones will return to the Daylit Lands-s-s. All our broodlings-s-s will make their own broods-s-s."

There was a hissing and agitation among the bone-skins, like ants around a corpse.

"Your Ones-s-s may not trus-s-st This One's plan. Your Ones-s-s may think This One's plan is flawed. You mus-s-st give This One time to show. Until then...." the last word he rattled throatily, "patienc-c-ce..."

The bone-skin called Patience circled over to the quivering, wriggling child, mandibles hungrily snapping. Drool slipped out from his jaw.

"Now... let's sample Dayfolk flesh... the first in many, many years-s-s."

Chev had been transfixed, nearly forgetting his own role in all this, but now he was suddenly reminded as a hungry jaw clattered toward the child. Imminent danger meant there was no time for reluctance—Chev gripped the sword, stood out from the brush, issued a battle cry, and ran toward the bone-skins with blade aloft.

Dozens of beady, oily eyes turned to him.

Surprised, perhaps. But they seemed more amused, as every insectoid head cocked curiously at the mad nightfolk charging by himself out from the forest. But Chev, without knowing it, was exploiting something true of all intelligent creatures. There's a dangerous moment between surprise and relief that leaves one completely disarmed. That was why none of them were prepared for the horde of nightfolk that began to pour out from the woods.

A titanic battle cry rose, arrows whistled madly into the gathering and planted into bone-skin carapace. A surge of moon-skinned nightfolk with axes, spears, bludgeons, and slings rampaged down from the shrubbery. Before battle was joined a rout had already begun.

Things were completely disorganized. Some bone-skins charged forward to meet the enemy, the others smashed into their fellows to escape. It made for a pyramid of snapping and clawing at which the nightfolk hacked. The sound of insectoid panic, horror and pain added a tumult of rage and bloodshed.

And Chev, in the center of it all, losing himself with every swing of his sword, somehow enjoyed himself.

His sword drove perfectly through the joints and carapace of bone-skins. Occasionally, one would break free from the tumble, and Chev would hack it, stopping it in its tracks. The battle high made him incredibly strong, fast, and confident, he was burning with up with it so much he felt he could take on beasts twice the size. There was little a bone-skin could do to stop the arc of the sword. It went through claw and mandible, and thrusts pierced through bony eye sockets.

All around him, axes crunched into bone, spears drove through bodies, arrows rained down with terrible precision.

It was a slaughter. Only a few scrambled out from the death pile to escape, but none left without missing limbs or horrid gouges on their bony plates, and many would die later from their wounds. The nightfolk stood over a sea of bone-skin bodies, spearing the dying, overwhelming those with any fight left in them. Chev was on the search, following the sound of a child's cry. He had to lever dead bodies away from it.

The child squirmed and wailed, her furry body wheeling around in search of something to hold onto. Chev, soaked and slippery with the blood of bone-skins, wiped off as much gore as he could before picking up the girl.

Just then, the clouds parted. There was no moon, just a sheet of stars. Eternal, as they ever were.

"*Starlight*," Chev said in awe. He looked at the child, scratch her little soft head. She had stopped crying. A gummy smile beamed. "Starlight," he told her.

A noise interrupted his quiet reverie. Something was trying to crawl out from under a heavy fallen body. It was a living bone-skin. One the same size as Patience.

The monster had promised Sana a slow, painful death. Chev didn't have the time to return the favor. In a brisk, efficient motion, Chev plunged the sword through the bone-skin's skull. There was a crunch and a whine, and it was dead. That was as much thought and care Patience deserved.

There was little else to do with the dead other than burn them. The nightfolk set out making a massive fire pit. One by one, the bone-skins were thrown in, crunching upon the empty, smoldering husks of their kin. Souring everything was the scent of overcooked flesh.

Varnas leaned against a tree, shovel over his lap. He'd done his share of work and more. Others tended to the wounded, dragged onto beds of moss. A host of dead monsters and not a single nightfolk lost. Chev couldn't help but admire their handiwork; he looked over it and sighed sadly.

No one had died, but few had come away unblooded.

Laven leaned over his friend Jaev. They'd stuck their spears into the ground and now tended to one another. Jaev had taken a blow—a gouge beneath the rib cage—and had grown sticky with blood loss. Laven ground an herb between his teeth, spat it out, and then smeared the mash on Jaev's wound so it mixed with the blood.

Between half-closed lids, Jaev's pupils found Chev as he gently laid the child on the ground and stared. He didn't seem angry or happy. It was a startlingly neutral face, expressionless, stunned.

Laven stood up, spitting out the remainder of the herb. "Hey, Chev," he spoke quietly, as though afraid he might disturb something.

Chev, for a single ugly moment, wished Laven and Jaev had traded places. But Chev kept silent, and his thoughts to himself as he approached.

"Whatever happened—and whatever happens—neither of us regret coming. It was a great thing you did. Even though... it was you who..." Laven didn't want to continue his line of thought. "The past is the past right? If you do something wrong, and you make it right again, it's like nothing happened at all. Right?"

Chev wasn't sure if it was true or not. He nodded at Jaev. "Do you think he's going to make it?"

"The healers said he would... probably..." Laven forced a smile, "But you never know if they tell you the truth or not. You know? Maybe it's easier if we don't know. Can you imagine knowing the very moment you would die? It'd be like torture every day."

Chev nodded. "I hope they told the truth. Thanks anyway, for what you said." He patted his shoulder and turned away.

"Hey, I was serious about what I said about you and Sana! I've talked up a storm about you. I know she'll pick you after me! I got a feeling about it!"

"Thanks," Chev replied softly, before waving him goodbye. "Tell Jaev I'm sorry."

Laven called after him. "Sorry? Sorry? Why? We beat them, didn't we?"

Darin was waiting for Chev at the edge of the clearing, one foot against the barrel-sized roots of tree. He was holding his unstrung bow, which now only looked like a poorly made walking stick.

Darin said, "The elders want to see you."

"I know, I know." Chev said impatiently.

As soon as the battle had finished, Chev had started thinking about his promise to the elders. To take whatever punishment they deemed fit for him. He couldn't bring himself to imagine what they had in mind, and turned to tend to this moment's most pressing demand.

The child was cradled in the roots of tree and resting in her new namesake: *starlight*. She made no sound as Chev took her into his arms. Some natural impulse had her little paws reaching for his neck.

"Leave the dayghost outside."

That was the warning Chev was sternly given. The guard by the elder's chamber brooked no argument, so Chev propped the child comfortably on the bare earth and stepped inside. Varnas followed behind.

"The elders want to see you too, Darin," said the guard.

"Why?"

"Just go in." The guard thumbed toward the door.

The chamber had been recently cleared. The ground was thoroughly treaded, any grass had been broken at the root stalk. The elders had climbed atop their stoops, perched high above the three men that stood before them.

"Darin, Varnas, Chev," addressed one elder.

Another elder cleared his throat, and spoke in a dark voice: "For actions in service to our community, your three names will be forever honored. Your stories shall be told to the children, and their children's children, and so on until there are none left to carry your stories. You will never be forgotten while our people live. Future generations will invoke your name for strength and courage."

The three men looked to each other. Varnas' silver beard seemed to have gone whiter, Darin's eyes shrunk to pinpoints, and Chev felt suspended in midair.

Darin was the first to choke something out. "This is a great honor—"

"We are not done," interrupted the first elder.

Chev could nearly hear three hearts hammering.

"For your selfish pursuit of glory, for lying to the tribe, for striking deals with the monstrous bone-skins, for dealing with dayghosts outside of the tribe, you will be punished. We've considered the nature of this punishment. In other circumstances, for such crimes, we would call for death. In light of your courage all three of you have shown, a more fitting sentence would be exile."

It took Darin a second of thinking, and hard staring, to realize he was included in the group of the banished. Even then, he couldn't quite believe it, "Surely you mean these two? It was Chev and Varnas who—"

"No, Darin. You had the chance to warn us before Chev and Varnas went on their mission. For this, you will share their punishment."

Darin's face dropped so hard Chev could feel his sinking heart. He was on his knees, his bow clattering to the floor. "You can't banish me!" Darin's voice modulated to carry panic and desperation. "I've only ever done what you've wanted! How can you do this to me!"

"We have already told you," an elder explained coolly, "and now you each will wander the forests forevermore, with the beasts and fellow drovers. You will have an hour to gather personal belongings and supplies."

Darin put his head to the dirt, his body and voice suddenly wracked with emotion. "No, *please!* I'll forgo the honors you give me! I just want to *stay!*"

Neither Varnas nor Chev felt the need to say anything. Darin already gave voice to it, his begging and pleading more than showed what mercy the elders would give them. Silently, Varnas brushed Chev's shoulder, a signal to leave.

Outside, they listened awhile to Darin's pleas. Whatever the elders had to say in response, it was no comfort to him.

Varnas sighed, idly scanning the village, "I don't think he's gonna take it as well as you and me."

"When they said it, I couldn't help but think of—"

"Sana?"

"Of course," Chev licked his lips. "But my mother, too. She doesn't have anyone else."

"That's not true," Varnas shook his head. "She's got the tribe. They'll take care of her. These people, they do that."

"I hope so," said Chev.

Chev emerged from his mother's burrow, drained and emotionally beaten. He'd waited as long as it took for his tears to dry before meeting Varnas outside.

"You holding up, boy?"

"Yeah," said Chev, though his shoulders were slumped and misery could be read all over his face.

Varnas draped an arm over Chev's shoulder. "Probably a whole lot better'n Darin is right now, so perk up."

"You did everything you need to?" asked Chev.

"Don't really have anyone to say goodbye to, honest. Come on, let's fetch Sourface and get outta here."

They marched through the village. Chev soon realized there was an audience. Nightfolk made a line in their dozens, each head cautiously following Chev and Varnas in their journey from the village.

Chev hoped and hoped that Sana would not join them.

But it was clear as they reached the center that the whole community had come out. Chev was swathed in furs, harnessed to his back was the sleeping child now called Starlight. In one hand he held a walking staff. On his belt he wore Ossen's sword, long out of reasons to hide it anymore.

And of course Sana would show up. Laven acted as her support, she leaned against him. They made two sets of sad eyes as Chev and Varnas made their slow course.

The wailing made Chev think that Starlight was acting up again, but suddenly Darin was pushed in with them, stumbling and teetering on two legs.

"Please," he begged through reddened eyes, "please, do something. I can't let Nalia see me like this."

Chev, in inspiration, wrapped a blanket tight around Darin's head. Both men took a shoulder, and made him into their burden, walking with him to the edge of the village.

Nalia was at the very end of the line, watching the shrouded man with open-mouthed curiosity. At the very least, Chev had saved Darin from the terrible shame of having his beloved see him like this. Chev understood that. It was like when he came back from that fateful trip, and how he would have traded his life so that Sana wouldn't see him.

And so, without goodbyes, or any other words, the three men disappeared into the blackness of the forest, from which they'd never emerge.

The Oracle

Part II

Chapter Nine
Two Minds with One Face

"DAY'S COMING."

It was obviously true, but as the two crested the hill Varnas still felt the need to voice it. Chev was about to bite back with a sarcastic comment; he was exhausted from hours of suffering Varnas' humor during their fruitless hiking. But he chose to keep silent, sneering to himself alone.

The view that the top of the hill afforded him was a flat forested plain with ghostly mountains rising far away on the horizon. He took a seat on a fallen log, looking sullen and already beaten by the journey ahead of him. It wasn't the distance, it was his burden. Strapped securely to his chest was the dayghost child he'd so recently named Starlight. If his eyes served him, the Daylit Lands were still very far away, and she would be with them for a while yet.

Varnas prattled on as poked a soft patch of dirt. "No shelter, but no matter. We'll do what we did last time. We'll dig outta pit, that'll do well enough."

Another pit. Chev would've rather slept on a bed of brambles.

A presence came shambling up the rocky slope. Varnas called out to it: "Darin! Hey Darin!"

The man had done nothing but follow their shadows as they meandered the woods. Now, he looked dumbly on the pair as though completely lost, his uneven blink looking more and more like the result of a wound to the head rather than a wound to his cheek. He was a portrait of what shock could do to a man.

Varnas held the shovel out. "You planning on being any use to us?"

Darin processed the shovel a second before he realized he was being offered it. He balanced it between two open palms and two shrugged shoulders.

Varnas mimed his instructions. "Darin, you dig with it. You dig. Geddit?"

Darin nodded, and plunged the spade into the earth. He followed instructions mindlessly, for what purpose Darin clearly didn't care.

"You thought I was crazy for bringin' the shovel, didn't cha? Well now y'see. Old Varnas knows a shovel is always useful."

Chev finally felt it. Something in him snapped. He chopped the air. "Varnas will you please—" *Stop referring to yourself in the third person. Stop making up stories. Stop being so damn happy. Stop-stop-stop...* "Just shut up Varnas. Please."

The child began to whine and cry. Chev shushed it while Varnas piped on.

"Are you kidding? Who's takin' this better? Me, or Darin, walking around like he just up and died? Boy, you better learn quick that they banished us, not killed us."

Chev took it bitterly, coming out in the way he rocked Starlight. "Yeah, *banished*. Away from my mother. Away from my friends. Away from Sana."

"When you see dung, make a brick my mother used to say. Banishment is the best thing that coulda happened. I'm not gonna see another twenty seasons, boy. All the comforts of life have been ripped out from under me, forcing me to go on a grand adventure for the last years of my life. If I get eaten by some monster tomorrow I got no regrets. Gods, why is it you younguns *act* so old?"

Varnas prodded Chev in the chest, and Chev didn't even have the energy to wave him off. "Stop it, Varnas."

"No! I'm gonna continue poking you until you do something about it."

Chev raked the air lazily.

"Missed me by a mile! You gonna let this old man beatcha? Huh? Huh?"

Varnas thumped his chest, hollered like a monkey, loping around on all fours. He made a big circle around Chev, prodding and jeering.

"Get some life inta you, boy! Go on, swing one at me! Show me your jab, I can take it!"

Chev whined. "Varnas... please!"

"Cheeks got dark... oh your blood is boiling I can see it! Come on! I ain't adventuring with some tepid-blooded ninny-nose!"

"Varnas!" Chev set the child aside and got to his feet.

"Rattle-brain! Crumb-eater! Bow-legged sow sucker!"

"Those don't even make sense!"

"When your mother gave birth to ya, she only meant to break wind!"

"You asked for it!"

Chev swung at Varnas' silver-bearded cheeks, and he caught it like a champ. Varnas stumbled a bit, spat out a lump of something, and stood right back up.

"That was it? Are your arms made of cotton? Do it again, and this time, get me off my feet."

"I don't want to punch you, Varnas!"

"Chicken! Squirrel! Doe!"

"Don't make me do it!"

"Slug-breath!"

"I'm warning you!"

"Dog-face!"

"Right!" This time, Chev went in for a real strike. One foot forward, a lunge for the cheek. The blow lifted Varnas off the ground.

Varnas had flipped, Chev's fist throbbed painfully. There was a moment when Chev wondered whether Varnas would get to his feet. But, one arm at a time, the old man dragged himself up. Oddly, he was snorting bouts of laughter.

"What's so funny?" demanded Chev.

"Did it make you feel better?"

Chev barked back angrily, "Yeah, it did!"

Varnas howled with laughter, like an old monkey, losing his balance like he was punched again. It was contagious; Chev began to smile, then grin, and even he let out a laugh. After a good, long session, Varnas clapped a hand over Chev's shoulder.

"You see, boy? You see? Better'n being dead. Even if Darin there don't think it."

"I see," Chev said.

Darin had dug up to his neck, like a man possessed. When dust raised, one eye was shut while the other darted around.

"We better get 'im to stop." Varnas patted Chev's shoulder before walking over to the man. "Hey, Darin!"

Darin let the shovel teeter over.

"How do you feel about givin' it a rest, hmm? Good man."

Darin nodded vacuously. They all crowded into the pit. Carefully, they placed a thick shroud of fronds over top. Enough where they thought the sun couldn't make it through.

"I hope it don't rain," commented Varnas quietly.

So, safe in the darkness, they waited for day to pass.

Starlight cried intermittently, and the best any of them could do was take turns sleeping. Mercifully, eventually even she was taken by exhaustion, and she rested peacefully in the swaddling Chev had wrapped her in. Furs gently rose and fell with her breath.

The leaves above finally dimmed with fading sunlight. It was silent and the perfect time to rest, but for some reason, neither Chev nor Varnas could take this last moment of sleep.

Varnas eyed the baby. "The one time she stops mewling, I can't close my eyes. What the hell."

"Now it's Darin that's crying."

Chev nodded over to the corner where Darin had curled up. He'd been muttering, restless, and squirming uneasily.

"Poor old boy," whispered Varnas, "You know, I really think that place was his life. I don't think he's ever gonna take this easy."

"I don't know if I will either."

Chev inspected Starlight's bedding. Finding something unsatisfactory about it, he adjusted it gently, pinching it into position until it was fit to smile at.

"I don't know what she eats," said Chev.

"Heh, well, part o' me didn't want to ask. I mean, they grow plenty. Maybe set her to graze somewhere?"

Chev's mouth twisted and he gave Varnas a cynical glance. "Can you see those little teeth chewing grass?"

"Well, I dunno," Varnas scratched his head. "I'm no dayghost expert."

"I gotta find something," Chev looked down, talking contemplatively, "I tried—sap, or ground up insects, or something..."

The old trapper suddenly looked uneasy, and for the first time, hesitant to say something. It came out slowly, cautiously. "Mmm... well, I don't want to get your hopes up, as it was a long time ago, but I might know where we could find out."

Chev looked up, his attention captured.

"It was a long time ago," Varnas now picked up pace, "and far away. I was young, bit older than you, and a nomad—near a drover, really, goin' place to place in search of a home. Long story short, I found a monster."

"A monster?"

Varnas waved his hand. "Not the sort you think. A smart, old monster, that knew many things. Enormous, more'n enormous, but real peaceful. It made me, uh... *tea.*"

Chev flinched at the unfamiliar word.

"Kind of an herb stew. You drink it. Never mind, it's not important. The important thing is, it knew a heckuvalot, gave me the answers I didn't know I was searching for, and seeing as it didn't eat me, it might be safe to look for him. I think."

"How long ago was this?"

"Oh. Fifty years or so."

Chev's eyes widened, mouthing the number back in disbelief.

"Well, that was why I didn't want to get your hopes up. It was a long, long time ago and who knows if the beast is still alive or not. And, even if it is, we don't even know that it has the answers you want."

Chev leaned forward "So? Is it close? You think we could get there before next dayfall?"

"Didn't you listen? I said it was far away, didn't I?"

"Doesn't mean we can't make it," said Chev.

That was when Varnas shrugged, and said something he instantly regretted. "Well, only if we *run.*"

"Slow down, you fool!"

Varnas had once again this early night nearly lost Chev. They had descended into a humid and mist-filled forest, streams ran through the valley, a waterfall at its center. Chev had made a beeline for it, climbing up a rise and onto a natural ledge running behind the waterfall. Varnas' voice was nearly lost by the crash of water far below.

Chev stopped, giving Varnas' the time he needed to chase him up the wet path. Wet mist blinded them as it blew into their eyes. Chev had to squint as Varnas edged across the slippery surface.

"You stupid boy. How do you expect to make it when you don't even know the way?"

"Hey, I'm just setting a pace!"

"That you are. Just wait for Darin to catch up, won't you?"

"But he's *walking!*"

"So am I! Trying to, at least!" Varnas flopped onto the rocks beneath him. "Rest a bit. You're gonna kill us all at this rate."

"Not when Starlight is hungry."

"You think she's happy bouncing up and down? She needs a rest too. Now, sit down."

Chev quickly checked her. Somehow, through all the running, she'd stayed dead asleep. Her head lolled lazily, burying her furry cheeks into Chev's chest, wet lips smacking randomly. But Chev saw Varnas' point, and after taking a breath he took a seat by Chev.

Chev asked, "So this monster... what kinda monster is he?"

Varnas scratched his head. "It's been a long time since I saw 'im. He was a big monster. Bigger than a ursar even. He was the shape of a wall, he was."

"Was he friendly? Do you think he would know what to do?"

"I don't know." Varnas nodded a direction. "And look, there comes Darin. Just in time."

Darin walked over a short rise, and there he stopped. But he didn't look how he did before. No longer was there that vacant look across his face, but one of determination, it was clear he'd done a great deal of thinking on the way. One eye closed and the other opened, and he stared at them for quite a while. Chev guessed he was communicating something, but the message was lost on Chev. Darin spun around suddenly, and back down the cliff he went.

It was all too strange. Chev said the first thing on the top of his head. "What was that?"

Varnas sighed. "I've seen that look before. He's near as stupid as you, that man. Nearly. He's parting ways."

"What? Why?"

"Who knows." Varnas flicked a stone down into the whirling waters below. "Just a foolish man, I guess."

"Does that mean we have to wait around for him?"

"Guess not." Varnas then realized what he'd just said. "I meant—no! Damn fool, Chev! You're going the wrong way!"

Chev had already sped like a hellion up the path. Varnas had to climb to his feet, sliding on slick rocks all the while, before he could run after him.

The terrain changed once again when Chev and Varnas scaled the cliff face. They found themselves flanked by conifers that loomed crookedly around a small stream. The air was dry, and the brook was cool and soothing on Chev's feet. Varnas had fallen silent, which could only mean he was thinking.

"It's coming back to me, this place," said Varnas after a long silence. "It almost feels like a dream the last time I was here. Hope you're not nervous."

"I'm not," said Chev.

"Sure you ain't."

The path followed the stream, waters tumbling over rocks and growing more gentle as they climbed the slope. The land leveled out into little plateaus like shelves, each topped with wild grass as thick and disheveled as hair. Trees became rarer and, after a walk, the path's end came to sight. A steep trail ascended a rocky hill and dipped into the mouth of a cave. A half-moon blazed overhead, the breadth of stars easily visible.

Chev was about to make a run for the top, but he was held by Varnas' tight grip. He shook his head, put a finger over his lips.

"Things get dangerous here, Chev."

Chev nodded, gazing briefly at the child sleeping peacefully at his breast, before they made a careful path.

Titanic slabs of rock made for natural steps up. Chev was about to step on one before Varnas hastily warned him.

"Don't," said Varnas, "it's a grave."

Chev looked down, confused.

The slab of rock wasn't natural. Someone had carved it out, the edges resembled those of an obsidian knife, though the rock was so big that Chev couldn't contemplate what force could have moved it into place. And as Chev stepped away from it, he realized that it was not the only one. Such slabs littered the valley below, and went up the cliff. The effect was dizzying.

"What *are* these monsters?" whispered Chev.

"You'll see. Come on now. Walk very carefully. We're being watched."

Chev twisted around to see what creature was looking at him, but there were only rocks and trees all around. Varnas pulled him insistently and they continued up the path. A sound that Chev had heard and ignored until now became louder and louder. There was bleating that Chev had never heard before, alien and slightly menacing.

"Whatever you do," whispered Varnas, "don't touch the woolbeasts."

"Woolbeasts?"

There was a rustle, Chev turned quickly with the Daysword half drawn. A monster like a cloud with legs trotted out from behind some rocks. Varnas quickly pushed Chev's blade back, whispering panicked warnings that were lost when a storm of the stumpy little monsters bounced across the path, bleating and whining all the while. Varnas kept his hand locked around Chev's arm as they stared at the surreal parade.

"What weird creatures," Chev remarked.

"Chev, you fool boy! You want to get us both killed?"

"Hey, you coulda warned me *before* I went up the path."

"Maybe if you weren't running ahead all the time like an idiot I would have the chance to! Just keep in sight, follow behind and *don't do anything*."

There was an unexpected cry of delight. Both the men blinked, and they looked down at Starlight, beaming a gummy smile with arms grasping toward the odd-looking woolbeasts. She was so insistent her feet pushed against Chev's chest and she leaned out from her harness to try and grab them.

"She likes these woolbeasts, I guess," Chev said, gently nudging the child into security.

"Maybe she's just trying to get something to eat," said Varnas.

Chev smiled as he imagined Starlight nibbling at a woolbeast's flank. "Come on. Let's get going."

Hoards of the little woolbeasts infested the landscape the further Chev and Varnas climbed. Now, the mouth of the cave loomed, after shooing a path through the creatures. Whatever monster called the cave home, it had carefully erected pillars by the entrance, supporting a roof easily six times Chev's height. He was forced to crane his neck to get a good look at the whole thing.

Chev's keen vision only pierced only so far into the pitch darkness of the cave. As they both peered inside, they found they were in want of a lantern, a torch, or even a stray firefly to buzz through. Even the smallest light would have helped in such a desperately dark room.

"It's in there," whispered Varnas, "he's watching us."

"Can you call out to him?"

Varnas turned to Chev, and shook his head slowly. "I dare not. You don't want to surprise them."

"But you said—"

"That he's watching us," Varnas brushed it off, "yes, yes he is! But... it's hard to explain. They're odd. Not like you and me. They are both observant and oblivious at the same time."

The contradiction almost hurt Chev's head, but he shrugged it off. Carefully, quietly, Varnas made a step into the darkness. Not in the lead anymore, Chev felt emboldened to follow.

The cavern was enormous, and must have occupied nearly the entire hill. Chev found himself spinning around to see everything. The floor was smooth and flat, made of hard-packed dirt and rock. In the center of the chamber, a black cauldron made an ominous impression in the darkness, with its lip coming up to Chev's eye level. Someone had built wooden furnishings and cupboards of immense proportions, hinting at the great size of this monster. From the ceilings hung dozens of herbal bouquets that filled the chamber with an invigorating scent. Free of dust or dirt, the whole place was maintained lovingly.

"Duck," said Varnas.

"Hmm?"

It was a cudgel of tremendous size, like a small tree trunk. It would have broken every bone in Chev's body had his instincts not kicked in at the very last second as he jumped away towards the edge of the cave.

"Friend!" Varnas cried, "Friend!"

Chev was spinning to meet the threat. But he could only see parts of the creature—an enormous veined arm, thick legs like lumber, a shadowed face with swooping beard. Chev dived for cover.

What followed was like an indoor avalanche; the monster skipped a boulder across the cavern to try to peg Chev. Chev sidestepped it, still not entirely sure which direction to move to either face the enemy or to escape it. In his breathless panic he even forgot on which hip he wore his sword.

"Friend!" Varnas continued to cry, "Friend!"

At the very least, Varnas drew the beast's attention onto him. A rain of rocks pelted across the room, and the cudgel swooped out the darkness like a scythe. Only sheltering behind the table saved Varnas.

Chev scooped up a rock and tossed it at the mass of flesh and muscle. He might as well have thrown it at the wall.

"Don't attack him, you might hurt him!" cried Varnas.

"I don't think he's listening," Chev went for his sword.

"I was talking to *you!*"

Chev put Varnas' words out of mind. He only could think how stupid he was to enter a monster's den with a child strapped to his chest— and of course poor Starlight was crying. But he lifted his blade, stilled it, prepared for the monster's inevitable charge.

It didn't come. Instead the cudgel shot out. Chev jumped back, but he was still caught by it and flung to the other wall, back thudding on the other side with his sword suddenly out of his hands. Starlight's continued crying came as a strange comfort as the world dizzily congealed.

The monster moved forward aggressively, cudgel raised to bring down on Chev. Varnas was screaming, in the chaotic vertigo Chev could only pick out a few words.

"Friend! Friend! Come on... come on... *Hlogas!*"

The name was composed of odd, drawling syllables, but it had the power to stop the cudgel in its path; Chev only got a rush of pine air as it stopped just before his nose. Carefully, he opened one eye after the other.

"*Hlogas...*" The creature repeated in a deep, echoing voice, almost mournful. "*Hlogas...*"

The monster moved in a sort of sad shuffle, slow and stooped over. Tree trunk feet slid over the stone floor toward one of the cabinets. He fumbled around, feeling for something, and retrieved an over-sized lantern that rattled with many loose parts. The workings were incomprehensible to Chev, he only saw this Hlogas fiddling around with the thing before it suddenly sparked with light.

The monster held the tiny flame up to see the nightfolk, also revealing his own ancient face. Lines crossed thick jutting lips, uncombed beard disguised a retreating chin, ram horns made disks over his brow, sunken cheeks seem to push his features out. He looked more like a carving than a person. What confused Chev the most were the two yellow eyes that peered from only one half of his face. Chev thought he must've been too rattled to see straight, but the illusion was reality. Hlogas had four eyes, two closed, two open, arranged in a V across his countenance. When Hlogas blinked, Chev stepped back.

"Hlogas," repeated the four-eyed giant.

"Yes," Varnas repeated, "yes, please, wake him up."

Chev was about to say something, a confused question, but then, he was captured by the transformation that occurred before his eyes. The giant dipped his chin slowly, and then, his posture changed, drawing up and down in trance-like rhythm. Slowly, the left eyes closed, and the right eyes opened.

Like he was newly aware of his surroundings, the giant blinked, looked about, and focused in on the two men before him.

"*Oh*, you again. I did think you'd be back." The giant's voice had changed dramatically, from a dumb drawl to something far more alert and bright. Even his movements changed, like vigor had infused him. He still shuffled across the floor to take a close look at the two men.

"*Hlogas!*" Varnas drew out his name happily, and came up to Hlogas to give a great big slap on the forearm. "Good to see you, old boy. I was thinkin' on it, how long it's been. I reckon fifty years thereabouts."

"Close. Fifty-three, and one-hundred twenty-six days. It was autumn when you tried poaching from my herd."

"Poachin'?" Varnas snorted dismissively, "Nah, you're remembering it wrong."

Hlogas rolled his two eyes. "You know, I was about to ask a foolish question—why you happened to be up so late."

"Ah, Hlogas, you know our kind better than that—"

Chev finally regained control of his senses. He made a determined stride forward, and caught the giant's attention. "Hold on. I want to know why you attacked us."

"Attacked you?" Hlogas boomed, drawing up onto his feet, "I wasn't aware. Did he bring a child in here?"

Varnas quickly stepped between them, but not before making a brisk gesture at Chev for him to silence the baby. "Understandable, understandable confusion. Hlogas, this is my companion Chev, son of Minda, and he does have a child here. That's the matter at hand. Chev doesn't know the nature of your species, the... uh... the... hmm..."

"We call ourselves *rondacks*."

"*Rondacks*, of course. Just as you said it, the word came back to me." Varnas lectured Chev while he bounced Starlight. "Hlogas is a rondack. A venerable race, descendants of the Great Folk just as dayghosts are nightfolk are. Every rondack has two minds, one rests while the other watches over their herds."

The rondack explained, "Argos has developed dementia. And he was never very social. The rights never are."

Chev just looked up at Hlogas in confusion. Hlogas' fat lips pursed out even further.

"Hmm... just see Argos and I as two different people who happen to share a body," Hlogas horned, "Please, sit. I'll put some tea on."

Chev was about to take to the floor when he saw Varnas sit on a strange object by the cauldron. Chev had never seen a cushion, but he immediately took it to be some seating implement and followed Varnas' example.

Hlogas pulled down one of the strange bouquets of herbs and threw it into the cauldron. Chev and Varnas both chewed on rations of jerky as they watched Hlogas work to start a fire.

"So..." Hlogas croaked as he bent over the cauldron, "I'm curious to how this child is supposed to be the reason for your visit."

Chev and Varnas looked to each other for an answer, but neither could think of manner of putting it. "Why don't we wait for tea first?" Varnas suggested.

"That unusual, hmm?" Hlogas rumbled as though his chest were a sack of rocks. "We'll do as you ask, but now I'm doubly curious."

Varnas swallowed nervously, and Chev found he had to force his food down as well. He knew why. This child, the dayghost called Starlight, with its bright endearing eyes and fur-lined cheeks, represented a terrible transgression. The people of day and those of the night were not supposed to interact. How Hlogas would take it, neither of them could guess.

It felt like a rock in his stomach. Chev had to think carefully of how he'd put things, though he was tempted to let Varnas prattle on in his own odd way. He seemed to have a way with this giant before him. But words were still dangerous. If the giant took things badly, there would be nothing stopping him. His nose alone would be the size of Chev's head. And that wasn't even considering his titanic gangling arms that stirred the cauldron, and the horns that spiraled over his forehead could smash Chev into a pulp. And the creature didn't even stand at full height, shuffling about with the hunch he had.

He went to his cupboard and, between three fingers, delicately squeezed two small cups. It was a mesmerizing operation as he used a ladle to carefully fill each with the brew, so deftly that not even a single drop spilled onto the floor. Chev and Varnas gratefully took a cup each. The giant sated himself just using the ladle.

There was a long, drawn out slurp as Hlogas sucked in the tea between near-closed lips, before releasing a pleased sigh like a swollen stream. Chev and Varnas followed suit. It was steaming hot, but had a pleasant aroma that had an immediate soothing effect on Chev's head.

"Oh," Varnas grunted, "you know, it's even better than I remembered. I always meant to make it myself, but I kept forgettin' how to do it."

Hlogas had a wide grin. "You throw herbs into a boiling pot."

"Heh, right."

"Enough. You didn't come here to share tea. I would like to rest again tonight. So please," Hlogas swept his arm in invitation, "please speak."

Both Varnas and Chev took the time to drink very deeply. Even after there was silence, and Varnas only answered after it was clear that someone had to say something.

"So my friend here came with this child."

Hlogas trumpeted immediately, "You have me at a loss. I have no children. They are not something I know anything about."

Varnas scratched his head, unsure of what to say next. But Chev set the wooden cup down and got to his feet, child to his breast. He told the monster, "Perhaps its best if you see it for yourself."

The giant clearly tried to think of a way to protest, but he sighed, resigned himself, and held his arm out. The child fit well into the palm of the massive hand, she was brought up to two yellow, inspecting eyes. He held her for some time, happy wet cooing the only sound.

And then, Hlogas snapped back in surprise.

"A child of the *dayfolk?* I don't understand... what are you doing with *this?*"

"I found her," said Chev, made nervous by Hlogas' confused tone.

"Well, perhaps you should have left her." Hlogas held his palm out, Starlight wriggling obliviously in the middle.

Chev took her back, giving a brief glance at her fat, furry cheeks and wide light eyes. Holding her tight to his chest came as an odd comfort. "Listen, I hadn't meant to offend you. I just need to know—"

Hlogas raised his hand to stop him. "There is no need to apologize. It is not my taboo you violated. I'm only worried for the poor child." Hlogas took a contemplative sip from his ladle. "I'm also worried for you."

"I would have left her, if I could," said Chev, "but I accidentally touched her, and since then, I've had the curse of the dayghosts—the *dayfolk*—on me. I am bonded."

Hlogas was definitely sure he didn't understand. He squinted and twisted his lips. "You're what? You're *bonded to it?*"

"I didn't mean to!" Chev defended himself, "All I did was pick her up, thinking she was an animal! And then like that," Chev snapped his fingers, "I'm cursed."

Hlogas had all four eyes closed for a good long time while he contemplated what Chev had told him. "I didn't remember that being how bonding worked," Hlogas scratched his head, and struggled to recall what he'd heard. "But you probably know better than I. It is not a custom of our people."

"Nor ours," piped Varnas.

"If you say so," Hlogas shrugged, quite sure that not all was right, but unable to think of why. "But no matter the situation, it's dangerous for you both to be together. It is a very bad precedent."

"I've heard that before," said Chev, flinching as he remembered Patience, "but no one has told us *why.*"

Hlogas' eyes no longer pointed straight at Chev. Instead, the two pupils made an uneasy trail across the floor. Hlogas was in deep contemplation. "You dayfolk and nightfolk, you are a brother races. One cannot live without the other. You know this well. Without the dayfolk watching, the nightfolk of the forest became slaves of the bone-skins. And without the nightfolk to protect them, the dayfolk go insane with fear of the darkness; they make easy, blind prey. Could you imagine what might happen if your races went to war? It would be a slaughter. In darkness, nightfolk slitting the throats of dayfolk. In light, dayfolk burning and pillaging nightfolk homes, dragging them out like worms into the sun. It would be just awful." Hlogas sighed. "A long time ago, when the nightfolk were the ones with armies and empires and the dayfolk were mere farmers, there was an edict passed by a great ruler. Any nightfolk or dayfolk caught together would be beheaded. This law persisted long after the empire fell, and lives on in your memory, even when the reasons are long lost.

"While you carry that child, you will always be in seclusion. This custom might be weak here on the fringes of civilization, but they have long memories in the Daylit Lands and the nightfolk there jealously guard the taboo."

Chev nodded. "That's good to know. We're going into the Daylit Lands."

Varnas twisted his head. *"We are?"*

"Where else am I going to find a home for Starlight? There's no one to undo the curse here, no one to pass Starlight to."

"Now, now," Varnas hooted his protests, "I know I said I wanted to go on a grand adventure, but I was hoping we'd confine things a bit *locally*."

"I share Varnas' concerns," Hlogas paused to make a great big yawn, hiding his gap-toothed maw behind the paw of his hand, "Sorry. I meant to say, the nightfolk of the Daylit Lands are very different from your kind. Many have degenerated."

"How do you mean?" asked Chev.

"They've come to be lazy, selfish, cruel. Many rely on banditry now. But if you are going into the Daylit Lands, you should see the Oracle."

"The Oracle?" Chev leaned forward.

"A wise woman, so I've heard. She might be able to help you with your problem. She makes her seat in the ruins of the last great city of the nightfolk. Once you enter the Daylit Lands, you should have no problem knowing which way to go. Apparently everyone there knows."

"So she can help end the curse, right? And she can tell us a safe place to take Starlight?"

Hlogas shrugged, and spoke sluggishly and tiredly. He rubbed his two right eyes as he spoke. "I suspect that this curse lies mostly in your head, Chev, son of Minda, and that you'll never find a safe place for the child. But the oracle may be able to help you see it."

Varnas looked benevolently at the giant. "You look tired, old friend."

"I am not nocturnal like you. I should be well asleep right now. We will talk again before you leave, but there is one matter of business left. There is another reason you have come. It should have been the first thing you said."

Chev understood what he was getting at. "We can't feed the child."

"Yes, no matter what race, young or old, all men lack that ability." Hlogas smirked at what he reckoned was a clever observation. "It's tough for me to do this, but I can see you two are in the greater need." Hlogas leaned toward the mouth of the cave, and bellowed, "Ma-ma! Ma-ma!"

Varnas and Chev had to cover their ears, but after the echoes died down there was just a long silence. After watching the darkness outside, a figure appeared as though it'd been pushed through a black velvet curtain: a little goat, trotting out proudly, its legs so stubby and fur so thick it resembled a piece of fluffy cotton drifting across the ground.

"Ma-ma has powerful maternal instincts. She'll follow you anywhere, and she will happily nurse the child if you wish."

Ma-ma shook her body agreeably, skipping happily deeper into the cave. She had this magnetic, psychic attraction to the creature Chev held in his arms. A long tongue slipped out from her tiny mouth. Chev got to his feet to keep Starlight away from the excitable goat, but once a pudgy arm shot out of the swaddling there was no stopping her. She did this hop to get at it, bumping and pushing against Chev as though he were nothing more than an obstacle.

"Get... it... away!" said Chev, juggling Starlight from arm to arm.

"Let her see the child," Hlogas said, his voice alight with amusement. "Trust her."

Chev didn't want to, not with that greedy, hungry tongue hanging out of the mouth. But Hlogas had been nothing but helpful, and he'd need to punch the goat to get it away, so he gave it what she wanted. He set Starlight on the ground.

Ma-ma came to sniff her, much to Starlight's delight. There was a soft cooing as Ma-ma buried her muzzle into baby fur, and a hairy paw drifted across the bridge of Ma-ma's nose. After some bonding, Ma-ma laid flat, and allowed Starlight to grasp her belly. Somehow, Starlight knew to nurse from Ma-ma.

"I... never... *thought of that...*" Chev could only speak in stutters—the idea of an animal nursing a person was a revelation.

"Ma-ma's a good girl. And now she won't leave Starlight's side. She's just that sort of goat." Hlogas lost composure as a big, enormous yawn broke out of him. "And now—I need to rest. Feel free to stay the day. I'll see you off in the morning—" Hlogas gave what he said some thought, "—dusk, rather."

Varnas nodded to Hlogas. "Thank you, my old friend. I knew we could count on you. If there was any manner which we could pay y'back..."

Hlogas brushed his eyes. "Do not worry about that. It does not take an oracle to know what the outcome of your journey will be. Chev is my investment, he will pay back far more than he owes, he just doesn't know it yet. I will see you at dusk."

Before any question could be asked, Hlogas was back to being Argos. Argos, slump-faced, mournful, slow, picked up his staff, and shuffled out like a feeble old man that he was. Until morning, the only sound was Argos' deep rumbling sadness; "Hlogas," he lamented softly, "Hlogas... Hlogas... Hlogas..."

Chapter Ten
A Guide of Talent

AS IT TURNED OUT, Hlogas' cupboard was big enough to comfortably fit two nightfolk, and so that was where Chev and Varnas stowed themselves away. The door was a slab of solid wood, it would've made a good thick table, but it was so skillfully hung, it needed to only a gentle shove to have it close softly on its own. The last thing Chev saw Starlight peering curiously around the cave until the slab of wood sealed completely. Chev's eyes remained open, like two lights in the dark.

"Go to sleep," moaned Varnas.

"I can't."

Chev kept his ear close to the gap. He waited for some sound, some sign, of what was out there. He heard something—a goat's baa and a child's contented cry. Relief came over Chev, and he gave away to sleep as he let himself fall back into the soft bedding.

As a matter of fact, Chev slept so deeply it felt borderline sinful. He had pleasant but unmemorable dreams, and after some hours he woke, rolling decadently in the furs to watch the sunlight peeking between the cupboard doors slowly fade. Varnas woke naturally as well, sometime before dusk. The distant chorus of day, with its bleating animals and singing birds, slowly gave over to the tuneless chirping of crickets.

"'Wise,' he called the Oracle," Varnas mused.

He and Chev were having the sort of groggy half-conversation that transpired when two people wake too early. Neither of them bothered sitting up, preferring the comfort of the furs.

Chev massaged his forehead with his thumb. "Hmm?"

"Don't you remember nothin'? Wise is just another word for useless."

"I don't think Hlogas knows that."

Varnas rolled his head side to side. "No. Nine times outta ten, when they say someone's wise, they're actually useless."

"Hlogas is wise, and he isn't useless."

Now Varnas shook his head more vigorously. "No. Hlogas is *smart,* he ain't wise."

Varnas' rules were getting confusing. But Chev dismissed them with a shrug. "Whatever. You just don't want to go to the Daylit Lands."

"'Course not!" Varnas stated it proudly, "Why would I go to the Daylit Lands, hmm? We're people of the forest. Us in the plains? It's like taking a fish right outta water. They say if the sun catches you out there, you're done. It's just grass and nothin' else to the horizon."

Chev thought earnestly on that, and gave an honest answer. "I see what you're saying. But what other choice do we have? We can wander endlessly as drovers, burdened by this dayfolk child, or we can try to get her back to her people."

And though Varnas grumbled and squirmed beneath the furs, he had nothing more to say.

Varnas and Chev once again fell to half-sleep until they were disturbed when the door opened abruptly. Something hairy, with heavy breathing squeezed in, then between them. As soon as Chev picked up the animal scent, and he went dead flat like a plank, arms rigid to his sides. He couldn't imagine how a wild creature could have snuck into the rondack's lair, but now it snuffled at his feet. Chev's rigid body became damp with perspiration—he debated whether to launch himself at it and try to kill it, or hope it took him as dead and left before going for the throat.

"Misty!" the rondack's voice boomed. "Get out of there!"

The wolf complied eagerly, knocking the door wide open as it left. Varnas sighed in relief, kicking off his furs, as did Chev. The rondack's four eyes drifted back and forth as it took them both in.

"Sorry. She's just curious." The rondack boomed with Hlogas' voice. "Time you were awake anyway."

Varnas, stubborn as usual, grunted and gave some lip with a side of good humor. "We *were* awake, we were just talkin' you big dumb oaf! If you'd given us just a *second* more we woulda walked out without you naggin' us!"

"Varnas!" Chev warned him. "Sorry about him. It was just that the wolf had us real scared."

"I understand. I know Varnas. He blusters when he feels he's been caught." Hlogas continued, talking over Varnas' incomprehensible protests, "Not a wolf. Just a 'dog', not many of them nowadays. I will walk with you to the edge of the ridge after you've eaten. Now, if you'd excuse me for a moment…."

Hlogas shuffled off to sort through a big chest. Starlight was lying peacefully near Ma-ma, Chev made a beeline for her and strapped her onto his chest in her padded harness. Varnas eased out into the clear night air at the mouth of the cave. Streams of stars drenched the horizon of the primeval forest with silvery light. Things sparkled beneath the night sky canopy, the light reflecting from streams and lakes that ran through the valley below. Though all was still for miles, things never seemed so alive.

"That's a sight you can get used to," admired Varnas. He suddenly he turned away and winced as though experiencing pain. He went over to Chev, who was tousling Starlight's fur. "Chev," he whispered, "I don't think I could leave this damned forest."

Chev looked to him and nodded in understanding. "It's alright, you can stay."

"I can't," said Varnas, "I mean, I *can* stay, but I can't leave. You know how it is, don't you?"

Chev shook his head.

"Darn it, Chev, you gonna make me say it out loud? You're gonna kill me faster if you go out into the Daylit Lands all on your own. But this is my home. You see what I'm getting at? See here, young man: We could spend our days driftin' out in the forest, trappin' and huntin' for everything we need, no elders or women or any of these wise fools tellin' us what to do. Or we could cross those mountains. And you know what's as them? I'll tell you straight: a sun-baked wasteland. We'll end up like the rest of 'em, living in a dayfolk's cellar, nothing to do but scrub streets and chase monsters. Which would you rather do?"

"You don't think I want to go home too? I'll tell you what I want to do. I want to be Sana's mate. And I can't do that until I break the curse and find a home for Starlight. And the only place to do that," Chev gestured grandly, "is beyond those mountains!"

Like a nervous tick, Varnas began stroking his beard. "What choice do you leave me then? What choice do you leave me? Go find an oracle, what a stupid excuse. You're just off to find Ossen."

Chev put his hand over his chest. "Ossen! Don't make me laugh! I haven't thought about him for years!"

"You have!"

"Have not!"

"Have!"

"Have not!"

"Have!"

Starlight erupted with a terrified cry. Hlogas bent his head down, sweeping a hand down his face with a disappointed sigh, despairing how Chev and Varnas provoked each other in turns.

"Are you done?" Hlogas was cupping something in his hand which, it looked at that moment, like a threatening fist.

The chamber was silent but for Starlight's forlorn cry. Hlogas seemed content to let the shame really sink through to Chev and Varnas. And it worked, they grew more sheepish by the second.

"I brought you some supplies. They should last until you reach the Daylit Lands," said Hlogas, unfolding his fingers and revealing a leather satchel so full the stitches might've burst. Varnas went to fetch it while Chev bounced and comforted Starlight until she calmed.

"Thank you for all your help. I don't know how I'll ever thank you," said Chev.

"That time will come," said the rondack. "Come. We can talk on the way."

"There is a pass between the mountains," started Hlogas, "that's the main route between here and the Daylit Lands. A small dayfolk city lies just at its mouth. There, you should find other nightfolk making the journey. Be wary. They do not trust tribals."

Every sentence was punctuated with Hlogas' staff stabbing into the ground as they walked. At full height now, Chev finally understood Hlogas' extraordinary stature. If Chev jumped, he would only just touch his hair-strewn chest. It seemed odd that such a beast would exude such placidity and have such a wealth of knowledge. Even after yesterday, Chev could not see Hlogas attacking someone.

Ma-ma the goat followed behind, her stubby legs hidden by a curtain of wool making her seem to more drift than trot. Ma-ma was little more than the size of an insect to Hlogas, but he was keenly aware of her, following her with his protruding nose and a benevolent smile.

"Ma-ma wants to go with you, it seems. I knew she would. A sweet old woman, she is."

Ma-ma bleated. She seemed like just an old goat to Chev, borderline silly. But the tinge of sadness in Hlogas' voice, matched by wistful smile, was very, very real.

When Hlogas sighed, it was more a breeze blowing through canyons. "Here we are. Good luck on your journey. May you grow on your way."

"We will. Thank you for everything, Hlogas. And thank you too, Argos," said Chev.

Hlogas, and by extension Argos, nodded, and, turning laboriously, started on the hike back toward the cavern.

The path circled around the cliffs where Hlogas made his home, and they were soon enough at a fork in the road where one path pointed in one direction heading back into the forest, and another went winding into the foothills that ascended into the mountains. Chev and Varnas came to face each other, neither quite ready to part ways and step forward on their chosen paths.

"This is it, then," said Varnas, "You going your way. Me going mine."

"I guess it is."

"Don't have to be," said Varnas, "plenty of game out here for two, or three. Sure we could find some dayfolk to trade with. They might even take in that little girl of yours. Starlight."

"I'm sorry Varnas. I have to go. But I'll be back. I'll see you then."

"Oh. 'Course. 'Course," Varnas nodded slowly. He stripped off Hlogas' satchel then, tossing it at Chev's feet. "He meant it for you."

Chev knelt over to pick it up. Holding Starlight gently on his chest, he put one loop after the other as the satchel settled on his back, and he seemed no slower for it. "I'll see you, then. Thanks for coming as far as you did."

"Careful with that pack. It's a heavy burden."

Chev nodded with a smile. "I'll keep it in mind."

"And if I see Darin I'll kick his ass for you."

Chev laughed. "That'd be a sight."

"I will, believe me I will." Varnas shifted uncomfortably. "Well, night's not getting younger and I gotta dig myself a pit."

"And I need to get to the Daylit Lands."

"Yeah, sure," grunted Varnas. "This goodbye has gone on long enough. Good luck, or sumthin'."

153

"Thanks."

They turned away from each other deliberately, and each walked away. A minute later Chev was now alone, except for a baby and a goat. The one thing going for him was that his path was clear; a trail winding to the first of the dayfolk cities, passage through the mountains, then the long arduous journey to the oracle. Chev hoped Varnas was wrong, that she could break his curse and lay out the guidance he needed to return to Sana.

It would be a journey made even longer without Varnas. He could be annoying sometimes; as a fact he was annoying *most* times. But time always went quicker by his side. Varnas had a talent for filling silence with constant chatter.

Things would be lonely from now on, but Chev reasoned, he always had been. Even back home, with the tribe, he was born an outsider. Ossen's banishment only furthered that. And now that he was banished, with no one by his side but this burdensome child, he was simply stripped of any illusion of companionship.

Chev tried to think of the solitude as liberating, in its own way.

Ahead of him the forest grew sparser. Clearings gave way to rocky outcroppings and fields thick with wild brush and flowers. Even further, vegetation gave way to rock and sharp cliffs, clashing with each other like petrified waves in a mounting, frozen storm.

Starlight was blissfully asleep, limp in her harness and lips pursed slightly. Chev combed back her fur and pointed to the horizon.

"Look, Starlight!' he whispered, "Your homeland! That's where we're—"

"Wait!"

Chev turned to the echoing sound.

"Wait! Damn you, wait!"

Varnas kicked up a dust cloud he ran so fast, leaping over branches and stones. He slid to a breathless stop, brushing himself off with a couple of brisk pats, and wheezed, "You little bastard. You meant to leave me there, didn't you?"

Chev was confused. "You said you were going your own way!"

"Oh, so you're not heartless, just stupid. You couldn't tell I was bluffing?"

"You were?"

"Close your mouth. You look like a brain-damaged walrus. The sooner we get to this oracle the sooner we can leave."

"So you *are* coming with me?"

As a response, Varnas snorted. "Don't get too cocky. I'm doing *you* a favor by going on this stupid quest of yours. Now, let's go!"

Varnas powered ahead in as brisk a stride as he could manage, eager to get this journey done. Chev let him walk ahead a little bit, he didn't want Varnas to catch him with the absurd smile that bloomed on his lips.

When the forest finally eased away to rocky foothills, a shudder went through Varnas. They both looked back at the vast forest they'd left, with all its shadows and shelter, food and water. Back in the forest lay the only home they knew. They looked at each other with quizzical, plaintive faces, and then they marched up the first of many ridges.

"Already feels colder," Varnas muttered beneath his breath.

The air was different here. It was dry and cool, making an unpleasant impression against the skin. It felt like the wind had run over the dead rocks of this forsaken place, picking up some of its lifeless chill. It was as though they urged them back from where they came, but Chev and Varnas ignored their own nagging doubt as they navigated the clearest path, a gentle slope leading into a gap between monstrous peaks. The rock faces crashed against one another, they looked like the teeth of a dead monster, gummed by stone and capped by ivory snow.

From a distance, it was difficult to understand the scale of the boulders. They formed canyons by themselves, like bleak hills, hard windblown things with lichen and moss for company. They forced the pair on constant detours into shadow-shrouded crags and little valleys caged by hard stone. When light came, they sought refuge in caves, only to begin again when darkness fell. One day's trek followed the next, with little relief. They found fish in mountain creeks and caught birds. Ma-ma was sure-footed and easily kept pace, nibbling mountain herbs and continuing to provide nourishment to Starlight, who began to thrive.

After many days, it was in a craggy valley they encountered the strange wanderer.

He was so unexpected and strange that both Varnas and Chev just stopped to wordlessly stare at him as he snoozed loudly in his rocky nest. He was dressed *absurdly*, with clothes that hugged close to his skin. He had, for some odd reason, *sleeves* over the legs and arms, like every inch of skin had to be covered. He looked like a nightfolk except for one strange feature: his ears were *rounded,* like someone had cut the points off.

Just then he started to stir, he scratched his head, pinched his nose, and blinked. His eyes opened wider as they tracked sluggishly toward the two shadowy figures in front of him.

He let out a cry of terror. Half-way on his feet, he picked up a contraption and it shot out something like an arrow which flew exactly between Chev and Varnas. His other hand shook an equally strange, shiny instrument that rang out tuneless, useless sounds.

"Tribals!" he cried, "Tribals! Tribals!"

In his rush to get up, he slammed stupidly into a boulder and folded up on the ground. Like a spring he was on his feet again.

He spoke in a bird's tone, immature and pitched. "Don't come any closer, or I'll shoot!" he warned, his feet already pointed in escape, "My friends are on the way! And you'll be sorry if you hurt me!"

Chev and Varnas looked at each other. Ma-ma bleated and found some wildflowers to chew.

"Did you just try and kill us?" said Varnas.

"And my friends will do worse! Go back to your bone-skin masters!"

There was nothing intimidating about this man, even with the weird wooden contraption that shot arrows. Chev stepped forward, the strange man shrank back, squeezing his back against the rock wall

"We're not here to hurt anyone. We're just trying to get through the mountains."

"Lies!" The strange man drew back further, dropping the arrow-machine and pulling out a long knife of silvery daysteel. "You're trying to trick me! Well, I won't let you rat us out. Your life ends here!"

The man made an unsteady lunge, each footfall unbalanced. Chev drew his sword, the sight of it stopped the man before a fight even happened.

"Oh, ancients of Manak!" the young man cried, dagger falling from limp, rubbery fingers, "Don't hurt me!"

Chev waved his blade. "Why would we?"

The man's hand twisted over a clump of grass, steadying him as he shivered and shook. "Please, please don't! I didn't mean to—"

Chev was going to step forward, but Varnas pinched Chev's arm, and whispered into his ear. "The man's mad. Best we leave him."

Chev watched him for a moment, how he shivered with fear at the blade still held out against him. A sense of pity took him; Chev sheathed his blade.

"It's a long way to this oracle," said Chev, turning to Varnas.

It seemed opportune to leave. They were about to make their way on the trail, but the young man lifted his face and relief swept across the expression of fear.

"You're pilgrims? You're pilgrims!" The young man laughed like there was nothing left to do in the whole world, and in his relief he pulled back his stark black hair. "Why didn't you say you were going to Manak!"

Chev twisted to him. "You know the way?"

The young man repeated himself in his excitement. "Of course. I mean—I mean—I mean, we're pilgrims too! I'm sorry, I thought you must've been tribals—clearly you are—but you aren't the sort to sacrifice people! Or maybe you are, but you aren't sacrificing anyone right now! And if you're going to Manak, you could join us!"

A wizened hand went over Chev's shoulder. Varnas whispered, "Come on, Chev. This one's no help."

Chev had already set himself to walk away from this man without Varnas' advice, but he was reminded of long, hard days alone, because everyone was scared to take him hunting until Varnas took pity. Memories made his eyes cloud up, shame flushed his face as he realized how close he had come to being the kind of person he hated. He turned, walked back to the young man on the ground, and Chev held out his arm.

"Chev," he told him.

The young man looked at the outstretched hand, and then to the man it belonged to. He took it, and responded in kind: "Tobi."

As it turned out, Tobi was a man possessed with wind and air, never breathless enough to pause his incessant chatter. Even the talkative Varnas was impressed. Up steep hills and down dipping valley, he yammered regardless of what anyone else said, and occasionally he asked questions like a child, forcing Chev's attention.

"So what tribe you guys from?" asked Tobi, loping up a steep path.

Chev was winded, his throat dry, and thoroughly done with talking. But he felt obligated to respond, if just to show Tobi that he wasn't ignoring him. "What do you mean?"

"You know... what tribe? Are you from the Pawcat Tribe, or the Ursar Tribe, or the Carcoons or Bear-rats or Ravens?"

"We're from the—" Chev interrupted his own sentence with a snort. "—the normal tribe."

The path opened up into a high ledge. Instinctively, they all stopped to catch their breath, but Tobi would make that difficult

"The normal tribe? How's that possible? You don't have a totem animal or anything?"

Varnas shrugged and shook his head.

"Well... what do you guys call yourselves?"

Chev thought about it for a moment. "We call ourselves the, uh, the *tribe*."

"That's it? The *tribe*? You don't have a name? That's stupid. How do you talk about other tribes?"

"We don't," shrugged Varnas. Chev nodded.

"Oh. You aren't proper tribals, then, are you?" Tobi sighed, as though deeply disappointed. He nodded to the next hill. "The encampment is just over there. I'm sure everyone's gonna be happy with two more members." That was when Tobi walked over to a boulder, mounted it, and shouted toward the hills, "*Hey! Hey guys! Hey! Hey! I found two more pilgrims! They're good! Don't kill us!*"

Chev and Varnas unplugged their ears. Still, the valley roared back with Tobi's voice, distorted into long, stretched, deepened sounds. Tobi looked back at the two, pleased with himself.

"That oughta do the trick," Tobi nodded, satisfied.

Varnas nodded to himself. "We shoulda left him," he said, with more certainty than ever.

"Come on, Varnas," said Chev, giving him a sharp eye, "Let's go see these pilgrims."

Varnas followed, grumbling, and Ma-ma was just behind him, like an animated mop swooping up and down the landscape, stripping away vegetation whenever a clump took her fancy. They marched to Tobi's peculiar swagger, dipping down the valley and ascending the next ridge. When he crested it, he stopped in his tracks. His jaw lost strength.

"Those are—they are—they're gone!" he cried out.

Chev saw it himself. All the ghosts of an encampment were there, ash from a fire, trampled grass, bits of bone and garbage, the scent of urine and cooked meat. Footprints and markings suggested fifty people thereabouts.

"They're gone!" Tobi marched around the camp in disbelief, as though hoping it were all some illusion. "They left without me! They did!" He stomped his foot and showed off a mouth of crooked teeth, with all the wrath of petulant child. "Oh boy, when I catch up with them I'm gonna give them a really hard time!"

"Seems like they had the right idea," whispered Varnas with a cocked brow.

"Shut up, Varnas," said Chev. He marched to the young man's side. "I'm sorry they left you. But we're going the same way, so it's not all lost, is it?"

He put a hand over Tobi's shoulder, and was surprised by just how much Tobi sank. The kid was as weak as a wisp.

"No, it ain't," the boy steadied himself, trying to put on a mask of cool determination, "You're right. We don't need them. Not when I have a pair of savages at my side. Any monster's gonna be real sorry they messed with us." It was then, without warning, Tobi started screaming into the winds, before Chev had the chance to cover his ears. *"You hear that! You hear that you guys? You're gonna be real sorry! I got savages on my side and you're gonna get eaten by monsters!"*

Tobi showed Chev a grin so big his eyes were near forced closed.

Chev regretted telling Varnas off about leaving Tobi. And Varnas must have known he regretted it, because when Chev turned to him the old man revealed an equally perverse smile.

As they marched over heath and ridge Tobi chattered on. It became ambient noise to Chev, like cricket chirps and gusts of wind. Chev was scratching his chin at the path ahead when Tobi repeated his question for a third time.

"Huh?" Chev looked at the young man.

"I asked: why do you want to see the oracle?"

It took Chev a moment, he'd been so focused elsewhere he couldn't retrieve the answer. "To end a curse," said Chev.

Tobi whistled, impressed. "That's dramatic. What kinda curse? Do you vomit insects? Are you forced to walk the day? Does the full moon make you mad?"

"None of those things."

"Well, what is it?"

"It's personal," said Chev, brusquely to show he was not interested in discussing it further.

"Well that's rude!" Tobi fluttered a hand over his breast. "I'll tell you why *I'm* on my pilgrimage. I want her to bring my sister back to life."

Chev glanced sideways. "Your sister is dead?"

"Of course! Would I want to bring her back to life if she wasn't?" Tobi swept his black hair back. "When she died of the gray pox, I vowed I would do whatever I could to save her, even if that meant going on a dangerous journey to the land of my ancestors: the Daylit Lands."

"I'm sorry to hear about your sister," said Chev, his voice heavy. *I thought so poorly of him,* Chev said to himself.

Tobi shrugged, a kicked a loose rock to the side. "It's okay. It's been a long time, and I'm not sad about it anymore. But my pa always said I gotta keep all my vows, so I'm stuck now, pretty much."

Maybe I didn't misjudge him, Chev thought.

"This oracle," Varnas grunted, "is she really powerful enough to bring back the dead?"

"Of course!" Tobi swept his hand grandly, "The Oracle of Manak is powerful enough to do anything! Whether she chooses to do it, that's a different matter. It's because she's so wise, she sees all possibilities and sometimes using her power upsets the balance."

"Yeah, she sure sounds *wise*," said Varnas, shooting Chev a grin.

But Chev wasn't ready to give up. He turned to Tobi, "But she has brought people back before, though. Right?"

"Of course!" said Tobi, and Chev looked relieved. But then Tobi elaborated: "Well, I never met them. And I can't remember any names. But people wouldn't say it if it weren't true!"

Chev hated the laugh that came out of Varnas; a mocking, whistling one. Though he did his best to salt the wound, Chev had to remind himself that Varnas was old and cynical, and would be suspicious of anyone and anything.

"It's the kid, isn't it?" Tobi asked.

Chev was jolted out of his thoughts. "What about the kid?"

"He's the cursed one," said Tobi, smiling faintly at the bundle tied to Chev's chest. "He's not been fussing, or moving, or anything. Dead asleep, and it's high night right now. That's not a healthy child. And why else would you bring a baby on a pilgrimage?"

Chev was silent, and that told Tobi everything he needed to see he was right.

Tobi tapped his forehead. "See? I'm smart."

It was several hours later when they scaled the next major ridge. Tobi had grown stiff and awkward, his stride turning into a half-waddle. When they paused to rest, he'd scratch at his chafed thighs and pronounce how much in pain he was.

"I could lay around for a million years," announced Tobi, resting briefly against a rock. Despite his exhaustion, he always found the energy to open his mouth. "Can't stop now. The city's just a short walk ahead. Just over the rise, in fact."

Varnas cast a worried gaze. "A city?"

"That's what I said, didn't I?" Tobi looked back on Varnas as though the man were stupid.

Chev's heart was throbbing, but not with anxiety—with anticipation. It was surprising how much he wanted to see one of these big dayfolk cities. Long-forgotten stories of Ossen's came to mind, how there were these places in the world where you couldn't see anything but buildings—little boxes stretching off into the horizon. It strained the imagination to picture it.

"Bunch of miserable little hovels," grumbled Varnas. Grumbling gave Varnas energy, it seemed, and he marched quickly up the hill. Whatever sight he saw in the next valley froze him.

"What is it?" Chev called out, running after him. Varnas didn't respond, but he didn't need to; the sight over the ridge spoke for itself. Centered in the valley before them, some goliath force had shifted earth and water to make artificial rivers and hills. Crops blanketed all available land, like an orderly profusion of life, patching the landscape. In the center of this quilt was a vast knob in the land, atop it an impossible jumble of structures, each larger than Chev had ever seen. Someone had strung together a forest for a wall, leafless logs that stood flush next to each other. It was an impossible sight.

Tobi huffed up behind them. "You like that? That's nothing. A little frontier outpost."

"A... frontier... outpost?" None of the words were familiar to Chev.

Tobi nodded. "Mmhmm. And the greatest city of them all was Manak. That crap hole wouldn't make a blip on Manak. Manak was *huge*. Ginormous. Titanic! You know, back when it wasn't a ruin like it is now."

Varnas grunted. "A bunch of nonsense, if you ask me. Come on. Let's go see this pile of wood and stone."

But as they came closer to it, the scale of the city began to dawn on them. The log walls were just as tall as trees, ten whole body lengths towering over them, and they stretched out so far that they couldn't see the end at the limits of vision. In the shadows of the walls were clusters of ramshackle huts, made from wood and crudely shaped stone.

"Big waste of time, this," snorted Varnas, "They coulda just dug under a big tree and saved themselves all sorts of trouble." At that, Varnas found a handhold on the wall, and began to climb.

"Hey! Stop, stop!" the young man cried out. Tobi grasped Varnas' free foot and tugged impotently.

Varnas kicked him off. "Why's that?"

"They'll think you're a raider. They'll kill you!"

Varnas folded his lips, like he was thinking over some belligerent response, but he thought better of it and let himself down. "If they didn't want that wall to be scaled, they shouldn't have made it so easy."

"Tobi," Chev got the young man's attention, "how do we get inside?"

"You go to the gate and you ask," said Tobi.

That's what they tried. It was a hike just getting around the wall, they had to wind through ramshackle huts and lean-tos, a sort of dirty little city in the shadow of its larger brother. They made it to a gatehouse, an enormous wooden box of a building like nothing Chev had ever seen before. He couldn't fathom any work of man dwarfing the trees around it, but here he was, staring at this strange structure. Little openings along the sides reminded Chev of clusters of insectoid eyes. Otherwise, it was faceless, lifeless. However, Chev could sense a presence watching him as he approached.

There was but one nightfolk guarding the gate, but he watched the party with a confidence that suggested he was not truly alone. He wore an absurdly bulky coat that made him out to be fatter than he was, and his face was lined, each wrinkle radiating out from a pair of watchful eyes. Those orbs glazed right over Tobi and kept careful watch of Chev.

It was true what they say then: nightfolk guard the dayfolk cities, and though it was strange to see with his own two eyes, Chev had heard of this. All dayfolk cities held host to nightfolk, keeping the town secure at night, ensuring the streets were cleaned and monsters driven off. They even built enclaves to house them. It was a strange thing seeing for himself one of Ossen's old tales, somehow it brought the old man so much closer.

"City's closed," the guard told them without pausing to look them over.

"We're pilgrims," said Tobi.

"Sure you are. We're full up on drovers and tribals. Go find a hovel somewhere else."

"Closed to pilgrims?" Tobi blinked as though he couldn't quite believe it. "We're off to see the oracle you know! Where's your sense of brotherhood?"

"Brotherhood's in short supply nowadays," the guard grunted, "and we're closed. Look around. You think people are living in those shacks like it's a choice? Shuffle off, and take your savages with you."

"But we're *pilgrims!*" Tobi was about to trail off into more incoherent protests, but he was pulled back by Chev and Varnas. They dragged Tobi all the way out of sight.

Tobi ranted obliviously. "Those jerks! I can't believe they'd leave their fellow nightfolk out to fester with all the monsters and savages out here! And to refuse pilgrims, too? Who do they think they are?"

"What's the plan now?" Chev asked them both, not really expecting an answer.

Varnas sucked his lips looking at the sky. "I'd dig a pit, but I don't like those clouds. It's back to the first plan."

"What was the first plan?" But before Tobi had even finished his sentence, Varnas had maneuvered Ma-ma onto his back and clambered up the palisade wall. Tobi shouted protests. "Hey! Hey! What are you—"

Chev shrugged, gave Tobi a grin, and followed Varnas up, finding the roughened timber effortless to climb. He tossed himself up and over, deaf to Tobi's protests.

"How am I supposed to follow you! Don't abandon me!" he cried out.

The city from this angle looked like a vast tortoise, with roofs of irregular shapes acting like scales and the streets like the veins between them. Varnas was already comfortably perched on one of these rooftops, when Chev clambered next to him.

Varnas read Chev's expression. "You aren't thinkin' of fetching him, are you?"

"I don't know," Chev shrugged. "He's useless at near everything, but he does know this place better than we do. This is a weird place."

Varnas made a noise like a thoughtful grumble, giving the side of his head a good scratching. He gave a suggestion as way of answer. "I'll watch Starlight for you."

Chev nodded, and descended the wall once again. Tobi was incensed with the earlier betrayal and cursed Chev to his face, but he still climbed on Chev's back as soon as it was offered. It was fine for Chev, he found him to be a lighter load on his back and more silent than he was on his feet and talking.

The party pushed through a small window in a roof. Among the wooden rafters and piles of boxes, they stretched out and made camp.

"We gotta be real quiet," Tobi, somehow, whispered loudly, "there's dayfolk downstairs."

They got the message real quick. No one was here to cause trouble. But trouble would come to them soon enough.

Chapter Eleven
The Sky Unfolds

VARNAS' INSTINCTS WERE RIGHT. Sometime in the early day they were half roused by the patter of rain atop the tiles. Chev looked about groggily from his little sleeping spot, a comfortable shadowed place between two crates. He saw only slits of tepid light emerging between the roof slats, and what looked like piles of discarded clothes where Varnas and Tobi slept.

He shut his eyes again, allowed himself to drift back to sleep.

It is that said when one falls asleep with light on their face it invites imps to drop strange dreams through the ears. Chev dreamed of a child's cry. He went through a sunlit void, where light swallowed all things but for the infinite black shadow cast behind him. He swam toward the crying, but he was confused when there seemed to be nothing. That was until he looked down. A monster dug talons into his chest, and its lips were peeled back to reveal wicked teeth. It gripped hard and went heavy like lead, there was a sensation of falling through reality and Chev burst awake.

Sounds. Too many sounds. Starlight was crying, and Ma-ma was noisily struggling to get to her. Something was shuffling downstairs. It took Chev a moment to understand.

"Damn!" he whispered out loud, understanding suddenly there would be danger. Starlight was tossing and turning, wailing. There was a blunt shockwave of light as a trap door was forced open.

Chev snatched up Starlight, rocking her swiftly. She locked in with her big, watery eyes, hypnotized by Chev's face. The comforting sensation made her fall silent and sigh. Chev was not so content; some creature climbed into the cramped attic, making cumbersome footfalls as it treaded over wood. It started a slow inspection, stabbing its head into corners and making sluggish rounds toward where Chev hid.

There was no avoiding it. It would find him.

The creature pushed its way to the little camp site. The hairy bipedal creature made a squat silhouette of scruffy fur, faint light shown within beady eyes.

He was certain he'd been caught. Kill or flight or freeze, and Chev couldn't pick between them. He waited for the end: a bludgeon, a dagger, an arrow. But the lights in the beast's eyes flickered oddly, and it slowly but surely shuffled away. The heavy latch clasped behind him.

It had to be a joke. A cosmic joke, or magic or a miracle that the dayfolk didn't see him. But it was simpler than that. The dayfolk simply couldn't see in the dark.

Chev sighed as he inspected Starlight, and it didn't take long to see what made her cry. Chev briskly tidied her up, and brought her to Ma-ma's teats—she slept peacefully after that.

"That was close," said Tobi, "*Real close*. Heck, you know, I didn't even sleep. I was frozen stiff in fear that the dayfolk might come back up." Tobi swept a hand casually at the child. "It's your little sister, you know, or your daughter or niece or whatever. It was dumb to bring her."

They'd all woken at the break of night, and Chev was working out of sight behind a crate. The little hairy baby was gurgling and kicking as Chev wound fresh linen around its body. "It's a *baby*," Chev said to Tobi, as way of an answer.

"It won't be a baby anymore if you bring it along," said Tobi, "it's gonna be monster food. And they can smell baby poop as good as I did last night. Yuck!"

"Shut up Tobi," said Chev, angrily putting the finishing touches to Starlight's swaddling.

"Don't get angry at me 'cause you don't wanna hear the truth," said Tobi.

"The truth is you're an ass," Chev said, briskly putting on the harness holding Starlight.

Tobi shrugged as he collected his gear. "Does it look like my feelings are hurt?"

"Just keep your mouth shut and guide us through the pass," said Chev.

"Oh, I will." Tobi slipped his crossbow over his shoulders and gave himself a good patting down, checking everything was in place, "But I'm going to tell you one last thing before I shut my mouth. If that baby brings trouble, I'm putting *me* first. I'm not dying for some savage's spawn."

"You won't need to," said Chev.

"Good."

Varnas edged in, providing a dead finish to their little argument. "Let's get outta this city. These places, they drive men mad, they do."

"As soon as possible," agreed Chev.

They scaled back down the city walls, Varnas with Ma-ma and Chev with Starlight. Tobi, clumsy as he was, made more of a controlled drop, scraping down the wall with a timid yelp. He got up slowly, poking fingers through new scratches in his odd clothes.

"The pass," he restarted breathlessly, "The pass is a short but dangerous trail. We need to hit the first rest stop before dayfall. It's serious trouble if we don't. Serious trouble. We need to get to the rest stop."

Varnas grunted. "What's this rest stop? Another one of your cities?"

"No," Tobi snorted loudly, wiping a scratch mark on his face, "it's a *tavern*. I know you two wouldn't know those sorts of places. I'll tell you about it on the way."

Tobi pointed to their destination. The mountains here folded into a sort of saddle, an uneven path curving up. There were rocks that littered the pass, each so titanic they played tricks with Chev's perception, like if Chev reached out far enough he could pluck them right out of the way. Two peaks leaned inward, spectators to the drama below, and other ridges and cliffs made razor edges, threatening to gobble up whoever ventured inside.

When they moved toward it, Chev was also moving against his better instincts.

Tobi interrupted the treasured silence. "It must be pretty bad in the Daylit Lands if we're the only pilgrims."

There was no response for Tobi, only a heavy air and hanging unease.

A boulder marked the entrance to the pass. It was covered with countless runes, each by different hands, some practiced, some shaking, in a mad variety of sizes. It drew their attention, and Tobi explained it offhandedly.

"Names of those who didn't make it," he told them. "There's a smaller one on the other side."

It was not a straight path up. By the time they reached the first serious incline Chev realized they'd be zigzagging up cliffs and ridges before they'd get to flat ground again. The boulders that looked like pebbles from afar proved to be the size of hills. They squeezed the party into narrow gaps between the stones. They moved between alternating deep shadow and starlight. Sodden by recent rain, the ground slipped and slithered like a living thing beneath Chev's feet.

Years of foot traffic had merely pushed aside the sharp rocks and thorny weeds that edged into the path. Even Tobi, with his big hardy boots, had to stop to dig a pebble out from his sole, and Chev and Varnas were barefoot. They were watchful at each step. Only Ma-ma seemed to have no difficulty, skipping over ridges and bounding back as though waiting for everyone else to catch up.

Not even halfway up the slope, Varnas furrowed his brow at some runes carved into the rock. He stepped aside for Chev, and invited him to come and translate.

Chev knew immediately their meaning, but felt the need to get close and run his fingers over the eroded engraving. "Monsters ahead," he read, "Day and night."

"Didn't need runes to tell us that," Tobi said, "Pilgrim's Pass is famous for its beasts. That's why people keep together in big groups. But monsters ain't no problem for savages. Right? Right?" Tobi repeated himself, insistent on the reassurance of an answer.

Chev gave him what he clearly wanted to hear. "Right."

Tobi chose to believe Chev. He visibly brushed off his shoulders like he had his doubts on there, and resumed his pace up the trail. Chev swore he heard Tobi whisper, "It's that damn baby I'm worried about."

Chev looked down at Starlight. Darkness had pushed her out of consciousness, and her furry cheeks nuzzled Chev's chest. He could only hope she would stay this way through the whole journey.

After a while, the trail was perilous enough even Tobi kept silent. It was especially dark this night, silver-tossed clouds obscuring swathes of stars, the moon nowhere to be seen. This came as a comfort, though Chev cursed himself he didn't ask beforehand what sorts of beasts he could expect.

Varnas' voice made Chev jump. "Maybe we shoulda left the child."

It was only a whisper, but Chev hissed back angrily. "Varnas!"

"We just passed a dayfolk city. We coulda left her there," Varnas spoke quickly, letting his mad eyes bounce from one shadow to the next, "That was her best chance."

"That's not an option," Chev hissed.

"Wasn't it?"

"No."

"We're not in the forest anymore, Chev. We don't belong out here."

"You're being loud."

Chev said it, but Tobi's pulled face repeated it. He waved over his mouth, and urged everyone forward.

It was Tobi who saw it first. He held out an arm for everyone to stop. But neither Chev nor Varnas could resist looking over Tobi's shoulder.

The sounds were horrifying. Snapping of bone. The wet sound of flesh torn. Gluttonous growls and full, chewing maws. A pack of creatures with muzzles buried into bodies. Only their canine eyes shimmered in those dark shadows.

They all backed off quickly. Ma-ma, mortified and silent, trotted behind them all.

Everyone turned to Tobi. His face was tense, his hand swept off the ridge of sweat that had formed above his brow. "Good, we're safe," he sighed.

It was so absurd Varnas nearly laughed. "We're *safe?*"

"Those wolves don't hunt twice. They'll scare off other predators. We're safe near them."

Varnas flashed a dubious smile at Chev. "You trust this idiot?"

"If they were hungry," Tobi nearly collapsed against the rock, "they woulda killed us by now. So don't argue with me."

"How many times has this fool *really* gone down this path? Huh?"

"More than you, dummy!"

"Stop it," said Chev, whispering urgently, "stop it, please! Let's just keep moving. Tobi, do you know a way around the beasts?"

"I wanna rest," Tobi said, plopping on the ground.

"Look at this fool. Take a rest, why don't you? Take a rest to the sweet sounds of people getting devoured. What a golden heart you have. You musta been a real comfort for your sister while she was alive."

"Hey, it's not *us* getting eaten, is it?" Tobi no longer kept his volume down, and he added, "And don't bring my dead sister into this! I'm on a quest to bring her back from the dead aren't I?"

"Quiet!" Chev hissed, drawing Starlight closer, but his words were lost in the back and forth.

"I already told you, we're safe!" Tobi raised his voice, and rummaged in his sack for something, "Pointed-ears. Nightlands or Daylands, you're all the same. You think you know everything, that you're better than all us round-ears, but you're not. I'm not the dumb one here!"

"And look!" Varnas eyed the wolves through a crack in the huge rock. "The fool's eating! Did the sound of beasts ripping apart raw intestines get ya real hungry?"

"Damn right I'm eating!" Tobi waved some jerky at him. "I *am* hungry! And if you two weren't so dumb, you'd take the chance to eat too! And rest!" With that, Tobi tore off a mouthful like it was some expression of anger. "You know, Chev... that's your name, right? Chev, your old man here is gonna get us all killed, what with his panicking and all."

Chev was glancing at shadows, ear pricked to the sound of wolves. "I don't know about that, Tobi."

"Oh," Tobi placed a hand over his heart, "oh so it's me whose gonna do it? Why, 'cause you think I'm stupid? Well, I'll tell you a smart move: leaving that sick baby at the city, just like the old man said. Or here's an even better one: end the kid's misery and throw her off a cliff."

Chev stepped forward, making angry pokes through the air. "Don't test me, Tobi."

"That baby's dead, genius." Tobi smacked his forehead. "Asleep all night and crying all day. That baby's sick. It's sick, it's sick, it's sick!"

"I will *beat* you," Chev came even closer, blood darkening his face and fist lifted.

"Sorry for being the bearer of bad news, Chev." Tobi pounced to his feet, and spat out his words. "The kid is dead, so throw it away!"

One, two steps forward. Chev invaded Tobi's personal space, and went for a blow. Knuckles dashed across Tobi's cheek. Starlight awoke and wailed, Chev was deaf to it.

One blow had Tobi on the ground, his lids suddenly welling up. He cupped his cheek and gave his attacker a venomous glance.

"I'm not dying for you!" said Tobi.

Chev loomed over. In his head, an angry debate arose how he'd hurt him. Part of him wanted to deliver a swift beating. An ugly side wanted his eyes gouged out. A gentle, calm voice demanded an end. Chev settled on a compromise. He gave Tobi a swift kick to the ribs, left him winded and that was that. Tobi was wheezing and doubled over, and Chev was left with Tobi's words poisoning him.

Varnas had not watched. His ears were pricked another direction. "The wolves are gone," he whispered.

Both Tobi and Chev fell quite silent.

Chev shushed Starlight asleep, and they edged toward where the wolves had been. It was grisly sight, half-eaten corpses strewn each way, pulled apart so it wasn't clear which piece belonged to which body. After a cautious approach, it was easy enough to see they had the manes and broad bodies of dayfolk.

The weapons they had drawn were of no use. Many of their swords, axes and spears were still tightly clutched in dismembered hands, gleaming silver as though unused.

All around them, the pass was silent. Only the distant echoes of other horrors ahead.

Tobi gave Chev a fearful glance. It only seemed to say they were no longer safe.

Ma-ma stayed flush to Chev's knees, only pausing to flap her ears at any unusual sound. He understood that she wanted comfort, but Chev wasn't in much better of a state. He looked around wild-eyed, throwing nervous furtive glances at crevices and darkened gaps between the boulders.

They approached a stage of the pass overgrown with tough, spindly bushes. Only an icy breeze rustled the vegetation here. All the world, even the insects, made themselves dead quiet. The loudest thing were their footfalls.

Especially Tobi's, as his big thick boots ground grit beneath him with each step, though he was oblivious to it.

Tobi suddenly stopped. His eyes twitched, he was trying to communicate something without opening his mouth. Chev found it hard to not bark angrily at him, to tell him yes, he knew they were in danger, and they should keep moving. But he didn't, only scowled at the pause in the journey. Whatever it was, Tobi seemed to understand, and he carried on. Chev couldn't help but note how pale and bloodless he looked.

Though they moved steadily, there was nothing to disturb the oppressive silence. For once Chev would rather listen to Tobi prattle on endlessly; there was an intense unease engendered in all of them. Like a terror lurked in every corner except the direction they faced. A pain embodied Chev's chest, a tightness surrounded his heart. He couldn't feel his own pulse.

Time moved at excruciating pace. Chev could mutter ten prayers in his head before he took the next step. The only thing in the world he wanted was for this journey to be over.

Something in the back of his head screamed danger. It had already put together clues that Chev hadn't yet noticed, and now he was listening to it drip pure fear into his veins. The anticipation was worse than any threat Chev had ever experienced. And he wasn't alone. It was a collective feeling.

Starlight mewled.

Dread melted his heart when he heard that child's cry. A minuscule, mild noise, but it was like a thunderclap in the blackness.

Chev heard someone whisper, "You should have left that kid."

There was a wild, errant rush of air. They all looked up to see the incomprehensible sight of the night sky folding upon itself. In the blackness there was a spot of richer blackness that moved in a way that none of them could understand, so oddly it was impossible to gauge how close it was. Chev only saw it grow, and grow, and grow.

"A dark roc!" cried Tobi, "Run!"

Chev finally put together what he saw. The sky wasn't shifting, a titanic bird was folding its vast black wings, tucking them together for a steep dive right towards them. In panic, the group split three directions, Chev rushing for rocks.

The monster crashed right into the ground where the three of them once stood. Plumes of dust arose, the beast lunged out, hovering around, flapping his wings, one gigantic eye tracking Chev as he rushed. It beat its wings and flashed out toward him.

Chev couldn't grasp the beast's scale. It wasn't any normal bird of prey. Black wings splayed out like a fan of swords, open maw large enough to swallow a man whole. All Chev had was his small size, so he scampered like a mouse between two rocks, a beak smashing behind him, dashing pebbles and dust everywhere. There was no hiding now—Starlight was wailing. Chev could only hope to hide in tighter and tighter crevices, but it turned out the roc's talons were well shaped to hook prey out. A talon scythed ahead and behind him.

It would take the bird just a second try, and it would have, except an arrow sprung from the beast's beak, shuddering. The roc raised its head, unhurt but annoyed. Chev took it as his time to run for it. He ducked down and, with no real plan, barreled into a nearby gap.

The roc screeched. It was an ear-piercing sound, Chev winced and would have blocked his ears had he not been so carefully balanced between two rocks. He could see the monster frantically searching for the prey he'd lost, leaping from one set of boulders to another, talons scraping into gaps.

He practically slammed into Varnas.

The old man held Tobi's bizarre arrow-shooting contraption in shaking arms. He was cornering a tearful Tobi, who whined and whimpered from the shadows.

"Tell me how to reload it," demanded Varnas.

"No," said Tobi.

"Tell me how to reload it!"

"It's no use!" Tobi barked back miserably, "You're never gonna kill that thing!"

Whether the roc heard the argument or not, the monster rose into the air, making a deep shadow in the night. Glowing eyes scanned all around it, and settled on their direction.

"It sees us!" Tobi squeaked, ducking into a shadowed path like a prey animal into brush. Chev and Varnas followed and dragged him back by his feet.

"There's no escaping!" said Varnas.

"We gotta fight!" Chev drew his sword.

"Are you all stupid?" desperate tears rolled down Tobi's cheeks. "It's gonna get one of us. That's the only thing we can do."

Tobi sprung. Chev didn't expect it, and he couldn't resist as Tobi collided with him, using a dagger to cut the harness. Starlight slipped off easy. Chev's sword swing came too late, and sparked against some boulders. With child in hand Tobi pounced atop the boulder, waving the child.

"Hey!" he cried, drawing the roc's piercing eyes, "Hey! Hey! Fresh meat!"

Chev was just scrambling up the boulder, his fingers slipping against the cold smooth surface, when he witnessed Tobi's next action through the time-distorting influence of intense adrenaline. An underhanded toss, the child arced up in the air, a bundle of wailing, panicking child whose life was about to end. She flew before the moon of scything talons and wide-open beak, a monstrous screech that could be felt in Chev's very bones.

The beast leapt after the child, plucking her straight out of the air with its mouth and landing safely to the ground on the other side. That beast was Ma-ma.

Chev cried her name in relief.

Tobi was now left wild-eyed at the roc swooped steeply toward him. His last words were, "What—no! No!"

A flurry of feathers and talons descended on Tobi. In the end, the roc tilted its head, letting the man's legs slide gracefully down its gullet. Only a boot survived to flop to the ground as the roc took off to darker skies, its enormous form a terrible vision for miles around.

Ma-ma was licking Starlight to tickles and giggles. Chev clambered over rock and stone, Ma-ma gracefully backed off, and Chev took her into his arms.

He was at a loss for how to thank a goat. "Good job," was the best he could come up with.

Could an animal beam with pride? Somehow, she did, before making good headway up the slope on stubby, hopping legs. Chev was hypnotized by her jaunty gait.

"We should run the rest of the way," Varnas said, breaking Chev from a stupor.

"Agreed."

Having lost their guide, the best chance was to make a break for it. And that they did, churning up new paths with how quickly they ran. Chev's tough feet had been blistered half-a-hundred times, and the only thing that kept him going was that he dared not look back.

They reached the crest, and it was now a long slope down, the valley opening up into the Daylit Lands spread before them for the very first time. The expanse was staggering, the horizon stretching so far it almost seemed like the whole world curved below them. And all of it was incredibly, unfathomably, *flat*, broken up by nothing but a few trees and houses that dotted the landscape of dancing grass. At the mouth of the pass campfires smoldered in clusters. It was dizzying to take in, like staring into a vast, bottomless pit.

They turned to each other at the same time. "Remember, don't-"

"You go first."

"No, you go."

"I was just gonna say we shouldn't tell anyone about Starlight."

"I was gonna say the same thing."

"Good, we're agreed."

"Good."

"Good."

Their conversation was premature. There was still so much ground to cover, and the path down would be miles. The roads were no better, but gravity was on their side, and they actually had to slow or risk tumbling down the ridges and sharp rocks.

They'd been running for at least an hour when they saw what looked to be a massive centipede making a zigzag path up the hill, in the direction of the Nightlands. After pausing to squint and work it out, it turned out to be mass of people moving so densely they seemed more like one creature than... hundreds? Thousands? It was a bigger crowd of nightfolk than Chev had ever seen, and if anyone had told him this was everyone in the world he might have believed it. The procession was endless, and breaks were simply small gaps between different groups. They came closer, and soon were within spitting distance. These people were akin to those same wretches that they had seen hanging around near the city gates, but here there were uncountable hordes. All sallow-cheeked, sunken-eyed, battered, bruised, with a different kind of defeat in every face. They kept their eyes to themselves, even as Chev couldn't help but stare in awe.

Men with bodies like stripped trees. Hunchbacked women with children in their arms. Those barely old enough to walk did so in bare feet and ancient faces. Animals trudged alongside just as listlessly. A cacophony of sneezes and coughs and splutters. Occasionally, there was a healthy man with a weapon on his shoulders, but they were in short supply.

Only one such man bothered addressing Chev and Varnas as he walked by. He bore some authority in his square shoulders, had more facial hair than any nightfolk ought to, and his question was very straightforward. "Monsters?"

Chev remembered what Tobi had called that behemoth bird. "A dark roc."

He grunted a thanks. "It will eat well tonight."

"Didn't that coward say this was where they wrote the names of those who died on the pass?"

They stared at the enormous boulder. It was similar to the one they'd passed on the ascent, but this one had far fewer names. A modest, sullen place, whipped by the mountain's winds.

"I don't want to write his name," said Chev.

"Go on," Varnas held to Chev a chisel, "it's their way, not ours."

"He tried to kill Starlight," he said.

"A giant damned bird tried to kill your kid," said Varnas. "Let's respect the customs of these city folk, and not get the wroth of their gods. Whaddya think?"

Chev sucked in a breath and gave a poisonous look at the little chisel. He wanted to make up an excuse, like how it was a wood and not for stone. But Varnas would see through it. Chev snatched the tool out of Varnas' hands and hammered in a hasty message.

Tobi the Coward, his final work read. The man would now be remembered for all time, though not in the way he'd want.

Varnas' draped an arm over Chev's shoulders, and ruffled his hair like he would a child. "Missing him already, huh?"

"Quiet, Varnas. You can't read anyway."

"Heh. That's true."

Chapter Twelve
The Trappings of Civilization

"What's this say?"

Chev squinted at the wooden sign hanging from a corroded chain. It squeaked with rust as it swayed to the wind, so Chev had to focus. But, even so, after reading it several times, he still gleaned the same incomprehensible message. "Says, 'The Happy Donkey'."

"What? What's that mean?"

"Don't have a clue."

"You can't really read, can you? You been making it up as you go along the whole time, ain't cha?"

"Still would be more than you," Chev grinned.

They had finally reached flat ground, away from the dark path, though it would be too much to say that Chev and Varnas felt *safe*. The settlement before them was not built with nearly the same deliberation as the one they'd left just that dusk on the other side of the pass. The crooked wooden palisades made a sad comparison, leaving large gaps where a large building was easily visible. At least it was brightly lit, exuding the scents of food, foreign music and laughter. The alternative seemed to be a haphazard collection of tents facing the tavern, a sea of soiled canvas and misery. Ghostly, wretched figures haunted the paths between.

"I know where I want to spend the night," Varnas quipped.

There was a gap in the palisade, watched by a guard armed with a padded jacket and sheathed sword. He took a glance at Chev's weapon and elected not to bother them. Past the gap, there were no ends to the bizarre sights. Two antlered beasts drank from a trough, their muzzles sucking water noisily, attended by two men chattering incoherently. Beneath the current of rowdy laughter and shouting, the frames of the building seem to vibrate with music so odd Chev couldn't picture the instruments. The wall opened up, a man waddled out, vomited, and collapsed.

Other than the cupboard at Hlogas' home, Chev had never seen a proper door before, but the demonstration was enough to have him figure how it worked. So Chev pushed until it swung open of its own accord. And the stench that came out—the stench was extraordinary. Stale smoke, underlined with this strange chemical scent that Chev could only describe as pure civilization. Bright lights fell on dozens of tables populated by the most bizarre cross-section of the nightfolk race, all in a desperate, disorganized competition to draw the most attention. Boisterous laughing and singing, violent arguing, and gloomy brooding; no matter they were under the same roof, each man was an island unto himself.

Hlogas had called these creatures "degenerates", and now Chev saw why. It wasn't just their behavior, few of them could barely be called *nightfolk*. They all had rounded ears, like Tobi, but that was where the similarities ended. Some had bloated bellies, others wandering eyes and crooked limbs. One man who walked by was of monstrous height, but another who looked on him with envy was barely the size of a toddler. A cloaked figure of reasonable proportions seemed normal, but then he went to scratch the rash of scales on his neck before returning to drink.

Someone slapped Chev and Varnas with an arm over each of their shoulders. They twisted to see a whiskered, small man whose gap-toothed smile seemed to leak the smell of fish. "Welcome! New here, are ya? Let me grab you a seat."

He talked so fast he allowed no room for refusal. Chev and Varnas were pushed on stools by the bar.

"So, what brings ya here? Onto Manak? Or coming back? Never you mind gentlemen, you can tell me everything as we drink. Barmaid! Two Cavian Ales, don't bother watering it down!"

He was odd, but very hospitable. Chev and Varnas joined him with blank faces. Two mugs full of froth drifted along the bar, wafting with the unpleasant, unfamiliar scent Chev detected when he'd first walked in. Varnas tilted the mug, inspecting it with a frown. "What *is* this?"

"Ha! Good stuff." The odd man clicked his finger and took a sip of his own Cavian Ale. "Now, seems to me like you need a guide. Someone who can give you a good tour, a lay of the land as they say. My name is Borin Corell. What do you two gentlemen go by?"

"Chev, son of Minda."

"Varnas," said Varnas.

"What unique names!" Borin laughed. "Now, as compensation for my services, I think that useless goat you're lugging around would be fair."

Ma-ma bleated.

Chev sniffed this 'Cavian Ale' and winced. "She's not for trade."

"And I don't get what this tour thing is anyway," Varnas pitched in.

That only seemed to make Borin even more excited. His wider smile let out more fishy breath. "Good. Great! All the more reason to my services. You definitely need it."

"We'll pass, thanks," said Chev.

Borin made an immediate metamorphosis into a monster. His mask fell into in shriveled, red rage, and in one swift movement he brought a long dagger shivering into the table.

"Give me the goat!" he screamed at them.

It all happened in a split second. Before Chev was even more surprised an arrow sprung between Borin Corell's eyes. Jaw limp, eyes rolled white, and Corell slumped off his stool and crashed to the ground.

The one holding the crossbow was a woman from behind the bar, and after Chev caught an eyeful of her, it was difficult to not to stare. She had a slender neck and delicate features, embossed with images of leaves and flowers running beneath her milky skin, like someone had carved them as part of her face. Her downturned lips and murderous eyes were a stark contrast. With the toe of the crossbow she tapped a sign behind her with businesslike authority.

It said: "Draw your weapon and die. No exceptions."

Varnas snorted. "You think we could ask for normal water?"

"Huh?" Chev had lost himself staring at the young, strange woman.

Varnas realized Chev's distraction, and he erupted with a sly grin. "Oh—don't tell me you were... you like the odd ones, doncha?"

"What? No! She's just real pretty!" Chev drank as a defense mechanism, but on sipping his eyes bulged out and the Cavian Ale exploded out of his mouth in a fine mist. "That's *disgusting*."

"I could smell it was," Varnas said. "Is this some sorta meeting hall? Who are the elders here?"

"Would it be rude to ask?"

Varnas watched someone drag Borin's body out of the way. "Don't think there's such a thing as 'rude' here." Varnas gestured madly at the pretty young woman. "Hey! Hey! Strange girl! You think you can help us?"

For a moment, Chev worried the woman would spin around and deliver another arrow right into Varnas' head. But she responded without even looking up. "Since you're a tribal I'll give you a freebie. This is a tavern. If you have plats you exchange them for drink, food and lodging." She flashed a strange, flat disc, about the size of the ball of the thumb. "We don't got no elders or totems or some such nonsense."

"Well, we don't got no plats," Varnas said, impishly mimicking the woman's affect.

"Sorry, that there's your problem."

Before Chev even thought of something to say, Varnas seized him suddenly by the shoulders. "Are you sure there's nothing you want? I got this young stallion right here. Good, healthy stock, unlike everyone else here."

"Varnas!" Chev cried out.

Varnas clapped down on his mouth. "For a just a modest meal and a waterskin, he'll sit in close so you have something nice to look at while you work. And, as a bonus, if you give a place to spend the day, you get a free half-hour with him alone for some friendly conversation, heheh!"

The young woman inspected Chev with a raised an eyebrow. "That's all?"

"So... interested?" Varnas struggled to keep Chev from breaking free.

"Deal," the woman combed her hair back.

"Good."

As soon as Chev was let free he stuttered to apologize. But the young woman interrupted him. "I'll have a spot put aside for you. Lodging's downstairs."

The woman was drawn away by some other business involving demanding customers. Given privacy, Varnas and Chev gave each other looks: Chev's exasperated, Varnas' mischievous.

"Why'd you do that?" Chev glowered.

"What do you mean, why'd I do that? I just got us room and board for next to nothing. Y'see, your trouble here is that you don't know how women work."

"I do," said Chev, "I just don't do the thing you just did. It was rude!"

"It wasn't rude." Varnas inspected the froth disintegrating off the Cavian ale.

"Well... it could've been! She coulda shot you!"

"Didn't realize you were such a wuss." Varnas shrugged, experimentally tipping out some ale onto the counter top. Finding nothing interesting, he vacantly looked around.

"I'm not a wuss, I'm *cautious*. Varnas, this is a foreign land, we don't know what kinda weird things these people believe."

Out of the blue, Varnas exploded with excitement, filled with so much excess energy he drummed the table and whistled. It all took Chev by surprise, for moment convinced Varnas had gone insane.

"Lookit that! An old friend. No, don't turn your head, Chev. Little suckerfish will slip right out of our hands."

"Who is it?" Chev's pupils drew to the side, ready for a surreptitious peek.

"Don't ask dumb questions, Chev. Just stand up, follow me."

Varnas didn't wait for further questions. He crept into the crowd, ducked and weaved past a group roiling with energy, coming close to an elevated platform where a nightfolk man strummed some bizarre instrument and sang an ancient song.

In a corner, a crooked figure was deep into his drink. A felt cap with a flopping brim fell forward on his head, concealing his features in shadows, his most distinguishing feature two pointed ears that poked from the sides of his head. He seized up as Varnas and Chev pulled seats.

Varnas had a wry grin. "Hello, Darin."

"Darin?" Chev looked closer.

The man sighed with defeat. He propped his hat up, lantern light falling on his face and characteristic scar. In the way only Darin could manage, one eye shut with exasperation while the other fluttered.

"You spotted me," Darin said. He dragged the felt hat across his face, into a ball in his fist.

Chev leaned forward to drink in Darin's familiar features. "Darin! What the heck—?"

"You and me both." Darin snorted, aligning his body away from the two of them, dragging his frothing ale with him.

"And you're dressed like a Daylander!" Chev looked over Darin's shirt and pants, so similar to Tobi's. "How did you get through Pilgrim's Pass?"

Darin paused to drink. "Same way you did, apparently. My question is, why are we talking to each other, boy? Aren't we even? I tried to kill you. You got me banished."

"Don't be petty, Darin," Varnas scratched his wispy beard, "We both got the same destination. Manak."

Darin squeezed his mug so hard it seemed to bubble. "How did you know that?"

Varnas inclined his head coyly. "Oh, I read the stars. It's one of my own old man powers." Then he let out a wheeze of a laugh. "Why else would you come here, you dolt!"

"I've heard of this oracle, once or twice before. I figured she was the only one who could help me undo the damage that's been done." Darin's one-and-a-half eyes seemed to persecute Chev.

"Don't blame the boy, he was just doing his best," said Varnas.

Again, Darin's body seemed to shift away. "I don't think even the boy thinks that. I can see it." Darin and Chev met eyes, Chev felt suddenly paralyzed by the abyss of the eyes, as his voice shook his bones. "I can see it in his face. It's natural, I guess, to not want to die. To be a hero. Two understandable, natural things, and both of which brought upon our community great danger. He was selfish. The right thing to do demanded too much from him, and he was too weak to follow through. I see he knows. That child he lugs around, *that animal*, that dayghost who should be with its own people beneath the sun. To Chev it's just a prop, an excuse to give him a little meaning and purpose, a little knot tying him to the possibility of redemption." Darin brought his clay mug to his lips, and sucked in a bit of the froth. "I didn't appreciate this Daylander drink at first, but it grows smooth, I feel it brings insights."

Varnas picked up Darin's mug and poured it over Darin's head.

Darin didn't struggle, he only looked mildly confused as ale dripped off his black locks.

"A big pile of bunkum you just said," said Varnas.

"Varnas," Chev's voice quivered with revelation, "I think Darin might be *right*..."

"Shut up, Chev, you're confused. You're too young to realize when a man is actually talking about himself. 'Course you acted selfish. Hard not to.

But this fool," Varnas swept his hand at Darin, "joined up with whats-his-face to kill your father and his family. Just 'cause he was little different. Well, Darin, if you'd showed just an ounce of compassion, none of this woulda happened. Chev wouldn't have been driven to go off in the woods alone to make for easy prey for bone-skins, and then he wouldn't have had to make a deal to save his life. And that kid did everything to make things right! What did you do when things went wrong, huh? Try and kill someone's family! That's what you did!"

Darin swept his hair back proudly. "You can't deny that if Chev had let himself be killed by that bone-skin he would have saved hundreds of lives—"

Varnas leaned over the table. "Guess what, Darin? Someone was eventually gonna make a deal with a bone-skin. It happens to every tribe, believe me. And Chev was the best person to do it, because he eventually got *you* off *your* lazy ass to fight them!"

Chev was reduced to blinking. Darin's mouth was flickering with angry retorts, most aborted before they even came out of his mouth. But it all came to a sudden end when the pretty young woman at the bar drifted by and smashed a couple platters of food on the table.

"Mashed potatoes with vegetable stock and rye bread, and a skin's worth of water, for both of you," she declared, "but I'm thinking of taking it back because so far, the view's not been too good!"

"Oh, right," Varnas said apologetically.

They rotated around so that Chev was in good view of the bar.

"Anyway," Varnas scratched around his ear, "Whose fault is what, that don't matter. Not a lick. Important thing is, Darin, you can help us reach Manak."

Darin was still high-strung from the argument, and came off as brusque. "Why do you need to go there?"

"Chev needs to see that the oracle's a useless bauble reader before he does the obvious. Apparently, you do too, so it's a good thing we ran into each other."

Chev drew up defensively. "Hlogas wouldn't tell us lies."

"Hlogas isn't lying, he's just plain wrong."

This time, Chev felt it more productive to talk directly to Darin. "I need to break the curse over me. I need to rejoin the tribe, I need to take care of Sana. Darin, will you come with us?"

Darin let his bad eye twitch. "It's more than a curse that keeps you and Sana from each other now. But if we're going the same direction," Darin cleared his throat, "I *suppose* it's safer together."

"Ah," Varnas nodded contentedly. "Don't worry, Darin. I won't rub your mistakes in your face *every* day."

Darin produced a scroll, and he weighed down each corner with a mug.

"This is a map," Darin declared.

Both Chev and Varnas leaned over it with bug eyes, following Darin's finger as he traced the route.

"There are four major dayghost cities on the way to Manak: Grainsea, Pock Hollow, Broken Rock, and Riverturn. Manak rests on the fork of the Sippi River, right here, in the center of a monster infested swamp. The journey will take at least twenty days."

"Twenty." Chev didn't like the sound of that.

"Shorter if we can find someone to transport us there. But it'll be hard going. The only shelter is going to be in those cities. And who knows what shape they're in, what with the war and all."

"War? This the same thing that happened to our dayghosts?" asked Varnas.

Darin nodded, slowly, considering the possibility. "The dayghosts do this sometimes. They go insane, burn down their own cities, assemble in fields to hack each other apart. They say the sun drives even them mad, eventually."

"We saw a whole bunch of nightfolk crossing the mountains around midnight," said Chev.

"Not just nightfolk," Darin gestured, "dayghosts too. All trying to go to the southern frontier to escape the bloodshed. It's bringing the monsters out. I suppose it's all easy meals for them."

Chev watched Darin, trying to read his expression. "So you're saying there's danger everywhere."

"Who knows what counts as dangerous to these soft, civilized folk," Darin shrugged. "But we got one thing on our side." Darin took out a little burlap bag and emptied dozens and dozens of little, smooth disks onto the table.

Chev couldn't help but pick one up: it was smoother than bone, with glossy texture that couldn't have come from plant, animal or stone.

"*Plats*," said Darin before Chev had the time to ask. "I don't know what they are, but the Daylanders are crazy about them."

"What do they do? Do you eat them?" Chev fiddled with one, found it bent slightly when he pressed it.

"That's the funny thing. They're completely useless, as far as I've seen. But if you give enough to a Daylander they'll do anything and give you anything you want."

"Food and supplies?"

"Clothes, for you two. We can't go far in this place looking like tribal foreigners." Darin tugged at his tunic. "Standing out, it's dangerous, especially with our pointed ears. People don't trust pointy-ears, and brotherhood means nothing here. They only see weakness."

"Good, we'll dress up like them, get something for the ears." Varnas nodded. "What else?"

"Weapons," Darin weaved his fingers together. "Chev's got his sword. We'll need something proper for you, Varnas, your stick isn't gonna hold up here. We'll need a spear."

Varnas affectionately petted Tobi's old crossbow. "I got this old boy right here."

"You know how to use it?"

"Sure I do. You point it at someone, it shoots out an arrow. At least, that's what I saw Tobi doin'."

Darin crinkled his brow. "Who is Tobi?"

"It doesn't matter," Chev jumped in. "Weapons, clothes. Then food and drink. Right?"

Darin let the matter of Tobi pass with a nod. "Sure. Sure. And shelter, too. I'm not sleeping in one of Varnas' pits another night."

"Well, if we're talking *literally*, it was one of *your* pits, since—"

Varnas had a lot to say, but suddenly the noise rushed out of the room when the door opened. Like a gust silence spread, and a host of figures made a careful walk inside. Tall warriors to the man, each step clacked with heavy armaments, and they wore—Chev couldn't quite accept what his eyes told him—whole *suits* of daysteel, arranged in strips over the breast. But there was no fight here. No sword was drawn, no hands over weapons. They ignored whatever mood they caused and took their own seats, each easing their helmets off and placing them atop the table.

"Stag riders, they call them," said Darin, "On account of the giant stags they use to get around, if it weren't clear enough. People don't trust them."

"Huh." Varnas saw something in them that was curious.

Chev had to ask. "What?"

"Oh, nothing," Varnas grinned, and touched the side of his face. "Just that they're pointy-eared too. Like us."

The woman from the bar fulfilled her promise. A bell was soon rung that was meant as a warning: the tavern would soon be open for dayfolk. Nightfolk left to their own tents or were herded downstairs. The pretty young lady personally guided Chev and group into one of the quarters.

"I hope you brought blankets," she told them as she opened the door.

Chev soon understood why. It was nothing more than a walled off patch of wooden floor, not much different from a prison cell. Varnas, Chev, and Darin would be packed in, and that was before Ma-ma squeezed inside and took up valuable empty space.

"I'll be back," the woman said enigmatically. And she shut the door. Chev remembered now what Varnas had promised her in exchange for the room.

Varnas, as he had a talent for doing, voiced what everyone was thinking. "Go outside to fart," he warned. He spent the next few minutes shuffling around, experimenting with the best way to stretch out and make the best use of what little space he had. Darin seemed entirely comfortable folding his hands together and laying like a dead plank. His new clothing clearly providing more warmth than the worn furs hanging off the bones of Chev and Varnas. Only Chev spent some time sitting up. He pulled out a smooth black stone from his pouch and let it dance in his fingers, the very same that Sana had given him when they were children.

It was terrible thing. In the best circumstance, she would be armless. Chev wondered if he'd left behind a village capable of taking care of her, or of Minda for that manner. He wanted to believe, after the attack by the bone-skins, the tribe would come together more than ever to support each other.

But, it was equally likely the stress of losing so many could tear them apart and bring everyone to blows. From them, Chev had seen both.

He looked upon Darin, who was sleeping, but not peacefully. Chev really started understanding how they were different. It was like what he heard sometimes, that some people couldn't "see the forest for the trees". Except Darin could only see the forest. And to Chev, the forest hardly mattered except the trees were in it.

Who told me that? Chev nearly laughed aloud as he remembered. *Ossen.*

Somewhere in the vast Daylit Lands, many fold larger than any land Chev knew, was his father. Why, then, did Ossen feel so close?

A little movement jolted him out of his thoughts. The sun would be out, and Starlight was rousing out of her slumber. Tiny, squeezed eyes opened one by one, hooking onto Chev's features.

But Chev had imagined it. In this darkness she was near blind. She sobbed slightly, and Chev quickly understood why. She had no idea she wasn't alone.

To comfort her, he rested his finger on her cheek. It sank slightly into her skin, and that was enough to calm her. A long time passed, and Chev did nothing but stare into those blind eyes.

Even in the dark, Chev could see Starlight's furry cheeks dimple as her gums spread wide with a smile and her emerging teeth sparkled. Little Starlight would have been monster food twice over if it weren't for Chev. Finally, it felt worth it.

The door opened. Chev stashed Starlight away as though she were contraband, hiding her beside Ma-ma. The pretty young woman looked through the thin gap.

"You wanna take a walk?" she asked.

In the dim confines of the tavern basement there was just a hallway. The only private place was the stairwell leading up to the dining area. The woman put her ear to the door, to close her eyes and relish the sound of furniture moving, grunting and bleating.

"Do you hear that? That's *dayfolk*, there." The woman put on a slight smile, and spoke in wispy, serene tones. "I know it's wrong. I know I shouldn't be listening in, but it drives me wild, just to think there's these beings so like us who we never see or talk to."

Chev had too much to say, so he kept silent as he watched her.

"I don't know if I should be telling you this, but you know, *someday*, I hope to meet one." The woman flushed, and put her pale hand by her cheek. "Oh hell, I'm telling you all this but I hardly know you."

"My name is Chev," he said.

"That's a handsome name," she said, "I'm Lily."

"Lily," Chev whispered to himself.

"Mmhmm. After the flower. Do you get them where you come from? They're the sort that float on the water."

The girl who sat in front of him with the sweet smile and lovely face could not have been the same that shot Borin through the head with a crossbow bolt. It simply couldn't have been. But they were identical, they both wore those odd, shapely dresses that went down to the ankles and swished as they moved. They had the same floral imprints on the neck and cheeks, the same warm eyes.

Before long, Chev had forgotten what she'd asked.

"To be honest, I didn't really want anything from you," said Lily, her attention fixed to the wooden door, "You aren't the first tribal to come around to these parts, and I always feel sorry for you. It never seems you come by choice."

Chev nodded mutely.

"I won't ask. But I can see something weighs on you. That's why you're going to Manak, isn't it?"

"Yes," said Chev.

She sighed. "Many go, but none ever seem to get what they want from there." For Chev's unspoken question, she turned to him. "The Daylit Lands eat you people up like that."

Chev didn't say anything. Soon, Lily naturally filled in the silence.

"We're a rough people, aren't we? Truth is, we aren't that much better than dayfolk with all the fighting and cheating we do among ourselves. It must be pretty peaceful in the forest, down in the Nightlands."

Chev's forehead scrunched on hearing the term. "The Nightlands?"

Lily nodded, making a soft sound. "Mhmm. That's what we call where you're from. The southern land, with nothing but woods as far as the eye can see. I hope to see it one day."

For whatever reason, Chev had never considered that his home might have a name to other people. The thought brought him to sit next to Lily on the steps.

"I've never heard it called peaceful," said Chev, sweeping back some black hair, "There's monsters and drovers everywhere, and deep inside the bone-skins rule. But," Chev had to think on things, "you can count on your people to support you. As long as you do things their way."

"It's the same here. If I leave this place, I'll lose everything. It's what keeps me here."

"You shouldn't let a place be your prison," said Chev.

Lily gave Chev a sad smile. "You don't understand us Daylanders. There's nothing more valuable than place here. You see, the dayfolk only need so many nightfolk, and if you don't find work, and hold onto it, you'll lose it. That's why the stag riders despise us."

"Those men that walked in, with the suits of daysteel," Chev suddenly recalled, "those were them?"

When Chev glanced her direction, he couldn't help but notice she was much closer than before, radiating a fire-like heat. Her whole body was twisted to face his. "Yes, silly. You didn't see their pointed ears? Like yours?"

Her own eyes lingered on Chev's pointed ears, giving them hungry look.

Chev's heart was thumping, but unable to do anything but pretend nothing was amiss. "I noticed, but... to me it's normal."

A finger on Chev's ear, and he nearly jumped. The attractive woman was burning, her whole body pushing against its confines. Her voice seemed to hum with music. "Please tell me you're not bonded."

Why does it feel so natural to turn and kiss her? But Chev couldn't help but be honest, even looking at a face and body that begged for a lie. "I am."

She deflated immediately, her face and body sudden going flat and cooling to a lukewarm chill. She kicked a leg over her knee as she pouted. "Ah, curses."

Chev twisted to her. "I'm sorry, really, I am. But that's why I'm going to Manak."

Her voice was a cool shadow, sounding by the minute more like the woman who shot Borin. "Why?"

Perhaps it was because Chev's heart still pounded from Lily's attention, or maybe he was simply tired of holding it in all the time. But Chev at the moment elected to make a serious mistake. He asked her. "Can you keep a secret?"

Chev quietly padded back into his room, and picked up Starlight from where she suckled greedily from Ma-ma. He gave her nose a little rub, and took her out into the hall.

"This is her," he said.

He didn't get the reaction he expected. He knew Lily would be surprised, but she was struck with silence, a deep one, she didn't even breath, and her neck shrank back between her shoulder blades. Her two eyelids shivered as she stared at Starlight.

The child cooed happily as two chubby arms stretched out to the new face in the tepid light. Chev wished he was just as blind and helpless as she was just then. The dread that he'd made a terrible mistake clawed at him.

"I don't understand," Lily could only say.

Chev said, "It was a mistake, I didn't look for her, and now I'm doing whatever I can to make things right."

Her jaw twitched, and couldn't seem to settle. "Chev, what is that? Is it a *dayfolk?*"

"You did say you wanted to meet one," Chev said.

"I was being cute," Lily stepped back in terror. "By my father's grave, I was just trying to be cute!"

"Lily, wait!"

It was too late. She had sprinted down the corridor, and slammed the door so hard it shook the whole building. Chev stared after her down that corridor, nothing in his head but for the blood rushing through it. He spent a restless night with one eye open the whole time.

The decision proved prudent. They woke to drawn swords.

Hlogas had warned them about how jealously the Daylanders guard the taboo. It became clear to Chev what Hlogas meant when he looked down the long, broad blade that was held straight and at a perfect angle to plunge between his eyes. There was an electric itch where the taper ended and his skull began.

"You," said a brazen voice, "you harbor dayfolk."

Darin and Varnas woke up quickly. Darin had his sword out before his eyes were fully open, but someone knocked it from his hands with a brisk swing. Fully hemmed in by a wall of blades, both of Chev's companions looked to him for answers as did the motley but well-armed militia before them.

"I'll say again," the man's deep voice didn't fit the wiry frame, "you harbor dayfolk. True?"

Chev's couldn't keep his vision straight, from sword to face to sword to face. Over the mercenary's shoulder, Lily watched, perched on her toes.

"Answer me," said the man.

Chev, seeing no other option, put his hand on the sleeping child behind him. His movement caused the armed men to squirm and shut their eyes.

"Don't look at it!" cried one.

"He's got it!" piped another.

Only their leader, the wiry man with the voice of brass, held steady. He only gave Starlight a jerking glance before he kept his eyes glued to Chev's face. "*You*," he hissed like a fading gong, "your kind does this, do they? Abduct children of the dayfolk?"

"I didn't abduct her, I *found* her!"

"You committed your crime when you picked her up," said the man. He tipped his head to his compatriots. "Take their weapons and drag them upstairs. Put the dayfolk creature in the basket and cover it up. I'll figure out what to do with it."

Seeing the sheer number of swords against them, they thought better of raising their weapons and gave up to the militia. The Daysword was taken from Chev with an unceremonious jerk, and the spindly rogue that took it held it with a greedy, misshapen eye. Another bound them with rope, working with dispassionate efficiency.

Most painful of all was watching the bundle that was Starlight being dropped into a basket. Ma-ma did her best, biting the linen and pulling hard, but the peasant militiaman just cursed it and booted the goat until she stopped. The basket was hauled with little tenderness, the sound of a child's wail fading upstairs as Ma-ma trailed behind bleating plaintively.

Unceremoniously, Chev, Varnas and Darin were dragged whole-bodied up the stairs, back to the tavern floor. Chev beseeched Lily as he passed by. She could only shake her head sadly, and tell him, "You gave me no choice."

Only a few stragglers occupied the tavern's bars in the early hours, each inclined to sit in the dark. Only a band of the stag riders were in any numbers, and they chose not to interfere, self-consciously absorbed in whatever discussion they shared among themselves. Chev looked at all of the murderous faces around him, quietly realizing his best chance might have been to fight his way out.

The brazen-voiced man announced his verdict, "You broke the treaty between dayfolk and nightfolk. You risked war between our people, and such an unthinkable crime deserves an unthinkable punishment. We'll leave you to hang beneath moon and sun, and we'll let the dayfolk know we upheld our end of the treaty."

"I had nothing to do with this!" Darin proclaimed, sweat dripping from his forehead, "I didn't take the child!"

"Darin..." Varnas breathed his name in disappointment.

The brazen-voiced man was merciless in his edict. "You allowed this to happen. You share in the punishment."

"What will happen to the child?" Chev called out.

The leader turned his iron eyes to Chev. "It is being disposed."

Disposed. Like manure or garbage. Chev found the energy to struggle.

"You murderers!"

"I said nothing about—"

The brazen-voiced man never finished his thought, as the most unexpected thing happened. The rogue who'd taken Chev's sword had just flopped onto a seat to better admire his new acquisition when the stag rider nomads suddenly took an interest. They all stood up, chairs clattering to the ground, their steel armor jangling as though alarmed. A nomad pointed at the rogue, "That's one of *our* swords!"

The rogue, suddenly wary, tossed the sword to the ground. "I took it from *him!*" he pointed at Chev.

All five of the stag riders drew blades. Swords shivered in threat, and the local militia hastily reformed to face the new enemy.

The leader of the militia stepped forward. "This has nothing to do with you," he told them.

The stag riders couldn't be cowed even by that powerful, iron-clad voice. "He's one of us!" a broad-shouldered nomad pointed at Chev and stepped forward, "You round-ears have no place to judge!"

"He was harboring dayfolk!" said the leader.

"Round-ear lies!" bellowed the nomad leader, "Release them or you'll face our justice!"

"Kill 'em pointy ears!" one of the militiamen cried, but it was impossible to say which.

"Murderous bastards! Charge!"

Suddenly, the five stag riders plunged into a melee with the local militia. Courage and audacity made up for their lack of numbers, as they cut and stabbed their way through an armed gang entirely unready for a fight. Daylanders plummeted to the ground before others could rally and provide a real fight. Things devolved into individual battles, nomad and Daylander wrestling and kicking and swiping at each other in chaotic, drawn out combat.

Darin wriggled out of his bindings, while Varnas and Chev both sat slack-jawed. They watched a nomad pound a militiaman's head into the floor until teeth clattered out like dice. Darin freed Varnas first, but hesitated before Chev.

"Promise me you won't be a fool," Darin said.

"I won't," said Chev.

"You won't be a fool, or you won't promise me?"

Chev just shook his head in response.

Darin frowned, but he tugged Chev's bindings loose. Chev ripped the ropes the rest of the way, and made a leap for his sword from amid the chaos and snatched it into his hand.

"Make a break for it?" Chev asked them.

"Make a break for it," they both said. And without further talk the plan was executed.

The door to the outside was across the melee. They ran for it, and the battle was so chaotic that they each could slip around to the other side, Varnas only detouring to pick up a new, shiny spear that he pulled out from someone's side. Chev reached the door first. Varnas and Darin both had to make several sidesteps through scything blades and axes.

Through the door they exploded into clean air, the night chill tasted like pure freedom. Already the battle had drawn attention, and a small mob of excited onlookers made a circle around the door to the tavern. For just one heart-stopping moment, Chev was sure he'd been cornered, but the mob merely craned their necks to get a better view of the carnage transpiring inside the building.

Varnas and Darin sped ahead. But Chev was indecisive, he looked back into the battle.

"Come on, Chev!" urged Varnas.

"Not without Starlight," said Chev.

Darin regarded Chev with an eye roll, but Varnas hissed at Chev, "Well, she's not in there!"

After some tugging and pulling, Chev was finally coaxed away. The mob parted naturally for them, and they rushed forward, nearly slamming into more curious nomads and villagers attracted by the sounds of battle. Still, Chev slowed, and he made it clear he wasn't leaving without his burden.

"I need to find Starlight," he said.

"Weren't you getting rid of that girl?" Darin said, "You're risking all our lives staying here."

"I don't care. I'm taking her to a safe place. She was left with me for a reason!"

Varnas was ready to placate Chev, but his eyes were drawn by some other sight. "That damn goat!"

Ma-ma bounced on stubby legs toward them. Varnas brightened up to see her, and he clapped hands, bent his knees and invited her right into his arms.

"Stubborn goat," Varnas weaved his fingers through the goat's silver curls, "bet you thought we were goners this time."

"Varnas," Chev's voice shivered, "now is not the time..."

Varnas seemed to pity Chev for a moment. "You are a little slow, aren't you? This ain't a normal goat! It's Ma-ma! Go on, go get her girl! I know you can do it!"

Ma-ma bleated, made several eager circles around them, and trotted in a direction. Varnas bid Chev to follow with a grand, meaty gesture.

"Come on, you dumb slowpokes!"

It was a short trot away, and Ma-ma took herself as fast as her short, stubby legs could take her, almost hopping across the landscape. Then they caught sight as two men with shovels heaved clods of dirt into a hole, their pace making it evident that this was something they'd rather not be doing. But it was here that Ma-ma stopped, made a circle around the group, and nipped at Chev's ankles to get him to move.

"It's too late." Chev deflated at the sight, the words died as they went out his mouth.

Varnas bent down to Ma-ma. "Messed up this time, old goat. All of us did."

But Ma-ma was insistent. She bit at Varnas' arm, and then got his necklace, and pulled him bodily forward.

"Ma-ma..." Varnas sighed.

But then something in Darin hardened. He made a ferocious, low grunt, and strode in front of the two of them, driven to impatience. "I'm not waiting around," he muttered darkly.

Chev would have sworn he was about to give up and walk away, but for whatever reason, he headed straight toward the digging men. The two men jumped at the motion and demanded explanations in meek panicked voices, to which Darin replied with a flash of his blade. Two slices later, both men were dead.

The display of sudden violence had Chev and Varnas cowed. Their approach to the pit came more cautiously, especially as Darin gave the bloodied sword a little playful toss.

"I can see why this was Ossen's favorite weapon." Darin's voice was emotionless except for a little sadistic glimmer.

Chev got to his knees and pawed at the ground, like a tunnel vision made him blind past anything to do with the pit. A few seconds sifting through loose dirt, and Chev felt the wicker weave of a large basket. Chev tried to pull it out before he'd even fully unearthed it.

"Here," Varnas stepped in with one of the abandoned shovels, and Chev cringed at the sight of a blade plunging into the earth near the basket. But Varnas knew what he was doing, and he very carefully levered the thing out. It was a delicate operation, Chev felt he was unearthing a sarcophagus.

His hands fell on the lid. Carefully, he lifted it off. The child was inside, and the sensation of light and air made her cry in alarm.

Chev's tears melted tracks of dirt that had settled on his face.

"That's the last time," her promised her. He picked her up and nestled her into his shoulder. He shushed her, stroked the back of her fragile head, and promised again, "that's the last time."

"There's no time for this," said Darin, suddenly aware of something approaching.

They seemed to move from danger to danger. The stag riders who had kept their distance now trotted in, clearly kin of the nomads who'd created the melee in the tavern. Chev twisted around, looking desperately for an escape route, but it was clear now they'd taken great care to surround them. In every direction, antlers stood like ghostly trees in winter, the stags trotted in with their heavily armored masters. The lances and shields seemed more suited to fighting monsters of legend than for this rabble of tribesmen.

One of these stag riders dismounted. Chev carefully put Starlight back into the basket and reached for his sword. But the nomad made no movement for his. He only walked up to Chev, scanned him from toe to crown, and said, "Greetings, brother."

Chapter Thirteen
The Nomad's Way

I T WAS HARD not to see the approaching warrior as anything but a towering suit of armor and gleaming weapons. But he called Chev "brother", and Chev was shocked into giving this man a second appraisal, past what he wore and carried. He was the same age as Chev, his narrow face giving him a boyish appearance and the impression he had a child's head with a man's body. It could have been either a friendly or nervous smile on his smooth face.

"You wield a knight's sword. You know that don't you?" the man asked, his tone suggested he looked for a specific answer.

"It's my… it's my…" Chev hesitated; he wasn't sure if these men had the same taboos as they had back home. But he could think of nothing but the truth. "It's my father's."

"Then your father was a *knight*," the boy nomad said, "and so you belong with us."

He took his helmet off, freeing his short black hair to toss in the soft wind. There was something familiar about his features. The Daylanders had slightly flat rounded faces to match their round ears, making them look slightly alien. This man could have been from home.

"What do you mean?" asked Chev.

"You are one of our people. You were lost, and now we've found you again."

"I'm sorry, I don't understand," Chev said, "We're not looking to be found. We're going to Manak."

The young nomad laughed, and stepped forward to slap Chev on his shoulder. "Luck of the ancestors, we have the same destination. You and your friends can come with us."

The nomad made a sort of whistle, at which his stag dutifully trotted toward them. Close up, Chev saw this was not the same animal he had once hunted in the forest. It was graceful and long-legged creature, with intelligent eyes and with its proud head raised it was taller than Chev by a good deal. Packed muscles radiated power, and its steady demeanor suggested it would not run from a fight. This was a beast of war.

The nomad, with all the grace of a practiced rider, mounted up. He patted the stag's haunches, an invitation to Chev to climb on.

Chev looked to Varnas and Darin for guidance. Neither had any to give him. Chev sighed, and decided on the spot it was better just to join for now.

"I'm taking this basket," said Chev, "and the goat, too."

And so Chev, Varnas and Darin shared saddles with these "knights"—as they called themselves—while they journeyed. Twenty men, each mounted to his own stag, trotted over hill and field to the ancient city of Manak. Most of the other men were like Wermac, fresh-faced, young, but leading the column were three older warriors, with peppered close-cut hair and cheeks bearing dramatic creases.

Chev scarcely believed what was happening. He didn't have the imagination to come up with such a tale, and though he'd walked through woods and mountains to get here he'd never pictured himself actually traversing the Daylit Lands, let alone adopted by a bizarre stag-riding warrior race.

Atop the stag, he could see for miles in every direction. What Ossen had said of this country was true: there was nothing but grass, only scraggles of trees bordering tended crops and the occasional dayfolk village. A half-moon beamed upon the empty landscape, as bleakly beautiful as it was slightly worrying; Chev had well-honed instincts to seek shelter from the sun, and there was nothing of the sort to be found out here.

The young knight with Chev must've noticed his nerves, because he turned to give Chev some words of comfort. "You gotta trust us," he told him, "We spend our lives out in these wastes. We know how to take care of ourselves."

"I know how to take care of myself too," said Chev, before adding quietly, "most of the time."

"My name is Wermac," the young man said, "I'm a novice. Why are you going to Manak?"

Chev wasn't sure how to word it. "To lift a curse," he settled on.

Wermac made a disappointed sound. "I'm sorry. Must be pretty bad, if it's taking you all the way to Manak."

"It's bad," agreed Chev, not wishing to elaborate.

There was a natural pause in the conversation. Wermac cleared his throat, and offered, "My people—before we can become adults we must go on a pilgrimage to Manak. We spend a year and a day there, on a quest to reclaim the lost city. You know the Old Empire?"

"No," answered Chev.

"Then you really are a Nightlander," Wermac set himself on an explanation, and he seemed to relish giving it, like he had the subject pinned in his mind. "The nightfolk once ruled the Daylit Lands. It wasn't called that then. It was just the Empire, the greatest nation on earth. Back then, dayfolk came to *us* for shelter. We protected them, not just from monsters, but also from the corrupt nightfolk who would do them harm. You've already encountered them."

Chev scratched the back of his head, and put out a wild guess. "The round-ears?"

Wermac nodded. "You've seen how treacherous they can be. Envy and greed is all they know. That's how they betrayed the Old Empire, and why the pointed-ears took to the wilds. Your ancestors fled south, past the mountains and into the forests. We knights stayed. We had sworn to defend the Empire, and now that it's gone we seek to rebuild it. So you see, a long time ago, our peoples were one. That's why I call you brother."

Chev couldn't quite digest what was being told to him. "Brother," he was called. Yet this man only shared his ear-shape with him, and a fable of a kingdom long past.

"How do you know my father was a knight?" asked Chev.

"Because that sword of yours either belongs to a knight or was stolen from a knight. If you were a round-ear I would think you a thief, but because you are a pointed-ear you must be a knight. Even if you don't know it." He said it as if this was the most natural logic, like how things fall and water flows.

Chev looked at his blade. He'd seen so few of these swords in his life, he had nothing to compare it to. He supposed they were similar to the kind the nomads held, but the Daylit Lands had proved so strange that such a detail completely escaped him. He still had difficulty comprehending the amount of *space* that stretched so far around him.

The mountains he'd left were just a bump in the horizon now. The place where Tobi had met his end was far behind them. He may have been far from the talons of the dark roc, but Chev felt in his bones there was much worse to come. The very land stunk of it, a stale breeze brought forth the scent of blood and burning.

These men — these "knights" — were not natives to a peaceful land.

Twisting and pitching, land rising and falling, the stag's swaying motion did something to the pit of his stomach. Chev turned his head from side to side, wondering whether he should warn Wermac or hold it in. It was a godsend when the whole group came to a halt. Wermac jumped confidently from the stag's back. He held his hand to Chev.

Chev politely refused, then dismounted like a fish flopping to the ground.

Wermac laughed, helping Chev up and beating dust off him with big, wide slaps. "Bet you don't ride much where you come from," he teased.

"We mostly just eat stags," said Chev.

Chev found his feet again, but they felt oddly rubbery, like the ground under him wasn't solid. He felt like a vessel that could be tipped out at any moment; his stomach lurched upward. Wermac must have noticed Chev's nausea, but he only smiled and pulled the stag toward a brook.

The knights had come to water their mounts. The brook was more stones than water, even so, each warrior and animal sucked greedily, the river trailing from their chins. Chev reckoned that if they drank any more vigorously they might dry up the whole stream. After, the riders filled their waterskins to the brim and secured them to their saddles.

Still, they had the right idea, Chev was running dry himself, so he stooped and sucked, and the cool water settled his stomach and brought back his strength. He took his fill, then washed his face and arms until the itch of that day spent in the tavern was well off him.

He didn't notice Varnas stooping next to him.

"You notice something about these men?" said Varnas, his voice quieter than normal, making it obvious he didn't want to be overheard.

"What?"

"They got no tools."

"So?" Chev was confused. "What's that supposed to mean?"

"Bunch of armored freaks with weapons enough to slaughter an army. Odd, wouldn't cha think?"

Chev released an exasperated sigh. "I dunno, Varnas. There's supposed to be some kinda war going on."

"I'm just sayin', somethin's odd."

"You think just 'cause you were right about Tobi it means you're right about everything? I'm not naive, I don't trust them completely, but it would be stupid to treat them like enemies just because."

"If I thought they were enemies, I'd say so, you lousy cretin you!" Varnas had a wheeze of a chuckle. "But now that you mention it, maybe it wouldn't be smart to trust them completely, you know?"

Things suddenly reversed, Chev tripped over his words. "I didn't—it was—you said—Damn, Varnas! It was you who was saying it!"

"Oh, I just said it was strange. The suspicion is all yours, and I think it's smart we watch our backs. Good thinkin', Chev."

Varnas gave him a couple of grandfatherly pats on the back, while Chev repressed an angry retort. In some strange way, Chev had been outmaneuvered. He turned his attention to the stream once again and scrubbed vigorously, annoyed that Varnas had been so skillful in planting that little seed of doubt.

Soon, all the nightfolk and the stags had their fill and preparations were made to mount up again. That was when Chev spotted the knight who'd taken Starlight's basket walking to him purposefully. That gave Chev all sorts of instinctive fears. The knight jerked his thumb to his stag.

"I think your animal's dead," he said.

"The goat?"

The knight shook his head. "The one in the basket. It stinks like carrion. Might want to throw it out."

Chev shoved past the warrior and to the basket. The lid came off easily, and Chev tilted it so the stars could shine their light inside. Chev didn't know what he expected to find—some limp thing or something bounced to a pulp from the journey—so he was surprised to see her sleeping, a tiny chest rising and falling beneath the cloth. Starlight was a heavy sleeper even though his nose curled at that smell the knight described. Starlight had soiled herself.

"Dung," Chev said, both a curse and a statement. He pulled the basket down and, in a quiet stretch of the stream, cleaned up the sleeping child and tucked her back into the safety of the basket.

The pilgrimage moved on. Chev had hitched the basket onto his stag, where its proximity made Chev feel comfortable. He felt less anxious, for a moment at least, and he could leisurely watch the landscape roll by. It had a sort of desperate beauty to it, with so much grass and space but so little to break the monotony. All there was for miles were flat plains, a tree here, a tree there, sometimes a little homestead with a few crops nearby. It seemed a complement to the sea of stars above.

Only a smell heralded a change to come; the scent of a long burnt fire, an undertone of something that was not meant to be burned. It was a stale, claustrophobic smell, like being locked in a room with cooking, rancid meat.

Others noticed it too. Wermac took a few sharp breaths, the stags protested by pulling at their reins, but the party moved on despite the unease. Up the path, a family of wanderers in their bare feet moved like tattered, animated shrouds in the dusk.

"Don't look at them," Wermac whispered.

Chev couldn't help but look. As the stags trotted by he saw a miserable band of pleading eyes in flat round faces. Exhausted mothers and ruined men, but mostly children, all with skin deeply marked with lines like knife wounds, filth spattered their cheeks, and emboldened flies orbited around, sometimes landing and crawling on their faces.

Chev reviled them, just as he pitied them. It was a contradictory emotion. Something in him wanted to help them, something in him wanted to flee. Seeing how Wermac kept his head stubbornly straight, he felt he had to act the same way.

With the sorry band was behind them, Wermac simply said, "Their kind are like the vermin that scatter when you overturn rocks. There is nothing you can do to help them."

And soon, they all saw their overturned rock.

It was supposed to be Grainsea. But there was no seas of grain, only an ashen waste where there had been fields, gray dust the shade of decaying bone. Coming closer a landscape of devastation unfolded—dead livestock with the flesh rotting from their bones, dayfolk bodies rotting and flush upon the earth, trees burned to their stumps.

For some reason, all the knights chose to dismount. Chev, Darin and Varnas followed behind, bare feet cushioned on soft ash.

One of the knights walked into the field and dipped his hand into the ash, letting it filter through his fingers. "Poison," he announced.

The band walked the rest of the path, and they all stopped at some sight. Chev didn't understand what they were looking for at first; the land around them was flat and featureless as ever. It was as though something was written on the ground, and that was when Chev began to see it as well. The ground had been burned to black, so completely it looked as if a vast pit had rent the ground. Stones were crushed together, the skeletons of buildings and streets and walls. Drifts of ash blasted across the dead landscape, disturbed by slight changes in the wind. Amid the ruins, bits of dead bodies strewn liberally, lodged in cobbles or laying naked on the earth. Dayfolk or nightfolk, in the face of this sort of destruction, they might as well have been the same.

It seemed no one could turn away from the place where a vast city once stood. One knight's comment broke through the indecision. "This land is cursed," he said, and with that conclusion everyone turned back to their mounts.

They took the long path around what was once the great city of Grainsea.

The knights marched far enough to escape the smell of the dead city before setting up camp. When they all stopped, Chev feared that they intended to sleep through the day in the open, but then the knights set about making shelter. They erected canvas buildings, big thick sheets of fabric thick enough to block out the sun, supported by sticks alone. Darin was fascinated and lent a hand as they constructed the shelters. Chev'd seen these structures from a distance before, but only now that they were erected before him could he see what they really were; it was bafflingly ingenious.

Varnas stooped next to him. "Cities of cloth. What a concept."

"Maybe there's something to it. Maybe if Grainsea could pick itself up and move it would have never burned down," said Chev.

"Maybe. But do you really wanna live in a sack?"

"Better than a pit," Chev answered with a shrug.

Varnas nodded, as though silently conceding the point. "Well, I'm sure they'll let you stay in one, being as they've all taken to you so quickly."

Chev tilted his head to Varnas. "Why do you sound so bitter about that?" It wasn't an interrogation—it was curiosity. Varnas had something on his mind.

And Varnas was quick to say it. "You think these folk will lead you to Ossen?"

"Varnas," Chev breathed out his impatience, "I already told you, I'm just here to find Starlight a home. And, you know what? Even if I was out here looking for Ossen, what's wrong with that?"

"What's wrong with it? You're dragging me along with ya, that's what!"

"It's the same as before, Varnas, you didn't have to come. You could have stayed in the Nightlands."

"I *did* have to come," said Varnas.

"Why?"

"Because I *had* too."

Chev now really stepped back to look at this old man. For the first time, saw an intensity that Varnas kept well hidden. His head was turned away, as though Varnas didn't want him reading too deeply into the ambivalent expression his face held.

"Some things you only understand with age," Varnas explained in an uncharacteristic flat voice, like humor had dropped from his personality.

A campfire flickered in the middle of the new camp. The stags were set to graze near a spring, and they pulled from the grass in greedy clumps with Ma-ma scampering between their legs. Wermac approached and made a welcoming gesture.

"We're about to exchange tales," he said, "You wanna join?"

Among the campfire of the knights, words were the only currency. Firelight illuminated the spiraling steam from many cups. They had brewed a stew—heavily seasoned with spice so it bit the nose and cleared the sinuses, but it was warming and went smoothly down the throat. Chev held his cup against his chin, enjoying how the hot vapors warmed his blood. Occasionally, whoever happened to need a good stretch would circle around with a ladle and pot, refilling the clay mugs.

The knights' faces glowed after each tale-telling, smoothed as worries dropped from them. Even the older ones seemed to shed years as all reminisced about younger days and told stories of long forgotten battle.

Across the sputtering campfire, Chev noticed one knight with silver eyes in a soft face of curious beauty. It took a moment to process his features, long snowy hair, and enigmatic smile. Chev ended up staring, much like one would try and makes sense of a puzzle by looking at it with no particular thought in mind. It struck Chev just then, he realized the knight was a woman. Just then, the moment was shattered by the rattle of chainmail, as a burly, thickset nightfolk rolled up the sleeves of his mail.

They called him Sargon the Brave, he was one of the older knights that lead the pilgrimage, and he exposed a forearm covered with images, the same strange bevels that Chev had seen on Lily. This time, it was not flowers, but snakes, fierce with flashing fangs.

"...And this one," Sargon rumbled, as though giving a tour of his own body, "this one I got after slaying the Great Basilisk of Rainswell Lake. I blunted my ax on that demon well and good, its scales were so damn thick, I had to wait for it to open its maw. A javelin down the gullet, that's what did it in."

"Basilisks ain't much to worry about. Getting them out of the water, that's the challenge," said a knight.

Sargon stroked a fringe of whiskers on his cheeks. "You didn't see this thing. This beast ate crocodiles, jumped out and pulled rocs outta the air. There was nothing easy about this monster, not luring it, not killing it."

Another knight nudged another. "Maybe it was best friends with the spider the size of a mountain."

There was rumble of laughter. Sargon took it with good humor, but still defended himself. "It *was* the size of a mountain. And its dead body makes a good landmark now, thanks for asking."

Chev was noticing a pattern in the stories, and he voiced the thought at the top of his head. "So you're all monster hunters."

A silenced was followed by general laughter. Clearly, Chev had grasped something they all thought obvious.

"We are *only* monster hunters," a knight said, leaning forward to grin.

"That's what defines us. A knight who does not slay monsters is no knight at all," said Wermac.

That was when the strangely beautiful knight with snow-like hair chose to speak for the first time that evening. Her voice was light and musical, and her eyes sprang to life as she looked to her fellow knights. "We have a unique treaty with the dayfolk. We promise to control the populations of night monsters. In exchange, they craft for us unique weapons. In thousands of years, the dayfolk have always been faithful to the agreement, and so have we." The knight unsheathed her blade and placed it in front of Chev. "The sword. The ax. The lance. The javelin. And the coat of chain. This is the knight's panoply."

She placed each of her weapons in turn. A practical armory was laid out, it was a miracle she seemed to wear it all so comfortably.

"It's a good deal for the dayfolk, too, because each of us can slay a hundred beasts. Basilisks, fiends, and yes, spiders the size of mountains." Sargon grinned as though a little drunk.

"Your sword," the beautiful knight continued, "is a knight's sword."

It was an invitation for a direct comparison. Chev slipped the Daysword out, and placed it opposite the knight's sword. It was, at a glance, entirely identical. To these warriors, it meant that Chev was one of them. Chev was not so sure, but saying his doubts aloud—that was dangerous.

It was supposed to have been Ossen's. For all he knew, Ossen stole it.

"You know," Varnas suddenly interjected, "this all makes sense now. The boy's a bit of a monster hunter himself."

Chev silently mouthed for Varnas to shut his mouth, but he'd already attracted every pair of eyes. All except for Darin, who looked to the horizon, anticipating the story that was about to be told.

Wermac exclaimed, "Chev! You never told us!"

"I didn't think it was that important," said Chev. It couldn't have been much more than a few weeks ago now, yet the battle with the bone-skins seemed like a lifetime ago even though it was very much fresh territory. He couldn't square his pride with the feeling that he'd brought the monsters on his tribe in the first place. The exile that followed—Darin clearly blamed Chev, and Chev wished he could blame someone but himself.

Varnas didn't know he was opening a sore subject. Or, more likely, he didn't care.

"Do ya'll get bone-skins around here?" said Varnas.

The knights seemed to all scoot closer toward the fire.

"A bone-skin! They were all driven south *ages* ago!" A young knight was awed.

"Well, me, Chev, and that brooding fellow over there, Darin, we all hunted a whole gaggle o' them once..."

What happened next was far too predictable. Varnas launched into his story, like it'd been pent up for ages, and he chose to start from the very beginning. It didn't take long for Varnas to insert his own embellishments, and each time Varnas' tale grew richer, Darin would just give Chev a knowing glance.

"...At that time, Chev, poor boy, none of the other men would take the kid out hunting, so it was left to me to show him the ropes. And, you know what? I realized this ain't the dull, lazy cretin everyone was talking about. No. It's like that kinda genius that makes you seem like a fool. That's what Chev has. I knew the first minute I laid eyes on the kid..."

Chev's instinct was to water down Varnas' little story, but Chev couldn't help but enjoy it. The initial embarrassment was turning to amusement, and Chev was laughing and reacting like it wasn't a story about him.

"...So we all found out that bone-skins are afraid of one thing and one thing alone, and that was fire. We set up torches—no, a bonfire! And then smoked them right outta their nest. And let me tell ya, you never seen nothing if you haven't seen a bone-skin throw himself at ya with rage and hunger in equal portions. At that moment, you stop remembering you're scared, you just get that pounding beneath you that tells you: *go, run, fight!*"

All the knights nodded as though they knew the feeling.

"That kid, right there," Varnas pointed at Chev, "One came up on 'em as big as one of your stags. I was pissing myself to run, Darin's bow shook in his hand. But Chev, he stared it down. Circled it, like a wolf contemplating a lion. I couldn't believe it. The struggle was fierce between them, and lasted the whole night, but in the end, he hammered an arrow through its eye socket, and it lay dead. I was in awe, shuddering as if I had won the victory myself, but the boy here looked down on it, wondering if it was even worth the trophy."

Chev was smiling uncomfortably at the expectations Varnas was setting. But for all the stretched truths, the knights were enraptured, captivated more by the teller than the subject, even as Varnas continued, talking about the Feast, and the counterattack Chev lead to defeat them. By the end, there was a hushed appreciation for the tale, and all around nodded and smiled as if each had eaten their fill of an exceptionally good meal.

"If that's all true," Sargon twisted to Chev, "this kid's a hero!"

"He really does have a knight's blood!" piped another.

"Listen, Chev, boy," Sargon leaned eagerly to him, "I know you were never raised in our ways, but I think all of us would agree that this tale is worth an *engraving*."

The other knights made noises of agreement, but Chev only furrowed his brow.

"What's that?" Chev asked.

By way of answer, Sargon pointed to the serpent image on his arm. "It is a tradition of our kind to be depicted with one's greatest achievements. The older we are, the more we have, and the closer the image is to our heart, the more personal and intimate the story. This tale is surely worthy to be worn on the arm."

"All who see it will know you are a killer of bone-skins," said Wermac.

Much to Chev's surprise, Darin chose now to speak. An enigmatic smile plied his lips, and he asked Varnas, "Old man, you've spoken a lot of our friend Chev. But what I want to hear is a tale about *yourself*."

"Myself?" Varnas grumbled, and shifted uneasily, "Well, I'm sure any one of these knights are eager to tell us their own stories. My throat's getting a bit sore."

"No," said Sargon, "I must admit I'm curious about you. We all are. If you have any other stories of your homeland, you have ears."

Varnas fidgeted for a moment, scratched the back of his head, rocked back and forth in indecision. "Fine," he relented, "I'll tell you a story. It's about a boy, and he lived with his mother, father, sister and brother, and they all lived out in the woods and they all loved each other very much. One day the larders were full of dried meat. And still his father walks out into the woods. The boy chases him out there, and the father turns to tell the boy, 'Don't worry, I'll be back. You see, we have enough for all of us, but I need something for the monsters. The monsters eat a very special kind of food, and I have to go get it so they won't take something precious from me. So you stay here with mother and sister and brother. I'll come home.'

"The boy had faith in his father so he waited patiently. When his father returned, he was not the same man. He was covered with thick liquid, dark with the smell of meat, and it dripped from his hands to ground. The boy asked his father 'What special food did you bring?' And father bent down, smiled, and smudged his cheeks with that substance. 'Berries,' he told him, and the boy trusted him.

"Some seasons passed and the boy forgot all about that incident with his father. His life was happy and all those questions went away. But it happened again. The larders were full and father still went out. This time, the boy didn't even question his father, and when he came back covered in that filth, that berry juice, the boy just accepted it. And all became normal as it was, and all as it should be.

"More seasons passed. Father did the same, and the boy told himself, 'father is going to feed the monsters.' But when he came back, he was not covered with berry juice, and father did not look happy. He moved as though a chill had frozen through him, dragging his feet across the floor, unblinking eyes with pin-like pupils. The boy thought, 'Something terrible happened,' and he went to his father to embrace him, to hope he might feel better.

"Father put his arm around the boy, looked into his eyes. Water rolled down his cheeks, crystal drops shattering to the floor. He told the boy, 'Father couldn't find the special food for the monsters.'

"The boy asked, 'It was never berry juice running down your arms, was it?'

"Father shook his head and told him, 'You always knew that, didn't you?'

"Father was right. The boy knew exactly what dripped off his arms, he had always known, but he didn't want to see it. He didn't want anything ruining his happy life, or upsetting the mother, the father, the brother and sister who all loved him.

"Father squeezed the boy tight to him, and said, 'Brother is strong. Sister is strong. We need mother. And they will not take me. Son, you are beloved, but you are also weak. That's why I ask you to make the sacrifice to save us all.'

"The boy understood. And the smart boy had *always* understood, even if he didn't want to, even if he'd do anything to be blind, or a fool, at that very moment, so that he wouldn't understand quite as well as he did. And as much as he tried to tell himself otherwise, he feared the sacrifice they demanded of him. Mother, brother and sister all embraced him with the worst sadness imaginable, knowing this would be the last night they would see him. The boy simply stayed silent, he had so many thoughts he didn't know what he was feeling.

"Day came, and the boy rose while everyone slept. He hadn't planned it, it was just his instinct before he fled as fast as he could into the daylight. He ran so quickly that all the beasts of the day couldn't catch him, and then with his bare hands, working beneath the searing sun, until heat flayed the skin off his back, he dug himself a pit where he could be hidden. That was where he curled up, closed his eyes, shivered and slept.

"Two days, and two nights passed. The boy was hungry, and he hadn't had a thought for a long time. He was just an animal at this moment, and he pulled himself out from the ground once again and wandered to where he might find food. He knew one place: his family larder, and he descended into his home burrow. In his daze, he wondered what his mother, father, sister and brother might be doing, and what they might say to him after being gone for two days and two nights. But when he felt what was beneath his feet, the boy's senses became instantly alive, and he would have done anything in the world to be in that daze again.

"It was the same sticky, wet stuff that had once dripped from his father's hand. And at that moment, the boy knew what he had done, and what he was responsible for. So he ran, ran so far he never went back to that place, and for all his life that boy wandered the world, taking shelter in holes in the ground."

Varnas took a breath, and nodded as though satisfied. "There you go. A tale about old Varnas."

Chapter Fourteen
Truly Named

WHEN THEY AWOKE the next dusk a swarthy, overweight knight pulled Chev aside and had him sit on a sturdy chair. The man communicated by grunting, and slammed Chev's arm onto a wood table, holding it fast so that he should stay still. Chev wondered briefly if he'd done something wrong and was now being punished.

"A bone-skin, right?" asked the big man.

Chev realized this was the 'engraving' he'd heard so much about. "Yes," he said.

The big man nodded, the sharp gesture causing the muscles on his arms to ripple. "Okay."

It was a strange process. The man had a little steel needle he used like a spear, dipping into a pan of odorous liquid before stabbing it repeatedly into Chev's arm. Where he stabbed, the skin swelled out, almost painlessly except for the pinprick.

"Looks good," said the man, inspecting his work.

Chev risked a glance. After a good ten minutes the man had depicted only the head. It looked more like an ant than a bone-skin. Chev considered his options, and thought it wise to keep his opinions to himself while he was confined to a chair.

"It *does* look good," said a soft voice.

Chev looked up. There was that enigmatic knight from the evening before. The one with the nice eyes. Chev screwed his gaze, piecing together why this person looked so strange.

"You're that woman," Chev concluded, more a thought than a statement.

The knight nodded, her lips stretching into one cheek in a lopsided but sure smile. "Yes. Of a sort."

Her wording was strange. "Of a sort?" Chev repeated.

"It's complicated."

Chev's confusion showed through the mild pain as the heavy man pricked his skin.

The female knight elaborated. "In our society, a woman can be whoever she wants to be, so long as she is willing to make a sacrifice. It's a bit like getting an engraving. There's a little pain, but you come out of it more yourself than you did before."

"I don't understand," Chev struggled with her turn of phrase. "How can you be more yourself than before?"

"If you don't understand that, then you will never understand, it's a simple as that." The woman smiled. "I am called Adar."

"I am Chev," said Chev.

"That was an interesting story your friend told. How much of it was a spider the size of a mountain?"

Chev bent his head, not understanding what she was getting at. "Hmm?"

She smirked, and asked more plainly. "How much of it was just a tale?"

"Varnas, well, he... uh..." Chev laughed a little uncomfortably, as though put on the spot. With that big knight looming over him with a needle it felt a bit like an interrogation. "He likes to make things sound more exciting than they really were."

"There's a saying I've heard. Bone-skins are dangerous to fight, and even more so to talk to. What do you think of that?"

"I'd say that's true."

The girl knight's next question seemed to spring from her lips. "Why would you say that?"

"I... uh..." Chev realized he'd been trapped. Distracted by the girl in Adar rather than the knight, Chev had talked more than he intended. A sheepish twist of the lips showed Adar what she needed.

"I see. So that's why you fled your tribe. You brought the bone-skins on them in the first place."

There was no wording things correctly for this. Chev vomited out words, his tongue getting tied up in tremendous knots. "I— I— I— was a fool. I thought I could trick it, but it only tricked me —"

Adar stopped him with a clean gesture. "There's no judgment here. We would all do the same. We all think we're better than the monsters. No one wanted to say anything, but the bone-skins scare us. We're used to giant snakes, rocs, and things that crawl in darkness. We understand a monster that ambushes and eats you without talking to you. Bone-skins, they're different. Their weapon is their tongue."

"I heard you drove them out from the Daylit Lands," said Chev, "Why not again?"

"Not us. Our ancestors. And even then it took the efforts of the folk of both night and day to do it. You think we can do the same now? Pointed-ear hates round-ear, and the dayfolk burn their own cities down. There's something everyone's been thinking but no one wants to say, that it's just a matter of time before a new monster comes into these lands, takes advantage of the division and war to feed on all of us. Just like the bone-skins once did."

Chev furrowed his brow. "Why are you telling me this?"

Adar shrugged, armor chinking with the simple gesture. "I'm just making conversation, Chev. And letting you know that there's more to you being here than simple hospitality."

She must have gotten something out of being so enigmatic, because even that sly smile across her lips provoked questions in Chev.

"Those knights are up to something," Varnas said, "I can just *feel* it."

Varnas was brushing down his new tunic, smoothing it out with aggressive sweeps of his hand. Chev didn't waste nearly as much time. He slipped his tunic over his head, letting the loose garment fall over him. The discomfort was immediate; the coarse threads hooked into bare skin, scratching him like a coat of nails.

Darin, already used to the shirt, slipped it on without a fuss. "Everyone is always up to something," he said, "so don't give yourself a headache thinking about it. And what you're doing with that tunic isn't going to do anything."

"It's just so damn *itchy*," said Varnas, picking at lint and loose threads.

"Just get used to it."

Darin had decided now was the time everyone looked like proper Daylanders, and that included putting on their excessive amount of clothing. Chev agreed it was better they not look like southern tribals, though he scratched and itched as much as Varnas. Chev still dreaded spending a whole day with it on.

"How's Starlight?" asked Darin.

Chev wasn't convinced Darin thinking of Starlight's welfare, he was just after assurances the girl wouldn't make herself into a problem.

"Dead asleep at night, and Ma-ma watches and nurses her in the day. That goat is a godsend," said Chev.

Darin nodded, satisfied. "We don't know how prickly these knights are about dayfolk, but they seem to be even stiffer about ancient laws than those round-ears."

Chev could see that. The knights seemed constantly aware of their place in history, like this empire they served only collapsed yesterday rather than thousands of years ago. It was alien to Chev, to have this odd commitment to a dead civilization, but perhaps it served to keep their society together, just as fear of bone-skins did back home.

"That's what makes 'em unpredictable," said Varnas, his complaint jolting Chev out from his thoughts, "they're not in the here and now, they're off being great warriors for a time long gone. And this shirt itches."

"Get used to it," Darin sighed, having already repeated himself. "Let's get a move on. These stag-riders are gonna get suspicious if we keep yapping like this."

"You go on ahead," said Chev.

Darin twisted to the boy, his voice lowering as though a reprimand. "We'll leave you behind if you dawdle too long."

"I know," Chev waved them off, "I'll catch up, I swear it."

Darin was about to utter some other warning, but Varnas seized him by the arm, and dragged him off into the main camp.

Behind the bushes, alone, Chev carefully took the basket, removed the lid, and pulled out Starlight. The child was just getting drowsy, still her tiny black eyes twinkled like mirrors to the night sky.

"Starlight," Chev said, "we're close now. I can find a place for you, I know we will."

The little girl squirmed in his hands, oblivious to the promises Chev was making. He realized, gazing into her mirror-like eyes, he was making promises to himself. He cast a gray, featureless shape in her dark pupils, the shade of the ashes of Grainsea.

They followed a path through a featureless and vast wasteland with little variation the whole night. The horizon would pull itself close, only to reveal an expanse very much like the last, fields of grass tossed by ever present winds. Mountains were distant and jutted out from behind the curve of the earth. The few trees and villages were too sparse to break the monotony.

Chev talked to Wermac when he could, but their conversation ran dry and Chev was left with his thoughts. At unguarded moments, Chev swore he heard words on blighted winds. A stag's grunt, a chill by the ear, a rustle from the grass, somehow each formed a warning. Something was begging him to turn back.

Chev wasn't the only one. Wermac's hand rested alertly on his sword, and he was a stiff as a statue. He would turn his head sometimes, a steely gaze at something far off like there was vague threat in some direction. Whatever unease affected him also affected the other knights, who kept grimly to themselves as they kept watchful eyes.

Eventually, Chev felt he had to ask. "What's wrong?"

He regretted asking, wondering if he'd broken some sacred silence from the stern look Wermac returned. But it wasn't in anger, rather in terrible seriousness.

"We're in the middle of civilized land," said Wermac.

"So?"

"So near a whole night has passed and we have not seen a single traveler."

It was taken as a sign. And then two nights passed absent any life. Any hope there was an innocent explanation was dashed. They came across the ruins of Pock Hollow, burned to the stones just as Grainsea was. The dusty desert in its place made a scar in this flat land.

Instinctively, the knights spread out to bear witness to the destruction. They trotted freely through what were once were streets and buildings, their sure-footed mounts clambering easily up and down.

Sargon gestured at a pile of rocks. "That used to be a big dayfolk temple," he said, like he was pointing out a curiosity. The big knight seemed to consider it further as he combed his chin hairs. "I remember it being quite impressive."

Everyone let Sargon's comment hang. Wermac used his lance to prod through some rocks, turning them over as though searching; Chev couldn't guess what he hoped to find, but the activity distracted Wermac and softened his face.

Chev unleashed a barrage of questions. "Is this normal? I mean, one city burned, but two? You think they did this to Broken Rock? What is going on anyway? Where did the people go?"

Wermac looked back at him with a glower. He understood Chev wasn't looking for answers, but he needed something to allay his fears. "I dunno. Never seen anything like this in my whole life. Dayfolk, they fight and fight, but never like this." He levered out a cobble with enough force it bounced like a bone. "This might be *the big one.*"

It was such unusual emphasis on those last words, and Wermac said it as though Chev would know what he meant. After Chev's silence, Wermac elaborated.

"You know. The war that ends the world? You don't have that legend?"

Chev shrugged. "Sorry."

"I thought everyone had some version of it, the last war. Only a few details change. At the fall of time, all the cities will be destroyed and millions killed, only Manak will stand. In the process, the nightfolk and dayfolk will be reunited, and the monsters will be driven out from the lands forever."

"Doesn't sound too bad," said Chev.

"I guess not," Wermac idly speared something among the cobbles, "but you have to live through the war first."

Wermac lifted his lance; at the end were some limp, rotted, half-burned scraps. But the Chev realized that its limbs dangled, its head lolled, and its button eyes came to life. It was a doll, caked with ash yet still bearing its oblivious, sewn smile. A morbid clue to what lay beneath the rubble. Wermac quickly tapped the thing from his lance as soon as he realized what it was.

"What sort of creatures do this to themselves?" Chev said.

Chev wasn't seeking an answer but Wermac gave one. "All of them."

The party had their fill of self-inflicted dayfolk atrocity. Faces hard, heads stiffly turned from the ruins of Pock Hollow, they marched toward the next city. With his heart in his stomach, Chev reflected on his promise to Starlight, and whether there would be any dayfolk left to adopt the poor girl.

There was none of the same chatter as the knights made camp. A tension hung in the air; Chev had thought seeing the city burned down might have stimulated discussion, but there was this feeling that couldn't be put into words. It drove everyone to deeper than usual silence as they puzzled it out for themselves.

After he'd finished assembling his own tent and hidden Starlight and Ma-ma protectively in its folds, Chev wandered out to the fringes of camp, lost in his own head. He half-expected to be alone, but Wermac was cross-legged on the dirt, watching something out in the distance. He sensed Chev's approach without looking.

"See out there," Wermac pointed to something, "see 'em. They're difficult to spot."

Chev leaned forward, focusing on the point Wermac gestured to. It seemed to be just dark grass moving in the gentle wind. But he trusted that Wermac was seeing something, and he tried doubly hard to pick out something. He thought he found it, something that could've been a figure, could've been brush. Only a slight movement betrayed there was anything at all.

"It's a rare sight. Some people don't even think they exist. But they do. The shadowed ones."

Chev looked harder, and saw it *did* move like a man, but its movements were that of a mad one, on all fours, jerking and scanning the horizon. Clearly a slave to animal instincts.

"Who're they?" Chev asked, now fascinated.

"They used to be nightfolk, like us, a long time ago. But they made a different choice and that changed them. Instead of allying with the dayfolk, they stole from them. And in long winters, when the silos were empty and the garbage piles dug out, they went to graves and feasted on bodies. They became masters of the shadows, but in doing so gave up on their civilization. There's nothing in this world better at hiding than them, squeezing into cracks and sewers with the rats and roaches."

"It's not hiding now," said Chev, watching this strange creature jitter from one copse of grass to another.

"It's not. Because the shadowed ones don't hide when they're desperate. Even rats hunt men when it's death either way."

Without much warning, Wermac picked up his bow, nocked an arrow, and aimed at the creature in the distance. The shadowed one halted, its senses must be keen to know danger from so far. Chev was caught off guard by the sudden eruption of light from its eyes, each of them like intense twinkling stars.

"It knows," Wermac said, the bowstring creaking in his fingers, "that if it moves, I'll shoot."

"Why not just shoot it?" asked Chev.

"I'm still not sure whether to kill it or not," said Wermac.

"It's a monster isn't it?" asked Chev. "You just said it might hunt us."

"Well," Wermac's face shivered. "I don't know. I should, it's the right thing to do, but I just don't want to."

Suddenly, Wermac let go of the bowstring. It arced through the air, and the beast ripped through the underbrush. The arrow landed nowhere close.

"That monster," said Wermac, "It's gonna go to its fellows, tell everyone this isn't a band of helpless peasants. They'll avoid us and wander the grasslands for a while, eventually they'll starve, grow weaker, and then they'll all die, because there's no dayfolk to steal from anymore. Doesn't make a difference whether I kill it or not."

Wermac put aside his bow in a deliberate manner, and leaned forward, like he was ready to fold himself up. "For thousands of years our people have stalked these wastelands, fulfilling our part of the grand bargain. Some say the ancestors abandoned us. Well, I say this is punishment for their crimes. We all know what they were, and no one likes getting reminded of it. But I think our purgatory is coming to an end. Someone has to sweep through this land, Chev, sweep through it to destroy evil and chaos. But to bring peace, order and prosperity in its wake—if not, what good is the destruction of evil?"

"I don't think anyone can do that," said Chev.

"Yeah, well, I believe." Wermac nodded, pleased with his own statement. "There's too many cruelties that good people suffer, nightfolk and dayfolk. Our two races divided because neither of us could trust one another anymore, we'd grown so wicked. But even in our division, and hatred, and anger, we still do great things. Imagine what we could do without this petty fighting and killing, imagine what we could do if we worked together, not separately. We could be like how the Great Folk were, with their cities and magic. Did you know they went to the moon, Chev? The moon! We could do the same thing. We step where they stepped, and then we can tell ourselves, truthfully, 'We are their worthy heirs'. Are you a good person, Chev?"

The question was odd and sudden. Chev didn't give himself much time to come up with an answer. "I think so?"

"I think you are. That's what I like about you tribals, is that you're uncorrupted, innocent."

Chev didn't have an answer to that. He'd already betrayed his tribe to save his own skin, risked the lives of his tribesmen for personal glory, and broken the greatest taboo his species cared for. The woman-knight had already seen right through him, and though she said she didn't care, he couldn't shake the feeling that the luster of his aura had tarnished, like he'd gone from hero to mortal.

"Oh, and Chev?" Wermac piped up, filling in the silence.

"Yes?"

"I don't want to get presumptuous, brother, but I've seen you looking at Adar. I'm going to save you a lot of pain when I tell you not to pursue her as a woman."

"Wermac?"

"It's not a command," said Wermac, shaking off whatever comment Chev was about to make, "just a warning."

"I got this depressing feeling about Broken Rock," said Varnas.

"What is it?"

"Can't say. Too depressing."

Chev sighed, securing Starlight's basket onto the stag's back. "Why'd you say it, then?"

"Didn't want you to get your hopes up," Varnas was noisily chewing something, and Chev didn't care to see what it was. "Any more blows to your dreams, I get the feeling you're gonna lose it."

At that moment, Chev violently pulled one of the straps that held his gear to the stag. Any tighter, it might've dug into his flesh. "Varnas, I *will* break the curse, I *will* find a home for Starlight, and *I will* go back to Sana. You can count on that."

Varnas shrugged. "Didn't say you wouldn't. But life doesn't just hand things over. Sometimes the universe is cruel. It's a thing you'll just figure for yourself, old boy."

"Right."

It had been a few days and there were still miles and miles to go. Ahead, by the Sippi River, was supposed to be the city of Broken Rock, within the night's reach at least. But despite brisk progress along the roads the mood was sullen, the saddlebags were getting light, as were rations. Resupplying was a necessity but no one was eager to find out what happened to Broken Rock.

As they came closer to the river, the land seemed to descend into a shallow slope. Little brooks and copses of fragile trees made wrinkles in this otherwise flat landscape. The ground was loose here, the stags treaded on cushioned earth. The air was heavier with moisture, and hot or cold, Chev sweated.

Not a soul was on the road. Occasionally, Chev glanced to his side, and saw what he thought was one of Wermac's shadowed ones crawl out of sight. Chev kept the feeling he was being watched to himself. He was sure if they were, Wermac would know something about it.

It was a relief, then, when they saw another group of a dozen stag riders

It was as though all the knights knew to dismount and embrace each other. Chev would have assumed them close kin if they hadn't all exchanged names. Wermac took the time to whisper in Chev's ear, explaining these men were from an allied tribe, and they were returning from their pilgrimage.

"It has been too long since Wolf and Hawk shared words. Greetings, Erren," Sargon welcomed their leader warmly.

"We are always eager to meet those of the Wolf clan."

After pleasantries were exchanged, a tarp was laid out, and the beefy knight Sargon sat with the elder of the Hawk Clan, tea steaming from both their cups. This was a deeply old man, his tended mustache much thicker than most nightfolk, and he brought more dignity to the armor he wore than power. There was clearly some ceremony that Chev couldn't unravel, but they were quick to pass through the formalities and drill down to business.

"Did you come through Broken Rock? What state was it in?" asked Sargon.

The elderly man responded in a voice that would have once been strong and deep, but now was close to a whisper. "We don't know. We took the long way around, after we saw smoke coming from their direction."

"Smoke," Sargon repeated to himself.

"If you're heading that way, don't expect much."

"We've learned not to. Grainsea and Pock Hollow were pulled apart, laid flat, destroyed down to the brick."

"The dayfolk have gone mad, then."

"And Riverturn... please tell me that place still stands."

"When last we left, it did."

Sargon nodded. "I pray to the ancestors it does. If not, we'll run out of supplies before we reach Manak."

The elderly man let the steam condense on his face. "I don't like the look of this land anymore. It used to be you could venture into the marshes, pick game up right from the ground, and there were dayfolk villages ready to trade in every nook in this land. Now everything's picked clean. The fruits of this land have been stripped bare, the animals hide in their hollows, the trading rocks are empty, and the monsters are forced to hunt one another. They say they're so desperate they'll even try for knights."

Sargon nodded. "We've still got to head for Broken Rock. We have to take our chances, we need supplies."

The elderly man turned away from Sargon for a moment, to gaze into the gray horizon where the sun had long set. "There's another thing, brother. There were rumors out from the west, and I don't know what to make of them. They say a new *Emperor* arises."

That word. That intonation, as though they spoke of the stars falling out of the sky. So *familiar.* It sent a shiver through Chev's spine.

"They say that every decade," said Sargon.

"I know. That's why I almost didn't mention it. But," the elderly man paused to sniff, consider his next words, "with times being as they are, if a new Emperor were to arise, it's going to be now."

"We have our own ideas about that," said Sargon.

"I know you do. I know you do," the old knight nodded thoughtfully before sipping his tea, "But maybe I shall not return home. I think I'll head west instead, see what this man is all about."

"It's a long journey, brother," said Sargon, "You know you might never come back."

"I've not got many years left. The best use I can do is to gamble my life on the hope that this man might be the one to restore justice and peace."

"I see I won't change your mind, but I hope it won't bring war between us," said Sargon.

"I would sooner drive my sword into my own chest than lift it against my brother, of that there's no doubt." The elderly man put his cup down. "It's time we parted ways. Any longer, and you won't reach Broken Rock by dayfall."

"May your ancestors protect you," said Sargon.

"May your ancestors guide your way."

The other group of stag-riders were quick to depart, trotting the way from which Chev and his group had come. It took Sargon and his band a little longer to depart, taking a few minutes to rest as they watched their brothers turn to dots in the distance. Even then, Sargon got to his feet sluggishly with a furrowed brow and an absent frown.

Sargon lumbered past Chev, mumbling something to him in confidence. "I'd rather face an unkillable monster." He wouldn't elaborate what.

"Sargon," Chev called out.

Sargon came to a stop. "What is it, brother?"

"What's this about an Emperor?"

Sargon cleared his throat. "Don't worry yourself about it, brother. Knightly politics are complicated, you're better off not knowing. I wish I didn't."

Varnas was right. It was depressingly predictable. Chev now was well acquainted with the scent of burned, broken cities, the only surprise left was that the place was not entirely flattened. Out from the marshes a blackened shell of a settlement rose, walls crushed like old bones and buildings pulverized by some terrible power. Chev had seen anthills crushed underfoot, and this was reminiscent of that. But there were still roofs, intact streets, places not completely consumed by fire. The place looked like a jagged broken labyrinth.

Sargon would not let indecisive silence fall over the band. He sighed tiredly, then waved his hand. "We'll search for supplies. Pair up, all of you."

It wasn't the city that captured Chev's attention, but the river that flowed behind it. Sparkling, vast and strange, it was the whole width of a lake, the distant shore a tiny black line in the horizon. He was drawn to its shallow banks more than to the broken city. But Wermac walked before him, turning his head to the city.

"Come on. There's gotta be something down there."

"Right."

The city was shattered into disconnected hovels and loose stones. Chev and Wermac had to clamber over a collapsed roof, the tiles slipping out even as they walked over. The streets were littered with detritus, burned wheels, torn fabric, barrels and crates thrown from windows and allowed to shatter atop the ground.

"It's much more intact than the other cities," said Chev.

"Must've not had the time to completely destroy it," said Wermac.

Already, pairs of knights poked around in the ruins, sifting through what looked like garbage. One pair discovered a cellar, and filed down eager for discoveries. Chev and Wermac found a small plaza, the blackened walls so close together it must have been positively claustrophobic when the city still stood. In the middle was a boulder, flat and gray with an impressive crack running through the middle like a bolt of lightning had turned to charcoal upon the surface.

"Guess that's the broken rock," said Wermac and he moved off to explore the surrounding looking for supplies.

Chev's attention was once again pulled to the river. They were on a slight rise which gave a good view of the slope descending to it, ruins like broken steps inviting him down.

Down the slope was Adar, she'd taken off her helmet and bent over something that interested her among the charred ruins. Chev watched her for a moment, not sure what he was looking for in her, but then she lifted her beautiful smooth face and brilliant eyes. They looked at one another for a good, long while, Chev's heart was frozen and beating at the same time. Her moon-shaded hair was tossed lightly by river-soaked wind.

"Really pretty, ain't she?" came a voice from the shadows.

"Huh?" Chev flushed, turned to Wermac.

"The river, the Sippi. When I first saw it, I thought that this was what they called the ocean, and that the other shore was Sunnam."

Chev looked back down the street. Adar had put her helmet back on, and had turned back to picking through the ruins.

"You know Sunnam, right? That's the continent across the ocean. We're on Norram, west is Sunnam. I was a child, I didn't understand Sunnam was a place so far away you couldn't just reach out and touch it."

There was a tremendous crash as Wermac lifted a beam of charred wood out of the ruins, raising a cloud of ash and making a small avalanche of stone. Whatever Wermac's objective, it only left him coughing and spluttering, batting the air to fend off dust. When things cleared, there was nothing of interest.

"Let's head to the river," said Chev.

Wermac scraped the last of the dust and ash from his face, "We're supposed to be foraging."

"This place is burnt to a crisp," said Chev, "We'll sooner find game by the river than food anywhere here."

Wermac frowned, considering whether to stick to his guns or relent. But as he beat his clothes free of dirt, something softened. "Just a little longer. Let's not hang out there forever."

It quickly became clear to Chev why he wanted to spend time by the river. Looking out on the shining eddies, the plane that was such a strange reflection of the night sky, he could only think of how Sana would want to see this. The little brook near where they'd spent their childhood was laughable in comparison to this. If there was a way to take this whole place and unfold in front of Sana's feet, he would.

"So we're looking for game, right?" said Wermac.

Chev had almost forgotten his own excuse. "Yeah. Look for burrows. There might be a hare or two hiding around."

"I sure hope you know what you're doing, forest-man."

Chev let gravity draw him to the shores. It wasn't like the rivers from the Nightlands, the banks were grainy and sandy, and the vegetation grew so thick that it made the river look more narrow than it truly was. Chev went to his knees by the shoreline, hand sifting through mud. Somewhere, he'd find a river stone worthy to bring back to Sana.

"I thought you were foraging," Wermac said, between huffs.

"I am! Just you wait!"

Chev didn't understand Wermac's problem. This marsh was practically alive, he already uncovered a toad that would go well in a stew. It escaped out into the rushes and Chev let it, confident he could pull enough food out from here to feed an army if he wanted.

His hand plunged into clay-like silt, and deep inside he felt something. It almost slipped away, but with lip-chewing concentration he carefully pinched it. Between his two muddy fingers was a little gemstone, rough but when looked at closely held a world of infinite detail. Chev twisted it, dunking it in water, cleaning off stubborn grime and clay.

"Look at what I found!" cried Chev.

"Can you eat it?" Wermac asked.

"Stop being so boring. It's beautiful!"

Chev was ready to run up to where Wermac was, but the young knight had an expression that made Chev shudder and that echoed through him. The young man clutched his sword and looked over Chev's shoulder with an ominous gaze. Chev quickly turned.

A monster rose up from just where Chev had been, from water that seemed far too shallow to contain such a creature. The flat, wide mouth opened, a tumorous tongue slipped out, veined by black, pulsing growths.

"Get out the way!" Wermac charged forward.

Two eyes bulged from the sides of its head, pupils were inhuman slits, face expressionless. It stood taller than Chev on its two short legs. Its tongue again pulsed, tensed, and moved explosively. A whip-like blur raced for Chev's chest.

But Wermac got there first. The knight knocked Chev aside and the beast's toothed tongue slammed into his armored chest instead. A cry rang out with the percussion of a bone-crushing impact. But Wermac stood, braced against the attack, grasped the tongue, and with one brisk arc cut a slice through it. The beast whined, shuddered, and in a flash slipped back into the waters, creating a brisk splash that went still in but seconds.

Wermac collapsed, his chest weighted down by the beast's horrid, veiny tongue.

"Wermac!" Chev cried.

Now limp and powerless, Chev dragged Wermac by the shoulders onto dry land. On the way, Wermac began to weep, shaking at the sight of the fleshy pillar emerging from his chest. When Chev next looked at him, his face was covered with a mucus-like film of sweat, black-ringed eyes wet with despair.

"It got me, Chev. It got me in the heart!"

"Why did you do it?" Chev pounded the dirt next to him, "I didn't ask you to!"

"Don't do this to me! Don't ruin things by being an ass! Please, Chev," a calmness went over him as his grasped Chev's shirt, "take my armor, my weapons, my stag, everything I have, and finish your journey to Manak. The Oracle," Wermac was interrupted by a gush of blood from his mouth, "the Oracle, follow her, Chev, I know in my heart what she'll tell you. Promise me!"

"I'll see her for you," said Chev.

"I know you will."

"Do you want me to pass anything on?"

"No," Wermac shook his head, in jerking labored motions, "They already know everything. I already—I already told them."

Suddenly, the young knight lost his power to move. His body went completely limp but there was still a glimmer of life in his eyes, but slowly that dim light faded and faded until they were dried like any common stone.

Sargon didn't touch the body. Instead, he leaned over and sniffed the dismembered tongue, snorting at it with a mixture of hatred and disgust. "A Xalaminder," he announced, "I wish so badly they didn't grow their tongues back."

What was Chev to do? Tell Sargon how courageous Wermac had been? He didn't need to. Wermac's bloodied sword was evidence enough, just as Chev's dry one was evidence of his inaction. His mind was full of unvoiceable curses at the stupid, brave knight, a tempest of alternating guilt and fury, each feeding into the other. The only way he showed his struggling emotions was how his jawline tensed from clenched teeth.

Why'd you sacrifice yourself for me? Chev wondered, Why? Why?

Varnas sensed Chev's bleak mood. He put a hand on his shoulder and whispered into his ear.

"Don't lose yourself, Chev," were his words of comfort.

Chev didn't know what Varnas meant by that, but the words resonated with him nonetheless. Darin simply glared at Chev from across the crowd of men, making Chev feel once more that he held the blame for the loss of another life. The old man Varnas gave him a few more comforting pats across the shoulders before he disappeared into the gathering.

Every knight had taken off his helmet, each head bowed. Here and there, tears and sighs, but none let himself linger long enough to be overcome with emotion. Two knights delicately stripped the body, placing Wermac's weapons and armor respectfully to the side. As they took off his tunic, an intricate engraving was revealed, radiating out from the center of his chest. His life story was drawn around the black, gaping hole where his heart had been.

Sargon bent forward. His fingers traced the pictures, and he narrated Wermac's life as though he read it. "Wermac, son of Jarvis, born to the Wolf Clan of Aras Meng. Third-born. As a youth descended into a cave to avenge the death of his brother Mingas at the hands of a cockatrice. Fell in love once. Left on his pilgrimage to Manak." Sargon stood, wiped his face. "That's it. Have his body burned. It will not feed the beasts."

Having said his piece, Sargon stepped over the body and walked a few yards to rinse his hands off in a nearby stream. Chev followed him, by the light of the growing pyre for Wermac's burning body the two men talked.

"Sargon... I'm really sorry. He was trying to save me, and I—"

"He knew what he was doing," said Sargon, letting water drain from his face and splash back into the creek. "Not everyone returns from their pilgrimage."

"Sargon..."

"There is one thing you can do," Sargon said, "A man whose life is spared by the sacrifice of another has an obligation to live their life twice over. He gave you his weapons and armor. I hope you'll use them to do great good in this world."

"Of course," Chev nodded, "I would do no less."

Sargon cupped another handful of water, long enough so that the water eventually was still, and Sargon looked into it like he would a mirror.

"Another thing," said Sargon, before Chev would walk away, "We didn't find any supplies this night, so we have to eat your goat."

Chapter Fifteen

In the Shadow of Manak

"IT'S GONNA LOOK real suspicious if you don't let 'em eat that goat," said Varnas.

Ma-ma bent her ear, curious and yet mercifully deaf to Chev's dilemma. What would the goat say if she knew they debated whether she was to live or die?

"I *need* Ma-ma," said Chev, "I could more easily cut my own arm off and have them roast that."

"What did you tell them?"

"What else could I tell them? One of their own died protecting me! I told him what he wanted to hear."

Varnas' mouth and eyes wrinkled with thought. "Hmm... I think I'm noticing a pattern with you."

"Anyways, I bought some time. Asked him if we couldn't wait for next night. Said that was his thought anyway. So I have time to think."

Starlight was let loose in the tent, and she started to wriggle her way over to Ma-ma, like a little doughy ball with arms and legs. She tugged at the locks of Ma-ma's fur, making a clumsy attempt to mount the little goat. Chev and Varnas, momentarily distracted, watched the tiny struggle unfold, punctuated by giggling and drooling.

"It's clear you've not learned your lesson, Chev."

"What lesson?" asked Chev.

"*Any* lesson," Varnas smirked.

Chev twisted to Varnas, giving the old man a dubious glance. "You think I should let them eat Ma-ma?"

"If that's what you've taken from this, you don't know me, boy." Varnas prodded Chev in the chest. "You should've told them Ma-ma's not for eating."

"Oh really?" Chev drew himself up, "How do I tell them that?"

"Make up a better lie. Like Ma-ma's venomous. Or she's got worms eating her up. Anything but another promise you can't keep." Varnas shrugged, sighed, letting his gaze follow as Starlight tumbled over Ma-ma the goat. "But it don't matter that much to me. It's your problem now."

Darin had been lying back, eyes closed, his head on a pack, but he chose this moment to make his contribution. "You all know what I'd do," he drawled, half-asleep.

"We do," said Chev like he was biting back, "and it's not an option."

"Goat's old, Chev. Meat's tough. Practically inedible now. Much better option to give that thing over than those supplies."

"What supplies?" asked Chev.

Darin snorted. "Forgotten already? You were the one that told me. That pack that 'rondack' gave you, whatever that is. It's still practically bursting with food. Been wondering why you've let it go stale beneath the basket."

Sargon was so eager to check the pack he split it open with his knife. Out like a spring bloom came a riot of foodstuffs—jerky, honey-soaked nuts, dry fruit, fine meal. The scent of it drew Chev's stomach into his mouth.

The more Sargon pulled out, the more the pressure pushed out yet more food. Sargon let a handful of oats filter through his hand. The look he gave Chev was not one of gratitude.

"You've been holding out on me," said Sargon.

"I... forgot," Chev told the truth sheepishly.

"You would've saved me a day's sleep if you'd come out with this sooner. But late is better than never. You must really care about that goat."

"She's of real sentimental value," said Chev, "I woulda been devastated if she died. She belonged to my grandma, you know. Looks just like her, too."

Sargon looked deep into Chev's eyes, clearly trying to read something. "Why didn't you just tell me that to begin with? I'll tell you right now that the goat still isn't safe. What you've given me will last until

Riverturn. If that city is gone like the others, then we're eating it, and that's the end of the story." Sargon thrust as much food as he could back in the bag, and then marched out of his tent to the assembled knights. "Breakfast is back on, boys!" he cried out, to much shouting and hollering.

A dried meat and fruit gruel was cooked. The taste was thin but it was filling and full of nutrients which fortified their tired muscles. That dusk, Chev was the toast of the campsite, full of thanks for food but conspicuously incurious about where Chev had gotten it all. The abandon with which these men ate revealed how bad things had gotten. Bowls were licked clean, knights sucked on bones for bits of marrow.

Chev ate too, the sensation of a filling stomach was better than any taste in the whole world. It seemed everyone had come by at least once, to put an arm over Chev's shoulder, to whisper something, sometimes just to give a nudge with some light teasing, other times to provide a brotherly squeeze of the shoulder. When it came to Adar's turn, she knelt by him, smiled pleasantly, and said, "Wermac was right about you, you know."

Chev didn't parse what Adar said. He was distracted by an odd impulse: to lean forward and kiss her, to take her by her lips. He acknowledged the feeling, but he didn't follow it, reduced to staring blankly at her like an idiot.

When it came time to get moving, the band did so with considerably more pep. The knights practically bounced atop their saddles, agitating to get to Riverturn in good time. Chev had just finished packing up the tent and getting his things together when Sargon approached him with a bundle in arms.

"Wermac's things," Sargon said, "I'll help you get suited up."

As it turned out, Wermac's padded jerkin and chainmail were a perfect fit for Chev. At least that's what Sargon told him, dressing him up between boisterous flattery. With all that heavy gear on, Chev felt like a swollen bear, his arms stiff and body top-heavy. Sargon either didn't notice Chev's discomfort, or he chose to ignore it.

"The armor's one thing, but it's the arms that make one a knight, Chev. It defines his role as a hunter of monsters. Here," Sargon's fingertips grazed over four weapons, "The ax, for beasts of thick and scaly hide. The lance, to charge enemies atop one's stag. The javelin, for cowardly foes. And finally, the sword. The noblest of weapons. For monsters disguised on two legs." Sargon frowned at Chev's blade. "I suppose you'd want to use your father's blade."

Chev nodded, "I don't know how to ride, either."

"I shall hold Wermac's stag then, until you're ready for it. Adar'll teach you."

Chev's heart pounded, "Sargon, I'm not sure that's a good idea."

"Don't be a fool. Just because she is who she is doesn't mean she's a bad rider." Sargon suddenly spotted something amiss with Chev's outfit. He pulled on Chev's chainmail, straightening to better suit Sargon's tastes. "There. Now you look like one of us. I'm sure you'll carry yourself likewise soon enough. The armor gets lighter with your back straight, boy!"

Chev straightened up like he was caught doing something wrong, and found Sargon was right. The weight eased off his shoulders, but now he felt rigid and restrained.

"Good, good. Let's get going, while Riverturn is still standing."

Adar moved forward on her saddle to give room for Chev to sit behind her. He was now used to mounting stags, and had no difficulty with that. It was the proximity to Adar, which gave him intense discomfort, as he wrapped his arms around her waist, and felt the heat of the skin beneath. Chev was quietly thankful for the thick padding of the armor.

She twisted around to whisper to him, "Don't worry. Silvertail is strong, used to two riders, and I know how to handle him."

"Thanks," said Chev, unwilling to say Silvertail was not his primary concern.

With a signal from Sargon, their march began. They followed the Sippi river, along a path well away from any marshes. Chev was thankful for that, because Chev saw those Xalaminder eyes even in the lowest, muddiest puddle now. They trotted over a trickling stream draining into the river, and Chev watched that even more carefully. Every little shiny stone seemed to move with predatory intent.

On the way, at irregular intervals, Adar would give some pointers. "There's no mount anywhere better than a knight's stag, I'd say. All you need to do is give the gentlest reminders of your will. A slight pull on the reins, a little pressure of your thigh on the saddle, and they'll do the rest."

Chev did his best to listen, but he kept getting distracted. Ma-ma, as she usually did, managed to keep up hopping on her stumpy legs, and sometimes Chev caught a glimpse of her, biting his lower lip, and knowing full well that her fate rested on Riverturn, and by extension so did Starlight's.

They made very good progress that night, and set camp on a slight rise, flanked by a wall of shrubbery and trees, and by the next morning near half the supplies Chev had given them were gone. Chev silently prayed they'd eat a little slower, so that they wouldn't look to Ma-ma like she would be their next meal.

As they readied themselves to leave, Adar stood by her stag, patting the saddle with a smile plastered on her face. It took a moment to piece together what she had in mind.

"Oh no," said Chev.

"Oh yes."

"Please don't make me."

"If you weren't listening it's your own fault. We of the Wolf Clan teach children to swim by throwing them into the Sippi."

"I've got too much on my mind. I'll mess up your stag, I know it."

"There's no way you can mess up Silvertail," Adar stroked the stag's muzzle, giving him a brief, benevolent smile. "Come on. There's still a lot to know about being a knight. Mount up. You sit on the front of the saddle this time and I'll ride behind."

That, at least, Chev could do. He took Silvertail's reins like he remembered, and jumped to throw his leg over. Chev nearly slipped—the stag was unstable, his trotters bounced across the ground in agitation, Chev felt he might be thrown off any second. Only Adar's gentle hand and light whisper calmed the stag. He didn't hear what she said, her hair made a wondrous distraction, an icy waterfall by the stag's milky white fur.

"Alright, I'm getting on there with you," said Adar. She mounted up, squeezed two arms around Chev's waist, and pulled herself close to him. Her breath was hot on Chev's neck, his stomach turned somersaults.

"You remember how to make him move, right?" asked Adar.

Chev struggled to remember, "Yeah, you slap his flanks with your feet."

"No, that's how you make him *gallop*—!"

Silvertail raced forward, leaping towards the horizon. Chev finally felt the stag's true power, for all the weight on his back Chev and Adar proved to be an effortless burden. The two riders, on the other hand, had to struggle to keep from being thrown off. Wind whipped around Chev's face and the landscape moved past at a blistering rate.

"Stop grabbing the neck! You're panicking him!" Adar cried out.

"Where am I supposed to grab?" Chev called into the wind.

"The reins, dummy! The reins!"

He grasped them, and now, a flimsy piece of leather was all that kept Chev from a tumble and multiple broken bones.

"What do I do now!" Chev cried.

"Pull it gently!"

"Pull it?"

"Gently!"

Chev arched his back to pull, the stag whined and made a complete stop. The two riders flew out of the saddle over Silvertail's head to slam into the ground. They tumbled like two sacks of rocks, rolling over one another, and made for two dirt-crusted figures in the rough weeds. Slowly, Chev got onto his elbows and crawled to Adar, who was writhing in the dust, her face pinched by pain.

"Are you OK?" Chev asked.

"It hurts!" Adar cupped her side, speaking through ground teeth.

"Let me look."

Adar nodded. It seemed natural at that moment to support her with his arms around her, if only because it was easier to get to the wound that way.

"This spot?"

"Don't touch it! It's tender."

"Give me a second." Chev unbuttoned Adar's padded jacket, just enough to peel it back and see the spot on her side revealing in the process a glimpse of bare, flat stomach. He touched her ribs gently, "Nothing's broken. I think you just fell onto a rock and got a bad bruise."

"How can you tell?"

"I just know these things. Been out hunting a lot, seen a lot of broken bones."

"Thanks."

And that was that. Chev made no move to cover Adar's stomach back up, and Adar didn't bother either. They were both aware of how close they were—Adar had wrapped her arm around Chev's neck, and Chev's hand felt the warmth of Adar's skin. Something magnetic was vibrating between the two them. Had they both had hands on their daggers staring each other down, there would be no less tension. But they had no weapons, just their stone-like paralyzed hands. Adar's expression fluttered, brows and eyelids like little hummingbird wings, hovering in indecision, she licked her lips and looked up at Chev. Just then, they both heard a faint noise which broke the spell.

Adar was the first who managed to speak. "Is that... is that a child crying?"

Chev immediately reacted. "Starlight!" he whispered. He practically tossed Adar to the side as he pulled away and made for the basket.

It would take Adar a moment to crawl back on her feet. Chev hoped it would be enough time to open the basket, calm Starlight, and return her to her hiding place before Adar could ask any questions. Chev quietly rocked and cooed at the little girl; the loudest sound was Adar's clinking mail as she struggled to her feet a few yards away.

"Look Starlight, it's me!"

The girl snuffled, her furry cheeks were wet with tears. Thinking quickly, Chev puffed out his cheeks. That did the trick. Starlight yelped with delight, and just as Adar wavered onto her legs Chev shoved the basket lid down and retied it.

"That *was* a child," said Adar, staring at Chev.

"Uh," there was no lie that Chev could summon, "Damn."

"*That* is what was in the basket?" Adar said, pointing, "A baby?"

She moved purposefully toward it, slowed only a little by her pain giving her an awkward gait. Chev tried to block her way.

"Please don't, Adar!"

"What are you hiding?" Adar made a move to push Chev aside, and Chev had to step back but kept firmly between Adar and the basket. Knowing Chev wouldn't be moved, she demanded: "Explain. And no lying this time!"

"Adar," Chev swallowed, shutting his eyes in a momentary meditation, "There are things I can tell you and things I can't tell you."

"Tell me first what you can," Adar lifted her chin and folded her arms, readying herself to judge Chev's excuses.

Chev's voice a half-whine. "You are right, there is a child in there. And she's the reason I've come to the Daylit Lands, to see the oracle. No, she's not mine. But she..." Chev paced a little, thinking of how to word things, "She needs my help, you know. She would have died without me. And now I'm stuck with her."

"Tell me now what you *can't* tell me," Adar asked.

Chev had a puzzled look on his face. "I uh... I can't tell you."

"You're a dummy, Chev, I know you can't! I'm asking what *question* can't you answer."

Chev nodded slowly, thinking he now understood. "I can't tell you what she is. I can't tell you how I found her. I can't tell you the nature of our curse."

Adar folded her hands as she paced slowly, her mouth quivering with some explosive emotion. The only way to keep it sealed was to tuck her lip beneath her teeth. "I hate lying, Chev!" she cried out. "You put me in a really bad position, you know. I'll pretend like I never heard this. Just be warned, if anyone finds out, I won't defend you. Let's get back to the camp and try to act like nothing ever happened."

Chev nodded. And so, quietly, sullenly, they got their things together, mounted the stag, and trotted at a sluggish pace back to the knight's camp. They could soon see some of them waiting in the distance.

"Another thing, Chev," said Adar, "when I became I knight I took a man's name and gave up the things that made me a woman. There's certain things I can't pursue. I know you understand."

"And I have a woman promised to me in the Nightlands. Her name is Sana. She's part of the reason I'm here."

"Good. Now that we know where we both stand, let's turn a new leaf. It's good to meet you, brother Chev."

Chev understood what Adar was getting at. "It's good to meet you, sister Adar."

Everyone was waiting for the scout's report. Chev had Ma-ma tucked into his arm, and he scratched her hairy little head. She was of little comfort right now. Chev knew if they didn't get the sort of news they were hoping for, it was her same hairy little head that would be on the chopping block.

"Please come back," Chev whispered to himself, as quiet as he could manage, "please come back, please come back."

With Chev's heart in his throat, he watched the scouts crest the hill and trot down a winding, tortured path. It took them so long Chev felt they might've been tormenting him had they not dismounted just in front of Sargon. The knights hit the ground, and walked to the straight-lipped knight commander.

"Well?" Sargon boomed, "What's the word?"

A knight stepped forward, helmet tucked beneath his armpit. He announced, "Riverturn still stands."

Chev couldn't help it. He sighed out loud, "Oh thank the ancestors!"

Chev half-feared the report was some joke, or mistake, especially as he spotted plumes of smoke in the distance. But it spouted from chimneys and chimneys alone. From a distance, the city looked sprawled out like a jumble of stone walls and paths, fanning out like a petrified landslide into a harbor. The dayfolk city made a proud image into the sky, but it cast a distorted, ghostly impression in the chopping waters of the Sippi. It was as if the reflection showed what might have been.

"Riverturn stands!" Sargon spoke in awe. Like Chev, it seemed he wouldn't believe it until he saw it. "Come on. Let's get to shelter before dayfall."

If Chev could have reach Ma-ma from the back of Adar's stag, he would've hugged and kissed her hairy goat brow. Instead, he could only beam at the grass-chewing goat, like he'd won some victory for her. "Looks like you get to live, girl."

It seemed like the stags trotted a little more energetically, and for a moment Chev could have believed nothing could go wrong from this moment. But sprawled out along the flat lands leading to the gates was a shantytown near as broad as the city. Haphazard and newly built, the materials had been foraged from broken stone and charred wood, heaps of woven weeds and torn sod made for roofs. The nightfolk residing here milled in doorways and alleys, alongside families and strangers, watching with absent interest as the knights wound through cluttered, muddied streets.

It was hunger and hatred in each pair of eyes. Judging from their tattered clothes and canvas-like skin, a goat and sword might as well have been silk and jewels.

Fortunately, none dared approach as they went to the gates.

Guards flanked the entrance to the city. Sargon descended from his saddle, approached with the sort of authority that weapons and armor gave any man.

"Entrance into the city," announced Sargon.

"Pilgrims only," said the guards.

"We're knights, as you can well see. Has this city avoided the fate of Broken Rock, or is that coming?"

One guard looked to another, and the one on the left ground the end of his spear into the ground. "They camped outside the city, they did. But then they moved on. Dayfolk must've decided the fight ain't worth it."

"So an army won't come in daytime, burn Riverturn to the ground, is that what you're saying?"

Guard nodded to the shantytown behind the band of knights. "They seem to think so."

Sargon seemed to like that answer. "Thanks."

The rest of the knights dismounted, and lead their stags by the reins through the city gates.

Adar whispered to Chev, "Have you ever been in a proper city?"

"No," said Chev.

"You're in for a treat," Adar then sighed, "but it's still a moth to Manak's fire."

The street sloped upward, and buildings erupted like orderly pillars out from the ground. Stories tall, brick and rock and wood masterfully shaped into civilization's unnatural terrain. Chev couldn't imagine anything short of an army of giants pulling these structures out from the earth. And in every street, a riot of activity. Markets, processions of stalls, inhabited by women, men and children, haunted by stranger figures of shadowed garb. Armed men stood by, slug-eyed despite the wonders about them. The smell though—the smell was awful. A knife-thrust of feces and rot straight into the nose, and it seemed to emanate beneath every street.

"Why did this cesspit survive," Sargon muttered, mildly repulsed the life around him.

Each knight put his hand on his pouch. Chev thought it might be some strange superstition, but when he felt for his, it was unexpectedly absent.

Adar noticed Chev patting himself down. "It's already gone."

"Did I drop it?"

Adar smirked. Chev imagined her eyes alighting with humor beneath the helmet. "You are from the forest, aren't you? Someone stole it."

"Stole it?" Chev shrugged. "It was just a few plats."

"Sure. Just keep an eye on your goat."

"My goat? What would they want with—"

A bleat erupted from behind, Chev twisted in alarm. A few dirt-faced children, having tossed a rope around Ma-ma's head, struggled in a mortal game of tug-of-war. Chev jumped after them until they scurried off, the urchins filtering through the alleyways like bugs down sewer grates.

Chev checked Ma-ma. The old goat gave him an affectionate lick, and after a few relieved pats they rejoined the rest of the band.

There was a fort within the city. A tower more like, squat and stone, it looked as though a mountain could break atop it. The knights took their stags into a wooden shack nearby and settled them with hay and water. The tower's interior bore only the lightest resemblance to that tavern outside of Pilgrim's Pass. There were tables and chairs with men deep in drinks in every corner, but there was no music, no laughter. Men kept to themselves in a stubbornly maintained icy atmosphere, where noises above whispers would reverberate like shouts. As if fearing to break this delicate mood, the knights filed in silently, and slumped around one of the big tables. A few knights raised fingers; this was apparently a signal, as a woman drifted toward them to serve frothing mugs from an over-sized platter.

"Why's everyone so quiet?" whispered Chev, to Adar.

Adar shrugged before dipping her lips into a frothy mug.

Varnas had somehow taken the seat next to Chev. He leaned over and grumbled something only for the Chev's ears. "Don't like this place."

"You don't like anything, Varnas," said Chev, "but now that you mention it, I don't like this place either."

It was quiet supper. For some reason, it felt natural that everyone remained quiet. It helped to digest the journey somehow. It was only after eating when some humor returned. Knights fell on each other, slapping shoulders and ribbing with each other in a way which reminded Chev of how the men acted back home, once they'd come back from their hunts.

Adar nudged Chev, telling him, "There's a room upstairs, last one on the left. Better take your stuff up there too."

They both glanced at the basket. Chev understood, and giving Adar a quiet thanks, he took both the basket and Ma-ma into the designated room.

Away from prying eyes, Chev finally felt ready to take the girl out from the basket. She was dead asleep, as she usually was at night, and instinctively she reached out to grasp Chev tightly by the collar.

Chev rubbed her soft little head. It was luxuriant, Chev found himself wishing he could make her into a pillow.

The door came open. Chev moved to squirrel the girl away before seeing who'd walked in.

"Oh. Varnas. Darin."

They both eased their gear off their shoulders to drop onto the wood floors. Darin immediately claimed his corner, while Varnas came to give Starlight a good head rubbing.

"That's a good girl," he cooed at her. "That's a good girl!"

Darin tisked in disapproval, but he chose not to say anything more.

Chev glanced out the window, out into a graying sky. "Manak. It's so close it itches."

Varnas had to tear himself away from Starlight, reminded he had something to do with his supplies. "Oh? Yes, yes. Gotta worry about the return journey now. We won't have a band of knights on the way back."

Chev's hand brushed Starlight's fur, and he gave a benevolent smile at her sleeping face. "It's a shame, isn't it? You know, a part of me hopes we don't reach Manak."

"Why?" Varnas lifted his head, like an animal suddenly aware of something odd, "Because this journey has been so much fun? Well, we can dance with rocs and Xalaminders at home, too."

"That's not what I meant."

"And I know it, too. Well," Varnas shrugged, "here's an option. You can accept your curse, go back to the woods, raise the little twerp. You don't even have to see a know-nothing 'oracle' to tell you that."

"Or you could leave the creature here," said Darin, not even bothering to open his eyes from where he reposed.

"I can't do that," Chev told Darin.

"Why not? Wasn't this what you were looking for? A standing dayfolk city. Don't know where else you'll find one in these cursed lands."

Chev gripped Starlight a little tighter, she made a carefree burbling sound. "Just because it's safe now doesn't mean anything."

"Chev," Darin sighed, finally deigning to open his eyes, "It was mad of you to give all those supplies for the life of a damn old goat. And now you'll toss yourself overboard for a baby you can't even take care of. For all these burdens you throw on your back, none of them have a lick to do with us. You've never said a thing about your responsibility to me or Varnas, and we're the two people that have done the most to keep you alive this whole journey. But no matter. Honest, I don't care what you do. Kid's your problem."

Chev drew himself up, and paced to the window, as though he needed fresh air. "Sometimes, Darin, you remind me of a friend I had. His name was Tobi."

Darin shifted in his corner, so his body faced the wall. "Well, this Tobi sounds like a smart guy, then. If you'd listened to him, maybe you would have found something for yourself already instead of wasting your time on fool errands."

"Manak is so close," Chev spoke into the light wind whipping the tower, and into the horizon which held the ancient city, "there's no reason I shouldn't go now. Right, Varnas?"

Varnas shuddered with annoyance. "Ah, hell Chev, why you askin' me?"

"So you agree with Darin, then?" said Chev, "You think it's a waste of time too?"

"I already told you, half-a-hundred times, I don't think you're getting what you want from Manak. It's those knights that want you to go. They got some designs on you."

Chev turned from the window. "The knights...? What do you mean?"

"It's a feeling I get," answered Varnas, cross-legged, casting a thoughtful eye to the wall. "After that young one died, I had this feeling. These knights, they live in their histories. Roaming around, fighting for some empire that doesn't exist. That's liable to make 'em act strange. Start seeing things only they can see."

"Don't be ridiculous. Tell me one mad thing they've done. They're as rational as we are," said Chev.

"You say," Varnas nodded at Chev, "as you wear their armor, wield their weapons, decorate your body with their art. Probably got cozy up to that lady knight, too. Chev, you can't see what we're seeing. But I'll tell you now, boy, if they can dream up an old empire, they can dream up a lot more'n that!"

A shudder through the tower. Knocking, shoving, shaking, shouting. Like it emerged from the floorboards.

"Sounds like a fight," said Varnas.

The three men grabbed their weapons and watchfully descended to the lower floor. It was Sargon they found, his shoulders square to a new band of knights who had come while Chev had been gone. With two groups that had taken both sides of the tavern, there was the atmosphere of impending battle but only two swords were drawn: Sargon's, and another knight's, equally big and imposing.

"Let me speak my piece," said this new, strong knight, "I have that right."

"I wouldn't refuse," Sargon replied, "Let everyone hear your falsehoods."

After nodding in a kind of gruff appreciation, the knight put one foot on a chair, and addressed the sea of hostile faces. "Wolf Clan! I am Val, of the Dolphin. I only come to give you good news. A new Emperor has arisen, the one who will unite round-ear and pointed-ear, and the kingdoms of night and day. He makes his throne in the west, in the greatest of the dayfolk cities, the city of Sunset. I don't ask for your faith. I only come with proof." Val, knight of the Dolphin Clan, boomed: "Peace in the west. That's my proof."

"The war is going westward," shouted one of the Wolf knights.

"What a stupid thing to say. Val, you say? Of the Dolphin Clan?" Sargon spat, and even that carried weight as it splattered to the ground. "Peace in the west? It's just as my comrade said: they're done here, and now it's the west's turn. The armies march downriver."

Val leaned forward toward Sargon, so that the chair he had his knee on creaked under the weight. It was all to unleash these words: "The new Emperor will stop the dayfolk armies."

The Wolves were loud with jeers, an appalled chorus. Val raised his hands for quiet.

"Don't matter what you think. Mark my words, this Emperor will do all and more. He knows the dayfolk better'n anyone."

"I don't like what you're saying. Dare I ask how he knows dayfolk so well?" Sargon asked.

Val narrowed his eyes at Sargon. "Because he's advised by one."

Even Chev, with little invested in either side, found himself on the tips of his toes. And the reaction that reverberated through the wolves was a shockwave of silence, heralded by wordless, open mouths.

Sargon stepped forward toward Val, his whole attention focused on every inch of his face. Only a steady pair of eyes met his. Sargon asked, in a voice quiet with amazement, "Your Emperor... consorts with dayfolk?"

"How else would he rule night and day?" Val said, "The people of the sun deserve justice too."

Sargon's already powerful, snake-like veins pulsed, and his eyes, already bulging, seemed to pop out further from his head just to get a better sight of this man. They came so close they nearly touched nose to nose, and still Val refused to move. "You shouldn't have told such a thing," said Sargon, "Only one of great virtue can be Emperor."

"And he *is*," Val replied, "It's that same virtue that demands he involve himself in dayfolk affairs."

"If what you say is true," Sargon came imperceptibly closer, so subtly it was impossible to say by how much, "then the ancestors will protect you from my sword."

As way of challenge, Sargon lifted his blade.

Val smirked. "I relish the opportunity."

The swords crashed between the two men, metallic thunder fell on all ears. The fight hadn't even begun, but even this test of strength was intense. Weapons locked, there was a struggle for dominance between gritted teeth. At some unchosen moment, both men released, springing from each other to bounce back into melee. Now they fought, clansmen on both sides watching from each side of the room.

There was no time to test one another's guard. They danced between tables, bounced in the tight confines of the room, expertly using chairs and stools to keep a good distance from one another. Their battle rhythm was like two crash waves, competing tides trying to wash out the other. One blow deflected, the next thrust deeper, only to be responded by a cunning counter-attack. These two men weren't just strong, they were strategists as well.

Peace was simply a pause between attacks. Val kicked a stool at Sargon, Sargon blocked, slicing it lengthwise with his heavy broadsword. Val rolled in to attack from beneath.

Val must have been confident he'd caught Sargon off-guard, but as his sword arced out Sargon knocked it aside with a kick. The blade bounced off Sargon's chainmail, but Val already had a foot planted in Sargon's gut. Barely acknowledging the strike, Sargon tried to spear him like one might a fish.

The blade shuddered into a wood floor as Val rolled out the way. It was deft somersault for a man so large, his sword already in position when he was on his feet. Sargon both retrieved his blade and tightened his face in annoyance, as though it were part of the same muscle movement.

"You're too slow," said Val.

"You're too lucky," retorted Sargon.

Val's eye twitched to something, as if he thought of a sudden plan. He launched himself from the ground and pounced of a stool, so that he flew through the air toward Sargon. Issuing a battle-cry, Sargon's blade should have been so low he would never have the time to defend himself. But he did. Sargon shifted slightly, and a razor edge sliced Val's legs.

The man plummeted like a bird torn from its wings. The cut was deep, and the blood which seeped through the chainmail gave the appearance of rust. Sargon, in an act of cool triumph, wiped down the sword and spun it back into its scabbard.

"Good fight," said Sargon.

"Seems you've proved me a poor champion for the Emperor," said Val, using his blade like a crutch to his feet, "but all you've done is delay the inevitable."

"The battlefield will have to wait, Val. I have many knights on their pilgrimage. I'd sooner drown in the Sippi than have novices fight my battles."

"Send someone west, to Sunset. Anyone who sees the Emperor will be convinced of his claim. I know it."

"Val," Sargon leaned forward, "There is no possibility the Emperor would break the laws of his own Empire. If I send a knight west, it'll be to put an end to this madness. For now, scurry off, and stay silent about your 'emperor'. It's hard enough to relax without you yammering your blasphemies."

The knights went to their respective tables, though with a cautious reluctance to turn their backs on one another. Chev twisted to look at that Varnas and Darin, leaning against the corridor.

"That look on your face, Chev," Varnas said, "I do not like it."

"What if—"

Varnas shook his head and his sparse gray beard. "You know it can't be, Chev. You know it can't. Best put that whole thing outta mind."

But the churning in Chev's head just wouldn't die. The idea had already been planted, and now it grew and grew, and Varnas saw it too. As they left Riverturn, the old trapper looked at Chev with some despair now. As the band marched over hill and trudged through swamp, it was not north, to Manak, that Chev looked, but west, where the last strokes of the sun faded to cinders.

The Emperor. The Emperor. It can't be...

It was so unlikely. The chance was so slim, but that made it all the more irresistible. Soon, Chev felt he couldn't return to the Nightlands without knowing for sure.

Adar, riding the stag next to Chev, patted his knee. "Look! In the distance! Can you see?"

Chev squinted north. An enormous shape loomed, like giants had carved a temple out from a mountain. It was impossibly tall, and if Chev hadn't looked closer he might've thought it was one of those storm clouds that piled impossibly high into the sky.

"You know what that is, don't you? *Manak!*"

Chapter Sixteen
There Are Only Questions

IT BECAME IMPOSSIBLE not to look at the city. The stags marched north, and the city climbed into the sky. Massive, blockish buildings of imposing breadth, slopes like mountainsides ending in plateaus that could hold towns. It was a structure of geographic scale, and though Chev could see it with his naked eyes it felt no closer.

Between the knights and Manak roared the Sippi river. The banks here were muddy, and jumbled piers and stilted shacks clung to them as best they could. Muddy-haired nightfolk dangled their feet from high places—rooftops, the ends of piers, porches—and they gave gap-toothed grins to the knights and incomprehensible gossip to each other.

"We'll rest here," announced Sargon, "gotta wait for a boat anyway."

It gave Chev and Varnas a chance to get their bearings, and unburden themselves of awe for the thing that lay across the river. "How is that a city and not a mountain?" Chev asked.

Varnas nodded. "I'd say if we went home right now, it'd be worth it. Just to see *that*."

"For a city full of Hlogas' it would be too big," Chev said.

"These civilized folk have fallen far, to go from *that* thing to piles o' brick on the ground."

"Maybe because in a million years you couldn't hope to tear that thing down."

"Maybe so. Turns out our friend Tobi was right. Nothing does hold a candle to Manak. Now," Varnas sniffed, "I'm just trying to puzzle out where everyone *lives*."

"The empire that built that must've really been great. Goes to show what we're capable of doing if we put aside our differences."

Varnas' mouth slipped to one edge of his face. "Not sure about that."

"Varnas, won't you stop—"

"Now, now boy," Varnas raised his hand. "I know what you're thinking. You think ol' Varnas doesn't trust nothing, always has to poke a hole in anything he sees. That building over there, sure, could be built with great cooperation. But great evil also gets things done. I look at that thing, something crawls up my spine. I don't like it."

"It's a ruin, they said," Chev pointed out, "Monster infested. Maybe that's what you're feeling."

"Maybe so. And maybe not."

Through the mists came a boat, a long, open vessel that bobbed to the strong and relentless current of the Sippi. Two boatmen on fore and aft expertly glided the ship along one of the piers. Without being told, the knights seemed to know this vessel was for them. They got up and, one by one, mounted the vessel, the stags following behind.

Chev knew rivers and lakes, but nothing he ever encountered in the Nightlands couldn't be forded or swum across. And just like he'd never seen a river quite as broad and deep as the Sippi, he'd never needed, let alone *seen*, a boat. It seemed as unnatural to board such a thing as it would be to mount a log, and even putting a foot on it, he feared it might slip out from under him and throw him into the water.

Chev took a bench, and Varnas and Darin took the seats next to him. He faced an oddly satisfied Sargon and an Adar, smiling even as she wrung her hands in a nervous ritual.

"First time in Manak?" asked Sargon.

All three of the tribals nodded, eagerly as though this would relieve them of discomfort.

"Of course. Look who I'm asking. It's a city of canals, you know. Each district mounted on a plinth of its own—like little plateaus. Bridges like you've never seen connect each one. They say you couldn't come up with something like Manak if you've never seen it. Makes you wonder what the place was like before it was a ruin."

The boatmen pushed off. Chev chafed on his seat—this new sensation, with the world sliding from beneath, was at once uncomfortable and alarming, and went straight to his bowels and gut.

"Don't worry," Sargon leaned forward. "You know something's wrong when the stags are afeared. And look, the beasts are stoic as ever."

The stags were given something to chew and looked on the retreating shore as though this were nothing remarkable. They seemed intelligent as far as animals went, and so Chev decided to trust Sargon. He still had to close his eyes, waiting for his stomach to stop churning.

It wasn't clear when the Sippi ended and Manak began. All Chev knew was the chill as the shadows of the ancient city covered him, like he could feel those old, wet stones. The walls of this place were alive with vines and moss, eating at the old engravings that covered each inch.

They told a story—a story that was losing ground to time, erased by the elements—but there were stretches where it could be read. There were runes, an epic's worth of them, but so strange in form, and so faded, that they were impossible to decipher. The images were what captured Chev. Some beheld grinning fiends, sharp teeth ear-to-ear, faced by knights whose still faces and raised swords they opposed. Others were more domestic, nightfolk in their homes, carrying on a long-lost way of life.

One carving was of a male and female, not nightfolk. Their image held impressions of shaggy manes, their posture proud, their arms wrapped in chains.

Chev pointed. "Dayfolk?"

Sargon shrugged. "Dunno. Never seen one."

Chev let that couple pass by, but he continued watch it, as though thinking through a puzzle without a solution.

And when Chev thought about it, he decided Varnas was right, something *was* wrong about this place. It was a smell—rotten vegetation. And a feeling—like things were watching from the top, and turning their heads just before he could get a good view. It only started to weigh on Chev that it would take an immense and terrible power to have transplanted these mountains into this swamp.

Like lice on a lion, some nightfolk had built a settlement here. The canal ended with haphazard jetties and shacks, and a steep, dubious set of stairs cut into the walls. It was here the boatmen guided the little vessel, tying themselves to a rotted little pile.

A city within a city. That was the only way to describe it. Atop the eroded steps were hundreds of little shacks arranged into their own little streets, laughable even when compared to Riverturn. They stood like broken teeth, each with gaps and uneven roofs, crowned by hay, wooden slats, even boats and carts, anything that would make do as a shelter. Sewage trickled freely in rivulets, bursting out over the edge into the canal.

"What a—"

"Cesspit," Adar interrupted Chev, "The best nightfolk builders are dayfolk."

"I used to live under a tree," Chev released this sort of short laugh, like he couldn't believe what he was looking at. "That's starting to look pretty good."

"The difference is this place is nobody's home. Look," Adar gestured at the city's inhabitants. Nightfolk, every single one. Sick, coughing, huddled together as though this would provide shelter in this swamp-city. "They're all here to see the Oracle. Thousands of people, sick or cursed, all without hope. And the Oracle only sees a few every night."

Chev twisted his head in alarm. "You're not saying—"

"No," Adar shook her head. "You're with us. That's a knight's privilege, to see the Oracle as soon as they come. But just once, and only once." Adar winked. "What I'm saying is you'll see the Oracle tonight."

Chev looked out onto the shantytown. "I don't think I could stay longer than that."

"Chev," Adar, paced away, biting her lip, "our pilgrimage requires us to defend this city for a year and one night. So yes. You get to leave."

"But you don't."

Adar nodded. "It's just a year. And then you're a true knight. That's the whole point in coming. I don't care about seeing the Oracle at all, I don't have anything to ask her. That's why we need to see her, because I need you to find your answers." Adar's eyes glinted enigmatically. "I hope you get your curse lifted."

"Me too." Chev, for some reason, couldn't face Adar. He had his back turned, captivated by a landscape of ruins: above the canals was a broken city, a pile of masonry so completely flattened it had its own stark, strange beauty. "Adar, I don't think I would've made it without you or your knights."

"That may be something to bear in mind once you see the Oracle," said Adar. It was an enigmatic answer, and Chev was still puzzling it out when Sargon suddenly approached.

"Come," said Sargon, "the Oracle is expecting us. I'm sure you have your own questions."

It wasn't all hovels and shacks. Deeper into Manak, Chev saw the ragged remains of what used to be a plaza, and patterns of streets pointed to a ziggurat in the distance. There was a scraggly, disheveled mob, milling about in an awkward, disjointed line peppering down the temple's sides. Chev couldn't imagine a more fitting place for an Oracle.

Sargon, walking beside Chev, sighed at the view. "The Grand Temple. Used to be the center of the Empire. Now its authority doesn't even extend past these city walls. You're lucky, you know. It takes years for a new arrival to get to see the Oracle."

"It's because you're a knight. Isn't it?" asked Chev.

Sargon shook his head. "No. It's because *you're* a knight. That armor—it suits you. It's extraordinary, how you grew into it."

Chev wasn't sure what he was getting at, but he nodded anyway. "I guess so."

"I guess so!" Sargon laughed, gave Chev a friendly shove. "Do me a favor, and act the part of a man who has killed some monsters."

It was the end of a long journey, but the trudging up the stairs was quite the conclusion. The knights dragged themselves up each step, their only source of energy remaining was knowing respite was so close. They passed by petitioners, a whole line of them, each one in murmured conversation, or introspective gazing at the stars. Round-ears and pointed-ears alike, frozen in their endless procession, watched by knights just like Adar and Sargon. Chev gathered the warriors he'd been traveling with would soon take their own spaces on the ziggurat's steps, statuesque sentinels with no purpose but to stand and keep order.

It seemed a strange and terrible fate.

After what seemed like hours of muscle-aching effort, Chev finally reach the top. It was such a relief that Chev felt like throwing himself to the ground and sleeping right in the open air. But the portal to the temple proper called out to him, festooned with carvings of proud knights and warriors. It was the ultimate reward, promise of a resolution.

Darin, Varnas, and the rest of the knights caught up. It may have been Chev's imagination, but the basket he slung over his back was heavy with movement. Perhaps Starlight was just as excited to get things over with.

Chev was ready. He waited for some sort of sign from the others, permission to go in. All seemed ready, lined up by the entrance. Except for Varnas.

Chev went to him, to his shoulder. "You aren't coming with us?"

"Nah." Varnas brushed off the question, "Pretty much know what's gonna happen already. Go ahead."

"You sure? You might never get this chance. Did you want me to ask them something?"

"Yeah. I want you to ask her your stupid question. Now get going so we can go home."

"Right," Chev said, facing the massive archway, "No more excuses. It's time to end this journey."

They entered a massive, shadowed hall. The echoes of footsteps carried with them the sounds of ancient voices. The walls, covered with murals of the old empire, knights arrayed in battle against one another, pulled the Wolf Clan's legends to the present. At the end of the hall, a withered figure sat on a stone throne, her feet barely long enough to touch the floor.

"How do I do this?" whispered Chev to Sargon, as though approaching some alien obstacle.

"Don't worry yourself. Let me do the talking," said Sargon.

It was an endless corridor, every pillar blanketed by history: nameless kings and gods all warring in their forgotten feuds. Armies clashed, cities built, only to fall and be rebuilt once more, maps of constellations long out of date. And overseeing it all was the strangest crone Chev had ever seen. A woman whose wrinkles and twisted back belied undreamed years. Her head was heavy with silver braids, twisted like ropes over her shoulders, ending in knots and beads. She struggled to open the folds of her eyes.

Even the bold Sargon slowed in light of her presence. At some undefined point, he came to his knee.

"Oracle of Manak! Holder of ancient secrets, heir of the Great Folk, she whose mind wanders the stars, I come with new pilgrims to honor you and knights to guard the temple."

The woman pointed her head toward Chev, in a slow, almost creaking movement.

"Is this the candidate you have brought?"

"Yes," said Sargon, "I—"

Before Sargon could finish, Chev went to his knee, so forcefully the sound of steel on stone rang out around the temple. "Oracle, I've come so far to see you. I—I—I'm not sure how to ask this, or even if I could, but the reason why I've come is for your ears only. Me, and my friend Darin, we've traveled from the Nightlands to see you. I ask, in whatever way I can, if we could have private audience. It's a matter of life and death."

Sargon looked like he'd been snatched from the air. The Oracle's hair shifted, as though gravity had altered.

"Sir Sargon of the Wolf Clan, do you know anything about this?"

"No, Oracle, Wisest of All, I do not."

The Oracle narrowed her eyes at Chev. "I'll need to talk to him separately anyway, so I don't see why I shouldn't right now. You may leave, Sir Sargon, and I'll summon you when time comes."

Sargon nodded, the band of knights marched out. The woman inspected the two left behind, Chev and Darin stood as still as condemned men about to be filled with arrows.

The last echoes of the departing knights died, and the woman spoke, "You say you are here on matters of life and death. But no one comes to me for anything less. You have no idea the privilege it is to gain my counsel without either earning it or waiting for it."

"I am grateful for whatever time you give me," said Chev, daring to ease the basket off his back. "I've been carrying this burden for months now, with no one to share it with, and no one who could help. You are the only one who might."

The old woman croaked, and circled an impatient finger in the air. "Please, many are waiting. If you tarry you will deny others this privilege."

Chev's hands rested on the rim of the basket. He took a breath, swallowed, and shivered before the imperious woman. "Oracle, I am cursed."

"Your curse is lifted," the Oracle gestured.

"Just like that?" Chev asked.

"Just like that," the Oracle said, "the power of the Great Folk's magic allows me to break any curse, you know. Is that all?"

"You... didn't even know the nature of the curse," Chev's voice shuddered.

"I didn't need to," the Oracle declared, pounding a little stick into the ground and producing a thunderclap. "Now don't waste my time! I would take it as an insult were you not Nightlanders who didn't know our ways."

Darin stepped forward. "I think I speak for the boy here when I say, this curse is not so simple."

"Darin is right. This is a different kind of curse."

The Oracle pursed her lips, taking on the facial features of a prune. "Fine. So tell it to me then, if you think it makes such a difference."

"It's better to show you, Wise Oracle," said Chev.

The Oracle braced herself, like she was ready for Chev to bend over and reveal some growth or infected toenail. But instead Chev lifted the lid of the basket, and now she leaned forward with simple curiosity. He reached in with both hands, and with thudding heart pulled out Starlight. The baby was held aloft to the Oracle's furrowed brow.

She knew not what to make of it, at first. Her head cocked, clearly thinking moonlight was playing tricks on her.

But the truth was a quick-acting venom. The cane fell from her grasp, she shuddered, and suddenly grew animated with her kicking and flailing to remove herself from the child. That look was one of utter horror, a shock so fierce it looked like it might tear her whole fragile body.

"Please," Chev begged, "she's just—"

"*A dayfolk!*" the Oracle cried, edging up her throne away from the snoozing child. "None have been in this hall for the past ten thousand years! *What have you done!*"

Chev and Darin looked to another.

"Put it back!" The Oracle cried out, "Put it back! Put it back!"

She was so alarmed Chev nearly dropped Starlight. But Chev complied. With the child gone, the Oracle regained some of her sensibilities, but she was still flushed and squeezed as though trying to maximize space between her and the basket.

"You have made a terrible mistake," said the Oracle, "no one must know the dayfolk was here. No one. Our lives depend on it. Why in the name of the Great Ones would you bring one here?"

Chev wasn't sure what else to say. "We thought that—"

"Is this how things are in the Nightlands? Have you started consorting with dayfolk? Do you know what that means?" The Oracle swept creeks of sweat from her face. "The knights don't like being reminded. They prefer to imagine perfection in the old Empire. Truth is, long ago, nightfolk enslaved dayfolk. Did you know they built Manak? Only dayfolk could build such a place. Nightfolk—great hunters, warriors, adventurers, but builders they were not. Wooden shacks are the best we could manage. The whole Empire came crumbling in a terrible war. Not a war—a series of massacres. No side could rest, because they would attack the other while the other slept. The chaos allowed great beasts to come into this land. The bone-skins the worst of them.

"The treaty, young boy. The treaty we signed *kept the peace*. Day to the dayfolk, night to the nightfolk, and no crossing over! Many had to be killed for the message to get across, but it worked. Since then, dayfolk and nightfolk being together was *unthinkable*. It was separation with the best terms—we would still trade and defend each other, but *none* was to cross that fragile line."

The Oracle sighed, and waved her hand at a series of runes at the wall. "There it is. Our treaty. No one remembers it but everyone *feels* it now. And, even as the star of the nightfolk descends and fades, and that of the dayfolk rises and brightens, we guard that treaty without envy. Our people live in their cities, eat their food, and live free lives." The Oracle sank into her chair. "And look. You walk in, not realizing you are the herald of a new era. Just like that mad Emperor in the west. The world really is crumbling apart. What possessed you to pick it up?"

Chev dutifully answered. "I picked her up, not knowing what she was."

"Not an excuse," the Oracle said abruptly, "You could've left it, and you should have. Just not told anyone. That's what everyone else does. There's nothing I can do to help you. I'll tell your knight friends that you aren't the new Emperor."

Chev digested that. But then Darin stepped forward, and talked without wasting a beat. "Oracle, I have my own question. I was banished—"

She made a sharp, cutting gesture with her withered hand. "I don't care. Can't help you either. Just keep silent about this, and leave Manak as soon as possible. Go now. Go!"

Her shrill voice pierced Chev's defenses. They ran in retreat, back through the vast corridor, refusing to look back.

Chev, Varnas, Darin and the knights all waited in anxious silence, and though it was only minutes it felt like hours. Sargon emerged from the temple on wobbling knees, blank-faced and stiff-lipped. The knights scrambled to their feet to assist him, even as Sargon lost the power to walk, he came to sit on the bare flagstones. He swept his fingers into the furrows of his brow, and let his helmet clang onto the flagstones.

"She said 'no'," he let out.

This engendered such a miserable mood that it infected Chev. Every face dropped like weighted rubber, and each man digested this little piece of news in their own way. Some hung their mouths in shock, some turned in shame, others openly wept. Even Adar seemed to lose herself, shivering like she was cold on this lukewarm night. The tribals just looked to each other in puzzled silence.

It was a dumb thing for Chev to do, but his legs, feeling more like sap than muscle, began to move. Varnas whispered some warning, but it was lost on Chev.

Sensing they were about to be addressed, the knights turned to the young man, each pair of rapidly blinking eyes finding Chev despite their grief.

"I'm sorry I wasn't the one you were looking for," said Chev, "If you'd just told me to begin with, I could have told you that."

Sargon was the only one of them who couldn't look up to Chev. He uttered: "Just leave."

"I thank you all for taking me to Manak—"

"Wermac died for no reason!" Sargon flinched, saving face by lifting his chin proudly. "Just leave!"

"I will." Chev nodded, unsure of what else to say, "And thank you. You've been kind to us."

As Chev turned, he tried very, very hard not to have one final look at Adar.

The knights, and the small band of tribesmen, turned away from each other, each marching to separate ends of Manak. Chev had shoulders of broken stone, walking away on peg-like legs.

"Well, that was what I expected," whistled Varnas.

"Shut up."

"Why else would they lock her up in this remote dunghill? So no one would have to put up with her 'wisdom'. Coulda told you that the first time I heard that fool title, 'oracle'. Never seen such a thing as long as I've been around." Varnas glanced at Darin. "You look to have a suckerfish in your throat, so I'm guessing things didn't pan out for you neither."

"No," coolly admitted Darin.

Varnas shrugged. "Well, long journey back to the Nightlands, then. Better get started."

"You can go," Chev said, his feet suddenly fixed to the ground.

"Ah... Hells. I even saw *this* coming. Ancestors save me." Varnas turned around. "Ever since you heard that name you've been chafing your bits to head west. Whaddya expect to find there? More 'wisdom' crap!"

"I'm still cursed, Varnas," said Chev, "I can't leave until it's lifted. Only then can I go back to Sana."

Varnas walked over to Chev, and vigorously prodded his head. "The curse is up there! Been so all along! And you ain't finding a home for that girl here. If I learned on thing on this damnable journey, it's that the Daylit Lands are seeped with evil and everyone here deserves each other."

"Varnas, I gotta try."

Varnas hissed. "'Try?' Maybe instead try not *lying!*"

"What do you mean?"

"This self-styled 'Emperor'. We had the exact same thought at the same time. I could see it." This is not Varnas' theatrical anger. He wrapped his arms together, stared down Chev in manner that pinned him. This was something rare from Varnas: real rage, hot-faced and ugly. "You think he's Ossen, don't cha?"

Chev lifted his hands. "Varnas! I told you, I'm not here for that!"

"Yeah, well, seems to me you were hoping to run across him on the way, thinking that wouldn't be so bad, ain't it?" Varnas shook his head. "Now you got a whiff of him and you race after the scent. You don't fool me, Chev."

"Yes!" Chev cried out to Varnas' withering expression, "Yes! I *do* think the Emperor is Ossen! And I *do* want to find him, Varnas! Who wouldn't do the same? Would you?" He let those words sink, and Chev found himself circling the old man. "But I didn't lie. I really am going down there to fix my curse. So if you want to go home, you're welcome to. But if you're gonna stay, stop whining! Because it's only you keeping you here!"

Varnas shivered, his milk-like orbs stuck to Chev like flies. And, angrily, he picked his things up. "Come on. Sooner we get to Sunset, the sooner we can go home."

Chev allowed himself a moment to grin. "And Darin, you coming along too?"

Darin's odd, uneven blink repeated across his face. "I didn't find what I was looking for, either. I don't have anywhere else to go."

"Good. Let's do the one thing the Oracle got right. Let's get out of Manak."

It was thoroughly unexpected. Chev, Varnas and Darin had already come to the pier, waiting for the next boat to take them. Over the din of business and quiet splashing, Chev's ears pricked to a voice.

"Wait, wait," it cried.

Chev turned to a sight that pressed into his chest. Adar looked straight at him from the path up to Manak, her armor glinting in moonlight. She raced down the ancient steps and joined the three tribesmen.

"Are you going west?" she asked.

They looked to one another. "Yes," they all seemed to say, in varying ways.

"Then I'm going with you," she let in a breath, "I'm going to Sunset as well. I need to see this new Emperor."

As way of answer, Chev gave Adar room to step next to them.

The four waited, watching for a boat to come into the canal. Come dawn, one would soon come, to take them all west, up the river, to the city of Sunset, to see the Emperor.

The Emperor

Part III

Chapter Seventeen
Of Neither Night nor Day

A T THE CUSP OF DAWN and the fade of night, the docks offered little but plenty of room to sit. Chev enjoyed how the water chopped just beneath him, cooling his feet and giving the momentary illusion of calm.

And wait they did. They all did.

Adar chewed her lip watching as the last ship slipped out onto the great river, bobbing to its swift currents. And Varnas had his fist buried into his cheek, casting a bored eye to the waterway. A low sun, just beneath the horizon, wiped the sky clean of stars, leaving a plain sky. And the harbors were just as empty. Only a few barges, anchored to weather the day, bobbed in the waters near the wharf.

Darin startled them all out of their quiet moments with his arrival. He distributed some sticks speared with crisp nuggets of meat, and gave Ma-ma a bit of grass and a carrot to chew on. The meat was some kind of amphibian, Chev guessed—and the soft texture proved it. It tasted like the fried bean curd his mother used to make.

Minda's sweet bean cakes. The reminder made Chev's mouth water. Somehow, in his mouth, the flavorless meat turned into little pastries.

"I don't think anyone's coming," Adar said finally.

Darin took his seat, grunting on the way. "Don't think so either."

"Yeah, well, where do we go? Huh?"

"You guys can go look for some shelter," said Chev. "I'll wait out here."

"In the sun? Alone?" Adar was surprised. "Come on, Chev. Don't be silly."

"Alone? No," Chev shook his head, then turned to stroke Ma-ma's patchy mane. "You'll sit out here with me, wontcha girl?"

Adar tugged on Chev's shoulder. "There'll be a ship that takes us tomorrow. Come on..."

Darin nudged Adar. "Kid wants to boil his skin off, it's his choice. This is his quest, after all."

"Yeah. If I want to boil my skin off, it's my choice," Chev agreed, "I imagine sun sitting has to be easier than sun walking."

"Sun walking? What does that mean—"

Adar was cut off with Varnas' ancient but brisk voice. "It means Chev's gotta feed his inner masochist, that's what. He don't feel right getting up in the dusk without punishing himself or moodily gazing off into the horizon. Me, on the other hand, don't wanna get sun sick. So I'm going to find a nice big rock to crawl under," Varnas drew himself onto shuddering knees. "Anyone who wants to join me is welcome to."

Varnas didn't pause for responses. He just walked off toward a jumble of ruins. Darin followed without comment. Only Adar seemed reluctant, her eyes torn between Chev and the rising sun. Finally, she broke. "I'll see you next night," Adar said, and followed the two older men.

Alone now, with no company but for a goat and a baby in a basket, Chev drew Ma-ma close and affectionately scratched the nape of her neck. The goat bleated pleasantly, and she shifted her head for better angles. But Chev still watched the mouth of the canal, glowing with ever increasing, ever more unbearable light. He hoped something would cut across suddenly. But he knew no dayfolk came to Manak.

It was fully day now, but Chev was still in the shadows of the deep canal walls, so deep that Chev felt he was in an island of night in this ocean of day. The contrast between the blazing light where the sun fell and the utter blackness where the sun was still hidden, was blinding by itself. Chev was left to squint, and hope the daylight would fade with time.

Enough light fell on the basket that Starlight began to squirm. Chev eagerly took her out and placed her on his lap, weaving his fingers between her supple skin and wondrously fine fur.

He hadn't realized how silent things had fallen until a sound finally broke.

Monsters. That was Chev's immediate thought, and he stowed Starlight quickly away. But the shuffling that approached him came too slowly to be an ambush, but too loud to be someone sneaking. Something was joining him by the docks.

The silhouettes, obsidian statues out in the blinding light, did not fit the dimensions of Varnas, Darin or Adar.

"Hello," Chev called out them.

There was rasp, like a voice filtered by a rattlesnake tail, and then a response. *"Greetings."*

"Are you dayfolk?"

"No," came the blunt answer, "Are you nightfolk?"

"Yes," said Chev.

"That's interesting," the voice said, low, methodical, rasping out each sound as though unused to it. "I was told your kind never come out in day. You are the first I have met in these lands. You are a very strange creature."

"I'm sure if I could see you," said Chev, "I would think you were strange too."

"We are certain of that. Do you wait for the *colony?*"

"Colony? What colony? Like an ant colony?"

"Then you do not know," the creature sucked in an airy breath. "Not ants. *Pimmen*. The pim."

"Pim?"

"You know not pimmen either? A pimmen clan travels the length of the Sippi. They have a barge for those who are neither nightfolk or dayfolk. You must be strange and desperate indeed to wait for the *pimmen*."

"I didn't say I was waiting for the *pim-men*," said Chev, struggling with the unfamiliar word, "But, yeah, maybe I will go with the pimmen. Haven't decided."

"You must choose soon. The pimmen are coming."

"The pimmen are...?"

At first, it looked like any other daytime illusion. Some obstruction shadowed the entrance to the canal, like the moon had suddenly entered a phase. Chev could not tell whether his eyes told him true, but it was the largest vessel that Chev had ever seen. The monstrous construction of wood and canvas nearly scraped the mossy walls of Manak.

"Am I dreaming or is that a floating city?" asked Chev.

"It is a *colony*," answered the rasping creature.

Its size played with Chev's sense of scale. Just as Chev thought it had pulled into the harbor, it grew larger and larger, a mass expanding out of control. Chev only realized how close it was when he heard wood and water straining against a titanic weight. Muffled and made percussive by the hull were many hundreds of small voices, melting into a single noise.

Chev barely made out a creature leaning over the ship's railing. "Starfarers!" it cried out with a squeak of a near childlike voice. "You call us! We come!"

"Starfarers?" Chev turned to his strange companion, to see that there was not one but five shadows of indeterminable shape. But only one of them moved to board the ship, as the other twisted to Chev.

"Where are you going, friend?"

"To the city of Sunset," Chev answered.

"That is not our destination," said the strange creature, "but it is on the way. The Pimmen will take you if you have the plats."

"I have plats," Chev said, "Not me, specifically. But my friend does. I have three of them. Will they take us all?"

The stranger creature, this *Starfarer*, repeated: "If you have the plats, they will take you."

It had, of course, been Darin that protested most strongly. "You don't know what they are. They could be carnivores. We might be paying them for the honor of being dinner."

"You can always stay behind, Darin. You got to see your Oracle, after all," responded Varnas.

Darin didn't have an answer for that, except he grumbled, "I want to see that Emperor too." He was outvoted, three to one, and if he didn't want to be alone he was forced to join them.

The nightfolk pulled Adar's big canvas tent over them, to protect them from the sun. One of these strange creatures, the "Pimmen" as Chev was told, came to meet them, guide them. They followed his incessant chatter.

"Nightfolk? Huh?" squeaked the little creature. Judging from his voice, Chev judged that he'd only reach Chev's knee, "Silly critters, hiding from the sun. A pretty day, and you don't wanna see it. Watch out—that's the gangway. I dunno how you can never ever see the sun. Seems a sad life. They tell me there's all kinds, though, so I don't question it. You guys, uh... like the dark? We could put you in the hold if you want. We also gotta cabin with a window—"

"Window," came the ringing response.

"Sorry, Gods forgive me for asking a question. Didn't know you nightfolk were so sensitive," the Pim drawled, "Just waddle that direction. Last door on the left. Hope it's big enough for all you."

Before the group could crowd into their new accommodations, the Pim shouted at them, "Oh, and when you wake up at dusk, we gotta few ground rules to cover. So talk to me, Captain Tips, before you do *anything*."

When Chev agreed to take Adar, he had been thinking with his heart rather than his head. Now, as his companions slept while his eyes were open, he finally understood those tightly sealed lips and disapproving glares both Darin and Varnas had given him. Chev was the one with secrets to protect. And now he was trapped on a foreign vessel with exactly the person to punish him.

The ship moaned in rhythm with the current of the river, emanating from the walls was the chatter of many hundreds of strange creatures, these *Pimmen*. Even so, Chev lifted his head slowly and carefully, as though worried he might disturb the room, and he lifted himself from the floor. He picked up Starlight's basket and with a gesture invited Ma-ma to follow.

The trotters click-clacked on the wood boards. Chev watched Adar for signs of movement, but his three companions stayed fast asleep, before carefully closing the door.

The length of the hall provided some idea to the scale of the vessel. There were three doors on each side of the corridor, each large enough to dwarf that cramped cellar beneath the Drunken Donkey.

Pimmen. Neither nightfolk nor dayfolk. Like Hlogas. But also like the bone-skins. Chev wondered if the pim understood or even cared about the taboo. That nightfolk and dayfolk were not to meet. Chev wasn't sure, but he knew the best thing was to not find out in the first place.

It was a strange thing, day. Even with no windows, even the darkness seemed lighter for it, like it was trying hard to press back against the whiteness that would swallow all. The hallway might have been empty of Pimmen, but he couldn't stay here.

Chev walked carefully. He noted a sliver of light, and realized there was a door ajar. When he pushed it lightly, he hadn't meant it to glide open so quickly.

The porthole was open, engorging the room with the sun's terrible light. But it was the sight that resolved before him that seized his heart. At that moment, the five cloaked figures that knelt in a circle seemed so sinister Chev imagined he'd opened into a room of unnatural evils. He shrank back, but the figures made no movement.

Ma-ma sniffed at the door frame, as though she might find some grass to pull at. It wasn't courage that made her trot into the room, it was that she didn't see any danger at all.

"Close a window for our friend," said the voice. It was the same creature Chev had met at the docks.

Chev instinctively shuddered, surprised at having been noticed. "I'm sorry, I hadn't meant—"

But one of the figures had already drawn up to pull the porthole's shutter closed. The blinding light was extinguished for warm, cloaking darkness.

"You didn't have to."

"We do not mind. We enjoy company. Besides, your basket is crying."

In Chev's surprise, he hadn't noticed. Ma-ma immediately got to work, nipping at the basket.

"Thank you," Chev struggled with Ma-ma as he spoke, "But, I would—*uh*—prefer not to intrude..."

"We will not mind," he repeated.

At that moment, Ma-ma had finally torn the basket from Chev's hand, and she got in quickly, cries turned to little giggles.

"You are accompanied by a child," said the figure.

Freed from carrying Starlight, Chev found himself pinned—like he had no choice but to answer the question.

"Yes," Chev said, guarded.

"But you do not wish others to see."

"Yes." Chev hesitated, wondering if explaining things would just make it more complicated. "It's a custom, you know. Of our people."

"The nightfolk take child rearing to be a private matter," said the creature to the other.

"Unusual for a communal species," commented the other.

Chev didn't like that exchange. Not at all. Like they were dissecting him, pulling him to pieces as a curiosity.

"Come sit with us. We do not often encounter nightfolk."

They had strange voices, rattling, like filtered through rushing grains of sand, and Chev realized that they unsettled him. It wasn't just that these shadowy beings were an unknown, it was that they also sounded so familiar. Still, Chev felt he needed to comply, and he squeezed between two of the creatures, who made no move to stop him nor make space.

"What is your name?" asked the creature.

"Chev," said Chev, then he asked. "And the pimmen called you Starfarers."

"It is a misnomer," said the creature. "We are not the Starfarers. We *follow* them. That was the purpose of our pilgrimage to Manak. We seek secrets."

"Secrets?" said Chev.

"Yes," the creature cleared its throat with an unmusical, dry sound. "My kind is one of the *fenderken*. One whose species devotes itself to the uncovering of ancient secrets. For the good of all the sapients of Earth."

"And that secret?" asked Chev, leaning forward as though hooked by the creature's words.

"It is as our pim friends said. We seek the secret of *starfaring*."

Chev had to pause, construct the concept in his mind. "You mean— *sailing between stars?*"

"That is precisely correct," said the fenderken.

"But—night is a veil, isn't it? And behind that veil is a sun. That's why the stars are bright, because there's holes in the veil."

"No," the fenderken said, "those stars *are* suns."

Chev's immediate reaction was to laugh, call it absurd, but the words died as he thought about it, as it made more sense the more it lingered in Chev's mind. The best he could manage was a thoughtful grunt.

"So," the fenderken's attention was suddenly drawn by something else. "Your child is dayfolk. That's very surprising."

Chev twisted around, a sharp pain stinging him when he saw Starlight's hairy paws stroking Ma-ma's muzzle.

"Crap!" Chev cursed, and jerked forward. Only a raised hand stopped Chev's movement.

"We do not share your race's taboos," the fenderken said, and then turned to his companion. "The nightfolk's reticence is now made clear."

"It has been noted," repeated the other.

"Stop doing that," said Chev. After seeing two cloaked heads, quizzically cocked, Chev felt obliged to explain. "She's the reason I'm going to Sunset. I'm cursed."

"Cursed? How?"

"By accident, I touched her. Now I'm bound to her. And while I'm bound I can't be with another."

"I see." The fenderken turned to his companion, to deliver another clinical note. "Some odd custom."

"I think it is idiosyncratic to nightfolk culture," said the other.

"An antiquated idea," offered the fenderken.

Chev couldn't bite back his annoyance. "Stop talking like I'm not here," said Chev. "Wait—you said something. Something about it being antiquated. Do you understand it?"

The fenderken looked quizzical and shook his head. "It is a common cultural artifact."

The other fenderken made the same sad gesture. "Sadly, it is not one we share. We cannot advise you."

We cannot advise you. Odd words that reverberated through Chev, in a way even he didn't expect.

At this point, Chev lowered his gaze, as though staring at the back of his hands. He watched as they popped with veins, a result of his now clenching fists. Out of his control, the frustrations of a long journey came to the surface, leaking into the tenor of his voice. "Advice. I traveled all the way to Manak only for that. And it turned out that old man Varnas was right. The Oracle really was just as helpless and ignorant as the rest of us. I honestly don't know what I was hoping for. If I'd known..."

Chev was about to say that he would've stayed in the Nightlands. But he couldn't bring out the words. He knew they were lies, and that he'd lied to Varnas without meaning or knowing. Ossen had drawn him here. Ossen and that man alone.

"He will not finish his thought," said the fenderken.

"He is in a state of high emotional agitation," said the other.

"I told you," Chev hissed, "to not talk that way!"

Respectfully, the fenderken fell silent, lowering their brows. It only made Chev feel worse, and he reflected how strange these non-nightfolk, non-dayfolk people were. Before Chev had come in, they had all been sitting in this circle, without moving, without speaking, each face cloaked by shadows and a hood. Only two of them ever seemed to say or do anything. Despite it all, they were courteous and had provided Chev nothing but help. Chev returned it with disrespect and hostility.

"I'm sorry," Chev said, "you didn't deserve that."

"May we take a look at the child?" asked the fenderken.

"We are merely curious," clarified the other, noting Chev's expression.

Why not? What words do you choose when you're about to pass a child to strange, otherworldly monsters? Yet, so far Chev was struck that these creatures seemed to be observers, not killers, and Chev knew if anyone was to glean something helpful it would be them. So Chev picked up the child, away from Ma-ma's udders, and held it to the fenderken.

The fenderken unfolded its hands from its robes and reached out. Chev shivered when he saw the alien digits. *Skeletal,* Chev thought. They looked to be made of bony plates.

The creature pulled the child close to it. Starlight's expression changed, from placid and cheerful to strained and dark with anguish. She released a cry, horrified as she stared into the monster's hood.

"Calm," urged the fenderken.

The hood started to fold back. It's skin was white, like snow, and its face was made of interlocking plates like reptile scales. A mouth—not a mouth but *pincers*—chattered excitedly with the tiny creature in front of it.

Like in a nightmare, Chev was suddenly surrounded by terrors. Monsters arose from the darkness. There was no safe place except behind a sword.

"A *bone-skin!*" Chev went to his feet, the Daysword whipping out from his scabbard.

In his panic, Chev stepped back, stumbling over the fenderken next to him. It didn't lash out as expected, it flopped with a dry rattle onto its side, the open hood revealing two dark pits for eyes. *A corpse!*

"What?"

Disoriented, the heat from his heart became feverish on his forehead, Chev tried to steady himself but his back hit the wood wall. He could feel the rocking of the boat, but now he felt it shake him into a nauseated, jellied mass. Chev was a stumbling danger, whipping around the room unable to stop waving his sword.

The two bone-skins rose, hoods fallen past their necks, clattering mandibles, unreadable alien eyes watched Chev.

"Let go of her!" said Chev, taking a wide stance.

These bone-skins were wordless, emotionless, Chev could see how close the pincers were to Starlight, how easy it would be to lean forward and crush the skull with their powerful jaws. But the fenderken moved not, except to make a cautious approach, and hold out Starlight's bawling little form.

A trick. That was all Chev could think. So he approached with equal caution. The fenderken held out the child, and Chev held out his sword, and they met somewhere in the middle. Like a fox snagging a mouse, Chev stole Starlight back, and he backed out into the hall, and shut the door with a kick.

There was no place to go. Chev couldn't risk opening any of the doors for fear of meeting new horrors, nor could he go back to his room where Adar would surely be sleeping. So he let his back slither down against the wall, and he set his naked sword across his knees, and while Starlight cried and Ma-ma comforted her, Chev kept watch.

"You mad, boy?"

A nudge in the chest with the toe of a boot. Chev let out a garbled protest, and rolled to pull up some furs but he only found hard floor.

"Wake up! Your lady-friend's gonna come out soon. Come on, boy!"

Both Varnas' voice and his toe got more insistent. With a sigh and a wipe of the eyes, Chev lifted himself from the floor.

"Whatsit?" Chev slurred. He twisted to see daylight no longer pressed against the exterior door.

"Put that damn kid in the basket!" said Varnas.

"Kid in the basket?" Chev turned his bleary vision to see Starlight's prone form next to him on the floor. Suddenly he shot awake. "Oh!"

It was just in time. Chev stuffed Starlight's sleeping body into the basket, covered it, and propped it upright. Adar came out of the room just seconds later, adjusting her chainmail when she was arrested by Chev and Varnas' guilty looks.

"Did I interrupt something?" Adar ventured.

"Chev always had a preference for hallways. Can't understand that kid," Varnas shrugged, made a meek laugh. "Needs a good *kick* every dusk."

"Ow!" Chev recoiled from Varnas' foot, getting quickly off the ground.

Adar watched as Chev brushed himself off, as if deciding whether to buy Varnas' story. "Listen," she said, "You have your own problems. If there's something you don't want me to know, it's your own business. I only ask that if it matters at all, you tell me. Would you?"

"Yeah," said Chev.

Adar, satisfied, walked away, as though sensing Chev and Varnas needed a word. When she disappeared down the corner, Chev whispered in Varnas' ear.

"She knows about the child."

"What?" Varnas' eyes went like saucepans, "You told her?"

"Of course not. She found out. Not anything about it being a dayfolk. She just knows we got one."

"If I knew that I woulda kicked you harder!" Varnas clenched his teeth, "When were you plannin' to tell me or Darin?"

"Darin? I was planning on telling *you*. Just hadn't found the time."

"Gotta tell Darin too," said Varnas.

"Why? So he can go tell me to feed her to some monster?"

Varnas' hand whipped out, boxing Chev over the ears. "It's not about what stupid thing he's gonna say," said Varnas, "it's about protecting *you*. That's important, you know!"

"How?" Chev rubbed his ear. "What could Darin possibly do?"

"Things neither of us can see coming. What do I look like, an oracle?"

The door burst open. Varnas and Chev twisted to see Darin ruffling his black hair as he stretched. His eyes blinked unsteadily, a result of both his strange cheek scar and having just woken up.

"What was it I could possibly do?" Darin looked to both of them.

Varnas made a noise, like snort and a laugh, "I'll leave it to you, Chev, since this whole thing was your peanut-brained idea."

Varnas' excused himself, past Darin and slammed open the doorway to the ship. Darin nodded to Chev. "What's this, then?"

"Nothing," said Chev, "Varnas is just worked up, that's all."

Chev followed Varnas with brisk stride. He wasn't sure how he'd tell him now about the bone-skins aboard.

Outside in the sedate light beneath the moon and stars, it was hard to pay attention to what the strange, short creature was saying. If Chev had been warned how strange the Pim were, he might have prepared himself. Instead, he watched as this hairless, wrinkled, knee-height creature aggressively lectured him with a voice distorted by thick, whistling teeth. It look like a pawcat with all its fur boiled off, or one of those dam-building rodents on two legs.

"There won't be any fighting on this ship, nossir, or hunting!" lectured Captain Tips, proudly puffing out its little chest, and as a result its sword wagging in the air, "If you want to eat another passenger, you gotta wait for port to do that! Everyone on board pays, and while they're paying customers they don't get hurt."

All the nightfolk, Adar, Chev, Darin and Varnas, nodded vacantly at the sight of this creature.

"Then," Captain Tips added, "The last rule, and most important of all: do not, I mean do not, and I can't say enough, *do not*, I repeat: DO NOT disturb the Queen, Blessed Be Her, the Clanmother, who makes her court in the very bowels of this ship. Now, what did I just say: *do* disturb the Queen, or *do not* disturb the Queen?"

"Do not," the nightfolk answered in unison.

"Good, good," the Pim nodded, satisfied, but it whipped out its little sword and pressed it threateningly again Chev's belly. "Because if you do— well, you may be big, but I've yet to see folk on this river who aren't just bags of blood waiting to be popped. You get me?"

"I get you," Chev shivered at the steel grazing his abdomen. "No fighting. No disturbing the queen. No... uh..."

"Distracting the crew! Making loud noises! Gambling with dice! Flirting with the lookout! And, Gods forbid it, but if you need to lay droppings do it in the bucket first and then throw it overboard, instead of sticking your whole butt out the porthole and doing it thataway! And if you do throw things into the river, not just but especially your nightsoil, shout a warning first!"

"What, to the river?"

"No, to the lookout!" Captain Tips shook his head. "Now, enjoy your trip! I'm going to bed."

Captain Tips weighed less in mass and more in authority, yet somehow he could push people aside like he was twice their size. Varnas, Adar, and Darin all stepped aside so that they wouldn't be shoved.

"Is Captain Tips male or female?" asked Darin. No one had an answer.

"I don't think flirting with the lookout is gonna be that much a problem," said Varnas.

"One wonders how it *became* a problem." Chev shuddered.

Adar went over to the railing. As large as the ship was, it was just a sliver swiftly tossed on the Sippi river. She clutched the wood, watching the shore drift by. "They are simple rules, right? Easy enough not to kill and eat people aboard. No one has any dice. Don't think any of us are noisy. It's gonna be a simple trip."

"Maybe not," Chev wondered aloud.

His companions turned to him. Chev now knew he had to say what was on his mind.

"There are bone-skins aboard," said Chev.

There was a collective doubletake, with knitted brows and open mouths. Adar nearly fell off the barge.

"You sure about that?" asked Varnas.

"Yes—no..." Chev paced down the walkway, sliding his hand through his black hair. "There are. But weird ones. They wear cloaks, talk about weird things like star ships, call themselves *fenderken.*"

"*Fenderken?*" Adar repeated, "One of the elder races."

"You know them?" Chev asked.

"No, not really," Adar let her words drift, as though deep in thought, "But people talk. They say they're these strange beings who wander around the world, collecting secrets, especially about the Great Folk. They're so rare hardly anyone meets them."

"No way," Darin shook his head, "There's no way a bone-skin could be one of these so-called *elder races.* Either they were trying to trick Chev or they're not bone-skins at all."

"They look like them," said Chev.

"Yeah, and they act like them, too. Tricking and confusing people." Darin went right up to Chev, nearly nose to nose, and prodded him right in the chest. "I know what kinda person you are, Chev, and I'm telling you now: don't take stupid risks. Don't think about whether they're these elder whatsits or plain old bone-skins, just avoid 'em. It's gonna be hard going keeping our noses clean as it is."

Chev watched Darin as the hunter strode down the walkway.

"You aren't friends, are you?" Adar observed.

"We have a history," Chev glanced at Varnas, signaling he was speaking for him too, "But it's not important. Adar, if these are bone-skins... I'm not worried about myself. But they—" Chev struggled with how to put it.

"—Like to eat children." Varnas put it bluntly

"Yeah," Chev said with an oddly sheepish affect. "And... so..."

Adar gestured boldly, cutting across Chev's words. "No matter what, Chev, I'm not going to let a monster eat a child, and you aren't either, I can see that. But that only leaves me confused. Chev, you don't seem like the sort to kidnap children, but I can't think of any other reason you'd not want me to see it. You're going to have to tell me what's going on."

"Frankly," Chev said, without thinking, "I'd rather you think I did kidnap it."

Chapter Eighteen
Children of the Sippi

THEY SENT CHEV out to dispose of yesternight's refuse. Rotten food, wood shavings, scraps of cloth, Ma-ma's droppings, like a cake of detritus stuck to the bottom of a bucket. It was such a strange contrast to the river's pleasing texture of shimmering water. It seemed a shame to disturb it.

He nearly threw it overboard before he remembered Captain Tip's stern warning, and not wishing to be "popped like the bladder of blood" as she creatively put it, he did what she asked. He let out a bland, flat warning.

"Look out, river," Chev said, "Trash."

A head popped out of the water. "Thanks!"

"Ah!"

The bucket slipped out from Chev's hand, making several circles through the air, and a mass of garbage broke over Chev. Nothing except the bucket went over the railing.

A head in the water. That was what he'd just seen. *A head in the water.*

Was the voice from his imagination? Or was it the head? Or was it all real? None were promising options, but they all mixed in with his thoughts as he crawled to the railing and peeked over the edge.

What he saw was a fish, except not. It moved through water like one, cutting through it with all the expected fins, except it was too big and oddly shaped. But it was only when the creature unraveled itself when it made sense: the tail was two legs, the little wings along the belly were webbed hands, and the big fin that seemed so serpentine retracted into the curve of a familiar back. Emerging from the river was the head of a bright-faced girl. A graceful, effortless glide was all she needed to keep up with the ship, even with the bucket dragging behind.

"You dropped your bucket." She said it like she'd caught Chev without his pants, as she tossed the bucket right back at Chev.

Chev caught it, no thanks to any conscious effort on his part. He was too busy puzzling out the being before him.

"What? You never seen a girl before?"

"Of course! Just not one that's… a fish! What are you?"

"What am I? Isn't that obvious? The lookout!" With no real reason, she punctuated the whole thing with a jump back into the depths of the river, before she erupted right in front of Chev. Chev had to throw up his hands to stop a plume of water from splashing him.

"Hey!"

One look at the girl's face—squirreled up with satisfaction—Chev knew it wasn't by accident. Chev searched for a place to dry his arms.

"Why so angry?" the girl said "The water is great! Air's so cold and dry, can't figure out why you'd stick up there."

"We'd drown," said Chev, finally resorting to drying his hands on his clothes.

"I'd drown too, if I never surfaced to take breath. That's why you surface sometimes, silly."

"Now I know why the pimmen said I shouldn't talk to you," said Chev.

The girl had a soft chuckle, and spun very slightly in the water. "That *really* what they told you? I think what they said was you shouldn't *flirt* with me. But that's fine. We don't have to flirt if you don't want to. We could talk for hours, count the stars, tell each other stories that we then have to guess if it's true or made-up! My name's Naia."

"Chev," said Chev.

"Chev. Chev. That's a handsome name." The girl drew up halfway out the water to puff out her naked chest, drop her voice, and screw together her eyes. "*My name's Chev.* Even saying it, it's very masculine, very strong. Think I just grew a hair on my chest."

"Naia's also very pretty name. I guess," said Chev, feeling more obligated to respond than anything else.

And Naia smiled, revealing the pearls she had for teeth. It must've been a trick of the light, because from a distance, they looked to be small, conical, and made for ripping. But that couldn't possibly be the teeth from a girl so whimsical and puckish. "Oh, that's cute. Say Chev, do you have problems expressing your feelings? That's the impression I get from you."

"Uh..."

"See, that's exactly what I mean. What was your gut reaction to what I just said? Did you get angry? Or was it more introspective? Did you finally see something you never saw about yourself? Come on, be defensive, angry, or break down and cry on my shoulder. It's dangerous to keep it all bottled up."

"I don't bottle things up, I just don't feel anything."

Naia gasped, mouth so wide and hand so fast over it she practically had her fingers in her mouth. "*That's even worse!* You don't feel *anything?*"

"What? That's not what—"

"Oh, thank every fish in the Sippi! I thought you were some sorta zombie or something." Naia hit the water, splashing at Chev and finishing it off a with a pout. "Oh come on, Chev, I'm not dumb. I know what you actually mean, silly night person. But it's no fun when you don't react strongly. Emotions make us special. It's the spice of the soul. Nobody writes a saga about Blandy Blanderson, who counts rocks all his old life."

What does this girl want? But Chev didn't even want to ask. He was getting the impression he was being fished for something, and the more he talked the deeper in the nets he was getting.

"Listen, Naia, it was nice talking to you," Chev glanced back, "but I think someone called my name. I gotta go."

"Oh, sure, see you." And Naia disappeared beneath the waves.

Chev couldn't believe it was that easy. And it wasn't. As soon as Chev turned to make his escape, Naia burst from the water and practically jumped on deck. Everything fish-like melted off in an instant—Naia was completely woman—two graceful legs, two long arms that vaulted right over the railing. Her skin and the air was peppered with gem-like droplets of water. Naia's form was concealed only by this new mist, and she was left nude as it spattered like rain on the deck.

"How would you describe me, Chev?" In a graceful, preening movement, Naia brushed back her thin, nearly ethereal hair. "A poet once said my skin was every shade of dusk and my eyes every blush of dawn. It was very flattering, and I've been waiting very patiently for a man to pay me a better compliment."

"I don't have the time, Naia!"

"We're on a boat, Chev. What are you gonna do, scrub the deck? Leave it to the pimmen. You're better off with me."

"I'm—I'm not a poet..."

But Chev already knew how he'd describe her. Her figure was much like any nightfolk athletic woman, but so subtly different. She was smooth and shaped by the water, like a stone pulled from the bed of a creek. It was much the same with her face, with her flat nose, smooth cheeks and eyes untarnished by lines—Chev didn't know if this was a result of her age or her species—her features would be dazzling except they were far too alien.

And when she smiled, Chev knew he didn't imagine those teeth.

"I can help you," she spun on her feet, every bit as gracefully as she did in the water. "Would you say I was more a light violet kissing the concept of red, or more a lavender that evokes tingly sensations of supple lightness, or a regal purple like a proud pennant fluttering in the wind?"

Chev sighed, "You look light-gray."

"Light gray?" Naia covered her gasping open mouth, "Light gray! I've never—you really do hate me, don't you?"

She made a pouty noise before stepping off the edge, diving back with barely a splash. And Chev stared down at the ripples of the river, unable to do anything but reflect on the bizarre conversation he'd just had.

"Told you not to flirt with her."

Captain Tips stood nearby and out of sight, evidently having watched the whole thing. He looked a bit odd with a proud, feathered cap that didn't align well with his mole-like face, but so would anything he might wear. The short, stubby little creature could still walk with great authority.

"I didn't," said Chev.

"Naia's a strange bird. I've never been able to figure out what she really wants. I think her kind are bred beggars, cheats and flatterers. Hundreds of thousands of years of nature has molded them into perfect manipulators."

Chev asked: "So, what is her kind?"

Captain Tips shrugged. "Don't care to ask. Anyways, she's safe in most ways but dangerous in others. She likes people to think she's stupid." He sighed as the conversation shifted. "Don't normally get into client's business, but you're headed to Sunset, aren't you?"

"Yeah. You know it?"

"It's where the Sippi meets the sea. The jewel of the western coast. If there's a bigger city in this world, I don't know it. If you stand in the middle of it, you'd think this whole world was nothing but Sunset. I'm only asking because I'm grateful to have nightfolk aboard."

"I thought you said I was just another customer."

"If you knew what the Sippi was like for us *others*, you'd understand. Sippi's been a very dangerous place, since the dayfolk war started. River's choked with pirates. But dayfolk don't attack nightfolk ships. You make us a lot safer just by being around. Still dangerous though. Monsters like you wouldn't believe are beneath those waters, but that's what Naia's around for. To tell us before some creature snatches us from off deck."

"I had a friend who was killed that way," Chev stung with the memory of Wermac. "It was a horrid way to die."

"That's what I fear." Captain Tips looked out on the placid course of the Sippi. "You anapim don't get that even though there's a lot of us, and more of us are born every day, we're all sisters here. It stings when we lose someone."

"Sisters..." Chev repeated, relieved he'd learned Tips' gender before he'd made some kind of mistake. And what Tips had said was true, there were *multitudes* of the creatures on the ship, the lower decks were practically bursting with them, every time they emerged they were practically on top of each other. And they worked like bees, too, how they would each find something to do—adjust the rigging, check the hull, empty the bilge, or wash the deck. And complex and inscrutable chatter rose wherever they went.

"You know," Chev spoke, "I was my mother's only child. It was strange even for my people. I can't help but think what it would be like to have a sibling. A lot less lonely, maybe."

"If you're asking what I think, I'd say you're both lucky and unlucky. I don't barely know the word lonely. But damn do these girls keep me up at night. I sometimes gotta wonder what it'd be like if I went away. Just went to shore and explored the world."

"Why don't you?" asked Chev.

"Because I'd get bored." For the first time, Chev saw Captain Tips' smile. A toothy, hairless, wrinkled one, but one that had as much love and humanity as Chev had ever seen.

After a week the rock and sway of the ship felt normal, and Chev didn't even realize he gotten used to it. He spent his nights watching the river, thinking over what he might see in Sunset. During the days he watched Starlight, with one eye always cocked toward the bone-skin's door. Between those two activities, sleep was sacrificed, and the regular hive-like activity of the pimmen became dizzying by comparison. Hordes of interchangeable little pimmen, in every shadowed corner and swarming every deck, always doing *something*.

When he saw Varnas participating in one of the pimmen's bizarre rituals, he knew he wasn't acclimating as fast as Varnas.

A line of pimmen secured themselves to the deck using rope tied to iron loops, each carrying a stick with a string lowered into the water. And Varnas was with them, legs dangling over the ship's side and humming like it was some leisure activity.

"It's like trapping, but for fish," Varnas eventually explained to Chev, "You get a hook, right, put something on the end, like a little squirming worm, and you wait for something to come along and give it a good old bite. Gets hooked, you pull it up. Genius. They call it 'fishing'."

"So, what's with tying yourself to the deck?" asked Chev.

"Oh. That's so that the fish don't fish you. Some beasts like to yank you right off deck, right into an open maw. Sippi has monsters that make ursars looks like chipmunks, it does."

"Monsters outside, monsters inside," muttered Chev.

Varnas had to think about that. "*Bone-skins.* Thanks for reminding me, like I needed something else to keep me up at night. What's eating ya, boy?"

"They're served by the pim, that's the problem." Chev rubbed his nose and made a cautious glance both directions. "They come in, bring in food, take out garbage. Are we getting that kinda treatment?"

"Suppose they got the plats," Varnas said, "That seems like the religion around here."

"Maybe. Maybe it's the plats. Maybe the pim don't want them hungry and angry. Maybe this is their deal, with us as their tribute. Maybe this boat is a little slice of the Nightlands."

"Chev, seems to me you're the only one who's actually talked to these creatures. But," Varnas absently waved his little fishing stick, "you're sounding an awful lot like Darin."

Chev raised an eyebrow. "Wait. Aren't you the one that doesn't trust anyone? Aren't I supposed to be the naive one?"

Varnas nodded. "Oh, sure still true now. I'm just sayin' you're starting to sound like Darin. What, you think I'm such a judgmental old ass? You're getting a bit boring!" Varnas made a pleased noise and his attention jerked away, "Ancestors! A biter! Look at this Chev."

With a jerk of the pole, Varnas pulled out a fish from the river. It hopped, tail wagging and struggling against the line. Varnas started furiously pulling the string, and in a moment he had two handfuls of big, fat fish.

"Never got suckerfish this big! I'm starting to like this river, you know, taking away the terrors that lurk within."

"That's a pretty big thing to take away," said Chev.

Varnas was oddly bemused, lowering his brow to deliver a snappy remark. "Oh Chev, there's always been terrors and horrors wherever we've gone. You were just used to them up until now."

Chev should have known something was in the offing when the next night the ship regurgitated its entire cargo of pimmen onto the portside deck. They made a mass so dense it was near impenetrable, and they chattered so rapidly that it merged to a single, indecipherable, musical roar. The ship eagerly made a sharp bank into a marshy lake, before the anchor was thrown. The pimmen watched the waters with the bated breath of children waiting for a surprise.

Naia lifted her head out the water. "Safe!"

That was all they needed to hear. The ship disgorged its crew into the lake. As Chev approached the railing, he did so with apprehension, like he didn't really want to know what was happening down below.

And what it was, was something remarkable yet entirely ordinary.

Apparently pimmen needed to wash like anyone else, and like everything they did, it was entirely communal. They formed great chains where one pim kneaded the back of the next, but sometimes one would break off to splash in the waters or just to swim. Still, it reminded Chev of insect spawning grounds where things just crawled atop each other in big, squirming layers.

It left him mildly disgusted, but then again, so did his own scent.

Chev last washed when he was with the nomads. And now, grimacing as he sniffed his own armpit, he judged himself ripe for another.

Varnas joined him by the railing. "I thought to do the same thing. It was a dumb idea."

"I never thought we'd get so filthy with so much water around," said Chev.

"A man once told me the sea was torturous because you're surrounded by water you can't drink," Varnas shrugged. "A bit far-fetched, if you ask me, that you can't drink it. Bit of salt's a good thing. But it makes a good saying. Just 'cause you're surrounded by something don't mean you can use it."

"Still true now," Chev said, twisting to Varnas with a big, lopsided grin. "You thinking of going down there into the water too? Looks like they might give good back rubs."

"It's too bad. Pimmen took over the last lake in the world. Yep. Over one day everything in the world just dried right up." Varnas gave him a friendly smack on the shoulder. "Come on, there's gotta be something for us somewhere down there."

Varnas had already set on going, but Chev grabbed his arms, and asked, "Aren't you worried about monsters?"

Varnas turned his head to deliver a twisted, gray brow. "What? Didn't you become some kind of knight or something? Aren't you some certified monster slayer? Did you forget what they put on your arm? Come on. The strange water girl says its safe, and I believe her. But on second thought, it might be safer with Darin."

"I doubt that," said Chev.

"Now you sayin' something without thinking it through," Varnas shook his head, tisking. "Let's get off this boat. I've started to miss dry ground."

They encountered Darin before they got off the boat. The hunter appraised them both with the same expression he might have given if faced with a small, unpleasant task. "I need some time alone," he told them, and went the opposite direction. It wasn't much a surprise, but Chev was still relieved. They wasted no time practically rolling off the boat.

And so, without much planning or thinking ahead, Chev and Varnas went on their own little expedition. They didn't have to walk long. Past tall grasses and chirping crickets was a lake of clear waters, too shallow and too small for anything dangerous. They quickly jettisoned their clothes and jumped right in.

The moon-drenched lake felt soft and embracing. It was so small Chev quite quickly paddled to the opposite end and yet he could still comfortably talk to Varnas.

Chev sighed, let himself lay back in the water and let his natural buoyancy do the work. "You don't realize how much you need a bath until you have one."

"Yeah," said Varnas, watching a water bug flit on the surface, "Been a while. You know. Not days. Weeks neither."

"Damn Varnas! Surprised you don't smell like a dead skunk."

"Heh. Well, it's there, maboy." Varnas made a wheezing laugh. "Call it lady repellent. Makes life uncomplicated."

"I'm sure you need it!" said Chev. He sighed, channeling stress through his throat. "It's a good kinda complication, though. If it weren't for women, I don't think I would've dragged myself from that hole in the ground."

"Y'see?" Varnas laughed, "That's how a young man thinks. Everything he cares about is right below the belly button. That's just how things are. You get to my age, you start really seeing things. Your whole life, you're so busy rushing around feathering yourself for this mate and that— that you don't stop, see how a blossom unfolds, how the insects move and live their own lives. You stop at that moment, but the whole world just swings around you like you can't do nothing to stop it. 'Sides, don't think I'd know what to do anymore if you dropped a lady on my lap."

"Cry out from the broken hip," Chev quipped.

"Ha! Yep yep, that's pretty much how that would go," Varnas lifted his head. "You know, I think I get as much fun from watching you navigate these rough waters."

"How do you mean?" asked Chev.

"It's just —" Varnas gave himself a moment to word things "— well, you got Sana. Now that lady knight's been thrown in the mix—"

"Adar!" Chev scoffed. "Please! She's practically a boy."

"Didn't finish, boy." Varnas carried on. "And now we got the river lady."

"Naia's not even *nightfolk*," said Chev.

"Looks like Naia don't care."

"Yeah, well, Naia's crazy."

"It's too bad, then, that they're all gonna lose. Naia, Adar, and Sana. You got one lady in your mind above all others."

Chev gave it a thought. "You can't mean Starlight."

Varnas laid back luxuriantly, sending ripples through the little lake, making an agreeable noise.

"I'm here because I'm trying to break my curse with Starlight."

Varnas sighed pleasantly. "It was the only honest thing that Oracle said. She really did break your curse. But what the curse was, it was your head buried in damn nonsense. That was the curse."

There was a movement in the grasses, something was edging through. Varnas and Chev both craned their necks, turning them in bird-like angles. A figure stepped forth.

"You weren't gonna invite me?" asked Adar.

"Didn't think to," Varnas said sleepily.

Chev did not keep nearly as cool as Varnas. He nearly flipped over trying to conceal his privates. "Adar! What are you doing here?"

"Joining you," Adar said, as though that were a stupid question. She disrobed.

Neither of them had known Adar as anything other than a proud knight and nomad, and now in the space of an eyeblink she was entirely, truly, supremely, blindingly naked. Her wholeness laid plain before Chev and Varnas, she was neither particularly ashamed nor vain, and as quickly as she'd stripped she was in the waters, paddling to shallows. Chev, meanwhile, was up to his nose in water.

"Forgive the boy," Varnas murmured, "He's a good man but innocent as a newborn."

Adar swept back her hair, giving Chev a bold look. "I'm not bothered. Chev and I know exactly where we stand."

Chev knew exactly what Adar alluded to—their conversation on the grasses, when they were both thrown from a stag. The time they both nearly did something they would have both regretted.

Varnas, being clever enough to pick something up, decided to shrug it off and move on. "Chev and I were talking about the Oracle and what a useless charlatan she was."

Whatever Adar felt, she chose not to take it personally. Instead, she combed through her luxuriantly white hair and wrung drabs of water from it.

"You're not from the Daylands. I wouldn't expect you to understand. The Oracle is our heritage, the last true Emperor's servant. She's the one thing that keeps us one people. Without her, we'd just be a bunch of mercenaries." She paused, "The water here feels almost silky."

The last comment was tacked on like it was part of the same thought.

"Didn't seem to help us any," said Varnas.

Adar closed her eyes, let the water gently float her. "A charlatan tells people what they want to hear. Clearly you didn't get that treatment, and neither did Sargon."

Varnas always had to get the last word in, especially in response to a good point. So he thought for a moment, lifted his head, and boasted, "Best charlatans use fear *and* flattery."

"Guess so."

Seeing he'd failed to impress anyone with his clever little comment, Varnas' head fell back with a splash.

"Well, *I* agree. The best ones do use fear and flattery."

It was far too light and whimsical to be from Adar, so Chev risked opening an eye. Naia beamed at him with her sharkish teeth, making it impossible for her not to look hungry.

"Naia! How'd you—"

"Please. Water's my domain. How would I eat if I couldn't hunt, and how would I hunt if I couldn't sneak? Hmm?" Naia, in a lazy demonstration, plucked a small fish from the lake and let it flap in the open air. "Too bad the only things here are bony minnows."

Still, she found it pleasing enough to drop in her throat and swallow whole.

"Aren't you supposed to be watching out for monsters?" asked Varnas.

"I did that!" Naia pouted, "Now I'm done, and hanging out with my new friends, the night people."

"Night *folk*," Adar corrected pointedly.

"That's what I said. Night folk. Night people. Pretty much the same thing. Though what makes you so special you get to name yourself after the night? You aren't the only nocturnals on two legs, and none them call themselves 'night people'. You should call yourselves the Eastern Hairless Finch-snouts or something. Much more specific."

"So what do you call yourself?" asked Chev.

"That's very rude," Naia lifted her chin proudly, and wrapping her arms, "Especially since you called me light-gray. But I forgive you. Your lady friend here told me that all males of your species are colorblind, which certainly saves you from a lot of embarrassment. But to answer your question, I'm from very far away. So as far as it's practical, you can just call me Naia, the lovely, elegant, charming, beautiful fish-girl."

"We're from very far away too," said Chev, before shooting a glance at his companion. "Well, me and Varnas at least. We're from the Nightlands."

"The Nightlands?" Naia puzzled over the name. "It's only ever night there? Is that what you're saying?"

Chev's mouth moved to one cheek. "Of course not. Is it only ever day in the Daylands?"

"Well, if it's not only night, why call it that, then?" Out of pure whim and the sense she'd done nothing odd for too long, Naia dropped her head beneath the water, blew some bubbles, and surfaced. "It's pretty silly."

"What's sillier is a look out who doesn't *look out*," Varnas said, though from his dreamy voice he clearly wasn't following the conversation.

"Why don't you go look out, then? Why's it always me? I'd like to have fun too." Naia puffed out a cheek. "Speaking of which, you nightfolk are about as fun as two bricks. Here we are, all naked under the moon, in a little private lake with nothing but crickets for company, and there's not an ounce of tension! I'm bored. Fishes have got to be more interesting."

She left the water with a splash, and slunk back into the Sippi soundlessly.

"She's very strange," said Adar.

"She's a real free spirit," Chev said, "I like her, but in a way where you don't actually want to talk to her."

"Can't figure her out," said Varnas, "I just feel like everything she says, it's all pretend."

"Yeah," Chev mulled that over, "but I don't know if it's all in fun, or if she wants something."

The voice of alarm was so loud that they almost thought Naia had come back. But the echos confirmed it came from the Sippi, and it carried one heart-stopping refrain

"Monster! Monster!"

They ran from the pond dripping wet, trampling over their own clothes before grabbing them and rushed to rejoin the pimmen. The creatures had retreated from the lake, standing shoulder-to-shoulder ashore, and now they were arrayed like so many pebbles on a beach, each transfixed by the surface of the lake, broken seemingly only by the natural chopping of the waters.

"Where is it?" Chev couldn't help but ask.

When Naia emerged, she drew every pair of eyes.

"Even I'm getting out of the water for this one," she said, practically a fountain for the dripping water as she pounced onto dry land.

There was only a moment to ask what was going on, but as soon as Chev thought to ask it had already passed. The waters leading into the lake began to boil and froth like a stew set over the fire too long, and the churning crept closer with a slow and steady pace, like a sneaking ocean surf. The whole mass of pimmen moved away from the shore in a shuddering huddle. Chev did the same, keeping the same sort of distance from the shore.

Staring at the gurgling and choking waters, they all were silent, even as it washed closer to the shore. Chev dared to lean forward, to get a closer look.

"What *is* that?" he uttered unconsciously. It was not something he expected an answer to. It was an exclamation.

"They look like worms," said Adar.

"They're called locust worms," said Naia, her eyes filled with the reflection of white, writhing, sinuous bodies, "But it's a bad name. It's really a *worm locust*—just one creature, and those are its tentacles."

That seemed impossible. What Chev was looking at, though he couldn't quite see it as a living thing, was tangle of wriggling tendrils, each no wider than a finger, but so densely packed that the whole lake seemed to have gone shallow.

This creature drove Naia's expressive voice flat. That was haunting by itself, but now that Chev could see the creature, he could hardly speak.

"You never see them so far inland, though," muttered Naia.

Adar said something, and she did so deliberately, quietly, as though the fearing the creature might hear. "I'm going to get my sword." And she didn't let her eyes off it even as she turned away.

Chev wanted to say the same, but he knew it would be a lie. The sword sat among his possessions, rocking on that barge, with an ever more daunting amount of water and monster between.

But, in Chev's momentary distraction, he hadn't noticed the tentacles emerging from just under his feet.

"Step back," said Naia.

Chev didn't step back. He looked down.

The worms were out of the water, with smaller, barbed tendrils for heads, like the edge of a saw. Just before Chev's toes they found something, speared the dirt, pulling out a crab right from the sand. Other worms fell on it, cracking open the shell, ripping out innards, meat, slurping ichor and pulling the husk beneath the water. In the space of that moment, Chev jumped back.

"If it doesn't find anything, it'll go away," Naia told Chev.

That was difficult to believe as the tendrils sifted through sand for the smallest prey, extracting sandy shells, breaking them open with sickening cracks, and sucking down the oysters, crabs, snails, and whatever else it could grab. The pimmen stood back, a silent wall, barely breathing and for once not chattering. Soon, the shore was pebbled with crushed shells, and the spearing tendrils had emptied the sand of life, and after a few attempts to probe for more, the tentacles retracted and slurped beneath the lake.

There was silence. The slimy sound of millions of worms slipping over each other faded. Chev dared to ask, "Is it gone?"

Adar came, clinking with sword and mail. Darin crept from out of the bushes with bowstring drawn. And Naia held out her hand as way of answer.

She was right to stop them. Because now the frothing came from beneath the barge.

"What's it doing?" asked Chev, watching tentacles creep up the hull like ivy over ruins.

Captain Tips shouted over, "Don't worry. The Queen's behind locked doors. It can't get to her."

"That's not what I'm worried about," said Chev.

"Chev!"

It was Darin who cried out, realizing what was about to happen. And by then Chev was already up to his knees in the lake. From behind erupted shock and violent objections, but they were lost when Chev dove flat into the water.

"It's suicide!"

"Don't do it!"

"What are you doing?"

Only a woman's voice managed to break through. "Come back!"

"I can't." That's what Chev would have said, if he wasn't leaving a wake as he swam through the waters.

The tendrils had squirmed their way up the hull, over the brim and onto the deck. But they had left a bare space that looked no more difficult to climb than any of trees from the Nightlands. With a leap that he didn't know he was capable of, he latched onto the hull, and straddled one of the worms as he climbed, taking only the briefest glances to make sure he would not lay hand nor foot on the creature. And that was the only time he had, because the slithering tendrils chased up his feet.

The deck was different story. In the time it had taken to swim and climb aboard, the tentacles had grown so thick there was barely a space to plant a foot. It was like the root system in a dense forest, except barbed and squirming for flesh.

"Left or right?" came a voice.

"What...?"

"I said, do you need to go left or right!"

Chev blinked, struggling to recall information like he had to pull it out from molasses in his own head. He needed to get to the cabin, whose door was —

"Left!"

There was the sound of a wooden chop, and in an instant the tentacles writhed and flung themselves about in their death throes. With more tentacles at his heels, Chev was forced to jump—his whole body rebelling as he squashed worms beneath his bare feet.

"More, more left!" Chev risked a glance overboard.

Adar had her heavy broadsword between her teeth, water stuck to her forehead like sweat as she paddled in a stubborn effort just to stay afloat. She did an awkward maneuver, grasping her sword and making a wild chop at the hull, severing the stalks of many worms just as she was about to sink. She put the sword between her teeth at just the right time.

"Get on board!" Chev shouted.

With the sword in her clenched teeth, she couldn't speak, but her eyes communicated helplessness.

Chev didn't even think long about it. He anchored his feet to the railing and swung himself down the hull. He grabbed her wrists, Adar responded with wide, stunned eyes.

"Push against the hull!" Chev shouted out of adrenaline, "With your feet!"

Adar understood after a second of blankness. She put her feet to the hull and scraped the side with the soles of her feet. It was just what Chev needed—he pulled her up, and she grasped the railing and shoved herself onto the deck. The sword bumped on wood. While it was between her teeth.

Chev's guts strangled, knowing full well what had just happened. She spat the blade out as she crawled on deck. Blood dripped and filtered between the planks. She held her cheek. With the amount of white in those orbs—she knew exactly what happened. Chev wanted to comfort her, but her focus came right back. She snatched her sword and cut right above Chev's head.

A mass of worms, braided into an enormous tentacle, fell headless and splattered onto the deck in mucus-covered gore. Its main body made a blind swing, like an enormous bludgeon, cracking railing and indenting the planks before sinking back beneath the waters.

Chev's hand lay on Adar's, in a silent offer to take the sword. Adar's face tightened proudly, pulling back her blade, a refusal. It was an odd image, with the blood on her sword matching what was smeared on her cheek. The dark texture hid the extent of the wound.

More knotted tentacles, Adar had to slice through three more in their path, and now they were appearing everywhere. Every side of the barge was being clutched and shaken, Chev could feel them pushing the vessel up, just like the barge had run aground. Running into the hold was not just their objective—it became a necessity.

"I'll—" Adar winced with the cut in her cheek, she touched it gently. "Get inside. I'll hold them off."

"Are you sure?"

Adar waved him off, before facing the doorway with sword held in both hands, disregarding the blood trickling from her cheek. After watching her slash another worm-tentacle, he was sure she could handle things, and rushed into the bowels of the ship.

For a moment, he couldn't remember which door was his. The cries of a child brought him to his senses. *Starlight.*

He burst in, practically kicking the door as he entered. The locust worm had already found the porthole, and it had its feelers halfway across the floor, feeling out the edges of the basket, tracing the edges of the Daysword. Chev cracked the worn wood of the deck as he launched himself at the sword. Like a child might draw a line in the sand with a stick, Chev drew his sword along the worm heads, decapitating a whole line of the creatures. They writhed and hissed for a half-second before some powerful force sucked the bodies back out the window.

When Chev picked up Starlight's basket—which was heavier than he expected—he suddenly realized he'd forgotten something.

"Where do I take her?" he asked himself.

The answer was nowhere. There was only one path. He would have to defeat the worm locust.

Even thinking about it gave him vertigo.

And at the end of the door stood the bone-skin.

He'd forgotten all about them in the rush to save Starlight's life, but they still had a part to play, especially as the creature watched him with that lack of expression only a bony, insectoid face could manage.

"Can I trust you?" Chev asked.

"We have never been what you've mistaken us for," said the bone-skin.

"That's not my question," said Chev in a more insistent tone.

"Yes."

He didn't want to believe it. He was incapable of that. Though either way he didn't have a choice. He held the basket out to the creature's skeleton-like hands. He took it.

"We will care for it."

Its words were undermined by the inhuman chitter that accompanied it. It gave Chev a sick feeling, but it would at least allow him to finish this unpleasant task quickly.

He barreled down the hall. Adar was already hacking at tentacles, barely keeping them at bay, when Chev arrived to finish a few more off. It gave Adar the luxury, however temporary, of holding her cheek closed.

"You're planning something crazy, I see it."

"Yes," answered Chev. And then he vaulted off the railing into the water, slicing through a mass of worms that would have batted him along the way. The water was not so forgiving. It slammed him, Chev rolled through it and lost all sense of direction. Time vanished as his awareness failed him.

Where am I?

The shock. It was so much worse than he would have expected. He didn't know enough to even realize it. He was enclosed by a cold, airless womb.

Should I breath? Can I breath?

Bubbles traced from his nose and mouth. Something thick and heavy dropped from his hand, landing on the lake bed and throwing up silt. It was a sword. Which confused him. Because as the moment passed, he recalled holding it.

I came. I came to kill the worm locust.

But now his sword rested far below, a shimmering dot in silt clouds, and there was no way to reach it. But something else did. A rope made from woven worms wrapped around it and dragged it upward. Chev watched the drama as if he had nothing to do with it.

If a webbed hand hadn't emerged from the murk, his sword might've been lost forever.

Naia wrestled with the tentacles, taking the blade by its two quillons and stripping it away. In a graceful somersault, she sprang towards Chev, urging him to take it.

Chev stared at the pommel. Frustrated, Naia slapped Chev with such force he nearly turned in the water. A brutal, effective method.

I need to kill the worm locust. That's what I came here to do.

The second thing Naia did nearly made him drop his sword again. She took him by the neck, and kissed him.

It was forceful, like an attack, but then Chev felt the oxygen rush into his lungs and he knew exactly what Naia was doing, with her smooth, oddly textured lips locking over his. At that moment, it was like his brain had finally flicked on. Now Naia just needed to give him a little room to work.

The weight of the sword stabilized him in the water. He watched the forest of worms, some probing the lake bed, other reaching to the surface, and still more sinking and retreating, only to shudder and regrow like an explosive shoot from the ground. But they all had an origin, they writhed as part of the same creature. Chev only needed to trace it.

And that creature was indescribable.

As any child, Chev had once turned over rocks and watched the things crawl out, like a menagerie of aliens. But the worm locust was not the same sort of creature. And though he'd seen wet things, shelled things, things with bulging eyes, things with a billion legs, he'd never seen it in one creature. Though all around it mortal battles were being fought, the creature itself drifted carefree along the river bed, manipulating the multitudes of great, branching stalks that made almost a living dome around Chev. The appendages crisscrossed the lake's surface like veins.

It was months ago, now, when he'd fought the bone-skin in the river, and drove an arrow through the eye. It may have been simple, but it hadn't been easy. With this creature, Chev wasn't even sure what to strike first. But like that bone-skin, the eye was good place to start.

As Chev pushed himself through the water he came level with the white, veined orb which twisted to focus on Chev. The stalk was an inviting target, and though it was difficult swinging his sword through the water, he made contact. The blade bit into it.

It wasn't strong enough. If they were above water Chev would have had enough leverage to cut it off, but he'd gone halfway and now a current tossed the dangling eye. Now the whole creature's body aligned to Chev, tentacles all swaying with respect to its motion. If he hadn't had its attention before, he had it now.

When Chev went for the other eye, something shot out of a gap in its shell, and a scythe like appendage parried the sword like it was made of steel itself. When it bounced back from the blade, Chev saw that it was a thick, stout limb, with an attached bone-like spur tapering to a dangerous point. Chev would need to fence it like he would a person.

So when he swung again for the blade's stalk, he was not surprised when a second came out to intercept him. He now faced two scything pillars, but it felt no different than how he might fight two enemies. And so, with two steel-hard bone spurs before him, Chev was on the defensive, deflecting thrust after thrust as the water provided nothing but constant drag.

Soon, he would need to take a second breath. But it would be lethal to even check if Naia was nearby. The fight demanded total concentration. Concentration which was rapidly fading.

Something strange happened. From the surface, which felt leagues away, came the strangest rain, little stones drift down to settle on the lake bed, rolling off the worm locust's chitinous armor, but bringing with it bruised worm tentacles—some even pierced by arrows—that quickly retreated deep below the surface. The creature made a high pitch whine as it slid back a few feet. In the midst of it, Naia slipped through a forest of severed and mangled tentacles, between the two bony scythes and right onto Chev's lips.

A second breath. For just one girl she certainly could fill Chev's lungs. It was enough to bring him once again in focus—just as the worm locust regained its balance and redeployed its spurs to deliver severing attacks. Chev was only just quick enough to weave and deflect the blows, but as far as he was concerned, they provided a barrier no more surmountable than a hundred meter cliff. Only a suicidal attack would get him through.

Suddenly a giant spear plunged into the depths, it's tip pointed directly at the worm locust, obscured by a veil of bubbles. As it drifted upward, Chev saw what it was. Adar, diving swordpoint first, using her rapidly falling momentum to cut through a tentacle and sink further and further. When the water finally slowed her right down, she struggled, making broad paddling movements to take her just a little further down.

She was just as confused by the beast as Chev had been. But the distraction she provided was priceless.

He had to take a risk. It would open him to a counterattack, but he had to try. He pointed his sword toward the creature's healthy eye. Adar lit up with understanding, and made a line toward it, gripping her blade with both hands, using its weight to sink towards it. It was only a matter of driving it into the flesh.

A shrill, drowned cry. All its tentacles convulsed at once, like how hairs stand on end. Even the scythes tensed. It was Chev's only chance to swim past. To deal the final blow, he would need to find strength on the way.

There was a fleshy gap in the shell, whatever was sheltered beneath it pulsed, arteries popping and retreating. Chev found a purchase partway, and reached for a swimming Adar. They glanced at each other, set their swords in the gap, and pushed.

The gentle rock of the barge made Chev's heavy head sway. They were on the river again, and that simple fact gave Chev great comfort. The chatter and labor of the pimmen felt almost like the lullaby of crickets and gently gurgling creeks. It meant Chev was surrounded by safety.

"Never thought you'd outdo yourself," said a voice.

Weathered and wry. It had to be Varnas. Chev's cheek split with a smile as he opened his eyes. Varnas sat along the railing, watching the river, practicing his newly found hobby—if the fat, silver fish lying still beside him gave any indication.

"Was I unconscious?" Chev asked, patting his forehead for tender spots.

"Were you unconscious?" Varnas wheezed, finding it terribly funny for some reason. "Boy, you climbed aboard, put your head down, and fell like a bag o' rocks. Your snoring's been scaring the fish away, I'll have you know."

Chev smirked. It wasn't just Varnas' grudging humor. After giving himself a good inspection he knew he was now unwounded if bruised, with just general ache of having exerted himself to exhaustion. "Expected some admiration from you, not jabs."

"Just keeping you modest." Varnas tugged his fishing rod, hoping he might feel something bite. "Especially when you get past the gauntlet of fawning pim, with the lady knight and fish girl nipping at your heels. You'll thank me later."

"Yeah right. Always trust you to make a molehill out of a mountain. Like drama was something I needed."

"You do need it," answered Varnas.

Chev tested his feet, and they took his weight, though not without rebelling with pain. But the pain was good. It meant that he was alive and what he couldn't believe he'd done really had happened. It wasn't just a dream.

Chev grinned. "I killed a sea monster."

He fell into a sing-song voice. And he might've turned it into a real song had he not walked into a slumped figure, whose head was buried in her knees and arms.

"Adar? You were here the whole time?"

She lifted her chin. And the wound on her mouth was nothing compared to what was in her eyes.

That look would've stopped any celebration, put an end to pride and light-heartedness, caused anyone to search through their lives to find what they might have done to wrong them. Eyes that would silence speeches, and yet be more deafening than any accusation.

"Adar?"

This was not meant to happen. It couldn't. Not after they'd won such a victory. And Chev couldn't have done it alone, just as Adar could never have done it without him. What had turned her so completely against him?

In any case, he needed to get out of the blistering fire from her eyes.

He strode inside the ship balanced on pained feet. Within, the *not bone-skin* sat cross-legged in the hall. In its skeletal arms was a pudgy, hairy child with closed eyes. Quietly, it turned its attention from the child to Chev.

It asked: "Your expression indicates shock. Have I done something wrong?"

Chapter Nineteen
The Secrets beneath Bone and Water

WHEN CHEV GOT the praise he'd sought, he found he wasn't hungry for it. The pimmen who would usually pass him by like he was no more remarkable than a piece of furniture stopped to batter him with questions. As he was right now, cornered by the creatures, who traded speculation with one another.

"The monster musta been a lot weaker dan we all tought," said one, "if just two of dese guys can bring one down."

"Maybe it was the rock-throwing and arrows that did it," said another.

"Nah. Never seen one of dem be boddered by rocks and such. Only way you get 'em is dive deep and open 'em up like a clam shell," said a third.

Captain Tips entered, and on seeing the scene before her she put two fists on her hips and adopted a stern expression. "You bunch! Pit, Rips, Bim, Tes, Isk, Neb, Ree, Flap, Wep, Sip and Cap! Not lounging hour. Wep and Rips, you're expected in nursing. Pit, go swab some decks. Tes and Isk, bilge. Ree, Bim, Neb, rigging. Flap and Cap, food prep. And you, Sip, it *is* your lounging hour, but don't waste it bothering our guest."

There was a collective, "Yes ma'am", except "ma'am" was contracted so far as to sound like "em". The pimmen scurried off in all directions like they knew where they were supposed to be. Afterward, Captain Tips gave a satisfied sigh.

"Curse their curiosity. How are you this evening?"

"Good," answered Chev, who, having sensed the Captain's words hang curiously, as though leading onto something, cocked his head. "You, uh, needed something?"

"Yes, actually." Captain Tips gave a full-bodied sigh, preparing herself for a difficult conversation. "I've never seen a crocodile eat vegetables, a bird walk on its wings, and a mole bask in sunlight. And I've never seen a nightfolk harbor dayfolk."

It was a strange feeling, being cornered by such a small, physically weak creature. But Captain Tips never acted like she was less than half Chev's size. As a matter of fact, it was the opposite, she had such presence that Chev could be physically intimidated by her. She tapped her foot, waiting for Chev to be the one to give answers.

"I know. She's the reason I'm on this journey."

"That right?"

Chev paused, mentally searching for a better way to put it. "You know when you see an insect drown, and you have no business saving it, but you do it anyway?"

"No," she said.

It was very final. Chev carried on. "Well, *I* have that instinct. I'm not here to undermine ancient laws or anything like that. I'm just trying to find a home for her. That's all."

"Well, I wouldn't care even if you *were*. I just don't want any trouble on this ship, as if monsters and pirates weren't enough. And I'm gonna tell you something—barges on the Sippi transport either nightfolk or dayfolk, never both. And for good reason. If it ever gets to be a problem, you're all getting off this boat."

"I understand," said Chev, but not before a nervous swallow.

"And you'll pay the plats for her, too. Double, as a matter of fact."

"Of course," said Chev.

"Excellent," Captain Tips moved to leave, but she suddenly stopped, remembering something. "Good job with the monster, by the way."

No heroic deed went unpunished, it seemed to Chev. Now that he'd slain a monster as terrible as the worm locust, he was made to feel like he'd done something wrong. Darin's sidelong glance was the last thing he needed. For whatever reason, the surly hunter had occupied the hallway in such a way to obstruct the door of the cabin, while he worked a new string for his bow. Chev tried to step past.

"I wouldn't go in there." Darin interrupted. "Adar is more dangerous than an oiled bear trap."

Chev's fingers lingered on the grain of the door. It still bore gouges from the fight with the locust. "What are you doing here, Darin? I mean on this ship? The Oracle told you there was nothing she could do. You think the Emperor is gonna tell you any different?"

"It's not about that anymore." Darin made a half-grunt, from divided concentration. "It's about finding a place. The last thing I wanna be is a drover in the Nightlands. It's not the fate I deserved."

"Yeah, well, I didn't ask for any of this either. Everyone acts like I didn't kill some horrible monster last night."

"You didn't have to," Darin shrugged, "the fish girl said it'd go away."

"Yeah, and let it kill an innocent in the process."

Chev finally got a superior smirk out of Darin. "Don't act like our world ain't filled with monsters. Hundreds of innocents are gobbled up each night, and you don't lift a finger for them. You had a responsibility to the tribe and you blew it."

"You did too—"

"And I know it," Darin's smirk dropped as he gave Chev a direct look. "That's the difference between you and me. I take responsibility for the things I'm supposed to be responsible for. I don't go on feel-good crusades to be a hero. The worst mistake I ever made was letting you talk me into it." Darin eyes fell to the floor again, the string was flat in his hands. "You've ruined my appetite for small talk. Go do whatever you want. Just don't involve me."

"You don't need to tell me." And Chev pushed in the door.

Chev already had goosebumps rising from his flesh, and it wasn't even cold. Adar wedged herself in the far wall, a sword held tight to her chest, glaring at some spot in the wall. The cut along her mouth, washed, sewn and treated, looked like a little bite on the left side of her lip, accentuating a sore expression. There was no movement as Chev entered, nor as Ma-ma the goat leapt to her little stumpy legs to give Chev's fingers a good lick. He gave her a little scratch before turning his attention to Adar.

Darin was right. Like a bear trap, he didn't even want to test it.

"Adar," said Chev.

He was hoping for some response, to knock her out of the black mood she radiated. But it did nothing.

"Please," Chev said, "talk to me."

She glanced at him—but with such a cold and awful look in her eyes Chev knew this was no invitation. With quiet indignity, she tapped the side of her mouth, where she was cut, and turned her head back to the porthole.

"If you don't want to talk, that's fine," said Chev, "But I want you to know that I have had only good intentions. I never meant to hurt you. And if I did, I'm sorry. And I'm willing to do whatever it takes to help. Just tell me."

She remained still but something in her face fluttered. Chev hoped he reached some part of her, but he also knew there was danger in pushing too hard.

The door was ajar, just like it had been when Chev first met the fenderken. He pushed the door just a little wider, opening to a strange scene. Two skeleton-like insectoids knelt over the Starlight, making strange rapping sounds like crickets were lodged in their throats. It was hard not to see the hands as hostile, reaching out to strangle, but they swept over the child's fur with an appreciation for the texture, like anyone else with a heart and wrapped in skin.

Whatever the fenderken were, they were capable of gentleness.

Still, Chev couldn't help but burst through the door, and the fenderken quickly went aside to let him pick the child up. Her little fat hand immediately grasped a link in Chev's chain armor.

"Thank you for taking care of her," Chev said, though even as he said it he could barely imagine it.

"It is our pleasure," said the fenderken, "We apologize for compromising the relationship between you and your woman. We assumed she knew of your transgression."

"She's not *mine*. She's a friend." Chev quickly realized the clarifying was pointless. "You've done a lot more for me than I was expecting. I was actually half-expecting for you to have eaten her. That's what a bone-skin would've done."

"We are not bone-skins," said the fenderken.

"Yeah. I didn't know that. You look like them."

One fenderken said to the other, "A related species to ours. Perhaps aggressive and predatory."

"Note it," said the other.

"Aggressive, predatory, and deceptive," said Chev. "They trick people. Their greatest weapon is their ability to speak."

"It is no wonder you didn't trust us." The fenderken added, "It is likely you still don't."

Chev couldn't entirely deny it. "Sorry," he shrugged.

"We would be happy to learn from the child, just as we might learn from you. We may also teach, while time permits."

Chev squeezed Starlight protectively, as though protecting her from unknown dangers. It was just on reflex. "What could you teach me?"

The fenderken said, "We fenderken have uncovered a secret of the great folk who lived so long ago. We have learned the secret of their blood. Blood we both share."

"That right?"

The fenderken rolled up his robe's sleeve, revealing a pale, unmuscled arm. "Eons ago, you and I shared a parent. To everything that lives on this earth, every plant that grows, everything the crawls beneath rocks, everything that flies in the sky, everything on four legs, two, or none, we shared an ancestor. All life shares this. Thus, if it is neither your father, mother, sister, brother, son, daughter, it must be a cousin. We are cousins, you and I, but so terribly far removed we would never guess it. This is not whole story.

"You see, 'humanity', as they called themselves, fractured. Population pressures, we expect. So a full half of them, who would become our ancestors, remained, while the other half fled into stars, to form civilizations on other worlds. They became the starfarers. But knowing that they would leave their brothers with a lesser destiny, they left a gift. The twenty-fourth code."

"What is that?" asked Chev, head swimming in strange ideas.

"We are made from twenty-four codes, Chev. 'Somas', we call them. They are inscribed in the one thing common to all of us." And at that moment, the fenderken produce a knife and made the smallest incision in the gaps of his bony skin. A drop squeezed onto the floor.

"Blood," said Chev.

The fenderken nodded, putting his knife away. "Twenty-three somas nature gave us. The last our ancestors gave. It made a part of us the gift of *language*."

Now Chev was really confused, with his brow wrinkling up so much it appeared to be jutting out.

The fenderken further explained: "We don't know it, because to us speech is so natural that it is as if we never learned anything at all. But it is not the same for the great folk. Theirs was a product of their society. Those born in different parts of the world could not even talk to one another."

"Like how people can't understand birds?"

The fenderken nodded. "It is an adequate analogy, yes. Just like how we cannot understand birds."

"Things must have been very strange back then," Chev stretched the limits of his imagination to picture it, "People must have seemed beasts to one another."

"Some things don't change," the fenderken chittered in an almost sad way. "In any case, without the twenty-fourth code, we would not even be able to speak to one another and be understood. We owe much to the starfarers."

Chev stared at his hand, eyes tracing patterns in them. "If there's somas in my blood right now... is that why you keep your friends?"

"Hmm?"

Chev gestured to the three kneeling figures, each so cloaked in shadow their hood revealed nothing but black. "Those ones. They're dead, aren't they?"

The fenderken nodded. "They are dead, yes. But that's the greatest secret of the somas, that no death is truly forever. Not while there is still a trace of us remaining. When we rejoin the starfarers, they will have the technology to bring each and every one of us back. All of us, Chev, are immortal. The smallest fragment of us has everything we need to make the whole. Until then, we must be caretakers of the dead."

"And if you're wrong?" Chev asked.

"In what way?"

"If there are no starfarers, no somas, if our blood's just water. If what you're saying turns out to be stories. What then?"

The fenderken gave it some thought, his head swaying. "At least we will have died with purpose," he said, and that was a fitting conclusion to the conversation.

Chev supposed there was no need for the basket anymore. And he relished the chance to take Starlight into fresh air, beneath the river of stars, to watch the shore drift by. It didn't take long for the child to take to sleep, and she relaxed like a ragdoll in his lap.

With his hand lightly ruffling Starlight's fur, Chev quickly lost track of time, undisturbed even by the pimmen who worked diligently through the night. For a while, at least, all the troubles with the pimmen, Adar, Varnas, Darin, seemed to drift off with that shore. Each problem he took in turn, examined it as he needed, and set aside to stew if he didn't come up with anything. Chev hadn't realized how desperately he had needed this time to sit and think.

He gave the door a cursory glance as he heard it open. Then he was a lot more attentive when it turned out to be Adar, out of her armor, with a simple padded tunic and sword. She shifted focus to the child on his lap with a disapproving twist of the lips.

Chev said: "I was going to hide her again. But then I realized: we all know now. So there's no point." Chev looked down on her. "But I can put her away if it bothers you. I just don't like her spending so much time in a basket."

Adar had no answer. She simply took in a deep breath, and took the part of the deck next to Chev.

"I was thinking," she said, and her voice sounded like the creak out of an unused door, the quiet cry of a spider with it web broken, a leaf falling to the ground, "about a lot of different things. Even before all *this*. Do you know who I am, Chev?"

"I know you're Adar, I know you're a knight, I know you have a great deal of faith in what you believe."

"If you want to become something else, Chev, you have to rid yourself of everything you were. That's the way of the knights, Chev, and it's not just ceremony. It's so that you aren't surrounded by reminders of what you could have been. Chev, I've done that. I've put aside everything to take up this sword, this armor, this ax, this lance. Chev, that was the beginning of my sacrifice." She swallowed something back, like she was a bow just plucked and was now only quivering. "You don't want to know, Chev. And this isn't what this is about."

"What is it, then?" asked Chev.

"I'm here to ask you a question. And I don't want you to ask anything back. Just like that night, when you told me I couldn't ask questions about this child. I want to ask if you're worth it."

There is a pause that happens before a conversation of great gravity, it is signaled by an unbreaking eye contact and a tension as still as a lake but seething from within. Like you might touch it and cause it to boil over. Chev and Adar both took this as a moment to collect themselves, so that they could both tread on the shores of the lake

"Am I worth it? Adar, what kind of question—"

Adar repeated herself, stronger, and with further, deeper emotion. "Are you worth it, Chev? That's what I asked. And I don't want clarifications. I don't want your interpretation of what the question means. It's a simple yes and no. Are you worth it?"

"You know, Adar," Chev looked directly into her eyes, "for some reason, I'm scared to answer."

"You should be. Now answer."

Her threat didn't encourage Chev. It only knotted him more, and now it was difficult to even summon the air. He had to take several breaths before he had enough wind.

"I'll answer. But I want you to know that I don't know what you're getting at, and I'm not agreeing to anything."

"Just answer," said Adar.

"Fine. Then yes. Yes, I think I'm worth it."

Adar had been holding her breath. She crushed her lids together as though this were some great release. "Oh, thank the ancestors. It's what I thought, too, Chev. I really did. I just needed someone else to say it."

"What would have happened if I said no?" asked Chev.

In that moment, that ugliness welled once again in her voice. "Don't you ever ask, Chev. From now on. Don't ask."

Though the nightfolk's room had been sealed completely, day somehow penetrated even this darkened cabin. But not the blinding light like raw sun, it was murky light that was somehow more obscuring than pure darkness. Like your eyes didn't know whether to adjust to night or day.

Within, where flecks of dust spiraled through the air like lightning bugs around trees, Adar meditated.

But her meditation was no more clarifying than this dust-speckled light. She was no more at peace than a hot wind circling a closed room. It was more that she'd contained herself, driven mental nails into her mental dam.

Are you worth it? She had asked.

Yes. He had said.

She had told him he'd said the right answer, when in truth there was none of the sort. Only two equally dishonorable, equally unpleasant tasks she had before her. She had to pick one, but she couldn't bear to take complete responsibility for what she was about to do. For what she *had* to do. Though she knew it was a mental trick she performed on herself, it helped to know somehow it would be on Chev's head. Even if just a little.

By even giving an answer, Chev would unwittingly take a portion of the guilt.

Now it was just a matter of waiting until all had fallen asleep. And it was through this time which Adar meditated, hoping to hold back the tide of conflicting voices.

It became obvious now that everyone was in the midst of sleep. Adar still didn't want to move. Everything just felt too heavy. Even her padded tunic.

So she took it off, everything, one by one. Clothes, belt, sword, boots, whatever could be taken off was. And then she stood up, and step by step left the room.

There were sounds, squeals of a child's joy. How evil intentions made innocent things so haunting!

The goat, whose nattered, ropy fur made a play nest for Starlight, cooing and gurgling like any nightfolk child would. But dayghost eyes flickered to her, and in the soft auburn fur split a smile with more gums than teeth. Children knew nothing of taboos. She had no sense that danger was coming. But the goat did.

It pounced onto it trotters, somehow its barred pupils issued challenge. Ferocious and determined it might have been, but it was still a little goat. Its charge bounced of Adar. There was a brief struggle but Adar had her on lock. She tried to smile at the baby, make it seem they were having cuddles, but hand went over snout and Adar did not let go until Ma-ma went limp. She let the goat fall from her hands.

"I'm sorry." That's what she told the goat. She would say the same to Starlight as she picked her up.

It concerned Adar that she should already be so used to contact with dayfolk, that she would be intimate with the sensation of their fur beneath her hands, she knew their scent and their bestial faces. It looked so much like a hairy nightfolk, like any child she might have plucked from the clan nursery.

That was not a comfort. It was disturbing, haunted by knowing a terrible deviancy.

And yet, this child didn't deserve it. It had no idea that it had shattered millennia of tradition and law. It had no idea the danger she posed.

The child was already in her hands, smiling and reaching for her lips and nose, but she still walked carefully, like she might wake it a second time. A careful push took her outside on the walkway.

A peek left. A peek right. It was hard to say whether the pimmen knew her intentions, being that they were so busy working, and that it was daytime besides and the whole world outside the shadows was afire. But they were far enough away that Adar was out of excuses. Each passing moment, someone might notice her.

She had to do it. She had to do it now.

The child had finally got a hold of her nose, and she squeezed with that surprising strength children had. When they made eye contact, the child's open-mouthed curiosity became beaming happiness.

"I'm sorry," Adar told her.

She dropped Starlight into the river.

Chapter Twenty
Catastrophe

ADAR DIDN'T SLEEP. She didn't even try, because she knew she would never be able to. As absurd as it was, she kept thinking she should retrieve the little girl, pull her out of the waters, though she knew very well how much further and further away the child was each second that passed. But the idea persisted, her heart pounded uncomfortably with it. She had to lie on her side so that it didn't feel like her heart was hammering into the floor.

When it was time to get up, she lifted herself with all the grace of something rising from the dead. She was stiff, wide-eyed, and she couldn't pull a loose thought from her head.

Everyone else was up to. Varnas yawned and cracked his joints. Darin had his usual burst of dark energy, rushing so he could seclude himself somewhere peaceful. And Chev came through the door so fast he nearly forgot which way it opened.

"Where's Starlight?" he asked breathlessly.

"Don't look at me," said Adar, like a flinch.

"She with Ma-ma?" Varnas asked, without a hint of alarm.

"Ma-ma... she's trying to tell me something. She's biting at my heels. I think something happened."

"The goat's not—" *...dead?* Adar froze before she gave herself away.

"Not what?" asked Chev.

"Not what? The goat's not hurt, is she? Maybe she fell into the river?" There was more blood in her brain than thoughts.

"Help me find her," said Chev, making a big, impatient circle around the room.

"We oughta look on the deck," said Adar, "maybe the goat left her with the pim?"

But Varnas had a simpler idea. He walked over to the basket that Chev had used for Starlight, opened it, and pulled the girl out.

Varnas was no magician, as far as Adar knew, and Starlight had no twin. So the noise that went out from her mouth was nothing she could control. Pure shock from witnessing the impossible, the sort of horror everyone feels at witnessing their first inexplicable miracle. A living, breathing, Starlight, little legs kicking in the air.

Chev made a sound of relief like someone had pulled an arrow right out of him. But that was nothing compared to Adar, whose gasps couldn't followed by words.

"How stupid of me!" said Chev, who pushed Starlight's furry little head into his shoulder, "I must have placed her in the basket! I can't believe it."

"If I lose something, I always check where I had it last," said Varnas, wry smile on his lips. "Hopefully that's the drama of the day over."

As Adar watched Chev and Starlight together once again, the strangest, most pleasant sensation drifted from her heart to the tips of her fingers like a balm. It was *relief*.

As soon as the opportunity arose Adar stormed onto the deck and shouted to the river: "Come out!"

The river was silent except for its usual slurping and chopping.

"Come out! Come out!" she continued to shout. "I know you're down there!"

Naia's head pierced the waters. "You don't need to call me twice, I've heard ya."

"It was you, wasn't it?"

"What?" Naia place a hand over her heart. "You're saying it like *I* did something wrong, and all I did was save a child's life, plus a goat while I was at it. And I'm so selfless I didn't even take credit for it!"

Adar steadied her breath, raised a judging eye. "You have no idea what you've just done. You should have stayed out of it."

Naia put a finger over her lips in a mockery of pensiveness. "Hmm. Well, you know, when I saw a cute little baby wailing and crying as it drifted to the bottom of the river, I hardly stopped to ask myself if it was my business to save it. Funny, I just knew it was. But I guess I was wrong. I guess you'd leave people to die even if it was super easy to save them."

"I've spent my whole life killing monsters," Adar drew up, "But not everything that poses a threat to civilization is a beast. Sometimes it is something innocent and blameless. Sparrows can sometimes bring disease. Hares can—"

"You're boring," Naia sighed, and slipped beneath the waters.

"Hey!" Adar leaned over the railing. "Hey! I'm talking to you! Get back!"

Naia lifted her head again, a little closer and sending up a spout of water. "You sound like one of those old butt-faces. And I traveled long and hard to get away from old butt-faces."

"Now that's just juvenile," said Adar.

"That's what stupid people say. Back where I'm from, people used to kill each other over the Big Magic Conch or Holy Pearls of Wonder or whatever. People were saying the same thing about me back then, that I was immature because I just didn't understand how things worked. Well, they're all chopped up like sharkbait, and here I am, alive and enjoying life. They can all stick their magic holy pearls you-know-where."

"This is different. This is about an ancient treaty, to end a terrible war between dayfolk and nightfolk—"

"Oh!" Naia clutched her head, "Sorry! I just had this flashback. Suddenly, you had grown a big ol' beard and butt-cheeks on your face, and you started blathering on and I forgot to listen because, honest, it sounds like the dumb ol' crap they used to tell me all the time. Sorry, go on. I'm listening."

Adar seemed to inflate a bit, like every curse she wanted to say was held back by her chest. But she unleashed it in one long exhaled breath and turned to speed off down the deck.

Naia was laughing, lazily kicking through the water. "Ok, really. Go on. Tell me."

Adar stopped, two hands clenching the railing, her gaze skipping like a rock across the waters. It was a while before she thought of something to say, but Naia waited with unusual patience, smiling as though lightly tickled by her own thoughts.

"Listen I—" Adar bit her lip, "Damn it, Naia, when I saw that girl come out of that basket I was so relieved. I don't want to be a murderer. But I couldn't think of a better plan. Even if you don't care to understand why, Chev needs to lose that child, for the good of nightfolk and dayfolk."

"Is this the part where you recruit me?" Naia was wry.

"Yes. Naia, it was right of you to save her, and it was wrong of me not to ask for your help. So I'm asking now. The child needs to go."

"What would you have me do?" Naia asked with a skeptical lilt. She was curious, not agreeing.

"You could take her to a dayfolk city. Leave her on a wharf in the harbor."

"Well now," Naia turned in the waters, and laid on it like a bed. "You see, *here's* where I say it's none of my business. 'Sides, I kinda think she's cute. We had some real quality girl-girl time, we did each other's hair and had a nice chat. Not sure I'd want to get rid of her even if I could."

"You're hurting Chev if you don't."

Naia seemed to think that was funny. "Don't get me wrong, Chev's fun to poke, but he's nothing special. I'm from a *social* species, teasing and flirting's like how we say hello. I had to learn how to hold back with you people."

"If you don't help," Adar declared, "you're in the way. We have nothing left to discuss."

"Sure thing." Naia was about to dive. "Oh, and Adar!"

Adar clearly didn't want to ask, but she felt compelled to. "What is it?"

"The dayfolk kid is not your rival," she said, "You can have Chev whenever you want."

And after Adar's indignant bristling and flushing, Naia laughed and slipped into the waters.

Adar's walk was purposeful down the hall, that was when Darin, who was near invisible leaning against a wall, addressed her.

"You did the right thing, you know," he said.

Adar felt the blood drain from her cheeks. "How so?"

"Don't sound so cold. You'll give yourself away if Chev talks to you." Darin gave Adar a jaded eye. He was stooped in the corner, vaguely remind Adar of how a tiger might rest in the shadows. "And I'm talking about last day. You did the responsible thing. You did what Chev or Varnas should have done had they been sound of mind."

"I don't know what you're talking about," said Adar.

"I understand," Darin smirked, "You don't want to say it. Just know whatever you tried, it was brave. I can't be bothered, if I'm honest. I already told them that kid is their responsibility and I wouldn't lift a finger to save it. That's as much as I can do."

Adar turned to Darin, silently beseeching him to continue.

Darin obliged, "I can't call Chev anything but well-meaning, but nothing changes the fact he's a man of passion. His father was forced out of the tribe when Chev was still at a very young age. Since then, he's done nothing but try and prove himself to everyone, but he only ends up making things worse. He's cursed alright, but it's not with some bonding. Everything he touches he destroys. He leaves misery in his wake."

Darin answered Adar's silent question. "If you're feeling bad, don't. Another thing about Chev is that he's very forgiving. Actually, he's naive. I tried to kill him once, did you know that?" Darin licked his lips as he smiled, his eyes made an irregular flutter. "He doesn't bring it up anymore. If I were him, I would have slit my throat in my sleep. But he doesn't do that. And if he ever finds out what you did, he'll be angry, he'll throw a fit, but a week'll pass and all's forgiven. In fact, there's no reason not to try again. If you fail nothing will happen, and if you succeed, you slip away, and save yourself the fate that all his 'friends' suffer.

"You don't have to say anything. I understand. Maybe you try again, maybe you won't. I won't judge you either way. Go do whatever you want."

And with that, Darin leaned back into the shadows and shut his eyes.

All in all, Adar wasn't sure she wanted Darin's approval, even less now that she knew his reasoning, and what he'd done. She remembered what she'd told Naia, and she still believed it, but in the conflicted way where one's heart and head were not the same place. Adar couldn't even figure out which wanted what.

She must've looked moody instead of contemplative as Chev opened the door. He had the same cautious expression as yesternight, when he tried to talk to her in this very same room. But he wouldn't be scared off like before. He stooped down across from her, moonlight beaming in from the porthole.

"You seemed so much better this dusk," said Chev.

Even the attempt at breaking the ice was so earnest and sweet, Adar couldn't help but smile. "Yeah. I wasn't doing well. I hadn't slept at all. I even took a walk out into the day."

"What was on your mind?"

"That it's impossible to do the right thing."

Chev stretched his shoulders as he digested Adar's words. "Sometimes. I think the right thing's like rabbit. It's hard to find. You have to stalk it, you might have to get on your knees and reach into it's burrow, but it's there."

"And makes awful good stew?" said Adar.

"Awful's right. At least my mother's. That's why her mate always hunted deer to eat."

"Your mother must not have seasoned things right." Adar licked her lips, as if tasting a decades-old stew. "Venison is good by itself, but rabbit takes in flavor. You need to put it in with the right herbs and spices. Wait— your mother's mate? Not your father?"

Chev waved his hands, as though defensively. "No no no no. He *was* my father. But, where I come from, the children were raised by everybody. It wasn't good to know exactly who your father was."

Adar's brow crumpled. "How odd. Things are very different in the Nightlands."

"They are. And as much as I hated it, I think about it and realize it made a kind of sense. It's not like here. In the Nightlands, the monsters could take advantage of that bond. You had to sacrifice people to save the community. It sounds cold, but the thing is…" Chev clutched his hands together. "*Everyone* was in that community. Everyone you loved. And if everyone was out for themselves, we would be like the savages in the deep woods. Hunting fellow nightfolk to sacrifice to the bone-skins."

"We live in a world of monsters." Adar leaned her head back against the wall. "Nothing's gonna change that."

"But *we* don't have to be monsters," said Chev, his voice suddenly gloved with conviction.

Adar shrugged. "I hear that a lot. Chev, I just realized something about you, but I'm not sure how to put it."

"Try me," said Chev.

"Where to begin? Chev, there's no word in my language for someone who is too courageous for causes he shouldn't fight for. 'Hero' doesn't do it. You're a *fool*."

She didn't say it like she wanted to hurt him. She said it like it was a fact.

"A fool?" Chev repeated to himself.

"Yeah," Adar nodded, "A really brave fool, who'll rush into mortal danger to save something that ought not to be saved. And I'm the opposite. I'll do terrible, craven things for the right causes." Her last statement put her into a mood again. She looked away.

"Hey," said Chev, "Hey, that's not true. You threw yourself into the lake to save *me*. I would never have killed that monster without your help. Adar, I think you're a fool too."

"You think so?" Adar split a smile.

"Yeah. We're both fools. Look at you! You became a knight, you traveled all the way to Manak, and now you're on a boat with a bunch of strangers to see some guy who calls himself Emperor? Sounds pretty foolish to me."

"You're right." Adar smiled, "I'm a fool. Why does that sound so freeing?"

"I dunno. Maybe because you don't have to worry about things that don't have to do with you. It's like what Varnas always says: 'wise' is another word for 'useless'. Maybe the most useful person around is a fool?" Chev already liked the way that sounded, judging from his satisfied smile that spread across his lips.

"Gods, that's so stupid." But Adar didn't drop that smile. "I'm gonna do something stupid Chev. What would you do if you knew I tried something awful?"

"It depends," said Chev, "But I've never killed anyone over anything, so it's not like I'm going to start doing that."

"And what if you never knew I tried something awful?"

"If I don't need to know, then don't tell me," said Chev, "The past's behind us all."

Adar's eyes watered as she clenched her lips tight, but it felt right to put her head on his shoulder, and he put his head on hers, so that her silver locks just tickled his nose. There was a satiety between them, like they had just finished a great meal. But neither knew that Chev was perfectly wrong about one thing. Tonight, he *would* start killing people.

But it wasn't obvious then. And it wasn't obvious even as Naia climbed up to the porthole, and spoke through it to the silent couple.

"Well, that's sweet. But you should probably get on deck, we might need your help. Pirates this time." Naia rolled her eyes. "It just never ends, does it?"

Chev and Adar burst on deck, already swords in hand. A more cautious Captain Tips cringed and swept her hands, communicating they should take the alarm down a notch.

"They're tollers, not raiders," she said, "They'll ask for some plats and move on."

"But you said they wouldn't attack while we were on board," said Chev.

"Yes. *Dayfolk* pirates won't. But *nightfolk* ones will. But don't worry. These ones aren't too bad."

That assessment didn't quite match the sight before Chev. Past a hedgerow of pim manning spears and crossbows was a Sippi filled with boats. Torches licked brightly in the dark, and in every spare space a man could be seen. Torchlight made deep shadows, intensifying the courses over each dent in their armor and bend of their weapons. Shouting, cursing, and guttural laughing drowned the continuous slopping of the Sippi.

"There must be a hundred of them," said Chev, spurring close enough that his knees nearly touch a pim's back.

"And you'd make a perfect target if they decide to shoot!" warned Captain Tips.

Chev saw her point, so he took steps backward, into the relative safety of the shadows. He didn't know how much good it'd do when they would pull their boats alongside the barge, as they started doing.

Captain Tips leaned over the railing. "Van, nice to seeing you again! How's that back of yours?"

"Better," growled a voice from below, "No thanks to you."

The barge was low enough in the water that the pirates could simply climb aboard from their rowboat, which visibly rose from the water as it disgorged a dozen armored men onto the deck. But they wore no armor like Chev had ever seen, it wasn't the elegant, seamless skins of daysteel the knights had. It was like they'd hacked bits of steel and sewn it into their garments, or taken ill-fitting pieces and strapped them on. It was not just the armor in disarray, but their faces as well. Darin's wound seemed a minor disfigurement compared to the burns, scars, and just sheer ugliness of these men, each of whom had oil-black stringy hair flickering with torch flame.

A thickset man, looking a bit inflated with all the padding he wore, pushed a punctured helmet more fully on his head. A smirk spread between two jowls.

"You finally got to shipping nightfolk, I see," the pirate Van said, already having spotted Chev and Adar in the shadows. "Knights as well? Didn't know the dayfolk pirates were so bad."

Captain Tips had to look up from the man's belly, but somehow, she managed to seem equally grounded. "Nightfolk are a little less brutal at the moment. And I see you got a lot more armored. Didn't know tolling was doing you so well."

"You're a harbinger it seems. War has followed you folk from the east. We took advantage, me and the lads had some shore time to do some battlefield looting."

"And they say birthdays only come once a year," Captain Tips said, "Well, do your headcount, but I'll tell you right now it's six passengers, three corpses, three hundred ninety-five pimmen, and one goat."

"Three corpses? Thought them starfarers came up with only one."

"Manak was not kind to them," said Captain Tips.

"I see. I'll relay my condolences when I see them," said Van, but in his slimy, greasy manner that hinted he didn't really care.

There was a brief moment, as the pirates spread out to search the vessel, that Chev could sidle close to Captain Tips. It was strange whispering to a creature who couldn't comfortably reach his chin, but since every head was turned at that moment, Chev realized it might be his only chance.

"Didn't you say they didn't like dayfolk and nightfolk being on the same boat?"

"Yeah?" It was like Captain Tips didn't know what he was digging at. But then she did, and her jaw dropped. "*Frick!* Why didn't cha— Damn it, you gotta do something."

"She's in my cabin. I—I didn't bother hiding her."

"Chev," Captain Tips spoke now in an urgent whisper. "Listen, you can't let anyone who sees her leave this boat alive."

"What? Like, *murder?*"

"Not *like* murder. *Definitely* murder."

"Hey," one of the pirates made a dull, tinny command through his helmet, "no chattin'."

They both knew they could really only afford to say one more thing to each other. It was just a matter who had the more important thing to say, and they both paused a brief moment.

"Follow them inside," said Captain Tips.

"Hey!" the pirate straightened up, a little more insistent, "Whaddid I say? Huh?"

"I heard you," said Chev, both to the pirate and to Captain Tips. He shot one glance before he made a purposeful stride into the boat.

The pirate chased him with a command, "Didn't tell you to move, either!"

Chev had just a moment before he was followed. His hand moved to his pommel, and as he marched he spoke to his heart in a futile attempt to still it. Blood rushed through him so hotly he felt feverish.

His cabin door was open. There were people inside.

Am I really going to kill someone? It felt unreal, like discovering you're marching towards a cliff and there's nothing you can do to stop yourself. His brain and muscles had already prepared themselves for the act, and as he turned into the cabin, he was ready to stab at the first thing that jumped out.

Three men, bulky with steel and leather, sifted through their things like animals rutting through trash. The basket was turned over. There was nothing in it.

And the men who lifted their heads from their tasks didn't seem appalled, only annoyed.

"Who let him in here?" shouted a goateed pirate, with a hand full of Darin's shirt.

And the pirate from outside rushed in beside him, clapped a gauntlet over his shoulder. "Told you not to move, fool. Gimme your sword, any more funny business from you, stag rider, and I'm pushing you overboard."

The pirate ripped away his sword. In shock, Chev didn't resist, and by the time he regained his balance it was too late.

"You damn proud stag riders, always think you're so superior. Well this is a robbery. You understand me kid? ROB-bur-REE. It means I don't care what you think. We're taking your things and there's not a thing in the world to stop us."

There was another open door, where the fenderken sat and meditated. He spotted a slight movement from under a robe. Like something pushing against fabric. Something like a child's hand.

They took Adar's sword too, and Darin's bow, and Varnas' spear. The four sat in a miserable line by the wooden wall, knees folded deep in their chests, watching as pirates marched past them with the strut of conquerors. Adar had an especially murderous glare aimed at one of the pirates. The thin, tall man, reminding Chev of a birch tree, wore chain and the sword of a knight, as he picked his nose without thinking and ran his hand over a round ear. Chev could only imagine how maddening it must have been to Adar.

A disheveled, helmeted pirate, the same who had pushed Chev out of his own room, now stopped before him, giving both him and Adar a glance.

"Stand up," he told them.

Neither complied at first. It wasn't disobedience, more that they were considering disobedience, waiting to see if the other would rebel.

"You two are the deafest. I said, stand up!"

The pirate pulled a small, sharp blade from a hidden sheathe. Now Chev decided it was best to stand, though his pace made it clear he was in no hurry. Adar followed behind.

"Now," the pirate grinned, "take off your armor."

"Armor is fitted for me," said Adar.

"Didn't tell you to talk."

"Unless you got a companion with a *big* chest I don't think mine will do you good."

"Take it off or I'll really open that cheek up, honey."

Chev could already feel it without looking. The violent tension that Adar exuded was not an expression but an aura. It was like her skin had suddenly stretched thin over her face, so that every vessel popped in jagged lines, her eyes were tight and focused so you could see the flesh just between orb and lid, and beneath the skin was a fiery rush of blood.

And she pulled off her chain with as much energy and rage as she might have stabbed him with.

"Good, good," the pirate turned to Chev. "Now you do the same, boy. Make it quick."

Now the knifepoint's near electric energy came to rest on Chev. And seeing Adar, proud and indignant, follow the pirate's commands, Chev felt in no position to refuse. He got out of his chainmail.

The pirate pressed the knife into his own finger, a grotesque smile on his indelicate features. And soon, two suits were laid before him. How Chev hated knowing he had had given this strange, abominable man his twisted expression of self-satisfaction. And the pirate was poised with another command on the edge of his lips—this next one would have been just pure humiliation—except Van noisily stepped onto the deck, Ma-ma tucked beneath one arm.

"That's my goat!" said Chev.

"My goat now," announced Van. And judging by how he held Ma-ma's snout in place, she wasn't agreed either. "Well past her prime. You really should've eaten her ages ago."

"She's a milk goat!"

"Can still eat a milk goat," said Van, with raised eyebrow. He then nodded to Captain Tips. "Madam Tips, honorable as always. Exact head count."

"After you're done robbing my passengers like you said you wouldn't, you can take your plats and go." With that, Tips threw a minor fortune of plats on the ground, with enough force and irritation a few scattered out of the bag.

Van made a simple nod with his head and got one of his goons to retrieve the money, "By the way, we're changing how we count heads, Madam Captain, not sure you heard yet. Instead of treating each pim as a quarter head, we're counting them as one whole head. I'm not sure why we made the exception in the first place. This way is much more equitable, wouldn't you agree?"

Those turned out to be Van's last words.

But only Captain Tips knew it at that moment. As things grew more pregnant with silence, it was more obvious that there would be violence. And that it would come suddenly and with great savagery.

Van was still nodding like a dolt when Captain Tips burst forward drawing her hidden knife, so quickly and with such decision he only had time to form an expression of mild surprise. Tips knew the precise place to cut and kill, so she cut Van's inner thigh like a slice of meat. A soft, bloody spot it quickly became, and barely a blink later Van's midsection was soaked with his inner blackness.

"Hnnngh!" A pathetic noise for a dying man to make. But it was the only thing in his power to say.

There was instant action. Ma-ma twisted free and trotted quickly to safety. Adar, with her honed combat instincts knew to shove the gap-mouthed pirate goon off the railing into the water, grabbing their swords in one swift movement into each hand. An underhanded toss later and Chev was armed, much of the battle was over by the time he was ready to fight. The pimmen were at arms, and seeing them fight was a little like watching prairie dogs muster to war. It didn't seem right that they should be holding spears and manning crossbows, using their numbers to force the pirates off the decks and right into the Sippi.

Adar found the time to drive her blade into the heart of the man clad as a knight, pushing her sword down like Chev had seen Ossen finish off wounded animals. But Ossen never seemed to relish it like Adar did.

As a matter of fact, having killed bone-skins and locust worms and every forest animal imaginable, the thought of raising sword against fellow nightfolk made his stomach churn. And such a battle was now sure to happen, because as much as they might have cleared the deck, there was river of pirates before them, cursing in surprise and enacting an impromptu battle plan.

"Repel the boarders!" Captain Tips was so covered in Van's blood that she barely looked pim anymore and more a predatory beast, with big gnashing teeth, a swarming, bloodthirsty piranha.

A half-dozen boats, each with a dozen warriors, fought through the water to be the first onto the ship. The pim demonstrated blistering discipline but none were fast enough to hold back all the boarders. Those that fell into the waters sank quickly by virtue of their armor. The ones that ascended found themselves slicing hedgerows of spears.

But no matter how organized the pimmen, the nightfolk brigands still were physically gigantic by comparison. And their blows demonstrated that. One man with a single swing of his mace knocked aside and broke several pimmen. Chev witnessed the creatures getting pulverized in unspeakable ways, crushed like bugs.

"Stop standing around," Varnas cried to Chev, "Pick up your damn sword!"

"Right!" Chev could do that, but somehow he couldn't bring himself to use its edge. He approached a pirate distracted by pimmen, and gave him a powerful slap with the flat of his blade, knocking him off balance on the edge of the deck. The pirate tried to grab the railing but cracked over it instead. His cry was cut off by a splash.

Bolts thudded into helmets. Pimmen, whole and in pieces, flew through the air. Adar's blade careened from one pirate's neck to another's arm. And though Chev hadn't been spinning around, it sure felt like it. The whole world was sideways.

A wet hand shot out of the water. The pirate scratched the hull of the ship.

"Help!" he cried to Chev. "I'm drownin'!"

Two more hands came up, this time to clap over the pirate's jaw and wring it like a cloth. A crack issued, and the pirate's eyes went blank and didn't resist sliding beneath the waters.

"You know," Naia said, "If you knock 'em into the water or cut their heads off, it's pretty much the same thing."

"Huh?"

"Gods you're thick. *They die*. The guy you knocked in the water? Drowned. So just hack 'em to pieces, won't ya?"

"Hack them to pieces," Chev repeated to himself.

Naia was already gone by the time Chev looked down. He was left with heavy blade in sweaty hand, and so many directions he could take it. The pimmen turned out to be fiercer warriors than Chev had expected. A pirate stumbled around with a pim holding his shirt and driving a knife repeatedly into his soft collarbone. More pimmen had thrown themselves on top of an enemy to force blades through gaps in armor. But as fierce as they were, they were still physically underwhelming. One pirate could easily kill multiple pimmen before getting killed himself.

So, rather like a dowsing rod, Chev let his weapon point him to pimmen in trouble. Two pirates, walking amalgams of leather and steel, clubbed and hacked at a ball of cornered pimmen, each blow splitting a poor creature apart.

Chev stepped forward, sword ready to be brought down in a terrible arc. A wasted second meant a lost life, so he told himself the man whose head he was about to split was a bone-skin in nightfolk form. The mental trick worked, it was surprisingly effortless when he finally did it.

Skull cracked, body went stiff, and the pirate fell dead. His companion saw it, twisted to aim at Chev with a cruel steel bludgeon.

"You killed Gav," he said, "Treacherous pointy-ear!"

It was a predictable attack, the way the pirate lifted his mace to bring down on Chev's head. Defending from it wasn't the difficult part, in an elegant maneuver Chev had parried it easily out the way. It was pointing the sharp end at the pirate—then thrusting. There was a natural resistance that had to be overcome, and an instinct to mercy he had to silence.

But his blade punched right through the enemy, and that was that.

There was no time for relief on the pimmen's part. They exploded forth from their corner and pushed back the pirates to their railings. Chev was still retrieving his blade, the pirate's armor and bone held a surprising vice-like grip over it.

"Come on," Chev prayed. He didn't want to step on the man's chest, he had an irrational belief he'd step right through the breastplate into a puddle of gore.

Chev turned to an alarming whine just behind his ear. A thin-faced pirate's mouth hung open, his knife's profile thin and short as it pointed right between Chev's eyes, but he wasn't stabbing. He was dying. A feathered shaft stuck from his neck and gravity did the rest of the job.

Darin stepped forward. "You're welcome," he said, before loosing another arrow at a warrior clambering over the edge.

Chev got the point. He pulled the rest of the sword out, the breastplate took his weight. He wrung it between his hands and joined the fight.

The pimmen, with the help of Adar's swordwork and Varnas' mad spearing, were winning. But the deck was slippery with blood. The battlefield littered itself with weapons and bodies. Chev knew it was now his part to repel any more boarders. Chev found an unguarded section of the ship and waited with sword in hand.

His mistake was obvious. The boat that drifted close was not full of fighters, but archers. Chev saw a bow shift toward him, at a distance he was sure to hit. Too late to dodge—Chev only could hope that it would wound, not kill.

But the waters itself blasted beneath the rowboat, the arrow went wild through the air, and in a bizarre spectacle the whole boat's worth of pirates slid right into the river without even a chance to cry out or protest. One moment they were above water, the next they weren't. Bubbles gave the only clue that anything had happened at all.

Naia came up. "Get in the boat, Chev!"

"Did you kill all those pirates?" Chev still couldn't grasp what he'd seen.

"I did. Get in the boat! They've got a catapult!"

"A what-a-what?"

"Listen, Chev, I haven't got time to explain modern military engineering to you—"

And Naia was right about that. Because it became obvious as a gigantic boulder came arcing right through the air towards the barge.

Whatever that cat-a-whatsit was, Chev couldn't imagine any creature so big it could toss a boulder so heavy so fast. It seemed almost magical, and Chev was awed even as it smashed right through the ship.

Gods! It was a sickening rip, like the breaking of bone, or the worst windstorms tearing through the woods. The whole vessel lurched unnaturally, beams broke and snapped beneath their weight. The flat floor beneath Chev turned into a slope.

From somewhere, Captain Tips bellowed: "Get the Queen!"

She didn't even need to say they were abandoning ship. The horrendous sounds already told that story. Chev could feel through the boards the sensation of weight as the ship's belly filled with water, and it seemed to slide further and further down. The structure was snapping beneath the strain.

The remaining pirates threw themselves back on their boats, but it was too late—the circumstances had changed. Now it was the pim who disgorged out, in such numbers they practically pushed the pirates out of their own boats. Adar, Varnas and Darin had the right idea, staking claim to a vessel of their own. With indistinct shouts and sharp gestures they urged Chev follow.

Chev couldn't. Starlight was still on board. He only hoped they would still be waiting by the time he got out.

Inside, the corridor was already slick with water, sloshing with increasing urgency as it followed the slope of the ship. It got deeper as Chev went, he had to walk as though treading through muck, the water proved too thick to simply wade normally.

That was Starlight's cry. It had to be.

The fenderken was waist-deep in water. Nestled in his arms was Starlight, bawling and little limbs desperately flailing. The creature knew what Chev was here for. He made a rasping sound that Chev could nearly call relief.

"Come with us," Chev said.

"I cannot. I've failed my brethren. They will die true deaths in this river. If they shall, so will I."

"I can take a part of you with me... give it to your people."

"And where will you find them? You do not know. Let us die with dignity."

Chev supposed he could have argued. He would have if the water wouldn't be up to his neck in a matter of seconds. It was also that the creature's voice brooked no room for persuasion. It knew what it wanted. And that was that.

"Thank you," said Chev, "You saved us."

"Go," the fenderken insisted.

It was good advice. Chev followed it.

By the time Chev saw the moon again, the deck had inclined so deeply that he would have slid down had he not dug in with his heels. He scrambled up toward the sky with claw and foot, and finally grasped the boat's edge like it was the end of a cliff. To some extent, it was.

"Get on!" was the cry.

Chev still had just enough energy. He launched himself over and let gravity do the rest of the work, skidding onto the rowboat that Varnas, Darin and Adar had claimed. He hit it hard enough that the whole boat bounced and splashed.

"Couldn't have timed things better!" said Varnas.

Indeed, the scratched, worn underside of the barge had fully tipped on one end. Bubbles rose as the last air pockets collapsed. The ship was on its last descent, and it was impossible not to watch. Even the pimmen, emotion ripping through them with cries and pleas, were transfixed.

Chev imagined what it would have been like if his own home had sunk into a swamp. A few months ago, he couldn't have imagined it. It seemed the very worst thing in the world.

And, as if the world itself was telling them to move on, their boat began to drift towards the shore.

But something wasn't quite right. The current was too powerful, and too straight, to have been natural. Chev had a hunch, so he looked overboard.

"Naia!" he said not completely in surprise.

She was acting like the boat's propellant, pushing the boat and undulating her whole body, but she was oddly languid about it, too. When the boat hit the shore, and nightfolk leapt out from it, Chev helped her out of the water just as Ma-ma emerged, wet and bedraggled from the water's edge.

Naia wasn't just tired. She was wounded. A feathered quarrel stuck out from her thigh, blood made a brisk journey across her smooth skin.

"It's not as bad as it looks," said Naia, whose throat suddenly contracted in an ominous way.

"I wouldn't say that," said Chev.

"Then you've never had a shark bite." Naia smiled. "Listen, help me back into the water."

"Are you sure? Can you swim? With monsters like the worm locust—"

"You don't help a fish by taking it out of water. Please, help me. I'm too weak to stand. Pick me up. Put me in the water."

"Naia," Chev looked into her half-shut eyes. "Thank you." And then he picked her up.

"Do me a favor, Chev," Naia had her hand around Chev's neck. "Settle in a place close to the water. If you don't, I'll never find you again."

"I'll try," said Chev.

"Goodbye, friend. I'll let you in on a secret. I only pretended to be stupid."

Chev smirked. "I'll let you in on a secret, too. I know."

He laid her out in the shallows, and she made her miraculous, but by now familiar, transmutation from girl to fish, and she wriggled out onto the river, kicking up mud as she went. Chev watched that mud cloud up and settle. For such an absurd person, she left an impression.

"She gonna die?"

Chev turned around. It could only have been Captain Tips, though Chev experienced mild surprise to see her alive.

Captain Tips nodded, having read his face. "Well, I guess it's nice that she's free now. Guess things aren't all bad. I have to admit, though, I thought it was you and that kid that would bring us the trouble. Not me."

"You attacked the pirate," said Chev, "Why?"

"When the noose closes around your neck you cut it. Simple as that. Off to Sunset?"

"Yeah," said Chev, "You?"

"We were never river people, yet we made it our home. That's just who we are. I hope if you've learned anything, it is to have strength like pimmen."

"I'm sure I will." Chev glanced at the horizon. "I'll find a home. But first, I have one last journey I need to make."

Chapter Twenty-One
A Hymn to Honor the Sun

"WE'RE LUCKY, aren't we?"

Somehow Varnas could practically chirp and skip up hills while everyone dragged with exhaustion. He and Mama, the two old ones, seemed to thrive on the harshness of the journey.

Darin responded as though cursing Varnas personally. "We're going to die."

"Of course we're going die. One night, we'll all die."

Darin shook his head, in place of exasperation. "It's not clever anymore, Varnas. You damn well know it might be this night. I haven't seen a tree since we got on shore. Come dawn this place is a deathtrap." Darin snorted, his head pulled to a curious bend. "It even smells like it."

Chev had been happy to ignore the chatter, but Darin's remark was strange enough that it grabbed Chev's attention. He sniffed, and found that something did indeed pinch in the air. It was a sour scent, like those burned cities they'd seen on the road to Manak, but fresher somehow.

"We're still lucky! Look!" Varnas swept his hand at the panorama, "We could've been one of them!"

Just over the knoll was a scene Chev could not easily believe, but the scent was too fitting, and the sight so strange, that it could not be a dream. They look like large rocks at first, like a beast had scattered masses of them across the grass, but boulders did not have eyes to pick at by crows, and flesh to devour by worse creatures. It wasn't that Chev had never seen the aftermath of a battle, it was the *scale*. New hills made by bodies, streams of tarnished steel, arrows thick as brush made porcupines of the land. Each speck, as boggling as it was, was once living, once breathing but now fallen.

Chev didn't realize there were this many people in the whole world, let alone enough to die on just one battlefield. If it was merely a number, as large as the numbers of berries on a bush, or fish in a stream, Chev could at least understand. But "large" was not fitting a word. This would be as great a task as counting the leaves in a forest.

Adar flinched when she saw it, as though prodded between the eyes. Darin had lost command of his jaw. And Starlight, usually so gentle and languid this time of night, began to cry.

"Shh!" Chev rocked her, and she fell silent. Which was good, because *creatures* stalked the dead. Monsters with two legs instead of four, the dangerous sort. They had to be the *shadowed ones*.

"We can't stay here," said Chev.

Darin snorted. "With the sun out? Best chance we have is beneath one of the bodies."

"*Or,*" Varnas jumped in with undisguised pride, somehow materializing with a shovel in hand, "we could dig a pit. "

Everybody took turns, not to save anyone's strength, but because the pit had to be dug as quickly as possible. As soon as someone started slowing down, they passed the shovel to the next, and a half-hour before dawn they finally had a pit they could stay in. Chev felt like he could roll in and sleep forever.

"So what now?" asked Adar, looking a bit apprehensive. Chev realized that she probably never spent a night underground.

"We get in," said Darin, wasting no time in dropping down.

"But... without shelter? What about—"

"Got that covered," Varnas announced, with a roll of grass over one shoulder, "had to walk a fair ways to find the right kinda stuff but it's always somewhere."

Varnas started laying down a cover of grass, occasionally fending off Ma-ma's attempts to grab a few pieces. In the end, it was only Adar still standing on the ground, warily looking into the black hole.

"Get in!" said Chev, "Sun's coming up."

"There's not a lot of space down there." Adar was giving meek excuses.

"You're telling me," said Darin.

Varnas put his head out into the moonlight. "It's safe down here! I dug it—well, most of it—but you can still trust it!"

Adar closed her eyes briefly, as though gathering herself, before allowing herself to be helped inside. Varnas sealed things up, and everything went entirely black.

"I never thought I'd be doing this," breathed Adar in the darkness, "Is this where you people usually sleep? In pits?"

"Actually, we usually make our homes beneath trees—"

Chev had only meant to be helpful, but Varnas grumbled at him for silence.

"We need to rest, lady knight. I know this may not be what you're used to, but I'll tell you that sleeping in pits has a proud and storied history. It's a tale for the dusk, though."

"Well," Adar made breathy smile, as though treating the situation like a mild joke, "I guess I'll give it a shot."

Adar would get almost no sleep that day. But neither would anyone else.

There was a rumbling through the earth. Thunder that came from the ground and made the pit tremble. A voice deepened as it moved through soil in waves. The four exhausted nightfolk, so recently having closed their eyes, were roused by the thrumming vibrations. The whole world, it appeared, had become an instrument.

They first waited to see if it would simply go away. It didn't. And Adar spoke when it was plain there would be no rest.

"A monster?" she asked.

"Do monsters sing?" Varnas lifted an ear.

"You hear singing?" Adar pricked her ear up, too.

It was a hum. Like distant moaning insects at first, but the notes lowered as it got closer. Something tapped on the drum of the earth, in rhythm. It could have been one extremely heavy footstep—or thousands upon thousands of smaller ones beating in unison.

"They *are* singing," said Chev.

"Shh!" Varnas lifted a hand to silence Chev.

Varnas wasn't trying to be rude. Chev had been stating the obvious, because the chorus that now boomed through became words, but so drawn out and with such power, that it was like the rocks were singing their own language. You didn't hear it, you *felt* it. It was a song that called to one's bones and demanded from the heart its rhythm. Chev had never heard anything that sounded at once so aggressive and so *mournful*.

Everyone listened, tuned their ears, and discerned these words.

"We hear our brothers' heaven cries,

We shear our mothers' earthen ties,

For everyone on this world dies, o Lord,

For everyone on this world dies.

Take me please to where there is no wont,

Where Father Sun forever shines,

Where golden water always runs,

Where hence my fallen brothers lie."

There was no comment to be made by the nightfolk. They gave each other blank stares from the bottom of the pit.

And the song continued. But not like it did before.

"Pray that the Gods should take me,

Pray that the heavens today I see,

Until then, there is one thing I say,

To my brothers who fight,

We are behind you!"

And out from the song rose one man's alien, dark voice, crying: *"Forward!"*

"A battle?" Adar rose to her feet.

"It's the dayfolk!" Darin said it as though cursing, "They chose this ground!"

"I'm taking a peek," said Chev.

"Don't!"

Chev didn't even know who rose the objection. But he clambered up the pit walls and lifted the very edge of the grass covering. What he saw in his sun filled eyes made him stare wordlessly, as though paralyzed. Varnas had to tug his leg to get his attention.

"What's up there?" he asked.

"We gotta go." Chev didn't say it, he breathed it.

"Are you crazy? It's daytime out there!" said Adar.

Chev dropped the grass cover, sealing them in darkness once again. "I'm not daysick enough to hallucinate *that*. Listen, we gotta go."

Adar was about to voice another objection. "How do you—"

"We have better chances in the sun than in here. But come on! Let's hurry! They're coming."

"Who's coming?"

"Them."

They all stopped yapping, because the tumult that suddenly arose commanded full attention. They were marching. They were close. Heavy breaths from chanting throats and drum-beat marching filled the air.

Varnas finally seemed to understand. "We gotta make a break for it. Which way we gotta run, Chev?"

"Which way?" Chev quickly grasped what Varnas was getting at. "The, uh, the dawn! Run for the dawn. Don't even look back!"

"When we gotta go?"

"Now!" said Chev, to whoever asked.

"Now?"

Varnas, took the initiative. At a pace unusual for his age, he clambered right out of the pit with all the supplies he could fit under his arm, crying, "Let's go!" One by one, they all followed.

If they took the time to understand what was closing in around them, they would have been far too slow to avoid the crushing pincers that came closer and closer. A glance was all they could afford, a glance at two walls of moving figures, distorted and made strange by the lashings of sunlight that fell on them. Were they dayfolk at all, or men of silver? Chev didn't have the luxury to stare. They had to rush for the gap in the closing wall, blinded by the light of the dawn in their eyes.

A whisper of sound and a narrow shadow flitted past Chev. He wondered absently if was an insect, but no insect he knew had feathers and such a long, deadly body. It was an arrow.

"Oh crap," Chev swore.

It was the drizzle that comes before a rain, a second arrow sped by, and a third stabbed the ground, and a fourth sailed into one of the armies and caused a cry of pain. Then they came like thick, heavy drops, thudding to the ground in patterns. The ground quickly became akin to the bottom of a bird's nest, with broken twigs and shed feathers all around.

Adar had to stop to let several arrows thud in front of her. She took a glance back at Chev, communicating a sense they would not be able to get out of the closing walls of warriors alive. And the missiles were only getting thicker, if the ominous, buzzing swarm on the horizon meant anything.

Chev wrapped his arms tighter around Starlight, checked to see that Ma-ma was following, and bellowed: "Into the lines!"

No one understood what Chev meant until he actually did it, and when he did, it was as mad as it sounded. He crouched into a run and skirted into the line. Two warriors made a clumsy attempt to chase him with blows, but they were too lumbering to hit.

Adar squinted as she checked the sky, to see that a swarm of arrows were alarmingly close. "Oh ancestors," was the two-word prayer she muttered before diving headlong into the battle line.

Angry bellows followed, acutely similar to her own language but simply incomprehensible from the chanting and marching and screaming that arose all around. She forced herself to move sinuously through a thicket of steel legs, knocking men aside before they had a chance to strike back. Stopping or being held up for a moment would have given the dayfolk enough time to take their weapons and end her there and then.

One thing worked in her favor. The dayfolk all sang like they were all part of a single brass instrument, and they turned their heads to the sun and *sang* to it.

"We are behind you," they intoned, *"we are behind you."*

When their voices reached a peak it created an overwhelming chorus. They sang as they fought, whether the one next to them died, or whether they absorbed an arrow, they still sang that simple little refrain. It gave them focus and discipline like Adar had never seen.

It was almost remarkable when Adar ran into Varnas.

Adar had never seen the old man "wild-eyed", but here he was, covered with discolored bruises, his ragged hair and beard further ruined by wind.

"Great stars, I'm glad to see you! Thought I was alone!" the old man said.

"Gotta keep moving," Adar breathed.

"That's right. Let's stick together."

As it turned out, Chev's instincts were accurate. Each warrior had one shield to the sky and one hand on the shoulder of the man in front, forming a solid line that moved in a halting rhythm with the song. Even then, arrows sometimes zipped between gaps, making a sharp tin sound as steel punched steel then flesh.

A warrior beside Adar was struck by a stray arrow, losing all strength in his steel armor. In a practiced, quick procedure the man was lifted above and a wave of shields seemed to sweep him quickly to the back lines. And he was hardly the only one. There were whole processions of dead and wounded that moved on this undulating sea of shields.

"Varnas!" Adar whispered, "You think we can...?"

"If it gets me outta here!"

And, like waiting for a storm cloud, they clambered up to meet the first moving shadow, and clung to it like a rock in a flood. They were riding atop a dead soldier as his fellows carried him back.

"Gods above," Varnas muttered as he was hoisted aloft.

They were atop the battlefield now, and it was as though the whole geography of the world had shifted. It was a plain of steel, made to look hot and dull by a low sun. Arrows shed down from the sky, their arc disguised by low clouds, so that they more resembled a force of nature than the product of men. Everything was vaster and more expansive than Varnas had ever imagined, and there was no end to it. Between the crushing continents of soldiers was a jagged fault line, a volcano of motion and a cacophony of cries that seemed to come from the ground itself. The battle-line. Sharp spears, swords, and axes scythed like teeth, followed by bloody severed heads and dismembered arms and legs. But, this landscape had its own terrain of pennants, banners, and idols which stuck their thumbs into the skyline.

"Have you ever seen anything like that?" shouted Varnas, an eye set to the sky for stray arrows.

"Knights war," Adar found a gap in the warrior's armor to slip her fingers into, "but it's nothing like this."

Even so close, a shout was a whisper. The dayfolk's hymn was constant, the rumble of a slow-moving avalanche. War had to struggle to be heard beneath their voices.

"I hope they don't drop us into a grave," muttered Varnas.

Though they were being pushed back along the river of warriors, it seemed they were only getting further from the front line. The sea of shields carried them past what was a heart-stopping forever before the arrows finally stopped and a few patches of hair-like grass could be made out. Adar let herself feel momentary relief, but Varnas held his face as rigidly and unpliably as it had been the whole journey.

"When there's no fighting," warned Varnas, "there's no distraction."

The line's end was coming. A line of crossbowmen, thick as a woven cloak, worked continuously to put as many bolts in the sky as possible, their faces each disguised by disfiguring metal helms that made them look like animated, unfinished toys. Between the infantry and the archers a line of bodies were laid out like gathered crops, some writhing with pain and others disturbingly still. They could see tenders buried in heavy robes and cloaks retrieving bodies from the top of the shields and laying them on the ground.

"We gotta make a break for it," shouted Varnas.

"At the next to last!" shouted back Adar.

And just before the body they laid on dropped into the hands of one of the tenders, they made a leap above the many craned necks. The momentary shock of the crossbowmen proved life-saving, as it allowed Adar and Varnas the time needed to push right through their formation before any of the creatures to could bring weapons to bear.

Varnas must have shoved his way through a dozen of the men. By the end, his hands were covered with a layer of grease and grime that had permeated his skin and got under his nails. Varnas watched as Adar just nudged past a dagger swipe from a particularly quick soldier.

They burst out of the back of the lines, bellows and curses following them, and they dodged a few hastily fired crossbow bolts, which hit the ground with such impact they threw up turf. Neither of them bothered to look back to see if they still had their attention as they dived over the next ridge.

If they'd known the monster waiting for him, he would've rather risked the archers.

Varnas had never seen anything like it. He thought it half-goat, half-stag at first, but it was taller than a bear and longer too. It was a mass of sleek, wiry muscle wrapped in a proud coat and mane. And the creature was strong, as it bore a dayfolk warrior clad in thick sheets of steel, a hammer by his hand, and thick riveted shield on the other.

"What is—"

"It's a *horseman!*" Adar screamed the answer before Varnas had time to ask. "Run!"

The warrior clapped the sides of the beast with his legs, and it made this confusing, bizarre sound like an angry, whining goat. The sheer oddness of it pulsed fear into Varnas and he spun on his heels faster than he thought he could.

The horseman had lungs like a bellows in a furnace, and his steed literally tore up the ground in pursuit. Varnas knew how fast it was approaching by the beast's frantic breathing. It grew louder so quickly that Varnas actually wondered if fleeing was even possible.

If it wasn't the spinning warhammer in the warrior's hands, it would be this beast's hooves. Varnas figured his best chance would be leaping out the way.

The man leaned from his saddle intending to bat Varnas with the hammer. Varnas was frantically calculating the best way to avoid it when suddenly an arrow sprung right out of the warrior's visor, causing him to tumble to the ground and roll with the horse's momentum right to Varnas' feet.

Luck? *Or...*

Varnas turned around.

"Knew it was only you who coulda made that shot."

Darin sniffed, pulling another arrow from his quiver without comment.

"Where's Chev?"

"Here," said Chev as he rose from a dent in the trampled grass.

That damn goat, Ma-ma, was draped over his shoulders, and that child was still in his hands, bundled up like a package.

"We in the clear?" ask Chev, between gasps for breath.

"Dunno. Gods, where are we..."

Apparently, surrounded.

The creatures who surrounded them only faintly resembled nightfolk. They had the similar faces and proportions, but their eyes held something alien and bestial, and they stalked naked like jackals. When Chev locked gazes with one, it provoked a hiss and bared teeth. But they weren't, like Chev had first imagined, sizing them up as prey. They were skirting around, edging closer and closer to the corpse of the cavalryman.

One of the naked monsters prodded the cavalryman's boot. Seeing no reaction, it ripped into its greaves with sharp claws and teeth. That invited a frenzy, a pile of the creatures ripped the corpse apart, stealing precious treasures; bones dripping with fresh marrow, limbs clad with flesh, viscera Chev hesitated to identify. They took him in pieces and fled with leaps and bounds out of sight, leaving a patch of grass soaked with blood and gouged with strips of steel.

"Shadowed ones," Chev said.

"They must follow the army," said Adar, "I've never seen them up so close."

As though a reminder of its presence, light blasted across the horizon as the sun inched its way a little further into the sky and fought through the thick clouds. All the nightfolk shielded their eyes from the harsh and blinding light.

"We need shelter," said Darin, his good eye half-open while his other was dead-tight closed, "and quickly."

"Where do the shadowed ones hide?" Chev wondered aloud.

It was an unthinkable solution, and the same grotesque expression spread across each their faces, but the sun was not something that could simply be weathered, and the decision came not from voiced agreement but from silence.

Darin sighed. "I'll look for tracks."

The dayfolk's chanting voice was haunting the distance now. The sound vibrated across the sky and clouds, while the battlefield became a stripe of white and black shimmering on the horizon. Chev craned his neck to watch; it was like seeing a rolling storm, with its own arrow rain and cavalry thunder. The clamor was changing. There was triumph on one side and despair on the other. Someone was winning, someone was losing, some got to live while others died.

Darin kept his head bent like a snuffling animal. In the ever intensifying light he couldn't see clearly without bending close to the ground. But his instincts and training taught him well—he shot up, pointed a direction.

"There!" he said, "Other side of the knoll."

Chev could almost feel them beneath his feet, clawing the earth like voles. It felt as if they were already burrowing through his veins, and Chev had to shake himself to exorcise that queasy feeling.

Judging from how everyone tiptoed, he wasn't the only one who felt that way.

There was a wound on the other side of the hill, it reminded Chev of an insect bite, not of the sort that might leave a mark, but that which ate the flesh. A million clawing hands had rented a tunnel into the earth, and looking down into it was a crawling reminder of the bone-skin burrow they once had emptied. Only Darin, having already resigned himself to whatever fate had in store, ducked immediately into the tunnel and knelt down in the comforting shadows.

"We'll take watches," said Darin. "I'll take first watch. Then Adar, Chev, then the old man. We'll rotate 'til it's dusk."

One by one, they all followed inside, crouching against the soil walls of the tunnel. Only Ma-ma was small enough to easily squeeze through and comfortably sit.

They were walled in now. On one end was the neck into the black abyss, which they imagined was full of rustling and clawing predators. On the other they were bottled in by impenetrable light. Chev already knew this was going be a very difficult day.

Rain?

Not rain. Hissing, spitting, and growling. It seemed like an ordinary nightmare when Chev opened his eyes to see a mass of pale, bestial faces, but there was nothing nightmarish about it. This was the real world, and the shadowed ones were really cursing at him from their cloak of blackness. Chev, still reeling from the reality of sleeping in a beast's lair, put his hand on his sword.

That simple act caused the shadowed ones to make quiet moans and retreat back in the blackness from whence they came, though Chev had the distinct impression they would be back.

Chev glanced blearily around. Only Darin had his eyes open, though he seemed more concerned with what was going on past the wall of blinding daylight than what was behind them in the depths of the darkness.

"What's that noise?" muttered Chev, before fully understanding he was even hearing something odd.

Darin shushed him. It was to better hear the din of battle rising up so that now it resembled more the sound a river rapids makes than that of a constant breeze. Muffled by the dirt walls, Chev hadn't realized how close the battle had moved, and how in the space of a few hours things had so dramatically changed.

There was not one chant now, like the drone from angry flies, screaming and crying punctuated the air and the pounding of footfalls marked drumbeats as they ran over top. Whinnying horsemen clopped loudly and added an alarming staccato beat.

Just then a loud and piercing cry was shouted into the tunnel. Chev couldn't tell if it was intentional, or if his head happened to be turned in just the right direction. A protective impulse shuddered through Chev, and he jumped on the balls of his feet. He wanted to *do* something.

Darin stood slowly and deliberately.

Darin might have sung like a thrush and it would have been less surprising to Chev, so all he could do was stare blankly as Darin pushed past the veil of light with sword drawn. There were sharp cries and the sound of combat, a muffled thud as steel hit flesh, and moments later Darin was dragging back a prone figure. It had to be one of the dayfolk, with his armored vest rising and falling. Had Darin *saved* someone?

Chev reconsidered whether he had been dreaming. This was so unlikely he made a face like he was appalled at Darin, but it was solely surprise that touched him. Darin pulled his shoulders back, seeming to take Chev's gaze in stride.

"I know what you're thinking, and you're wrong." Darin didn't whisper, but he kept his tone cool and quiet, "I knew you were gonna rush out there like a fool, so I thought it would be easier if I just got it over with."

Darin was wrong. Not even *Chev* knew what he was thinking, and he drifted into half-sleep as confused and muddle-headed as ever.

Sleep had never felt like such an ordeal. Chev had hard nights before, but this time, the dangers were very real. They were resting just beyond the hungry longing gazes of cannibals, and on the edge of a battle for life or death. The only thing keeping these dangers at bay was someone else's watchful eyes and steady blade.

Dusk came like a long awaited release of breath.

No one needed to be woken. As soon as the tunnel's mouth darkened they started to move on their own. Chev felt around for blade and gear. Everyone did the same.

"He's dead," announced Darin.

"Who?" asked Varnas. The same question on was Chev's mind.

"The dayfolk warrior," Darin said, "told you there was no point saving him."

After briefly checking Starlight and his gear, Chev stepped over the fallen soldier. His helmet had been eased off, revealing a face Chev knew he was not supposed to stare at. Even in death he looked like a proud creature, cheeks of rich fur punctuated by closed eyes, a prominent nose and stiff lips. He was framed by a mane, of carefully tended hair made ragged by battle, stretching from chin to forehead.

"No one asked you to save him," said Chev. "Though, I'm happy that you tried."

Darin spoke quickly, defensively, "It's as I said, I already saw what you were going to do. I just decided I'd rather do it myself. Let's go. Not sure I can take another night of this."

"How far is Sunset, do you think?" asked Adar, averting her eyes from the corpse.

"Dunno," shrugged Chev, "But at least we know the direction."

It was as if that whole day had never happened, the sight before them was identical to the one yesternight. A topography of carnage, infested by shadowed ones and worst. Except now they were in the thick of things, navigating between canyons of carrion. A scavenger's dream.

"Ancestors!" Chev cried as planted his foot to the ground, found it marshy with gore. Adar glided quickly to his side, and whispered a comforting word in his ear.

"Let's not stay, Chev." Her voice had a soothing effect. "Come on, let's keep going."

An arrhythmic nod was the answer, and Chev let her gently pull him along.

They were going to Sunset. And as it turned out, they would not be walking long. They trekked over heath and hill for hours, but as they did, the air changed, getting smokier and saltier by the hour. Surmounting the next hill, they saw a horizon of dark and light, a new field of stars, contouring a drowned geography. Buildings speared the skyline as though aiming to rocket upwards, and in such multitudes that it seemed there was a structure for each man that was at that last battle. Chev finally understood how so many people could have come to be.

"Sunset," Chev whispered, "it has to be."

In the back of his mind, he knew Ossen was somewhere down there.

Chapter Twenty-Two
The Sunset Emperor

F ROM A DISTANCE, it looked like those times when Chev as a child would harass ant colonies, rousing rivers of insects out of their nests by his disturbance of their carefully constructed space. But the creatures in the tide moving out of the city gates were not ants but nightfolk. They created a sluggish meandering stream out of the city, some carrying everything they owned on their backs. For some that meant a towering pack that erupted like a tumor behind them, while others the rags transformed them into hunchbacks. The stream trailed off to the east, where the horizon was as black and starless as coal.

Seeing that they would have to fight their way past a tide of refugees, the party camped out on a hill overlooking the city, watching the spectacle like one might watch petals drift across water. Varnas certainly found it food for contemplation, and like all his contemplation, he did it aloud.

"That's the biggest one so far," said Varnas, "And gods, it's endless! Never seen anything like it. Strange times, strange and trying times."

Darin had found piece of grass to chew, which made him look meditative. His response was a thoughtful but dispirited grunt, as he twisted the grass blade between his fingers.

"Bad sign, though. These folk know something we don't," said Varnas.

Chev could have told him that. Nightfolk were abandoning the place like it was already on fire, and they were about to wander right in. Foolish by any measure.

"Chev."

Adar's soft voice pulled him from his thoughts. Something warm and moist tickled his neck—her breath. It was so lingering it nearly felt like a bruise.

"Chev, there's something I don't understand."

Chev's jaw tightened imperceptibly, bidding her to continue.

The lady knight had lost everything that made her a knight—everything but her sword, that is—and she seemed so oddly vulnerable in nothing but a padded tunic. By her gentle expression and voice, she might've felt it, too. Her lips squeezed together, and her eyes searched for a point to focus on the ground. "Why are you going? Really?"

"To Sunset?" Chev asked.

"Yeah. You know I'm here to see the man who claims to be Emperor. But I don't know what you'd want with him. Chev, I had this crazy idea—that the child you were transporting had something to do with the Emperor. But then I learned the truth, that it was dayfolk, and now nothing makes sense about you. Don't tell me about a curse, Chev, because you know I know you don't believe it."

"You'd think me stupid if I told you the truth," said Chev.

"Try me."

"It's not based on any prophecy. It's just a feeling that I have, that this Emperor might be a man I know. I mean to say," Chev sighed, "I think he might be my father."

Adar's eyebrows made a little surprised dance. "That's... different. But what about Starlight?"

"What about her?"

"How does she fit in?" asked Adar.

"She doesn't," Chev shrugged, "I just have nowhere else to take her."

Adar took a moment to put things together. "So, you found a dayfolk child, and that spurred you to try and find your father?"

"I wasn't lying about the curse," said Chev, "I really am cursed. But I thought, if I'm in the Daylit Lands anyway, might as well look for him." Then Chev said to himself, gritting his teeth as though fighting through a pulse in his heart. "Gods, he feels close. I can't explain it. But, I just know he's in Sunset."

"What are you going to do?" Adar asked, "When you see him?"

Chev's breath cut short. "I haven't thought that far ahead, actually."

It wasn't that that the crowds pouring out of Sunset were getting any thinner, it was that if they waited much longer they'd have no time to find shelter. There was a strange strength in the desperate, huddled masses. Dirt-faced children, old folks, weak men and tired women all had a presence that pressed against Chev without his even having to touch it. It was as if a physical manifestation of their hardship made others step aside out of respect. It was hard enough with just one such group marching down the street, but the gate was full at all times with nightfolk.

To carry all those people, Sunset must have been bigger than whatever Chev's limited imagination could conjure up. A sponge can hold a lot of water but it still couldn't make a tidal wave.

Moving forward, they were forced to the sides of the road, where they could finally make headway through the throng. When they finally reached the gates, they had to struggle against the tide so fiercely they exploded out the other side of the gate.

"This is it, then," Varnas sniffed the air, deciding whether he was going to be impressed, "*Sunset.*"

"They say the city looks out onto the ocean," Adar seemed oddly wistful. "I've never seen the sea."

Varnas summoned something to spit from the back of his throat. "Let's see this Emperor, then."

Chev had gotten so relaxed around Adar and the others that he'd near forgotten that there was still the taboo separating nightfolk and dayfolk. Starlight was still a terribly dangerous possession. He stopped abruptly to make sure her linens were tight over her and the cover of the basket fast before they wandered the city.

And what a city Sunset was! Chev could only compare it to Riverturn, and Sunset had thrice the number of streets, each at least four times the width of Riverturn's dingy alleys. Yet the buildings, madly enough, were even more crammed together, so narrow and so tall the whole building must have been staircase. Runes and drawings decorated each wall, advertising services that Chev couldn't wrap his head around: "barbers", "grocers", "lawyers", "physicians". Life spilled out onto the streets from the buildings into carts and stalls. It all smelled a pleasant kind of awful, a place which had been lived in and thoroughly abused. In the air there was smokiness without fire, an undercurrent of stale ale and outhouse, food fresh and rotten melded together to form something both repellent and mouth-watering.

For all the signs of life, it seemed a place in need of a population.

Everything living had fled, or near enough to everything. The skittering of rats and scavenging dogs seemed the only movement. They felt eyes in doorways and windows, but what they hoped to glean from watching them walk the empty streets, Chev didn't want to know. He hoped it was simply because there was so little else to look at.

They found a man dressed as a guard picking his teeth in a doorway, and Adar walked up and asked where the Emperor made his court.

"You mean Osmond the Mad? He's no Emperor. Maybe to you pointy-ears, but not to me."

Osmond? The first syllable sent a little vibration up Chev's spine, but the second one stopped it dead. Chev wasn't ready to say if the similarity in names meant his theory was more likely or less.

"Be that as it may," said Adar, "we'd still like to meet him."

The guard gave Adar a quick appraisal, blowing thoughts out from his cheeks. "You're welcome to go to the Court, but don't believe Osmond's promises. The dayfolk are coming. They will destroy this city like they've done all the others. You won't see a trace of me the night coming. He holds audience in the big temple. Keep going up this street and over the hill. You can't miss it."

They followed his directions.

Chev had trepidation before he saw the Oracle, but even that hadn't made his palms sweat, his heart ache, and his feet wobble all foolishly. The building they faced was no less imposing and impressive than the Oracle's, but there was something intangible and unreal about being here. Perhaps it was that they had passed through so many empty streets. Perhaps it was the threat of a mad dayfolk army burning the whole place to the ground. Perhaps it was the hunger and hardships they had endured for so many months. Perhaps they were simply at the end the journey. But Chev knew well enough it wasn't any of those things. He had an idea of the secrets buried between the proud columns and austere statues. The cold stone, and the colder eyes of the knights who flanked the doorway, leeched the heat right out of him.

Chev had no idea if there was some ceremony or propriety they should know before simply wandering in, but if there was, the guards didn't enforce it. They joined the others moving inside the building.

Some people had taken their weapons inside, and seeing that Chev and Adar's swords were those of a knight, made a closer look. Their inspection stopped at their pointy ears.

"You are lucky," said one of the warriors, "The Emperor has an open hall tonight. Few are allowed to simply walk in and see him."

Varnas' ear flicked as it tuned itself to music emanating from beyond the stone. Someone within was playing with some skill, a peaceful tune that seemed to invite the listener to draw up a chair to their own inner fire.

"What's the occasion?" Varnas asked.

"The Emperor is celebrating his ascension," the warrior explained, "in a few days he will prove to all his courage and righteousness."

"*Right*," said Varnas. Chev could easily hear dubiousness leak into his voice.

They moved with the crowd towards the sound of the music.

And so this was where the remainder of Sunset's life had fled. It was as though someone had taken the model of the tavern by Pilgrim's Pass, stretched it in every imaginable direction, and stuffed a thousand people at each newly wrought table. Round-ears sat alongside pointed-ears, passing food, sharing private jokes, and turning an ear to the harpist who played so beautifully it hurt.

Yet, the party's approach was slow and cautious, rather more like entering a silent bear's den than a festival. Blindness seemed to mark each person, as they stumbled drunkenly across their paths, or shouted loudly past their ears. Each pair of lips were stained with grease.

To those who had been on the road for months, it seemed appalling decadence.

There was one focal point to this chamber, and one raised platform was not enough for it.

A stone seat, like an obelisk whose back melted into the ceiling as a pillar, rested on multiple layers of skillful masonry. It seemed impossible that there could be a single person in the world with enough bearing to bring dignity to that throne, but there he was. He was dressed as a knight with a regal fur mantle. He had thin, severe lips and piercing wolf-like eyes, but the years had buried them under folds of skin. He rested his craggy, pallid face on his fist, cheeks indented by age. It might have been mistaken for boredom had it been anyone else, but this man was deep in thought. His eyes could drink the world.

To say Chev hadn't seen him in many seasons felt too small a word. In the time they'd been separated, the moon had once gone dark, awful beasts had risen from the world, and one boy had traversed the known world. Too much had happened, and simply describing the passage of time didn't seem enough.

Those wolf eyes caught him.

His fist dropped from his cheek. The other hand gripped the side of his throne. He launched onto his feet, a pair of pointed ears shuddering with the energy of his jump.

The Emperor cried out: "Chev!"

The whole chamber fell silent. The final sound was a harpist's last note drifting off into the void beside the echo of his call.

Ossen looked no frailer than back in the Nightlands, but still he wobbled on his feet, and used the throne and tables for support as he clambered down the steps. His heavy boots made sharp claps against the stones, echoing on the walls and out into the night.

Chev let Ossen cup his cheeks—Gods his eyes hurt! The same man lurked beneath the sterner lines and furrowed cheeks. Hands drifted across Chev's face, pushing his skin back taut, before inspecting his eyes one by one, as though they might be different from each other.

Then Ossen turned away.

Chev felt the blood rush to the tips of his ears, but Ossen simply gestured to a servant. "Set a table for my son and his friends," he commanded, and with a flick of his wrist bid the music continue.

With a startled expression, the musician picked right up where she'd left off. Ossen used it as a cloak for his voice.

"Chev," his thin lips cracked a smile, "Chev... I feared the day I'd die and not see you a man."

"I needed to see you too, Ossen," said Chev.

"I'm not Ossen anymore, I'm Emperor Osmond now. Chev, I can't help but think the ancestors guided you here. The next few days are going to be extremely eventful. I really don't know where to begin."

"Emperor Osmond? Ossen, what's going—"

"Please," Ossen, or Emperor Osmond, gave a wry smile, "we're not in the Nightlands anymore. Call me father."

So far from the elders and Minda and everything else, that word was still not easy.

The Emperor then looked more closely at Chev's companions. "Varnas!" he exclaimed, "You haven't aged, old man."

"I've been keeping it easy. You, on the other hand, look like an old shawl."

There was a note of alarm on the faces of the knights and servants close enough to overhear, but the Emperor's cheeks readily balled up in good humor. "You were always the best among them, Varnas. Never thought I'd see you out of that place." The Emperor drew his attention to Adar. "A knight? I've never seen you before."

Adar's stood taller but tried to keep her face impassive; she was actively trying to seem more guarded. "Not many people realize that when I'm out of armor."

"You bear yourself like one. There's no time for tea, so I must be rude and ask directly your name."

"Adar. I'm of the Wolf Clan."

The Emperor made an intrigued noise. "Someone of the Wolf Clan! I was hoping I would meet one of your sort. We'll have much to discuss." And finally, the Emperor's gaze drifted to Darin, and to him he said nothing. He simply made a few short steps his direction, and gave him a stern appraisal. Darin, proud as he was, threw his own jaded eye right back.

Chev chafed to intercede, but how to end a conflict that hadn't even begun?

"I recognize you," Ossen said coolly, "One of Feska's thugs. You missed out on a good, clean death when you didn't show up to kill me."

"I was supposed to be there," Darin uttered, refusing to break eye contact, "but I failed to kill your son."

"Darin!" Chev cried out.

"Were you curious, then, about what I do to my enemies given the luxury of time?" The Emperor turned to his guards, "Throw this man into the dungeons."

"Osse— father, he's not the same man as he was! He's helped us across the Sippi and the Daylit Lands—"

Chev's defense was breathless, but Darin didn't welcome it, he held his head proudly askew. And Ossen seemed deaf to Chev's entreaties.

"If he's loyal, he'll have to prove it," said Ossen. "But I won't have him spoiling this celebration."

The Emperor confirmed his command with a sharp gesture, and a pair of knights whisked Darin away. The hunter would not allow himself to be dragged—he pushed their arms away and walked proudly and unhesitatingly through a nondescript doorway.

Varnas narrowed his eyes. "You know, in the space you've been gone, he's also saved Chev's life. And not just once, either!"

"A drop of wine in a barrel of sewage is still sewage." The Emperor gestured to a table. "I'd be honored to sit with you."

The stools and tables looked fresh from the carpenter's shop; Varnas could practically blow sawdust off them. But it was like everything in this hall. Manak, in spite of its ruin, had dignity from its great age. Here, the freshness of everything—from the polished furniture to the clothes of such quality they seemed to shine—was in search of tradition but in wont of antiquity. The Emperor took an especially splendid seat and waited, expectant of a great tale.

But Chev was in no position to tell a story. He couldn't overcome the strangeness of this—the man who was once the figure in his daysick hallucination, was now sitting on a throne with a twist of a smile on his lips. But, there was something else, and that really tugged at Chev as he struggled to figure out where to begin. He knew this story he was about to tell wasn't yet over.

"The truth is, father, I didn't come to the Daylit Lands just to see you."

The Emperor leaned back in his chair and steepled his fingers. And the other faces around the table, worn and ruddy from travel, seemed to shrink.

"It's better if I show you," said Chev.

Chev carefully placed the swaddled child on the table.

Something about being removed from the warmth of the basket roused the child. Her hands began to swivel, as she started to make sounds, like small, mournful animal waking from slumber. The Emperor did not unwrap the child. He lifted her wholly out, letting the cloth fall from her naked body. Now Ossen looked the part of a proper Emperor. His nose was raised as he inspected Starlight, expressionless. The sound of the harp was the only sound in the hall as every eye followed his. He gave ample time for Chev's heart to quicken and fear to pit in his stomach.

Then the Emperor had seen enough. The child was lowered back on top of her swaddling in the basket. It was then the Emperor seemed to become Ossen once again, in the way he could be thoughtful and deliberate. Chev knew his father, he was patient. But Adar was flushed and her chest moved with her heartbeat, and her fists clenched with pure nerves.

Ossen shifted in his seat. His booming voice addressed the whole room. "I have something to say," he announced.

The whole chamber turned toward his voice. Chev noted the simple people, and the nobles. One table of seven ladies wore shawls so heavily embroidered it was remarkable they could sit up so straight. Yet others wore tattered clothing and were purely grateful for food and respite from the trials of life.

"You have remained in this city because I have promised that I will save Sunset. And I will. What has walked into this hall this night is a vision of the future. The young man that sits at my side," Emperor Osmond pointed at Chev with a sharp nod, "That is my eldest son Chev, who was born to the Nightlands during my exile. He has come from that land in search of *place*. Our culture would have Chev believe that his act of heroism is one of the worst crimes our people can commit.

"My son has taken in one of the dayfolk. A defenseless child he rescued from the devastation that surrounds us. For his courage and self-sacrifice, he has been banished, and hounded from the Nightlands and across the Daylit Lands. He is now with us, and he should know: we do not judge by ancient laws, but by intentions and the heart. There is no taboo here but cowardice and injustice. Moon and sun shall finally wax and wane together. We build here a new Empire of Sun and Stars. Let us toast to him, not to his bloodline, but to his wisdom and strength." The Emperor thrust a goblet into the air, sloshing ale out from the rim. "To Chev!"

The whole hall followed suit, lifting a roar with each cup, "To Chev!"

They all drank together.

All made their toasts. Even the seven ladies, who rose from their seats and lifted their glasses but failed to smile. Their lips might have been curved and teeth all pearly white, but their expressions could never have been mistaken for grace.

As Ossen took seat and sipped out from his goblet, Chev leaned in. "Ossen, who are they?"

Ossen's eyes looked in the direction of Chev's comment. He swallowed carefully and wiped his lips with his forearm. "Them? Oh, those are my wives."

The night continued in the same jubilant tone. Chev was the toast of the whole hall, Starlight rested in open view of the whole court, with nightfolk even approaching to admire the child, and there was food and drink in such quantities that made it hard to think that hard times were ahead. But that was precisely the thought that Chev dwelled on.

Things felt so *strange*. Like he was still on that day-lit path, deliriously sunsick and conjuring up phantoms. Everything felt too easy, too convenient, to have been real. Mere nights ago, people had been trying to kill him for what he held. Now he was a hero for it. It would have all been easier to understand if Chev had simply been chased out of town.

His father leaned over, boasted something. A proud compliment, the kind only fathers could give. But Chev couldn't hear it. The music repeated in a manner that pricked at Chev's nerves. There was something crawling up his spine. He felt the hall's broad dimensions shuddering inward like a slow moving trap.

Without much warning, Chev rose from his seat.

Chev thought he was going to make it outside but the Emperor himself saw fit to intercept. A firm hand gripped his shoulder, his gray eyes questioned him.

"Is there something wrong?" Ossen asked.

"I don't feel comfortable, Ossen. I think the journey's just getting to me. Maybe I need some rest." Chev wavered. "Um... Ossen?"

"Yes?"

"I heard a rumor you were advised by the dayfolk. If you could allow it, I'd like to talk to one."

Hurt passed over Ossen in such a brief moment that lightning would have lingered longer. But Chev's request had been simple, reasonable. There was no reason to feel as *strange* as he had.

"Yes," Ossen said, releasing Chev's shoulder, "Of course. You only need approach. He's at the end of the corridor, behind the large door. Be sure to check if he's sleeping, sometimes it is hard to tell."

"Thanks," said Chev.

He left through the same nondescript door that Darin had walked through only a short time ago. As soon as it closed, the sounds of revelry faded and the celebration felt miles away, distorted as though filtered past a waterfall. Chev identified the door Ossen had described, and for some reason, that didn't dispel his trepidation or feel comforting.

A light push had it swinging open on well-oiled hinges.

Far from the great hall's candlelight, stars blazed through an archway and gave the whole chamber a soft, otherworldly feeling—light glazing books, scrolls, a cloak thrown over a chair, and scintillating the dust flying over a desk. Somewhere in this room was one of the dayfolk, and he had all the presence of a mouse. As cool as shadow, the creature's white fur blended into the clutter, a chameleon who could hide amid snow and books. His eyes were closed, Chev presumed, but then he saw a slight shift in position and it glittered in the pale moonlight. No—this creature had eyes of milk, and ears that pricked to alertness.

He had a voice like a northerly wind. "Sit. Your feet must hurt."

"How did you know?" In fact, it was difficult to think of anything other than his aching feet. It was like it had been pulled right from his mind.

"You dragged your feet," the creature explained, "But you're not heavy. And you walk too straight to be drunk. I presumed that meant you have traveled a long way to be here. And you sound like a young man, so that means it has been a very long way indeed."

"I've traveled all the way from the Nightlands," said Chev, finding a stool, and letting it creak as it took his weight, "But it wasn't to come here. Not specifically."

"So was it curiosity that brings you here? I'm sorry to disappoint. If you've come to meet one of the dayfolk, I am as alien to my own kind as you are." The walls seemed to bend to accommodate his winter voice.

"I have so many questions. What should I call you?"

The dayfolk man paused, and without any physical motion or expression Chev could read, he seemed outright eerie. Like he'd turned to stone in the middle of his thought. "Mitradiates," he enunciated.

"Mit-ra-die-uh-tees," Chev struggled over the unfamiliar syllables.

"Mitra suits me fine," said Mitradiates, cutting off an awkward exchange before it occurred.

"Mitra, then—I have a story to tell."

Chev told him *everything*. From the Nightlands, to finding Starlight, to the battle to with the bone-skins, to the journey to Manak and finally the journey to Sunset, ending where they ended now. And Mitra listened in a way that it was not clear whether he was awake not, as he remained very still and gave little in the way of encouragement or interruption. Only the piercing nature of his questions revealed what a skilled observer and listener he was.

"And... why did you come here?" asked Mitra.

Chev was confused. "I thought I told you. Didn't I? I was looking for—"

Mitra shook his head. "No. You'd already made the decision, boy. You never had to come. People have been giving you answers your whole journey and you've refused them all. This is the end boy. This is where you realize what you've known all this time. The only answer you've ever be able to accept."

Chev waited for Mitra to say something more, but he wouldn't. The hair on his face was coarse and unmoving, rippling across the lines of age. There was no sense of discomfort. They might have have sat across from each other all night if Chev hadn't spoke.

"I have to take care of her," said Chev.

"*Yes,*" Mitra's quiet voice seemed to indicate approval, "Yes. Abandoning the child would have been a small evil, by the measure of these times. You never had to take the shame and violence thrown at you, but you did. I am only sorry you journeyed so long and so hard to find out that you already knew the answer. I can say that this sort of revelation is far more common than most would think."

Chev bent forward, elbows on his knees. "I hoped that Sunset would be different. That it would be safe. But the war comes here too, doesn't it? Do you really think the Emperor can stop it?"

That strange pause again. Chev thought he'd said something wrong, something to offend Mitra. But then he continued, "I am... blessed and cursed with clear thinking, Chev, son of Minda. But I am also an aberration, you see, to me, the sun is simply a pleasant warm tingle against the skin. But, I cannot fathom the world that my people live in. The *colors*, Chev, oh how I hunger to know what they are! How can something untouchable like the sky be blue? What is *green*, that which is the purest expression of life? I want to understand the royalty of purple, the rage of red, the wealth of yellow, but I've never experienced them. I can't even know the absence of color.

"My people, you understand, are night blind, but to them every blade of grass is a different, wondrous shade, the sun sets and rises in a hundred by hundred different layers. It is how we communicate, it is how we express meaning. Colors are words that populate our day-lit world, Chev, and I can't even fathom them. I hated that. While the others like me grew to love music and sound, I came to appreciate silence. The absence of things. Along the way, I diverged dramatically from my people, so I did not adopt their hysterias. This war is a hysteria, Chev, like a pit of mating vipers, and reason can't penetrate it. I'm only glad I'm not a part of it.

"I do not know if your father can stop the destruction of this city. But I would readily accept death just to see him try."

Chapter Twenty-Three
Games of Shadow

A SALTY WIND PICKED up, lightly picking at the bottom of the curtain, brushing the room with a fresh scent. It was bright and burning outside, and Chev lay awake on his mattress, fingers woven over his stomach. He'd never had a room to himself and he couldn't recall when he'd last felt so clean.

He listened to the dayfolk. The city outside the window churned with business, things must've been eventful because the streets were all a mumble. Sometimes, Chev picked out an individual voice, but it was stretched out by distance, transforming into a long wavering note.

Starlight was somewhere. He presumed her whisked away by admiring maids, somewhere in the belly of this place. And though he couldn't seem to get his eyes to close he had to take it on faith that she was safe. The only other option was to accept that sleep would never come.

Even when the day seems so long, the dusk and break of night comes eventually and suddenly, it creeps up and ambushes you. The coming of darkness meant it was time to get up, and that was something Chev was not ready for.

The tunic he slipped on was much nicer than the one he'd gotten on the road. It slid right over his back and didn't itch or snag with loose threads. He was so pleased with it that he took no care opening the door, and someone launched away with a scurrying of feet. He was only quick enough to see the flap of a cloak disappear out of a corner. It seemed a man acting the part of a rodent, hiding and sneaking about, and that was strange to him. Why would anyone wish to linger at his door?

He moved freely about the fortress, grabbing some bread left over from the feast yesterday. Adar was with his father outside the hold. The woman had changed a lot on the trip from the Sippi, thinning and growing tired. But after the good sleep, bath and nourishing food, she looked so like her old self. Chev almost could believe this was all happening back in Manak. In the course of a day she'd acquired new armor, her snow-white locks were brushed and braided into order, and she resembled the proud knight Chev met in what seemed like a previous life. She met him with her eyes, and gave a deep smile when she caught sight of him. Chev realized he'd not seen anything like that from her recently.

But Ossen, that man looked different. He was armored as Adar except he had a cloak wrapped over his shoulder like a scarf. Cloth patches hung over the shoulders of his armor. Chev figured they were indicators of station and they gave Ossen an air of pretension he'd never seen out of him.

"We're going to the walls," Ossen—Chev still could not see this man as Emperor Osmond—said, "I think it would be profitable if you came with us. But you should don some armor first." He signaled at a servant to bring over armor and fit it on Chev.

"Is this a military expedition?" Chev asked as he struggled into the armor and glanced at all the knights in full battle gear. A half dozen of them at the ready and others at a distance and forming a rearguard.

"It could be." Ossen made a flick of his wrist. "Let's go."

But it wasn't just warriors. Children followed out, a troop of boys at most half the age of Chev, wearing padded coats that made them look bulkier than they were, like waddling penguins. Back home, the boys were overjoyed to attend hunts and were all smiles. These young boys had cheeks stuffed with petulance, and walked with a stiff symmetry inside their jackets. It looked like they had better places to be.

"Do you remember our hunts?" Ossen's privately whispered words brought Chev back in the moment. "Stag hunting in the Nightlands. I don't think you realize how good you were at that. I actually thought, if I hadn't had to leave, I'd see you better than me in just a few years. How embarrassing would that be, huh?"

Ossen smiled like he wasn't used to it, punched Chev in the shoulder like he was seeking ways of being friendly. And Chev might've been better at pretending, except he was so distracted by all the oddities pulling at him: the sounds and smells of the city, the children wrapped in duty, the delicate scent of the ocean, most of all, his own father acting like a stranger wearing a costume and playing a role.

Ossen had a wistful sigh. Chev had never heard anything like that from him. "And Minda! She loved you too. What a sweet woman she was. A treasure of the Nightlands. You know, when I saw you, I almost expected her to be right behind. And what about Sana, hmm? I always sensed there was something between you two. Did she ever become your mate?"

"Yeah," Chev said. He hadn't meant to lie. It was just easier to say than the truth.

"I suppose it didn't work out," Ossen made a guess from Chev's tone.

"She got hurt," Chev quickly added, "A bone-skin got to her. She..." The mental image brought to mind made Chev's voice waver just a second, "it attacked her. And—"

"Yes," Ossen interrupted, "I understand. It must've been terrible. To see all that."

Chev didn't just see it. He knew it was his fault. But he had unburdened himself yesternight on Mitra. There was no point in doing the same to Ossen.

"Who are the children?" Chev asked, sensing an opening to change the subject.

Ossen hesitated through mild embarrassment, releasing a breath like a hoarse cough. "There's a lot I haven't told you, Chev. Those aren't just children. They're my other sons. And your brothers."

"Oh." Chev couldn't summon any expression other than surprise. He peeked backward—seeing the line of children like he laid eyes on them for the first time, feeling something indescribable. Part of what weighed on him that moment was the strangeness of it all, but also something darker, and more piercing—horror at not knowing what kind of man Ossen was, horror at not recognizing these children for who they were, and thinking so little of them, and the residual shock of simply being *here* in the first place. Chev felt he needed to be somewhere else just to unpack these feelings.

The wall's steps eased up a tower. It was already as high as Chev had ever been, enough to feel the night's raw wind strip his hair of structure, but the horizon was dominated by taller, monolithic structures that seemed ready to fall over and crush swathes of streets and buildings. But while Chev admired the city's interior, the rest of the party were focused on the tents that peppered the hillside, strewn like rocks across a wasteland.

"Do you know why they build keeps for the nightfolk here?" Ossen would soon answer his own question. "We keep the beasts of the night out. These walls were built as much for us as they were for them." Ossen pointed over to the tents. "That's the dayfolk army out there. Are they beasts or men?"

"Men?" Chev wasn't sure he was giving the right answer.

"Men," Ossen repeated in agreement.

Chev wasn't sure what Ossen was getting at, but it only added to the host of things on Chev's mind.

"Ossen, what's your plan? What do you want?" asked Chev.

"I'm not ready to unveil anything," said Ossen, "There are too many spies yet."

"That's not what I meant," Chev stepped in front of Ossen and looked him in the eye. "You have the marry with seven women, you have —" Chev made a brief check, "— *dozens* of children. Ossen, what's—"

"*Father!*" Ossen growled the name, pushed Chev aside and laid his hands on one of the battlements. "*Father,* damn it. No one should be calling me that name anymore. If you aren't my son or daughter, or my wife, I'm Emperor Osmond. Those are my names, and nobody has any right to call me any different."

"So what's Minda to you then? What's she supposed to do?"

"You fool kid. Didn't you understand? I think about her constantly, she's the string that's always pulling. I feel like a damn fish at the end of a line. What about her? You think I can just thrust everything aside and go back?"

"I wasn't saying that..."

"So why bring her up, then? It drives me crazy thinking how she just let that rotten place hold her down. But she wanted to be a flower among weeds, so I let her be! What else do you want?" Ossen growled his complaints into the cold air. "My Empire will be a revelation, Chev. I'm not just going to restore Manak, I'm going to make it greater than it ever was! To do that, I need a great deal of children, to administer the Empire, to marry into powerful clans. Chev, draw closer, I won't say this loud."

And Chev did, leaning over the very battlement the Emperor did. And he didn't whisper, but he spoke, quietly, and let it float into Chev's ear alone and the rest blended into the wind.

"You have a special place, my son. They all think they will be the next Emperor, but it was only ever going to be you. You are the only one with any sense of courage or justice. You are the only one I truly care about."

What a strange thing for him to say, and even harder for Chev to take deep into the heart. Yes, it was a father's pride, but also something ugly at its root. Chev reeled back as though his father had spoken nonsense.

And looking into his father's eyes, gray as slate and bearded with lashes like frost, Chev dredged through his memories, and found something he didn't want to see. Ossen was strong and distant and stoic. He was slow to anger but he could be a vengeful thunderstorm when it was summoned. He had faith in a few and the rest he didn't trust. And Emperor Osmond wasn't like that at all. The Emperor Osmond *clung*, like a beam that couldn't stand on its own, desperate for reinforcement. Ossen never needed to be told he was loved and respected, he carried it inside himself. But Emperor Osmond *fished* for it.

They had the same face, Ossen and Osmond, but they were different. Chev couldn't recognize this man.

I can't be that. The words were in Chev's lungs, but a hard fatherly slap across the back beat the words out before they were spoken. Perhaps Osmond knew that a refusal was coming, and he wanted to head it off before it came out.

In a more carefree time, Chev might have wanted to see the ocean out of pure wonder. Now, he *needed* it, like he might needed a balm to soothe him. After he left his father's side, he watched the ocean for a long time. Comparing the vast plane before him to the Sippi was an exercise in quiet contemplation. Whatever conclusions he came up with were drowned out and washed away by the churning of the sea. Water brushed his feet. Here, there was nothing better in the world.

It shouldn't have been a surprise that Adar might come here too. She had said that she hoped to see the sea, and as she plodded down a dune with an airy tunic and breeches, she had to stop her in her tracks and admire the sight.

"Is it like anything like you imagined?" asked Chev.

"I thought it was going to be more like the Sippi," Adar looked out at a distant spot, as though stretching her vision just a tad beyond the horizon.

She had that queer tone, the sort you get when things turn out not like you expect.

"You sound disappointed," said Chev.

"Not in the least," said Adar, "It's beautiful. Sometimes, you realize the world's a bigger place than you imagined." Adar let herself plop on the sand beside Chev, turned to him to ask an earnest question. "You ever feel like that?"

"Yeah," said Chev, "In fact, I've felt it so often lately that I don't know how to feel any different."

Adar watched the same distant point, and sighed. "It seems a little silly by comparison. War. Killing. Emperors and prophecies and destinies. You know how I feel? Like a little firefly trapped under a cup, just seeing there's a big world out there but I can't do anything to change it."

"Hmm..." Chev had nothing to say about that. It was like the waters that splashed his feet washed away whatever was on his mind.

"So the Emperor was your father." Adar didn't pose it like a question. More like a spark for conversation.

"Do we have to talk about this?"

"No," Adar said, "but I'm a firefly in a cup and that's all I can worry about right now."

Chev licked his lips, uneasily pulled from his thoughts. "I used to sit by a stream with a girl from my tribe. Sana, she was called. It felt just like this does. Just quiet. Peaceful."

"You told me about her," said Adar, leaning back on the sand to look up at the stars.

"Yeah. Something terrible happened to her. She was... I guess the word was 'eaten'."

"What?" Adar twisted her neck, "Chev! I thought you said she was *waiting* for you."

"It's not like you think. It only got her hands. The creature that did it, you see, it didn't want to kill her. It just wanted to torture her." Chev shook his head. "That's wrong. It didn't even want to torture her. It wanted to torture *me*. Sometimes I sit, and hard as I try I can't hate that monster. I just think about how brilliantly evil it was. It's like *admiration*. And what does that say about me?

"Adar, all I wanted to do was impress Sana. I didn't want her finding out I'd made a deal with a bone-skin to save myself. I thought, if I went out to kill it before it hurt anyone, I could turn my cowardice into heroism. And when I went out and couldn't find the monster, I lied. And I ended up causing the death of a lot of people." Was Chev choking? His face didn't show it, but he spoke like there was a catch in his throat. "I could've destroyed my tribe, Adar. The worst part of it was that this *villain* called Feska said it. He said I was selfish enough to put the tribe at risk, and he was right. Darin was also right."

Chev's eyes traced the crude image of the bone-skin imprinted on his arm. It was by a man who'd never seen a bone-skin, and could only guess what they looked like. "I don't deserve this. I bring monsters wherever I go. I don't slay them."

"Chev," Adar said, slowly, soft-voiced, with two distant eyes, "I can't rightfully say that I've never done something cowardly or stupid. In fact, as you spoke, I could only compare it to what I did."

"You killed that worm locust," said Chev, "You can't be a coward."

Adar nodded, "You killed it too. And to think how good I felt afterward, like I was a hero, and it all turned right to ash when I laid eyes on that creature. That child of the *dayfolk*."

"No one can blame you for that," said Chev.

"You're right, in that Darin was right," Adar swallowed hard, as she watched waves lap at her bare feet. "But not what about what you think. He said you were forgiving."

That was so absurd Chev had to laugh. "Darin paid me a compliment?"

"He didn't mean it as a compliment," Adar flashed a light smile. "Chev, the real hero in this story is you and Naia. If it weren't for you both, Starlight would be dead."

Chev was thinking of a way to deny it. "Maybe. I can hear Varnas already telling me that I did something no one would do. But I wouldn't give Naia the credit you deserve."

"Gods," she cursed, and she muttered darkly to herself, "It's coming out. I can't not say it now." With a dreadfully flat expression, she told him: "Chev, Naia rescued Starlight, and she didn't tell you."

Now Chev's eyes flickered toward Adar. The truth was coming out, like a river gushing out from a broken dam, Adar couldn't stop herself. She could only bend the truth, so that it was more tolerable to Chev, so that it was more tolerable to *herself*.

"Starlight went overboard," Adar said, "and it was my fault. I had taken her out one night, without your knowing. And—I dropped her over the side of the ship. I thought she'd died, Chev, but Naia saw her and saved her. And she didn't want to embarrass me, so she didn't say anything."

While she was speaking, Chev's lips dropped and lost form, his eyes blinked and he looked utterly lost. And when she'd finished, he let the moment hang, twisting his head slowly back to gaze at the sea.

"Why didn't you say anything?" he asked after a long pause.

That could not have been the first question on his mind. It wasn't even the question she most feared. But Adar took it.

"Chev—" The sweat on her brow, her thudding heart, her bloodless fingers and toes, all made a haze that Adar found difficult to speak through. She did her best, and managed to get some words out. "Isn't it obvious? I thought if you found out, you'd hate me."

Chev's tone became a note darker. "Is that why you told me that Darin said I was forgiving? Were you priming me?"

"Chev, I—" she didn't know how to answer. It was as simple as that.

After a few beats, Chev knew that Adar wasn't going to come up with anything to say. There was a tale between the two of them, and after Chev took a moment to gather his emotions, he simply moved on. "I had some good news. I learned that I'm not cursed," Chev was speaking as though Adar were some goat or wooden post, "I thought I was bonded to Starlight, but Mitra sat me down and explained it to me. I feel really dumb."

Chev stood, beat the sand from his breeches, and addressed a stone-faced Adar. "I suppose you could have never told me. I'm happy about that, at least."

And at that, he plodded over the sand dune and back into the city.

There was something going on.

Chev entered the Emperor's hall, where so recently they had held a raucous festival. But now things were cool and quiet. Emperor Osmond and a handful of his knights stood around a table, gesturing at a map and making whispered plans. Silence fell as Chev's footfalls fell like sharp cracks across the stone floors.

The number of turned heads made Chev feel as though he were intruding. It was only his father's insistent voice and snapping fingers that brought them back to focus.

"It's only my son, and we're in private now."

"Are you sure he can be trusted?" said one of the knights in a weathered voice, "he might be a spy of the Hawk Clan, or—"

"He's a child of the Nightlands," the Emperor quickly dismissed, "They're a simple people. Let him in. I think it's time he learned."

It wasn't Chev's plan to join his father. He wanted to check on Starlight, it had been a near full night since he'd seen her. But he was roped in now, and the men around the table made space for him.

"While you were with Mitra last night, I had a discussion with your friend, Adar," the Emperor's eyes traced the map, "Very interesting woman. We had a long and fruitful discussion. Chev, you should know that an Emperor's most important duty is to bring peace and justice. There are others who want the mantle just as badly, they fight and war with one another but only the True Emperor can take power simply with his words. I made a shameful mistake, Chev. When I first sought to become Emperor I did so through the sword. Now, I will prove my station by bringing peace."

The Emperor put his finger on the map so hard it thudded. A finger drew across some glyphs, representing the very same tents and camps they'd spied earlier that night. "We will bring peace between the dayfolk. There will be no siege. Not a rock will be flung at Sunset."

"How would you do that?" Chev asked.

Osmond's response seemed unrelated. But to Chev's mounting horror, it wasn't. "You brought the dayfolk child. A better sign of the coming time I have not seen."

"Please, just tell me the plan," Chev said.

"The taboo has come to its natural end. We nightfolk have been drawn into this conflict whether we want to or not. Our people burn alive as the dayfolk destroy their own cities, forcing us into the wilds, where we suffer from hunger and disease. I know I don't need to tell you how we've suffered, you've seen enough it just by journeying here. Neutrality ends tomorrow night. Tomorrow night, we'll drive off the dayfolk army."

Chev leaned over the map, and suddenly it seemed to click into place. The markings: troop movements. The runes: locations of enemies and allies. So that was what it was. Emperor Osmond prepared for battle, not against nightfolk, but *dayfolk.*

"That doesn't sound like peace," said Chev, "it sounds like *war.*"

"If we do everything right," and now the Emperor paced away from the table, from his advisers and toward the moonlit window, "it won't be."

A rattling noise interrupted them. A servant came in with a tray of wooden goblets, and carried it with trembling hands across the room.

"Set the tray on the table," said the Emperor.

The woman either didn't listen or didn't hear. She made a beeline for Chev, who had to shoot out a hand to receive the goblet she gave him.

"Stop," the Emperor said.

The woman had her head bent down, so that her hair covered her eyes. But Chev could see her clearly: and fear was written all over her face, and cold sweat was dripping from her brow and dampening the corners of her wide, white eyes.

The Emperor approached, his chainmail clinking heavily with every step. He addressed her with an authoritative brass tone. "You know better than to give drinks directly," he told her, "You allow your masters to take their goblets off from the tray of their choosing."

Her voice was a mouse's. "Sorry, Emperor. I thought it would nicer if—"

"Since you touched the goblet, you get to drink from it." The Emperor snatched the goblet out from Chev's stiff hands, and thrust it before the servant. "Go on."

"Sir..." Her fear was so palpable Chev felt it melt into the air and poison him. She trembled, he shook, she couldn't breathe, he couldn't breathe. The whole exchange was painful and terrible to witness.

"Drink," he repeated once again, "I'm sure you would have picked only the sweetest wine for my son."

All her defenses were taken down: she raised the tray with both hands right to her chin, and Emperor Osmond casually stripped it away. Two empty hands, with fingers clipping together like crab claws, and she had nothing to do but take the goblet.

She did so. She sipped. And she put her hand to her chest, coughed a few times, struggled to the floor with some invisible enemy, and died.

The Emperor sighed, as though he had anticipated this, and put the tray onto the table. "The nightfolk have had no courts for some time. Even our assassins have gotten awful. I can tell you one thing, Chev, one of my wives is responsible, and I'll find out which. Mark this, I'll find out."

Chev couldn't answer. He was frozen and speechless, consumed by the dead eyes of the servant.

"But do take a drink," the Emperor lightened, "the other ones will be safe."

Chev let himself leave the room as quickly as he could, heading back to the rooms where they slept. He nearly ran into a woman zipping past with a bundle of crying baby.

"She won't stop crying," the woman said in a harried voice. "I tried to get her to sleep but I can't. She won't drink any milk!"

He could hear Ma-ma's trotters before he saw her, and that tiny hairy goat seemed to hover around the corner waiting for it to be safe. Chev picked her up and tucked her under his other arm.

"I need to sleep," the woman wearily said, and she dragged her feet in the opposite direction.

Chev watched her go. In his familiar arms, Starlight started pawing at his chest, finding loose pieces of cloth to tug at with an iron grip. Her big bright eyes looked up at Chev in wonder, lips spread revealing her sweet smile.

"I'm so glad to see you," said Chev, "Come on. Let's go see Varnas."

In response, Starlight blew a raspberry, chasing her smile with spittle.

Varnas had his own room too, and Chev used his shoulder to knock the door open. The old trapper had his hand wrapped around a pillow on his stomach, his back against a cushion, his sleepy face sunken behind his wispy gray beard.

"Sleepin' in the middle of the night," Varnas sighed pleasantly, "What a concept. And here you've come to ruin it."

"We gotta get out of here."

"I know," said Varnas, "but these beds are so damn comfortable! I gotta get me one of these mattress things, or stuff a sack full of hay. These things feel like damn clouds."

Ma-ma began to struggle, so Chev set her down, absently watching Varnas' closed eyes. For once, Varnas looked the part of an old man, still and frail above the sheets. His normal breathing formed a sort of snore even while he was half awake, as though breathing through a heavy cold.

"Are you sick?" asked Chev.

Varnas' eyes sprang open, he brow curved with annoyance. "Am I sick? Of course I'm sick. I'm an old man and I just finished a journey across the known world! Am I sick? I can't even get outta this bed to save my own life. Literally!"

"So you think—"

"—That your father's plan is full of crap? Yeah, very *wise*. He thinks it's some genius thing to attack dayfolk in the middle of the night. It ain't. It's cowardly, and there's a reason why nightfolk don't do it."

Chev was taken aback. "How did you—"

"Stones carry noise," Varnas answered simply, "Everyone here is deaf."

There was a momentary distraction as Starlight gurgled, pulling Chev's shirt, reminding him that she was here. He adjusted her in his arms and stroked her soft head, but it didn't put the usual joy into his heart. His had only concern.

"This place is awful," said Chev, "Everyone's watching me all the time. They tell me sweet things and then try and kill me. This is the sort of place that drives people crazy. I can't spend another night here. This can never be my home. It's like I traveled all this distance just to figure out the obvious."

Varnas weighed that statement by tilting his head. "Yeah. I suppose it's half-true. You did come a long way, you didn't find what you thought you were looking for, but you got something else."

"What?"

Varnas snapped onto his feet like a lightning bolt went through his ass. "An adventure!" Varnas clapped Chev's shoulder, pinched his cheeks to make a dumb smile. "You do it for its own sake, boy. Everyone needs at least one big adventure in his life. This ain't the one I woulda gone on, but it turned out better than expected. But now we've traveled the world, it's finally time to go home."

And then Varnas threw his things on his back, as though they were just going to march out the gates.

"Varnas," Chev licked his lips and shuffled his feet.

"Don't like that tone of voice," muttered Varnas unpleasantly.

"We can't leave. Not yet. What about Darin? What about Adar?"

The pack dropped from Varnas' back, clattering on the stone floor.

"Ah, you're so predictable, you know that!" Varnas made a string of indistinguishable curses as he paced around the room. "Adar—can't say I know that woman too well, but she sure fits that armor well, and she'd never drop that knighthood act for even a second. And Darin didn't come for the adventure. It should be obvious by now, but knowing you, I guess I have to spell it all out. Darin is *not* a good man."

"But you saw him rescue that dayfolk," said Chev, "And he's loyal to the tribe. You can't fault a man for that. He doesn't deserve to rot in a dungeon."

"It's as Darin said," Varnas motioned toward the window, "He saved him because he knew you were gonna charge out there. And that dayfolk didn't survive 'til morning anyway. I ain't sure he *doesn't* deserve a prison cell."

"You can't say that," Chev stepped forward as though in defense of something, "Weren't you the one that said I should make peace with Darin?"

"You forgot, boy! That was for *you*, not for him! I needed to make sure you'd do nothing as stupid as make a deal with bone-skins again. But..." Varnas released a stuttering breath, "I suppose, if you're stubborn on this, we can go rescue him. Just in case, thinking this might happen, I already came up with a plan."

Half an hour later, Chev was desperately clinging to a wall, his feet dangling over a lethal plunge. The wind conspired to shove him, and only crumbling mortar provided any handhold. His arms were tortured, his bare feet scratched near to bleeding. And just a little above, Varnas was hanging on the stones with his beard blowing like leaves in a storm.

"There's that window!" Varnas cried out to Chev.

This was the problem with agreeing to a plan before listening to all the details. He'd mentioned sneaking into the dungeon. He hadn't mentioned it was from the *outside*. Perhaps the old man had assumed the keep's wall wouldn't be much more difficult to climb than a tree.

Still, Chev knew this wasn't beyond his abilities. It was just going to be painful.

Varnas grasped the open window and threw himself inside. When Chev came close, the old man took his arms and pulled him into a dismal place. Corridors crisscrossed and fled into dark dead ends. There were doors everywhere, dizzying numbers each a precise distance from the next. Muted steps carried notes of chainmail and duty. Guards were afoot.

"Don't step," whispered Varnas, "slide your feet across the floor."

Varnas showed by example, slipping across flagstone, raising only the lightest scrape across the dry, dusty ground. Chev followed closely behind, back hunched over and peeking every direction.

"Look under the doors," said Varnas, "You take the left corridor, I'll go for the right."

"Are we splitting up?" asked Chev.

"Are you slow, boy? How else are we gonna search this place? Get to it!"

And so they did. Chev took the left hall, Varnas the right. It was strange, crawling on his hands and knees like a madman or a child, peeking beneath doors. He could only make out quiet shadows in each, he kept searching to find one that held an interesting shape.

He was about halfway down the corridor when he found something which might prove interesting.

"Darin?" Chev whispered.

Something moved on the other side of the door. If Chev were in the forest and hearing this between trees he might've guessed it was some panicked wounded animal. But the gray, twisted hand that slipped into moonlight was very much a nightfolk's, though Chev could scarcely believe his own conclusion.

"Gods, Darin!"

Chev pushed the door; it didn't budge. Chev was confused because he'd only experienced doors that opened. He assumed the contraption simply didn't work, so he made what he thought was the simplest, most obvious entry. He levered the hinges off with his bare hands. Putting the door to the side, he ventured right in, waving madly as though that would rid him of the throb in his fingers.

"You're not Darin," said Chev.

And yet, Chev recognized him, though he hadn't expected to.

The prisoner pulled his back up against the wall, flattening his shoulders against it in an expression of salvaged dignity. Chin pointed high, breath steadied, long, pointed ears tucked back, this man had the bearing of a knight. The sight of his worn face transported Chev right back to the road to Manak, when the strong Sargon chatted with a fellow warrior on the road. One who said he was going west to see the Emperor.

"Oh," the old man spoke hoarsely, "You were with the wolf clan, weren't you?"

Chev bent beside him, "Erren, was it? You were the one going to meet the man who claimed to be the new Emperor."

"I expected a familiar face, but not yours. But neither did you expect mine. I hope our interests align."

"I do too." The old man's sunken cheek and pulled lips caused Chev's back to shiver, he resembled a skeleton, but Chev tried to address the man trapped inside of it. "But I can't be sure. The Emperor is my father."

There was a dry, dusty laugh. "Oh, what wonder circumstance is! To have crossed paths with you before. Listen, boy, I won't survive an escape, so come close. I am long delayed and now the Hawk clan will send a warband for me. If you see your father for the man he has become, then don't tell my clansmen I'm here. They must stop Emperor Osmond. You tell them that. Tell them what he has planned."

Chev nodded. "I can, at least, do that. But, how would they stop him? What should they do?"

Erren paused. "I don't know."

Not words of comfort.

"I trust you will think of something," the old man spoke so quickly it came out like a breath. "Go! The guards patrol will come through soon, put the door back up and balance it there. We are lucky they do not open my cell."

Chev sensed a goodbye would not be appreciated. He did as asked, and put the door back into place, which felt like he was sealing a man behind a boulder. But one last glance in to see whether what he was about to do the right thing, and Chev saw a glitter of hope in the Hawk knight's eyes. Not a drop of fear.

When they met back up, Darin was over Varnas' shoulder. Any relief at seeing him was diluted by what he saw: imprisonment had changed this man. He was weak, and the hunter's scar seemed darker by twilight, the same shade as his eyes and that lanky hair which covered his forehead as torn drapes. No emotion passed his face when he locked eyes with Chev.

"Stop staring at each other," hissed Varnas, "we have a lot of wall to descend."

Darin refused all help climbing back down, and so the descent was done in silence and with patience. Darin took to solid ground with the same stolid pride as he had his walk to his prison cell. But his blank, unreadable eyes called attention to themselves as they blinked in Darin's strange, unique way.

"A bit of gratitude would be nice." Varnas was thoroughly done. The old man had his hands on his knees and his back against the rough stones of the keep. His breath half-wheezed, suggesting he couldn't quite get the air he needed.

"I'm waiting for you to tell me what you need. You didn't do this out of the kindness of your heart," said Darin.

"We did, actually." Chev was at Varnas' side, rubbing his back as though easing the breath back into him, "My father's moving against the dayfolk army. We're leaving town before that happens, Darin, and we couldn't leave while you were trapped here."

That was when Darin's eyes shrank to little pinpricks, adding the suggestion of suspicion to his eyes. In the odd light by the side of the keep, he seemed not much more than a ghost falling on shadows.

"So you'll abandon your father? I doubt that." Darin turned, ready to limp down the other side of the street. "I'll take the freedom you give me, and I'll thank you for it, whatever your motive."

It was an odd way to say goodbye. That was the only impression Chev was left with as Darin evaporated into the city.

"Ungrateful bastard," Varnas hissed it out, hand over his throat as he watched him disappear.

Chev, without even thinking about it, rubbed great circles over Varnas' back. He could feel the knots of his spine, the old ragged scars, the canyons between the ribs. "We did the right thing," said Chev.

"I can't be sure of that. This whole adventure took a bite out of me, and that took what little I had left. I think it's the air here. It's the salt, dries the throat, tightens up the skin." Varnas, finally gaining some composure, sighed in the way only a man spent and worn could. "Boy, I just wanna see the Nightlands again."

"You will," said Chev, glancing into the patch of darkness into which Darin evaporated, "You will."

It felt like the moment when Chev and Varnas had first arrived, there they were standing outside the keep, the gate an open maw and the weight of masonry all around them. Then, they were eager to be inside to cast off their long journey. Now, even the promise of food and warmth was poor encouragement, the fire that roared deep in the throat of the castle looked less and less for light and more and more to burn and consume.

Chev and Varnas exchanged a long glance. He looked older than ever, that man, the lines dug deeper into his face and the thin tracing of lips around his mouth ever more toothy and snarled.

"You wanna get your girl, you have to go in there," said Varnas.

"I don't know how I'm gonna do it," said Chev.

"You felt it, I felt it. Nice as the beds are, it's hard to sleep when you can imagine everything around you turning to rubble and ash. This is your part, Chev, I've never done anything like this and I've run out of ideas. Don't have a word to give from these *wise* lips."

"Varnas," whispered Chev.

"Yeah?"

"You're not wise," he told him.

Varnas flashed more of his lipless grin. "It's the wrong time and place we all are in now, but I see what you're digging at. Anyways, there's a glimmer on the horizon. Sun's coming. I'm gonna leave the city. Make myself a nice old pit."

"Make it enough for three!" Chev shouted at Varnas as he turned back.

The old man flicked his arm, and he was gone. The keep stood before Chev. Inside he could hear laughter, the wafting scent of meat tried to lure him to the drifting music. None of these things helped Chev in his climb up the steps. It felt like approaching a bone-skin's den. Staring down that hall, with branches into so many chambers and corridors, was exactly like those labyrinth of tunnels Chev so desperately feared to tread.

But this was different. Starlight was in there. And she wasn't going to crawl out herself.

Chev made a ------------------------steady and cautious pace inside. Lamps burned in alcoves, flickering like dying stars, casting improbable shadows down abyssal corridors. The stones carried wild laughter and drunken speech. And inside, Emperor Osmond was on his throne, his fingers dancing impatiently on the armrest, his subjects so thoroughly lost in their revelries they didn't notice whatever sour expression their ruler happened to have. His wives looked more imperious than he did, and the children sated their appetites with abandon.

The Emperor did not miss Chev's entry. As a matter of fact, Chev seemed to be the only thing his eyes roved for.

"Chev!" the Emperor exclaimed, before launching out of his seat like a young man. He put a heavy arm around Chev. "I sent for you, but my servants said you'd gone. I was expecting you to come out from upstairs, but you walked in from the outside. You must've been out on a walk, which is your right, mind you. But still, I was waiting. Where is Varnas?"

"He left Sunset, going back to the Nightlands," said Chev. It was close enough to the truth that Chev could say it without withering or equivocating.

"A shame." The Emperor pulled Chev toward a table populated entirely by knights. "He was going to be useful in the coming fight. I want you to meet someone."

The man the Emperor practically pulled out from his seat could barely fit into his armor. He was at a gangling, awkward age where he had the frame of a man and the face of a child, his skin shredded by bumps and boils and he looked at Chev with the darting eyes of a child suffering mild terror.

"This," the Emperor pounded the boy's shoulder as though he could withstand it, "is Jarv, my second eldest son." The Emperor added with a flick of an eyebrow. "Your brother, too."

It was hard to see the "brotherness" in this boy, as he couldn't even meet Chev in the eye. He'd shaken vines with greater strength than this boy's hand, each dip causing an equal and opposite shockwave across the boy's arm. He stopped before he broke something.

"It's nice to meet you, brother," said Jarv.

Being called that was so odd that Chev couldn't even pretend. He wasn't even sure what he was supposed to pretend. He looked at the boy with an open mouth, limp and wordless.

"Jarv isn't old enough to fight. He'll be carrying my weapons for the battle next night."

Jarv dipped his head in ascent, but there was no smile.

"Emperor—"

"*Father*," the Emperor's correction was stern, but followed by a smirk.

"Father," Chev swallowed, and picked words carefully, "you said this was going to happen next night?"

"If we wait any longer, it would be too late. They'll destroy the city the next morning."

And that statement chilled Chev to the bone, summoning beads of cold sweat across Chev's brow and draining the blood from his hands. This was all happening a lot quicker than he'd thought. And, Chev didn't forget Erren's plea. In the rush of all the competing things he had to do, he remained silent, his mind empty of logical thought, and his effort to think produced nothing.

"Are you sure?" Chev asked.

"Am I sure?" the Emperor reeled back by the inanity of the question, "I've been waiting for this day for a long, long time. I'm sure as anything." The Emperor moved on quickly, again draping an arm over Chev's shoulder. He now spoke in whispers, cloaked with conspiracy. "Chev, I'm glad you've come tonight. For you, I will give everyone a sample of my justice. But you won't need to do anything. I want you to find a seat, relax, watch, and learn."

This was not what Chev wanted. He wanted to grab Starlight and go. But he'd been locked into a terrible circumstance. He had no choice but to satisfy his father's whims until he could again sneak out of sight.

He didn't spot Adar at first. But she had seen him, and she quickly averted her gaze elsewhere. This was no time to play games, so he stole an empty stool and inserted himself between her and whoever she had been talking to.

"Chev!" Adar could have said it in either surprise or annoyance. Chev couldn't tell, and he wouldn't care to sort it out. He leaned to her, and whispered directly into her ear.

"I'm leaving the city, Adar. I think you should too."

Now her eyes rose to look into his, and there was no confusion that this was surprise. "But your father! Does he know?"

Chev's eyes darted to the other people at the table. Drunk knights, who wouldn't notice a bone-skin if it landed on top of them. "The Emperor can't save this city. And in the way he wants to, he shouldn't. He's going to bring this war to the nightfolk."

"He's right, though," Adar looked more into her drink than toward Chev. "War is already on us."

"Adar, you can't say—"

"It's too late," she said, watching her ale ripple to the perturbations through the table. "Nightfolk live in these cities too. If we don't save them, we're just as homeless."

Chev scooted further in closer to her, his stool scraping noisily. "Adar, can you imagine what would happen? Dayfolk dragging us out into sunlight and slaughtering us. Nightfolk raiding dayfolk in the dark. It would be a *nightmare*."

"It's already a nightmare. The way things are, it can't get any worse. At least the Emperor has a solution."

"A solution with only the faintest chance of working."

"But still," Adar finally looked up, "a chance."

Her gaze was dark and sad, and Chev found few things to say to her. It was a relief when the Emperor himself provided a distraction, as temporary as it would be. Osmond rose from his throne, the mere act casting the room in silence.

Servants weaved across tables, setting cups before every knight, child and wife.

"There are many things I wish to raise my goblet to. Many things indeed." Osmond's narrow eyes scanned every corner of the chamber. "Emperors, they say, bring peace. They bring order. They bring *justice*."

To this there was great cheering and the raising of goblets, all which died as Osmond raised a hand, making it clear he was meandering his way toward a point. Chev noticed Osmond's left thumb, white hot, nail driven into the stain of the throne.

"Someone in here panicked to see my eldest son alive."

If the room was already quiet, it was now deathly silent. The whole chamber went white with fear.

"I hoped that I would see it on someone's face. That way I wouldn't have to do this." There was a strange weight as the Emperor shifted toward his wives. "One of you arranged to have my son poisoned. One of you has been served with what he would have drunk. The rules of this game are simple. Whoever among you confesses, or reveals the culprit, doesn't have to drink."

The table where the Emperor's wives sat became a line of stone faced gargoyles. As the seconds went by, their faces eroded; the young women shriveled up as though suddenly old, the older women had masks which turned as smooth and pale as youth, and every subtle movement, every finger that traced lines in the wood or shifted grip on the stems of their goblets, quivered.

Justice, the Emperor had called it. Justice for a crime against Chev himself. Yet, there was no satisfaction in this. Chev's chest was as frozen and solid like one of those goblets which sat waiting.

The first voice rose came from one of the youngest wives. She sat at the very edge of the table, her hands and feet tightly bound. "If the culprit confesses, then we don't have to drink?"

The Emperor shook his head. "Whoever confesses *doesn't* have to drink."

"This is madness," a more matronly woman spoke, expensive fine shawls demonstrating a great deal of station. "Osmond, is this a trick? Please tell me it is!"

"No trick," Osmond weaved his fingers over his lap. "I'm simply giving you the same choice that you'd give to another."

"Osmond, I'm your first wife! If had betrayed you in any way, I would have done so years and years ago. Don't treat me as though I'm one of these newcomers!"

There was an audible mutter from one of the middle wives. "Shut up, Fiora."

"I didn't say anything when you *adopted* this strange boy." Now Fiora, the eldest of the wives, pierced Chev with a horrid gaze. "If I wanted rid of him, he'd be gone already."

"You talk too much Fiora, you incriminate yourself." The Emperor made an emotionless scan of his other six wives. "Do any of you have anything else to say?"

The youngest of the wives, the one at the end of the table, turned a darker and darker shade, her grip on her thigh growing tense, her forehead bled sweat, blinking rapidly, lips tightened. When the Emperor's gaze moved onto her, it all boiled out.

"Emperor, I—"

" —It was Vemma," spurted one of the middle wives.

"Dierdre!" The woman who was clearly Vemma called out in shock.

"Sorry Vemma, Lanie was about to say anyway. It was her. I heard her talking about it with one of the maids."

"Don't listen Emperor, it's a lie!" Vemma stood up from her seat, knocking over her goblet so that it spun through the air onto the floor. "It was Dierdre, she did it!"

The Emperor, in bland recognition of the fallen goblet, said, "You can drink Dierdre's, Vemma. And if you continue to act out you can choose another one to drink as well."

"Emperor, I'm—" There was a quick calculation of chances, her eyes quickly darting over each mug, wondering how many she could afford to risk. "—*I'm innocent.*" The plea was silent and under the breath.

The Emperor's next command was delivered with the cold of granite, and from sunken eyes and thin, twisted lips. "Now, drink."

Even Dierdre, who would drink nothing, looked like she'd swallowed a serpent's worth of poison. She shrank into her shawl, and tried not to look as the other six women put clumsy, reluctant fingers around the stems of their goblets.

It was too much for even Chev to bear now. He'd been leaning so hard on his foot it had gone numb, and now he sprang on it. His words came out faster than he'd could think of them.

"Emperor Osmond—"

"*Father,*" the Emperor once again corrected, more as a growl from the back of his throat.

"Father, I don't need this. They've learned their lesson. They've—"

"Enough!" Osmond made a fist on the armchair. "This isn't for you! There *will* be justice. I *will* be obeyed. They *will* drink."

Through Chev's pounding heart and flailing nerves, he misspoke once again. "*Emperor—*"

And with a volume that shook every crow off every branch for miles upon miles, the Emperor cried out: "*Father!*"

There was shockwave of even deeper silence that spread out from the throne. An echo barked back, like an enraged ghost calling out. And then the Emperor settled, his eyes cold, his breath a rasp.

He whispered in the silence, and it was deafening. "Drink."

All but one of the wives took her goblet. All but one swallowed. All but one set her goblet on the table. Fiora let hers tumble from her hands onto the floor.

It was a very hollow sound, stone against goblet. The matronly woman put her fingers to her throat, and her nails left dark trails across her slender neck. She made animal noises and opened her lips. It was hard to say whether she was crying out or trying to breathe. Possibly both.

Jarv, from across the room, jumped out of his seat so quickly that it smashed to the flagstones. There was horror on his face as he watched his mother writhe and shrink within her shawls, limbs jerking and reaching for something faraway and untouchable. She continued to suffer as the Emperor sipped the froth from his ale, his interest focused on a point halfway up the wall.

"And that," the Emperor declared, "is a sample of my justice."

There was no further communication between Chev and Adar. They ate in silence, and when the meal was over, Chev moved silently to his room.

Ma-ma was chewing on some hay in a box in the corner. He whistled at her and she trotted up to him with trust in her eyes. Starlight was wriggling in her crib when he snatched her and held her close. Chev moved quickly, straight out of the keep and straight out of the gates of Sunset with Ma-ma not far behind. He didn't stop until sunlight stung the back of his head and compelled him to turn and seek shelter.

What a strange thing it was to see Varnas, shovel across his knees, face gleaming with all the effort he'd gone through.

"Why have a bed when you can have dirt, eh?"

"Thought you would've gone beneath by now," said Chev.

"Ah well, if I had, you might've walked right past. Come on boy. Let's rest up. The Nightlands are damn far away."

Chapter Twenty-Four
The Sky's Measure

CHEV WAS UP BEFORE Varnas. He wanted to watch the sunset.

As the Great Burning Orb dipped just below the horizon, turning the diamond clouds into the ash of a long dead fire, he finally understood how the city got its name. That far off star and the city spires seemed so perfectly aligned, the way the ocean's waves seemed to transport the sun's wealth to the harbor. He could drink up that scene forever if his eyes didn't water and his skin gone calloused and hot.

Out from the gates, a little fleck of movement in the haze, someone was walking towards them. If it were a nightfolk, he would have gone out in the streets on just the cusp of dusk. It would be some time before the figure reached where Chev and Varnas had rested.

Chev descended from the rock, wiped away the feeling of sweat and cracked skin, and saw that night had started to fall upon the Dayfolk camp. Movement had died down and silence was descending.

A head popped out of the hole. "Didn't take you for a sunwatcher."

"Must've picked it up from Starlight," said Chev.

Varnas grunted, as a means of communicating that he didn't quite approve. "Eh. Almost forgot what a sleepless day was, with that girl giggling and such. Thank you a million times for reminding me."

"No problem." Chev said it absently. His attention was drawn back to the figure, now clearly marching quite purposefully in their direction, and he waited until it was close enough to resolve into something.

"So? Whaddya think, boy? Long journey back to the Nightlands. Think we can get started?"

"Yes," Chev said. Varnas gave him a long, strange look like what he'd just said was madly out of character. "There's just one thing left to do."

"Thank the ancestors. I thought someone had stolen you in the middle of the night and replaced you with a shapeshifter." Varnas went to Chev's side, curious to what he was staring at. "Who is that?"

"I think it's Adar."

"Adar!" Varnas' smile was sly, and his comment breathy. "Boy, she really does like you."

"Shut it."

The old man's laugh was more like a wheeze, but they both fell silent, watching Adar's form slowly expand and shape into that of a hurried, exhausted woman, slightly bent with an invisible weight, bloodshot eyes carrying a day's worth of nightmares.

"You were right," she proclaimed, her pack dropping from her shoulders. "After what I saw last night… I was a fool, Chev. I wanted to believe someone could bring peace and order. Not just to us. To the dayfolk, too."

Chev sighed, his glance shot off a million miles across the plains, and his voice was weighted down by reluctance. "Adar. I can't tell you how glad I am that you've left that place. Varnas and I are going to the Nightlands. I'm sure you'll want to go back to your own tribe. But—" Chev paused a moment, to bite his lip, and really consider his next few words, "I don't think I can go back having done nothing to stop what's coming. No one but me has to do this. But if you could stand beside me, I can't think of a presence more welcome."

The sun's blaze finally sank completely from the world as he spoke. Instead of the inferno of day reflected in his eyes, came the silver ash of the rising moon. Nightfolk eyes were deep and bright of their own accord, and could shine as intensely as stars.

Her braids were frayed, she'd barely slept and she'd hobbled out from the city risking everything in the light of the fading sun. But she knew what he meant.

"I'll stand by you, Chev. But I don't think I can do anything but fight."

"I'll hang around too," Varnas said, "but I don't think I can do anything but look real pretty."

Varnas, as he always did, couldn't help but fit in the last word.

All dayfolk armies were protected by a nightfolk contingent. These were not part of the army, they wouldn't do the fighting. It was monsters instead they drove off, and monsters they always expected.

They did not expect a female knight, a young man, an old trapper, a squat goat and a tightly wrapped baby in a basket.

In fact, the sight was so bizarre a crowd seemed to congeal together to watch them approach, and they were met by a half-dozen or so curious faces.

Chev stopped before them, took a quick breather, and told them plainly: "You're about to be attacked."

There was no real leader among the sparsely armed men. The best there was, was a quartermaster, whose big cleaver was mounted firmly above the butcher's table rather than in a scabbard by his side. He took in the story with a wide variety of dubious blinks and squeezed brows, and Chev was never quite sure if the man believed him.

"A strange story by a strange group," the man's voice was bloated and slightly bovine, "But 'tis impossible. Anyone who wants to be Emperor knows they oughta follow the ancient laws. And the most important of all: night is for nightfolk and day is for dayfolk. The world isn't so far gone for *that* not to be true. And, 'sides, I don't think a pointy ear would betray another pointy ear. No offense."

There was something unfathomably tired about Chev's slow, painful blink. His breath turned into a half-sigh, his mouth opened for a multitude of arguments he didn't want to give. *Why would I lie? What's the harm in being cautious? Come, just come look and see!*

But this was the same species of obstinacy that he'd encountered his whole life. The same lack of imagination, the same foolish denial. From the elders of his tribe, to Tobi, to the Oracle, to Emperor Osmond. And Chev was finished with it, simply and completely. And so, he told him: "Fine, I'll just go face the Emperor myself." And he marched out the tent.

Adar was quicker to his side than Varnas, she rocketed out to chase him, leaving the tent flaps open by their own motion's breeze. She whispered quickly, desperately, "What are you doing, Chev? That's certain death!"

"I already knew what he'd do. Which was nothing. Adar," he turned to face her, and by instinct he ran a knuckle over one of her snowy braids. "I don't plan on dying. But I can't think of what else to do. A whole army is gonna march out those gates, my father is gonna see I stole away in the middle of the night, and he's gonna start a war between nightfolk and dayfolk. I haven't the clue what I'm gonna do or what to tell him. But I can't not try. Can't I?"

"He murdered one of his wives, Chev." Somehow, Adar's slight hand had fallen on his shoulder, and another clutched at his chest, where his pectorals and ribs joined. "I don't know that man but if he's willing to do that—"

"I know. I know." Chev didn't wish to be reminded. He turned away instead, and started down the sodden path toward the city. He shifted his shoulders so that his tunic fell more comfortably on his shoulders, and he pulled his belt tight so his sword was even closer at the ready. "I know when I face him I'll think of something. I have to."

Adar bounded across discarded gear and the detritus of army life. "I'll come with—"

"Not yet," said Chev. "Let me talk first. There has to be something I can say."

The view was like the edge of pit holding the dying embers of what was once a bonfire. The gates were closed and bolted and full of dreadful possibility, and that was where Chev sat and watched.

The grass was tall and full of life. Insects rustled as they navigated through their little jungle. Tiny things chirped near and far. Everything moved by the brush of the wind except that gate: solid, unmoving, silent. It seemed to hold things inside as much as it kept things out.

Soon, there was no light but the cool radiance of moon and stars. Nothing to see but plenty to hear. From behind him, he could sense the guards beginning to gather. They might have been curious. They might have been afraid. They might have been thinking they were watching a man going mad. Mutters stirred the silence, making eddies among the winds, and they carried rumor and speculation.

Chev's mind drifted, carrying him back to the Nightlands. Ossen's kind face was warmed by the smolder of a camp fire. He remembered how the light crept up trees and made Chev realize then how huge the world was. But now he knew, that as much as he was a speck compared to that tree, that tree was a speck measured up to a mountain, and that mountain a speck compared to the sky. And he had no way to know how he measured compared to the sky—that thought was so wild it caused vertigo. Like he might truly fall upward thinking about it.

In his memory, in the ash and by the light of that fire, Ossen had drawn a rune. "What does that mean, Chev?"

"Brother," Chev had answered.

"And this one," Ossen scraped another rune in the ash, hastily drawn, so that there were echoes of the previous word.

"Sister," Chev had answered.

Then, Ossen took great care scratching out a new rune, each soft curve delicately formed. It looked like two arms cupping a small human, it evoked magical feelings of safety and warmth. He asked: "What does this mean, Chev?"

"Mother," he had answered.

Again, in a few quick wipes the rune was wiped away. And for the next, Ossen had taken the greatest care: strong strokes, each deliberate, and dramatic, and enclosing. A complex thing that Chev had never once seen before. Chev looked to Ossen in confusion—something in Ossen's face had broken. He stared at the runes like he had sometimes stared out at the mountains, thinking about the Daylit Lands.

"What does this say, Chev?"

Ossen's voice was heavy. Chev hadn't wanted to give the wrong answer. But to Chev's eyes, it hadn't looked like anything.

"I don't know," Chev answered truthfully.

Ossen's face split again, sadness budded out. "I know," he had said. And in a few moments he'd wiped that rune away, turning it from meaning into a flat plane of ash and dust. Chev hadn't even the time to commit it to memory.

A wind picked through that ash, clumps were drawn and rolled, and soon the whole event had gone to fog in Chev's memory. He couldn't recall what came after. It was so very long ago.

And back in the present, the gates had creaked, shuddered, and with a metallic sound they whined and split open. A ghastly breeze followed them out, carrying a scent of fire, grease and salt. And staring through that open gate was as blinding and intolerable as staring right into the sun. But Chev watched as the man once called Ossen, cloak billowing from behind and mounted on a proud, tawny stag, trotted out into the plain. Behind him came more armed men on stags. Behind him came an army.

This wasn't like the long parades of refugees, drifting in clumps like bits of pollen, trailing across a landscape as though they were a part of it. Behind Emperor Osmond the knights marched in a column of three to a row, spaced and paced so perfectly as to impress in others that they were unified in purpose and oblivious to death. From a distance it would have been difficult to say they weren't part of the same monstrous animal. Osmond and Jarv cut stern faces among the crowd, but in different ways. The Emperor lifted his chin and let his lips tighten even further. Jarv's brow lowered, throwing his eyes into shadow.

The Emperor came close enough that Chev felt the gusts of warm breath from the stag. Osmond the Emperor dismounted, flicked his reins to his servants. After a rich carpet was laid out and tea placed in cups, the cups found homes in awaiting hands. With a hasty kind of ceremony, the Emperor lifted his sleeves and sat. Chev looked at him and did the same, taking his tea cup and a seat before his father.

"I'm not a statue, you know," said Emperor Osmond, "Nor am I a rock, or a clod of dirt. You slap me across the face, it hurts. This betrayal cuts deep. You could have told me of your dissent."

"You killed someone in my name," said Chev. "I didn't ask for that."

"It's justice, boy." Steam touched the Emperor's cheek. "A damn rare thing in our world."

"You didn't even get the right person."

"The right person? Bah!" The Emperor's grin was ugly, hungry and dark. "You think there's magic or machine out there that can tell the innocent from the wicked? The punishment's the fear, boy. The fear! Knowing that every crime will be answered in time. That's what stays hands from daggers, fingers from purses, blasphemy from lips. They all know well now that I will cut away the things I love for what I know to be right. And there's nothing in this world safe from that."

A shudder ran through Chev's breath. He had so much to say, so much of it appalled and angry, but the Emperor's reasoning was so novel and twisted the ideas he spoke were like wisps breaking against a gnarled bramble. In his hands, the untouched tea rippled, and the steam undulated in a hypnotic, serpentine manner. The man who sat before him: you could rip the bark off trees and beneath see a face as wooden.

The sides of Osmond's mouth dipped in unpleasant reflection.

"I don't mean for you to be my enemy, Chev. If you can't do this, you are welcome to stand aside and watch. But this will be done. Though now," the Emperor dipped his head in the direction of the camp, where the nightfolk defenders had formed a thin spearline, "you've made this much bloodier than it had to be."

"I get angry too, you know," said Chev, quickly, the words tumbling out of the tip of his tongue, "You think I don't wanna scream about how awful and screwed up this world is, how my heart breaks when I see cities burned down and people eaten like… like… like rabbits! It makes me wanna give up, lie in a pit somewhere and never get up! But I know, the way you're trying to do things, you'll be no different than those evils. Father, you're acting like *Feska*."

And to this, Osmond's wooden face broke out in rot and rage. "*Feska!* We are nothing alike! He tried to kill you!"

"As you will try and do."

"Chev! I would *never*—" Osmond couldn't finish. His face fell, his eyes went glassy, and he either saw clarity or terrible delusion just then. A subtle sound—it was his teacup cracking in his grip, and now the hot liquid filtered through his fingers to drip like rain on the carpet. In a quiet, almost fearful tone, he whispered: "Yes. Yes, I see what you are trying to make me understand. You're right. Of course. I should have seen it myself. Chev, I hope you don't forget whose sword it is you wield."

"Would you like it back?" asked Chev.

"I wouldn't dream of it."

Not a drop of tea had passed their lips. And now it was over. The Emperor stood, letting what was left of his drink dry from his fingers, and he made a long, deliberate march back to the line of stag riders. No one bothered to roll the carpet back up.

Slowly, Chev lifted from the ground with heaviness pulling at his every movement. Watching him was a sparse line of nightfolk guards around the dayfolk encampment, spears leaning against their shoulders. They tried to approach Chev, but Chev only addressed a silent Adar and Varnas.

"I think," Chev began, "we should prepare for battle."

These men were not supposed to fight soldiers. They were supposed to prod their spears at beasts, scare them off with hooting and shouting and go back to their campfires. They were not soldiers. They were guards.

So, when it was clear on the opposite end of the field, that heavily armed and armored riders were arraying themselves into battle lines, there was a shudder of disbelief and panic. The snorting quartermaster who'd raised his piggish nose to Chev's warning now had his hand frozen beneath his wet lips, looking at the scene in disbelief.

"What do we do?" he asked Chev.

The man was physically and now mentally a ball of clay. If Chev had asked him to tumble about in the grass, he might have done it on the blind hope it would do something to stop the enemy army. But Chev had nothing to tell him; this was an alien situation to him too.

Only Adar was prepared to act.

Using her sword to conjure up great battle lines she got the few dozen or so men to line up. The line was irregular and full of gaps, their postures were awful and they used their spears as support rather than weapons, but it gave them some form to face the enemy. That those men might withstand a charge from a line of knights was a real challenge for Chev's imagination.

As the stags trotted forward, pennants fluttering among a line of lances, the guards had already begun to run.

Some had dropped their spears, squealed like babes as they made clumsy leaps over crates and supplies, to disappear into the darkness. Adar shouted after them: "They're just gonna run you down!" but she wasn't convincing. And when she turned back to her enemy, it was clear just by looking at her that she didn't have much hope.

Chev didn't know much about history. He knew that the past was distant and mostly forgotten, he knew the future was impossible to imagine. He could never conceive of people studying the past as historians did, so he would never know that the coming encounter, to him a nameless coincidence of events leading to the fight of his life, would come to mean something.

But to Chev, that a charge from breathy, murderous stag riders might be remembered was very last thing he considered at this moment.

He looked to his left and found one or two unsteady men, and to his right, the same. No one here stood a chance. Chev's decision was split-second, and he didn't think before voicing it.

"Adar," he cried out to her, "we have to run!"

"No!" came the answer. Adar's command was desperate, and she said it like an instrument out of tune.

"Only chance we have is behind cover," Chev shouted.

It seemed Adar finally grasped what Chev was getting at, though another refusal was at the tip of her tongue. Pride burned in her face, even as she waved her sword, crying, "Fall back!"

If the command was given but seconds later, it would have been too late.

The retreat of those in the fore was performed in as organized a manner as Adar could manage. Even still, some men turned their backs wholly on the enemy. Some dropped weapons and kept running, out into the veil of the night. And surrounding them all was the increasing volume of the pounding hooves, like thunder rolling in the sky, and nobody dared stand up to it. Not even Chev, though he knew duty and responsibility would force him to turn around.

The knights had now overrun where they would've set up their battle line, and now they were filtering through, bursting between tents, lancing the slower soldiers and leaping across whatever happened to be in their path to eradicate resistance.

Adar was the first to turn around, and steady her blade in her hand.

"We hold here!" Adar shouted.

Chev might've kept running if it weren't for her. The way she leaned forward, sword in hand, was like a challenge to stand ground. And it was issued as much to him as to any of the soldiers.

In the end, it was Adar, Varnas, Chev, and a handful of shivering spears. And the stags and their riders were leaping just into sight. It was the strewn rubbish and disheveled tents that saved them: alone, at full speed, a powerful stag could have easily overrun any one of them. But they had been slowed just enough to engage.

Adar set out to prove it. Out over a barrier of canvas and wood erupted a stag and rider, lance pointed toward the sky. Adar cut the air in front of her, as though reminding herself of the weight of her sword, before taking a step forward and cutting across the furred chest of the stag. Dark liquid rushed forward, there was a terrible whine, and the rider had to leap from the back or risk being pinned down by the body.

The lance was tossed aside and sword drawn. The enemy knight's blade came dangerously close to Adar, as she recovered from her attack. Now was the time for Chev to step up.

He'd cut down those pirates. A knight in the heat of combat shouldn't be so different, but Chev still had to squelch a sick feeling as he buried his blade into the knight's soft side.

"Dishonorable—" the knight gurgled.

A quick hack across the face put the knight down for good. It was only one, more were coming, and their tiny force was already struggling for breath and soaked in blood. More hooves beat across dirt toward them.

There was little time to recover. Adar wiped the blood from her sword but not her face, leaving flecks like dripping freckles. In the distance, stags dashed from tent to tent, so quickly even their shapes were difficult to grasp. Sounds of pain and fear haunted the individual melees, people being run down, speared from stagback, clinks of chainmail as knights did their work on foot.

Out from the darkness more came. This time Varnas stepped forward, thrust his spear into the proud breast of a stag. The beast was valiant, and struggled which only served to bury the thing deeper, so deep Varnas had to abandon his spear and use a dagger to finish the job. The knight didn't have a chance to show what sort of fight he gave, one of the soldiers made a skillful jab just beneath the helmet.

There were more, but they came as individuals, and they were cut down the same. A stag was taken down by blade, and the rider came on foot. Some were skillful, some were clumsy, and some ran. In this one eddy within a tide of bloodshed, fortune was on their side. Soon, the ground was slippery in stag blood and crawling with wounded knights, inching their way into the darkness.

But Chev refused to believe the battle was turning. To get ahead of himself would spell death.

"Stand!" Chev cried out, "Stand tall!"

To cry out victory now seemed hubris. They were only holding out for a miracle to save them.

Varnas roared a hoarse battle cry, shoving his spear into another man. The man's own weight had him sliding off his stag. "Chev! It's been good journeying with you," Varnas called out.

"Don't talk like that!" Chev pulled his sword from someone's belly.

"Don't know how else to talk!"

Adar fought fiercely too, cutting down a man who had limped over a low wall of dead beasts and men. She had lost count of the numbers she had fought this night. Fresh blood made a continuous drip from the hilt to the tip of her sword.

"Ancestors save me!" someone cried. It was desperate and pleading, and it could have been anyone. Chev felt it could have even been him, within a moment of blind panic.

All the blood, the bodies, the wailing beasts, the dismembered bits that couldn't have belonged to anyone. With such a whirlwind of carnage, it was hard to believe that a miracle had happened. Varnas, Chev, Adar, the handful of soldiers that had stood with them, they all lived. Covered they may have been with dark reflections of the wounds they'd inflicted, none of it belonged to them. They were unscathed. And in this moment of surreal peace they could finally look at each other in awe and relief.

There were no knights in the darkness, no stags, no battle cries, just silence. It was almost like they'd all been fighting ghosts up until this point. But their weapons were still up, ready to slice and stab through any apparition. They were all animal instinct, thumping hearts and heaving breasts. But, in time, even those steadied, and exhaustion was allowed to set in.

"Is—is it over?"

It was just like the elders had once said: nothing summons trouble like thinking you are safe. The heads of a dozen stags emerged from the darkness, with coal-like eyes that smoldered and their riders swaying to the strong stride. At least one came from every angle, and two blocked every way out. There were not enough weapons between them for every enemy that came to surround them, a blade pointed at one meant three others went unthreatened.

And their lances stayed at their side.

One more stag strode out of the darkness. Across the Emperor's right leg were dots of blood. Wiping his face made streaks of grime and blood, looking like comets. There was no chance he hadn't killed someone this night. Behind him, Jarv cut a sinister, brooding figure.

He addressed his eldest son with the same tone he might to the servant cooking his meal or cleaning his floor. "You learned to be a fierce warrior. I am proud of you for that. But you helped me learn something, son. An inconsistency in my character, which I've since excised. I favored you. And had we not conversed before, I would have spared you. But how cruel and unjust would it be not to avenge the knights that have fallen by your hand? Blood is nothing compared to loyalty. That's what justice is. I thank you for teaching me."

"Bah!" Varnas walked forward, between Chev's silence and Osmond's switching stag. "That's a real pretty speech. Surprised you had time to think o' it while you slaughtered fleeing men."

"You're a worthless old man, Varnas. You should've never come." Osmond's voice was an emotionless drone.

"I agree with you there, Osmond. I should've stuck in the Nightlands. But poor Chev here wanted to see his father, and instead he saw a craven half-wit dung-for-brains with delusions o' grandeur. I hope he remembers Ossen, instead. That man was fierce and intelligent. You ain't that man no more. You're *wise*."

Osmond's nose curled up. "That stupid platitude of yours. Wisdom mean 'useless'? Only a fool thinks that."

"I learned something else too," Varnas spat, "Wisdom don't mean 'useless', it means a whole buncha people think you got something you don't. For you, that's *justice*."

"Justice!" Emperor Osmond barked a battle cry, and his lance snapped forward in his hand. "You don't know anything! Your time is about to come!"

Osmond clapped his feet over the stag's thighs. It rushed into a charge, the lance was lowered, and Chev knew that even at his quickest he'd never be able to deflect it from Varnas' chest. The lance point dropped, and Chev rushed forward with sword drawn, but nothing could stop a spear with the whole weight of man and stag behind it. It came out Varnas' other side, like a stick running through a cage.

But there was no panic in Varnas' face, only a smile that grew into a maniacal grin, growing so his teeth looked a part of his silver beard. Now something strange unfolded: the maddest trap as Varnas' joy translated directly into Osmond's growing dread.

Varnas said: "I got you, you stupid ass."

He grabbed the lance and leaned forward. The genius of Varnas' plan started to unfold before Chev's very eyes. Varnas was using his own body-weight to lever Osmond off the saddle. At this late point, not even letting go would save Osmond, the lance was firmly angled under his arm and into his shoulder.

The stag carried forward while Osmond hung in air, a slave to gravity and the powerful mechanical forces that now spun him across the camp. His body jerked so violently that his helmet flew from his head. He made a tumble through the dirt, scouring a line on the ground.

"Save the Emperor!" was the battle cry.

The other knights didn't waste time rushing forward with lance and stag, driven by a panic that their Emperor was now in danger. There was no surviving this melee, Chev already knew. But there was nothing left to fight for. At the very least, he might stop his father from killing Varnas, already risen to his knees with sword in his hand.

If Chev hadn't had to fight to save his own life, he might've reached him in time.

Responding with pure reflex against the charging knight, Chev cut through the collar in an impatient motion and finished things off with a kick. By the time he regained his balance and turned back, the melee was already finished. Varnas' spear was hurtling toward Osmond, and Osmond's blade was coming down on Varnas. It may have been death for death had it not been for Osmond's armor. The spearpoint sheared off to the side. The sword did much more damage.

Blood flowed out from his mouth, his ancient eyes were screwed up in pain, Varnas made a picture that could have only come from a half-forgotten nightmare. Face forward the old man fell, a shudder in the dirt then absolute stillness, and Chev found himself screaming hoping to wake up.

The Emperor was back on his feet. The carnage behind was like vague background music. And Osmond and Chev faced each other, weapons drawn. A shadow crept from behind wielding a tooth of gleaming steel in hand.

"She was my mother!" A boy's forlorn battle cry and last mistake echoed through the camp. By reflex Ossen spun around and stabbed at the sound.

It was Jarv.

The blade had punched through steel, chest and bone, escaping out the other side, the sword's taper acting as a gully for blood. It seemed neither Osmond nor Jarv could quite believe it, though Jarv's dagger was still tight as steel in his hand as he fell to the ground.

There were probably no curses blasphemous enough for this moment. That might be why Osmond stayed silent and shivering, as he pulled out his sword as though his son were any other dispatched foe. He had enough possession of his senses to stand until the sword was back in his hand. But then, Osmond could no longer make sense of anything around him. He turned his head every direction, even away from Chev, eyes tracking the alien landscape of the battle he'd caused. Fire flickered in his empty eyes.

"This—this can't be happening."

A quiet, psychotic mutter. And then he staggered up and wandered through the debris of battle, wherever his feet might take him.

Everyone had fallen. Adar had taken so many with her she was practically buried in bodies. With the last reserves of Chev's strength, he pulled corpse after corpse off her. The lifting and shoving took as much effort as looking away from dead faces.

Chev rolled the last of the bodies to its side. A pair of panicked eyes flared open, framed by white hair that had gone patchy and dark with blood.

"Am—am I dead?" Adar's voice was pitched with madness. Something had broken inside of her.

"If you are, I am too. Here, take my hand."

He helped her up, and supported Adar who was unsteady and shifted constantly on his shoulder. It wasn't physical—it was all mental. Wobbling knees, pounding heart, even from where he was he could feel the beat of her heart. Chev would easily believe that it would never slow down again.

Adar was raw and emotionally worn, right down to the point where she could only express plain fact through a flat, tortured voice. "This is *horrible*."

"I know," said Chev, "Varnas is dead."

"Why are we here? Why did we do this? Chev, answer me!"

"I can't."

"Where are we going?"

"I'm taking you to a safe place."

"Don't leave me alone. Gods, don't leave me alone!"

"I have to. Only for a little bit. I have to find my father."

"I'll go with you."

"You can't."

"Why not?"

"Because you'll die."

"I promise you I won't die."

"You can't keep that promise."

"I can. And you can't stop me."

"No, I can."

Adar looked uncomprehending into Chev's eyes. And then Chev kicked her just below the knee. There was a stomach-turning pop, Adar howled. She chased Chev with hoarse and desperate curses. But her curses were all to Chev's benefit. If she kept whining and yelling, he would know exactly where to find her. But whatever courage she had in her heart, Chev knew there was next to nothing she could do to help. This was a task for him alone.

The night sky was clear, not even a streak of cloud dusted the sky, but every direction he looked was shrouded in fog. Chev's own beleaguered senses were failing. He couldn't comprehend the sights around him as he wandered about the dayfolk camp, even as his mind was singularly tuned to catch sight of his father. He was present enough to be confused by two knights fighting from their stags, but he couldn't piece together from his fragmented memories what was truly happening. The battle drifted into a distant blur. Chev followed his father's trail.

At the end of this path was one man, stumbling around islands of carnage as though on peg legs, a once resplendent but now tattered cloak dragging across the mud and blood. Chev could move only slightly faster, but where Ossen moved aimlessly Chev's battered feet carried him with purpose to his father's side.

Chev's arm went round his back. It wasn't a blow, but Ossen was still toppled by it, his blinking, mad eyes darting around before finding Chev's face.

Ossen's voice was halting, and though he seemed to be looking straight into Chev's eyes, his pupils shivered in a manner a sane person could not imitate, "I had this nightmare, Chev, that I was in an enormous rotten tree, surrounded by crows. And as the crows flew around me and I tried to kill them, and I stabbed and slashed and did whatever I could, but every time my sword found Minda. I'd cut her. And I would wake thinking: 'I'm so relieved this didn't happen' and then I'd realize it really did happen. I did cut her. Every night I'd dream this, Chev. Every night!" Ossen grasped Chev by the elbow, but those once steady, experienced fingers were thin, twisted and quivering. "You must understand, I truly thought that I was becoming greater than that man who had cut Minda. I didn't know that I was growing closer to him. And in the end, I saw what I'd done, and what I'd become. Please, Chev... Chev! Have mercy on me. Kill me, don't let me live and allow nightmares to torment me, please don't say out loud what I just did. Gods believe me, I know nothing will ever let me forget. *I know.*"

Chev did not know what to say, so he stayed silent. He nursed his father, stroking his head on his lap, and as he leaned over his tears splashed onto his father's cheeks, the mail on his chest, and dashed upon his cloak.

Finally Chev said to him, "It's time to go home."

"Gods. Where?"

"To the Nightlands."

"The Nightlands were never my home, Chev. I never had one. Do you know what my father used to tell me? He said I would make a home in my destiny. Gods, Chev, I hope you never have anything as terrible as a destiny."

Chev shook his head. "Then just come with me. To wherever I happen to go."

"I think it would be better to leave me on this field, Chev."

"I can't do that."

A moment of serenity fell over Ossen, his vision drifted to distant places and other possibilities, and he let himself be carried in his son's arms. For a moment, at least, he'd been absorbed by the emptiness and immaterial, like he was a sheet of paper in an unwritten book.

Some strength trickled back into Ossen. His eyes steadied once again, and he resumed some control over himself. "Very well. I think I will follow you."

Chev helped Ossen to his feet, and Ossen draped his arm over his son's shoulder. They walked together like a three-legged animal, the world around felt distant and cloaked in irrelevance.

Ossen's next words were so simple, and yet so expressive and surreal that Chev would never forget them. There was a sense that he was marching somewhere to find a missing piece of himself. That his next journey would be the only one with any real significance.

He said: "I am glad to be going with you."

And then they both felt it and heard it. A twang and whistle, like so many that had happened during this battle. And the impact had them both lurching forward, but only Ossen fell to his knees. Chev felt him slip, catching him was like trying to snatch a dandelion seed adrift in a strong wind.

The arrow stuck out from the side. That side belonged to Ossen. He was face down in the dirt. And what came so swiftly to still his slowing breath was death. Moments passed slowly and with disbelief.

A man approached. Chev could not connect Darin to the arrow, even as he leaned forward over his father's body. Darin looked Chev directly in the eyes, pulled the arrow out and cleaned it on a muddy cloak.

"Arrows are valuable," Darrin said blandly, letting the undamaged shaft drop in his quiver.

He was armored like a knight but the suit didn't fit him, not just physically, but in attitude. There was no nobility in Darin's countenance. He seemed to regard Ossen like any kill he might've made in the Nightlands.

"My vengeance is done, Chev." Darrin was already looking toward another horizon. "If you want revenge, too, you can come and take it, I really don't care anymore. You'll find me in one of those taverns, learning the exchange rate between plats and ale. I don't expect I'll do anything different until the moment I die."

Into the darkness he walked. Chev could have followed and taken Darin up on his offer, but he didn't want to loose that last bit of warmth before it drained from Ossen. He wanted to collect it, as much as he could, before it dissipated and seeped into the cool earth.

Chapter Twenty-Five
The Last Journey

THERE WERE A few facts that Chev simply didn't care to learn, but he did. Who told him when and why, he hadn't bothered to remember. But the facts rattled in his skull like loose, useless pebbles.

The Hawk and Wolf clans had arrived sometime that night, and defeated Osmond's knights in battle, keeping the dayfolk out of the fray. Without defenses, the keep was taken, and Osmond's surviving wives and children were scattered among the commoners to meet what fate had in store for them.

When dawn broke, the besieging dayfolk army attacked the city of Sunset. But the walls stayed erect and the dayfolk of Sunset protected their territory, and the attackers were defeated. The fate of so many destroyed cities was not to be the fate of Sunset. It would stand to serve as the center of civilization for a time.

And Osmond, who Chev had known all his life as Ossen, was dead, his side punctured by an arrow. Osmond's dreams of an empire died with him.

Chev left early the following night. The last most anyone saw of him was traveling southeast, cutting across hundreds of miles of scrub land. His only company was a goat bearing a child on its back, and a dead body in a cart wrapped in canvas and bound with ropes. Chev was his own draft animal, pulling the cart up rocks, hills, fields, and whatever else happened to be in his way.

Adar was the last person to have ever seen him.

She followed the twin ruts in the packed, lifeless earth for a long time, along patches of ground so dry that they'd begun to crack like old skin. She was so focused on the markings that she nearly missed the cloud of dust, kicked up by what looked to be an old man pulling a cart, flanked by a goat with a basket mounted atop it.

The sight may have fooled anyone for a pack of refugees, but Adar knew better than that. Glee spurned her forward, bidding her riding stag to practically gallop across the desert. She had found what she'd looked so hard for.

She trotted alongside for a while, hoping to draw Chev's attention, but he kept his head stubbornly turned away. Eventually, she ventured a greeting.

"You need some help?" she asked.

"There's nothing you can do," said Chev. He glanced her direction, and quickly looked away, lost in his own mental journey. Only a look at his strong, lineless face gave any hint he was young.

"I think there is something I can do." With that, Adar hopped off her stag, stepping in front of Chev she put out her hands in invitation. Chev inspected those hands, then her face, and her hands again, before finally letting her take the handles. Adar picked it up with a grunt.

"So, it can't be Osmond in this cart. So who is it?"

"Varnas," said Chev.

"Varnas? And not your father?"

Even without the burden of the cart, Chev still walked with a slight bend in his back, dragging his feet through the dust as though they were leaden. "He only ever wanted to go home. To the Nightlands. I dragged him halfway across the world. For what? To find out what I already knew. And so," Chev sighed, "I remember what the fenderken taught me. That while a part of you lives, you can be remade."

"Is that why you're going through the desert instead of by boat? Because it's dry?"

"Yeah," said Chev.

"It's pretty silly of you. The badlands are filled with dangers, you know. Sand traps. Razor lizards. The vultures don't even wait 'til you're dead to eat you."

"I haven't had a problem so far," Chev said neutrally.

"I think that attitude invites trouble," said Adar.

Chev's pupils squeezed to the corners of his eyes. "I don't think you've come to such a dangerous place just to help pull my cart."

An uncomfortable snort of laughter escaped from Adar. "You are right about that. Chev, there was a gathering after the battle. The defeated clans and the victorious ones all drew up a new treaty. After much discussion—too much discussion—it was decided, seeing your conduct in standing against the false emperor, who was your father, and seeing that you demonstrated such great honor and wisdom, that we would make you Emperor. If you wished it."

Chev didn't make a sound. The desert insects chirped, the dust rustled across the ground, and the bushes itched with life. But Chev let them all speak before he would.

"Chev—"

"Give me my cart back," said Chev.

"Chev, they all know about Starlight. And you know what? They all agreed that what you did was a rare act of self-sacrifice—"

"Give me my cart back."

"Listen to me, Chev."

And Chev shoved her. It was completely unexpected, and she had put up no defenses least of all to steady herself against it. She folded up along the dust, kicking up a cloud. It proved hard even getting to her feet, she was turned around, and by the time she faced Chev, he'd gone a ways up the road.

"Chev!" she cried out, "Chev!"

He didn't listen.

"Remember everything we went through! Remember the Sippi! Remember that time we were alone in the grass! You can't just walk away from that!"

He didn't listen.

"Don't make me chase you to the ends of the world!"

He didn't listen.

Even before Adar had caught up, Chev had nearly given up fighting to let himself die in the dirt. There was no shelter from the sun but beneath the cart, and that dawn Chev went on his knees and elbows, slithering like a snake and using the packed earth as a bed, the sun's diffused heat serving as a blanket.

There he rested. And come night, Chev couldn't will himself up.

Insects moved in, the sort with clicking claws, and strange canines investigated from a distance just over the rise, and the vultures circled round and round. And Chev wouldn't move.

The goat did. Ma-ma nibbled at Chev's collar, tugging and pulling. And Chev didn't move, except to lift his head, and drone out: "Leave me to die. Please."

But Ma-ma insisted. She pulled and pulled, nearly ripping Chev's shirt with all the force she could muster, and by inches he was drawn out. But that didn't help to revive Chev. Hungry creatures moved ever closer. They had smelled his despair and weakness. Drool fell like rain.

Chev had saved Starlight so many times. Chev knew he would have to always, and he would have done it over and over again, even knowing full well all that pain and hardship would bring on him. But Chev never imagined that Starlight would return the favor. That she might save his life one day.

The pulling was soft, but insistent. It pried Chev's eyes open.

Two tiny paws grasped and tugged on two different clumps of black hair. Starlight had climbed out of her basket, and now Chev looked into her familiar furry face. There was an intelligence there. No different from any nightfolk's.

Chev propped his chin up in the dirt, smiling softly. "Hey. Ma-ma teach you that?"

The goat bleated.

"I see your point. Let's go home, Starlight."

He placed her back into the basket, and they traveled home. The mountains served as their only guide.

Hugging the mountain range, dipping into misty valleys, and other days crossing windy highlands, drinking from streams, boiling lichen for food, hunting rabbits. This was a journey that felt longer than all the others combined. In the dusks and dawns they rested, volumes could have been filled with Chev's thoughts, though it seemed more fitting if it could all be forgotten and lost to time. The journey to Manak, and then to Sunset, seemed a dream now, the most concrete reminders being shapes in clouds and mist.

Chev's mind and body became molded to the shapes and sounds of the wild. He was beyond thinking in words but composed everything in images and pictures. He was aware of every change in the climate, felt his need for water, food and shelter not in his body, but in his spirit. He sensed intelligence in the smallest lizard, soul in every insect, and the heart-breaking sorrow in every wolf's eyes.

The journey was arduous, tedious, and nearly erased Chev. The external things that had held him together were now gone. He had an identity untethered to any expectations.

He nearly forgot he had a destination. And seeing it coming closer and closer was the very last thing he had. Yet he kept moving forward. At the end of this eternal journey he was but a shard of the man who had set out so many months before.

It was not Pilgrim's Pass anymore. It was now paved with the bones of nightfolk and dayfolk, and the monsters that haunted it were hungry for the slow, weak kind of prey that refugees provided. But Chev wandered the valley unmolested. The beasts didn't like the leisurely pace this man adopted. It wasn't that he was confident. It was more he didn't even require confidence. They watched with burning eyes as Chev left their domains and entered the Nightlands. The place Varnas once called home.

Familiar trees, familiar sounds, familiar paths. Chev ventured into a clearing and dug a pit Varnas would be proud of. After he was done, he stuck a shovel into the dirt, and let the handle shudder a bit.

"Varnas, I kept my promise. I took you home, old man."

Now the canvas and ropes were laid out before him, and Varnas' body was like a cord of fallen wood. As Chev breathed Nightland air, he wondered whether what he was feeling was happiness or sadness. He wished Varnas could take in those old scents that made the forest so rich. Moss and fresh water had a way of filling the nose, and it was only after being so far away that Chev really appreciated it.

"Damn you Varnas. What I wouldn't do to hear you tell me how stupid I am right now. Come on Varnas. Get out of that sack. Tell me I'm a fool. Tell me I'm wise. Share with me your pain. Make me feel better."

Chev buried his head into the canvas.

"Please, Varnas, *please* tell me that you're somewhere. Please tell me you made it home. Please please *please!*" And after that, Chev howled like a wolf into the moon, nearly ripping the canvas under his fingers. "Varnas! Why? *Why?*"

He couldn't say goodbye. The sun was out and he still couldn't do it. His hands made spiders over his eyes, his palms provided gullies for tears. His skin burned by the light of a young day. He didn't even notice.

Things went black, or white hot, in Chev's state they were very much the same. The bag was beneath the ground and buried, and yet Chev still sat on a rock.

There was a creature standing in front of him.

Chev took her into his hands, feeling her soft fur mold to his palms, admiring her beating heart, the strong, warm blood that ran through her was vital and young.

"I'm sorry Starlight," Chev told her, "I'm blind."

"Ba-ba," answered Starlight.

The first little words out of her mouth. *Ba-ba.* Simple and innocent, and all the same it broke Chev's heart. It was the voice of the girl he failed.

"I can't take you home. There's no home. I lied to you, like I lied to Varnas. I'm *so* sorry."

"Ba-ba."

"Don't call me that."

"Ba-ba."

Little paws reached out, feeling for the softness of Chev's eyes. She gently pried them open, lid by lid. His vision was filled by the sight of the soft-furred child.

"Why do you look so hopeful? Gods, don't smile at me like that!"

Chev turned his head in shame. And Starlight pulled his chin right back. Now her palms were buried into his cheeks, pushing them together to make fat imprints on his face.

"What should I do then, Starlight? Please tell me."

"Goooo," said the girl, "gooooo!"

It wasn't the mindless noise that Starlight usually made, and that was clear. Chev suddenly realized she was pointing his head somewhere. Toward the goat.

"Ma-ma!"

The goat was staring back, the tail flitting about like it might in agitation and curiosity. Upon being noticed, Ma-ma clapped up in the air, and pounced away over the hills.

Not knowing what else to do, Chev followed.

Ma-ma guided him back to trails so familiar they were nigh ghostly. Even in day, the cliff sides were shrouded by mist set afire by the sun. It was blinding but condensed on Chev's skin. It cooled him, giving him the strength to follow the little goat's trotters.

He followed Ma-ma. And soon he faced an old cave that Chev would never forget. It was here things had really begun.

And so, with Starlight in his arms, Chev trudged up the hillside, following a mournful sound.

"Hlogas," went the mournful cry, "Hlogas…"

The source was just over a rocky outcropping. It was the rondack, so long gone he seemed like an old friend, but he was not himself. The great big creature faced an open pit. Two of its eyes were weighed by sadness and fear. The other two were slanted and closed in manner that was deeper than sleep.

"Hlogas?" Chev called to it.

The rondack's nose and beard seemed to wave at the sound. Seeing Chev, it drifted in slow movements, absent of purpose or intelligence.

"Are you Argos?"

The rondack dipped its head in affirmation. It wiped its two open eyes and sniffled.

"Is Hlogas around?"

The rondack shook his head.

"Is Hlogas *gone?*"

And that was that. Argos trumpeted in misery and pain, placing his hand over his two shut eyes, running his fingers over them with affection and loss.

"Oh, *Argos*," Chev went to the creature's side, burying his hand into the creature's coarse fur. "I'm so sorry. I've lost someone too."

Argos' head made a sad dip.

"Come on. Let's take you home, Argos. You're gonna get sunsick if you stand out here. Even more than me."

And they slowly went up those steps, all the way back to Hlogas the Rondack's former home, crossing herds of woolbeasts. But another proud creature stood at the top on a flat rock watching them approach. It was a powerful, intelligent-looking, smaller than a wolf, peaceful in demeanor and yet vigilant. It made a wolf's bark, and propelled itself off its hind legs and down the mountainside, circling Argos several times and hopping and nipping.

"Misty… the dog," Chev recalled. Chev didn't know why that should cause him to smile.

Yet inside was an even stranger sight. Until this point, Chev would have believed that only terrible magic could stop his breath and throw into question everything he thought he knew. That instant, he realized everything had been foreseen, that it was always known what path he'd take, even that it would lead back to this point. It would forever burn in his heart and give him a strange new faith. If Varnas had been alive to see it, he might have found something to finally make him believe in wisdom.

It was a chair, not a rondack's size, but Chev's. Over that was draped a cloak, also Chev's size, and leaning over the arms was a herding staff. Again, Chev's size.

Seeing that there was little else for it, Chev put on the cloak, picked up the staff, and there he sat.

Epilogue
The Names of the Colors

HOW DOES ONE express anxiety?

So much of it was in the hands. The thumbs might wheel, the fingers weave together, blood would pool in the flesh and the joints would ache. For all the wonderful things she missed, and for all the infinite textures she had to commit to an increasingly distant memory, it was only these tense moments that reminded Sana what it was to have hands again.

She wished it was something else, like that moment you reach out to touch someone and you can't, or when you so desperately want to feel something between your fingers, like cool grass, soft soil, or the fractal texture of bark, but Sana had gone through that pain and felt it ebb over time. But nerves made you remember. It made you want to hold onto something and there's this awful sinking feeling when there's nothing with which to hold.

In these moments, Sana imagined her hands back, caged together in her lap. The conjured limbs seemed just as real as the old ones.

There was a time when Sana wished she could trade her feet for her hands. She actually prayed for that very outcome, that one day she might awaken with some great God having accepted the bargain. That was a long time ago. That was still when she walked about on her own power. Now, it was her tongue that did her walking, just as it took the place of her hands.

There were four warriors that carried her palanquin, and Sana had taken to calling them her Feet, just as the women who attended to her were Hands. She used none of her limbs, but it wasn't some beast that stripped Sana the use of her limbs, but the blessing of status. Power, Sana recognized, could be just as destructive on the body as teeth and claws.

"We'll rest here," she addressed her whole band.

The whole party came to a stop. Spears planted on the ground. Bows were unstrung. Her palanquin was set down and her warriors dutifully took this moment to rest. Their neutral expressions communicated they were indifferent to whether they took the break or kept going.

Sana leaned over to her Hands. "Head west until you reach a stream, then follow it as it grows narrower. You'll find a turn where the stream digs into the hillside. Amongst the roots of an old oak are some evil-looking mushrooms. They are skeleton mushrooms. Take the caps. Despite how they might look, they are good for the liver. We'll wait here until you come back."

The Hands nodded wordlessly, and took their leave. The rest waited in silence for their return.

It was a brief but welcome respite, as they would not have one for quite some time. The land began to incline, the trees grew short and hardy, squeezed between the titanic rocks of an earlier age. This was a place few from the Confederation had ever ventured. Here was the dwelling place of monsters and drifters. Only the woolbeasts existed here in any number, and so too the wolves that preyed on them.

It was as the scouts had described. There was a winding, rocky path howling with ghosts and littered by sharp, treacherous stones, at the very end a cavern opened like a dark maw. Sana would normally be grateful for the bright, waxing moon, but the light played tricks here, making the mist glow with strange shapes that evaporated on inspection. It seemed a fitting place to find a lost hero, but a strange one to find Chev, an old unforgotten love. When she saw him in her remembrances, he had a distant untouchable smile, always with a brilliant blue flower cupped in his hand. He was always in the shine of health and youth.

It would be hard seeing him after so many cycles had passed. His isolation might have made him cruel and wizened, like an old toothsome man. Equally, she feared he would be as beautiful and untouchable as she remembered him being—that might break her. This was what made her phantom hands ache and twist.

Over the valleys, rustling the trees, came a ghostly moan: *"Hlogas, Hlogas..."*

"It's the beast!" cried one of the Feet.

Her palanquin tilted on a wave of fear. Mutters drummed across her entourage. Sana was forced to command everyone like they were a herd of animals spooked by thunder.

"Hold!" she yelled. "Hold!"

It was soon apparent that the ghastly moan seemed further away than it truly was, because the giant that trudged out from the mists was mind-bogglingly large. Sana had only seen trees as tall, and even if she sat on the shoulders of the tallest of men, Sana wouldn't reach the beast's chin. A prominent nose, comparable in size to a fallen log, was the first thing to emerge out of the mist into reality. Warts, scars, and bruises made for its coarse texture, expanding in horrible detail as it grew closer.

This thing stepped out of her nightmares, and one of her Hands took her thought and made it into words.

"Monster!" someone cried.

Spears were raised, warriors surged forward to protect their charge, as the palanquin quivered on unsteady shoulders. The giant turned the mists into ropy strands and revealed two bright yellow eyes on one side of its face. When Sana saw another two shut eyes on the other half, making four in total, she was sure she'd gone mad.

"Don't hurt him!" The cry was shrill and childlike, yet powerful enough to freeze weapons in midair. The giant stopped moving, its two sad eyes coming to rest on a tiny figure by his feet.

The girl was no taller than the giant's ankle. She held him fiercely, as though she were his chosen protector.

"Don't hurt Hlogas. He's very sad," the girl enunciated, calmer this time, but still fierce in her proud gaze.

"Hlogas," the giant agreed mournfully.

The girl stepped forward, and as the mists drifted away from her, she struck all with an existential terror that ripped all thought from their minds. If she were merely a monster, a warrior would know to fight or run and hide; that was true no matter how large, fierce, and terrifying that monster might be. But the girl was no monster; she was a revelation, for which none of the nightfolk's well-honed survival skills held any solution.

The tiny creature, with the captivating eyes, long hair, and thick fur covering her body could have been nothing but one of the dayfolk.

"Turn away!"

"Don't look at her!"

"Dayfolk! Dayfolk!"

On the palanquin that turned and shifted with panic, Sana had to hold out her arms to steady herself. She was the only one who kept her gaze fixed at the girl, as her whole world shifted like a storm-tossed sea beneath.

"Calm!" she declared.

And with that, the sea had calmed. Her Feet held fast, and her Hands forced themselves still as they all gazed downward to avoid the sight of her. The only movement came from Sana's thudding heart. It was not the creature was that had her blood rushing but what her existence implied. The golden fur, with copper highlights, a mane exploding out the back of her head like a lion—she was Chev's girl! What memories she evoked! Like the way they said your life flashes before you as you die, Sana saw herself kneeling on the bank of a stream with Chev, skipping rocks, talking nonsense, laughing intimately. It was as though that had been the only thing to have occurred in her whole life. Any fear she felt was erased by her captivation. She could feel a smile spread across her lips.

"You must be Starlight," said Sana.

The girl nodded sharply. It was interesting the way she stood by Hlogas, at once defiant but also half concealed by the giant's thick leg. The girl knew her high ground, and she wasn't about to concede it. In any case, Sana now knew exactly who she faced. Her lips parted slightly to let out her quickening breath.

"I knew a man once. His name was Chev. I think you might know him."

The girl did her best impression of fierceness, but there was something wrong. The girl's eyes were somewhat unfocused yet moving as though she were trying to find a particular star in the sky.

"Starlight, can you see me?"

The girl's cheeks blew up pridefully.

"You can't see in the dark, can you? You must be very brave to come out at night."

"Baba says I can't go out at night without Hlogas," said the girl.

The matter-of-fact way she spoke was consistent with a child's eroding mistrust. Few children could maintain suspicion like an adult could. Sana was starting to see a way forward.

"Is that right? I think that's very smart. Do you know where Baba is right now? Can you show me?"

The giant shifted slightly. The whole party wrenched back as it lifted it arm, but it was only to scratch its ugly, pitted nose. The distraction made the girl give a comforting scratch at the beast's calves.

"There, there," Starlight said softly.

Had the girl lost focus already? Impatience boiled over in Sana. She knew better than to voice it—but it was her heart she fought against now. For so long and hard she'd searched, and now he was so close, she couldn't help but erupt. "Baba, Starlight! Do you know where he is?"

Starlight's little face crumpled, clearly not liking Sana's tone. Still, she answered. "He's here. He's watching."

At that point, the whole party twisted their heads to a figure looking down on them from a huge mound made from a collection of fallen rocks. He wore a cloak that shielded him from the wind, and a staff that steadied him on his perch. Long, clumpy locks of hair swayed freely from his head. Even from this distance, his gaze was bright and piercing, and the sheathed sword at his side was notable. Only one man, spoken in the tribe's stories, wielded such a weapon.

"Chev!" Sana whispered sharply.

Whatever time might pass, there was no mistaking him.

"Lower the palanquin," she commanded.

"But Wise One..." one of her Feet protested dutifully.

"Do it," she commanded, hoping she spoke darkly enough it would quiet any dissent.

The palanquin was lowered. Handless, Sana had to rise onto her feet in a manner that seemed clumsy but was actually skillful. Still, it provoked all sorts of alarm in her entourage and a half-dozen of her Feet and Hands rushed forward to balance her, help she accepted. She set the pace as she clambered up the rocks, a warrior at each shoulder.

Chev was unmoving atop his perch, letting the wind whip his robes about him, watching with detached interest. His features were muddied by distance. It was only when she was face to face with him that she saw him clearly. He was not a withered limb of a man, nor was he the same person from her memories, untouchable and beautiful. It was rare in her society to know who fathered which child, but she could see the Ossen in him now. His face had narrowed and grown distinctive with maturity, his eyebrows were nearly as wild as his hair, and he bore himself with a lonely pride. But there were differences. He still had features as soft as his mother's—his lips, skin, and the reflection of his eyes. Even with no particular expression on his face, Chev looked much gentler than his fierce, wolven father.

He had an effortless soft smile which reached to his eyes. It was the way his face happened to be put together. It was how Sana knew he recognized her.

"I'll take her from here."

His voice. *That* had changed. Like a worn instrument it was slightly out of tune, but deeper and more resonant from use.

She gave both her guards a glancing command, and they both abdicated Sana into Chev's arm. He slipped his arm around her back and put a firm hand beneath the armpit. From here, they meandered a gravelly path downhill, away from the entourage, away from the cave. And there was silence for a long time, except for Chev's staff crunching against loose stones, and cricket song piercing the gray mist.

It felt perfectly natural. Somehow, the years of absence just melted away. Nothing had happened. The shadows shifted while they walked, revealing a formless, purposeless path. Eventually, the mists cleared, opening to a vast vista of forest clawing at mountains. It would have been heart-wrenching had Sana not already felt her heart wrench several times.

"We should say something to each other," said Sana. It wasn't a joke, but she laughed like it was.

"I would rather not," said Chev.

"You know we have to."

"I know," Chev started, "that you didn't come with all these people for a personal visit. But I hoped to make myself believe you had."

"If you wanted to see me," Sana sighed in the middle of her thought, "you should have just visited yourself."

"I was banished," Chev said.

"'I *was banished...*'" Sana repeated it, mocking it, "Chev, you really think that's how people remember you? Most everyone who gave you that sentence is gone. The new generation remembers you as a hero."

"Well, I'm not."

That was so stubbornly stated that Sana couldn't help but laugh. "Aren't you tired of punishing yourself, Chev?"

"It's not punishment," Chev said, "I just have other responsibilities now."

There was a weight to his voice that was poison for Sana's smile. She made a concerned frown—this was one of those moments when she very dearly wished she had her hands again, so she could touch the nape of his neck. Her impulse was so strong she had nearly forgotten she couldn't.

Instead, she shifted so that her forehead rested on him. It must've been a comfort, because he breathed a contented sigh and didn't move for a long time afterward.

It was a while before they'd made a leisurely path back. They were on old lovers' time, and everything moved to suit their clock. Only the merciless cycle of night and day compelled them to move onward.

With Chev's arm around her back, Sana finally saw there was some advantage to having no hands. It was then disappointing as matters turned toward bleak reality.

"What happened to my mother?" asked Chev.

Sana let out a sad breath. "We were going to talk about this eventually, I suppose. Chev... I can't say it any other way. She... disappeared."

"Is that right?" Chev's voice was startlingly neutral, but Sana took it to be shock.

"I want to tell you we know what happened, but we don't know. We looked for her, but there was not a hide nor hair of her. I'm sorry."

Chev nodded in a steady way that drew Sana's interest.

"You don't seem upset."

Chev revealed a knowing grin. "I was just curious what you thought."

"Curious...? What I thought...?"

It was terribly cryptic but Sana would soon get her answers, just over the crest of the hill, where the maw of Chev's cave lay. Sana's feet ached from the unfamiliar act of walking, and the last few meters proved the hardest of all, but soon an amazing scene was unveiled before her. Down the rocky path her entourage waited by the palanquin, but near the mouth of the cave the dayfolk girl howled and giggled as she ran in bold circles around the giant. There was a third figure of note, seated on an old log, bent over with a singular focus on the girl. The old woman tilted her head to them both, revealing a surprisingly delicate face. Even at a distance, there was no doubt this was Minda.

"Ancestors..." Sana's shock was genuine. It was like seeing someone back from the dead.

Chev guided Sana insistently down the cliff and against her shock. Soon, she was face to face with this specter. What was especially haunting was how *different* she seemed. The old woman, who once was isolated and haunted by memories, now seemed serene and content. There was a mysterious smile on her thinning lips, but it was the pupils of her eyes that put Sana off. They took quite some time to track her.

Chev told Minda, "This is Sana."

"Ah. Sana." Minda's voice was drier that a frog's croak. "It's lovely to see you."

The pupils. Bounding and searching, pointed to Sana's direction but unlooking. The realization came swiftly.

"I think you mean it's lovely to *hear* me," said Sana.

"Oh. The artifacts of youth die last." Minda's smile deepened with her wrinkles. "I'm sorry I caused you so much worry."

"You disappeared one night. We had assumed—"

"That I had ended it? Or that some pawcat invaded my burrow and dragged me off? I understand that. I had meant for you all to think that. I did not know if you'd come to this place with hands empty or grasping spears."

A defense built itself in Sana's mind, but it relented. "I understand why you'd think that. But we're different now. That's why I came. Is there any place where we can sit and talk, Chev?"

"Out here is perfectly fine," said Chev.

"Minda," Sana said, "would you mind?"

Chev interjected. "I'd prefer it—"

"No, Chev, it's alright," Minda lifted her hands, "Private matters are your own. But then you have to take yourselves someplace else, because I can't leave."

Understanding, Sana allowed herself to be led by Chev some distance away to a shadowed place on a rise. Still in sight of Starlight, who currently occupied herself by tossing rocks blindly into the fog. Sana sat cross-legged on the cold stone, and Chev leaned from his perch.

"You come at a fortunate time," said Chev.

"I agree," said Sana. "So much has changed since you left. Since even your mother left. You wouldn't even recognize us now."

"I was worried that they would have mistreated you. But I see you now, surrounded by helpers who answer to your every beck and call. I don't know what to think of it."

Sana's gaze drifted pleasantly to Chev. "When you lose one thing, you focus on another. I lost my hands, but I still had my head. So I have done nothing but gather knowledge and wisdom, because what else was there to do?"

Chev looked grimly off into the distance. "I can't imagine how it must be to rely so heavily on others."

"It was humiliating at first, I won't lie. But I realized we all rely on one another. It's just not always as obvious as it is with me."

"Sana, do you sometimes blame me for what happened to you?" Chev asked.

Sana's smile concealed a serious contemplation. "I did at first," she answered honestly, "But you didn't cut off my hands, Chev."

"Sometimes, it's hard to remember I didn't. I was a fool, then."

Again, Sana treated this with serious contemplation. "It's impossible to say what would happen if things were different. All I can tell you, Chev, is that we don't remember you as the one who brought the bone-skins on us. We remember you as the one who lead us against them, and sacrificed to defeat them. After you left, we went far into the deep woods, we discovered more people like us, and we heard stories of the bone-skin's predations wherever we went. We knew, then, what you did was force us to confront something that was coming anyway. Chev: the banished hero. His deeds blazed a path to a new nation of nightfolk. One that would see their people free."

Sana searched Chev's face. He hadn't moved much while Sana talked, and his face seemed stolid like carved rock at that moment. Chev reacted to the tale with a quiet nod.

"I am glad that I inspired you all," he said.

"That's it?" Sana leaned closer, nakedly watching Chev's expression. "I'm at a loss. I was expecting you to jump at the opportunity."

"The opportunity for what?"

"To rejoin society!" said Sana. "If it's Starlight you're worried about, it's fine. They'll accept her. Times are changing."

"I appreciate the offer. But I decline."

Chev's answer was so plainly spoken that Sana felt her heat rising. Despite her past relationship to this man, and knowing what sort of person Chev was, she was *offended*.

"Chev! I don't think you understand. There are so many challenges we face, we *need* your guidance and wisdom..."

Chev's lips curled at the word, 'wisdom'. "I understand, and it looks like you are doing quite well. I feel you wouldn't need me. But I have too many promises I must keep. Besides, it's peaceful here."

"*Peaceful?* Chev, this land is *haunted!*"

"That's a foolish thing to say, Sana. This my home. It's where I raise my family and my woolbeasts. So many rely on me. I'm a caretaker here. What would I be to you?"

"Chev, I was hoping your sense of responsibility might draw you back. I know you have a conscience. You would save many lives, provide guidance for many hundreds of children, build a society that kinder and greater than the one you left. But I can't force you to be a part of it. All I can do is sit here, and beg for you to see reason."

And with a placid but unmoving expression, Chev drew his eyes to the valley, watching as the girl below sifted through rocks and said indistinct things to the giant that lumbered after her. The girl, with her strange furred skin, was at once so odd and so perfectly normal. Her dress swished playfully behind.

"It's fortunate you came," said Chev, "I will consider your invitation. In exchange, I need you to do something for me."

"Anything," said Sana.

"Starlight is getting older. She's asking questions I can't answer anymore. It's the colors, Sana. She wants to know the names of the colors. I know blood is red, grass is green, and so on, but then she points to the sky, or the bark on trees, or a flower, or a rock in her hands, and I don't know what to tell her. If you would, I'd be honored if you would sunwalk with her, and tell her all the names of things I can't see."

It was a strange emotion that passed through Sana. She had to bury the impulse to sob—but it came in a whine in the voice. She spoke as though pleading, "Chev, is that *all* you need from me?"

"That's all."

She agreed to Chev's request, and spent the hours before dawn sitting on her own with impatient dignity, allowing one of her Hands to apply sunleaf oil to her skin. Her heart thudded, time drew on so slowly, like she had to prepare for battle, and yet never would she be able to name the reason for her distress. Even in the months that followed, when she would reflect back on this single moment.

Dawn was coming. She watched the sky lighten with mechanical detachment, envying her servants who set camp now and would rest beneath canvas. She would not feel too sorry for herself. After all, she'd dismissed many offers of help. But even a word of comfort would be as welcome as a kiss.

With great care that came with knowing she might not get help if she happened to run into danger, Sana climbed the hill. Atop, Chev's girl waited, watching. As the sun pierced and burned the fog, the first rays of brilliant light cast themselves onto her face. The dayfolk girl didn't even flinch.

"Good dawn," the dayfolk girl said.

Sana put on her smile. "Good dawn to you too, Starlight."

"Baba said you'd teach me the names of the colors."

"I will," Sana said, finally finished climbing. She turned, admired a landscape waking up to the first of a newborn day. The woods still clung to muddy darkness, the last place from where night retreats.

The girl gave Sana a casual inspection. "You have no hands."

"I lost them," said Sana.

"How?"

The girl certainly didn't mince questions. Sana laughed in a way she hoped would make seem it was not such a painful memory. "It's a long story. Maybe I can tell you once I've finished teaching you the names of the colors?"

Starlight nodded, clearly thinking this was sensible. "What color am I?"

Sunlight was just starting to blaze on her. Sana gave her a long, poetic eye.

"You are beautiful auburn. Like gold reflecting fire."

The dayfolk girl smiled to this, a hint that the girl was warming to her. And the next minute, they sat alongside one another. Not in Sana's wildest dreams did she see herself sitting next to a dayfolk, teaching—of all things—the names of colors. And they sat up together for hours and hours and hours.

"What color is that?" Starlight asked, pointing to a wildflower that stubbornly grew on the rocks.

"That's blue."

"But it's different from that flower," Starlight complained.

"You have a good eye. That's cyan. Very close to blue."

"What's that color?"

"Pink."

"It looks like clouds over the dawn."

"I think so too."

"What color is that?"

"I think it's purple."

"Are you sure? It looked more blue than that other purple thing."

"Stubborn girl! I think you might have better eyes than me."

"Maybe. What's that color?"

"Orange..."

And so Starlight learned hundreds of names, and for those hundreds of names, there were thousands more shades subtly different: the shadow of a blade of grass, the blackness of overturned soil, the hue of rain-spattered stone. It was an important lesson, that beneath the blaze of day, there was far too much in the world's resplendent variety than mere words could catch.

Author Biography

William Scott Martin was born in Kuala Lumpur, Malaysia, to an American mother and New Zealander father. Growing up, he lived in Kathmandu, Seoul, Auckland, Madrid and Washington DC. After graduating from Christopher Newport University in southern Virginia, he did everything from journalism to burger-flipping—but always focused on his primary passion of writing. Will currently lives in northern Virginia.

Dayfall

Mother Night
I left thinking you stole sight
But I come now blind;
Here your son returns, to bury hisself away,
And stare into blackness 'til the sun's echo fades
And sweeps clean a fire that persists with eyes closed,
In which burns the shade of
What I've seen.

I can say now: in the naked gaze of sun, which boils even shadow,
Man's evil is not held fast by shame,
And what's done in dark is done in light,
Only here are ghastly deeds laid bare
For all to be made witness
And cleansed then of innocence.

Mother Night,
Save me from Father Day,
Conceal from sight the evils that men do,
Disguise their acts under shroud and metaphor,
Be my cloak, my shield,
And lay me beneath your cooling shadow.

Black are the bones,
Violet are the talons,
White are the crows,
Green is the blood
From which red grass grows,
And orange boils the sky, floating coal islands,
Into ashen offerings spiral down,
down, down, down,
where their spirits fell.

www.ingramcontent.com/pod-product-compliance
Lightning Source LLC
Chambersburg PA
CBHW060138260626
47160CB00001B/30